IDOL

'This is the epitome of a compulsive
read. Glamorous and riveting'

'Smart, gripping and scarily relevant'

'A brilliant read – totally in touch with
the current zeitgeist'

'Delicious drama with a dark and
twisty storyline'

'Compelling and suspenseful; I felt
almost breathless at times'

'Unputdownable'

'A biting look at influencers, at self-
perception, at our modern world'

'A thought-provoking masterpiece'

'An utterly brilliant examination of the
fine line between truth and deceit'

www.penguin.co.uk

Also by Louise O'Neill

For Young Adults
Only Ever Yours
Asking For It
The Surface Breaks

For Adults
Almost Love
After the Silence

IDOL

LOUISE O'NEILL

PENGUIN BOOKS

TRANSWORLD PUBLISHERS
Penguin Random House, One Embassy Gardens,
8 Viaduct Gardens, London SW11 7BW
www.penguin.co.uk

Transworld is part of the Penguin Random House group of companies
whose addresses can be found at global.penguinrandomhouse.com

First published in Great Britain in 2022 by Bantam Press
an imprint of Transworld Publishers
Penguin paperback edition published 2023

A CIP catalogue record for this book
is available from the British Library.

ISBN
9781804990865

Typeset in Dante MT Std by Jouve (UK), Milton Keynes.
Printed and bound in Great Britain by Clays Ltd, Elcograf S.p.A.

The authorized representative in the EEA is Penguin Random House Ireland,
Morrison Chambers, 32 Nassau Street, Dublin D02 YH68.

Penguin Random House is committed to a sustainable
future for our business, our readers and our planet. This book
is made from Forest Stewardship Council® certified paper.

For Anne, Brian, and Ciara Murphy

They ask me to remember
but they want me to remember
their memories
and I keep on remembering
mine.

—Lucille Clifton

I.

◎ 2,868,635

Samantha watched the girls as they filed into the event hall, tilting their heads back to stare at the ornate vaulted ceiling with its oversized chandeliers dripping silver and blue crystals. They elbowed one another in the ribs, mouths open, as if to say – *Look at that! Can you believe it?* Her publisher hadn't wanted to hire this space for her book launch. They said it was a waste of money, money that could be used more 'efficiently' for marketing, subway posters, targeted ads on Instagram, and she had simply waited until they'd stopped arguing, waving their Excel sheets and projected budgets like white flags, pitching other, cheaper venues, and when they had worn themselves out, she'd smiled sweetly and said, 'It has to be the Ballroom, I'm afraid. My girls deserve the best.'

And look at them now, she thought, staring at the monitor screen backstage as they unbuttoned coats and shook out hair flattened by the cheap berets they hoped would make them look sophisticated, even French, perhaps, tucking their *New Yorker* tote bags under the red, velvet seats. They were young, in their early to mid-twenties, and pretty with their winged eyeliner and red lipstick. They wore heeled booties from Forever 21 and ribbed dresses from Zara and they were mostly white, but that wasn't her fault; as her manager always reminded her, it was just the demographic for this sort of event. Really, it had nothing to do with Sam; she'd always fostered an inclusive atmosphere in her workshops, insisting that everyone was welcome regardless of race, sexuality, or gender identification. But in the end, it was *these* girls who had come to her – these nice, white girls – and Sam knew it was her responsibility to help them the way she wished someone had helped her when she was their age. It was over twenty years since she'd limped off that cramped, overnight flight from Utah with nothing but the memories of all she had lost to sustain her, yet despite everything she'd been through, she had refused to become a victim. She'd been determined to bring this city to its knees and make it hers. And look at her now. Look at how far she had come, and she had done it all by herself.

'We're about to hit a million views,' Jane, her manager, whispered in her ear. 'You are a goddamn genius.' Samantha reached one hand up to cover Jane's and she smiled in relief. She had been right to trust her instincts, then, to argue that a little controversy never did the first week of sales any harm, no matter what her gun-shy editor had thought. It was like she always told her girls: if you follow your heart's truth, you'll never be led astray.

The stage was in darkness except for the screen against the back wall, emblazoned with the word CHASTE in giant neon letters. 'Is it a bit much?' she'd asked Jane earlier, when she saw the set for the first time. She was always like that before a big event, antsy, restless, wanting to make sure everything was perfect. 'If it's good enough for Beyoncé,' her manager had shrugged. 'And the girls will love it, it's very 'grammable.' A spotlight switched on now, particles of dust dancing in its heat, and there was a ripple of energy moving through the audience, like a wave crashing on the stage and lapping at her toes. Sam pressed her fingertips over her ears to block out the excited muttering, the half-stifled laughs, the rustling of skirts being adjusted and seats settled into, until all she could hear was a faint echo of her own breath. She slowed it down, visualizing a bolt of lightning running through her, turning her to flames. She would set this place on fire and burn every person here alive; they would be born anew once she was finished with them.

'Happy New Year! Welcome to the Ballroom for this very special event!' A male voice, deep and loud, reverberated in her bones. 'Samantha Miller,' he said over the loudspeaker, waiting for the applause to die down before he continued. 'Samantha Miller is a *New York Times* bestselling author who travels all over the world as a motivational speaker. Her first memoir, *Willing Silence*, was released by Glass House Publishing in 2011. After Oprah called it her book of the year, it went on to sell over ten million copies in the US alone,' the man said. 'She set up Shakti, a lifestyle brand with a spiritual focus, in 2013, and the website's podcast regularly tops the iTunes charts. Her four-part documentary series, *Shakti Salvation*, premiered on Netflix last year. We are thrilled to have her here tonight to celebrate the launch of her fourth book, *Chaste*.' He could barely be heard over the roaring crowd now, the chants of *Sam! Sam! Sam!* growing louder and louder. She would never grow tired of that, she thought – her girls, calling her name. It was all she would ever need to be happy.

'Here's Samantha Miller!'

The cheers were deafening as she walked on to the stage, the cream silk jumpsuit clinging to her five-foot-nothing frame, her butter-blonde hair curled to fall over one eye. It had taken the best make-up artist and hairstylist in the city two hours to put this together – 'I want to look *pure*,' she'd instructed them, 'it needs to be on brand for the new book' – but now that she was here, Samantha forgot all of that; the styling choices, the mood boards, the look books. She cared only about her girls.

She held her arms out to the side, embracing everything they threw at her – their appreciation, their love, even their desperation. She would take it all and offer it up to the Universe in their names.

'Welcome, my loves,' she said, gesturing at the crowd to sit down. They did so immediately, staring at her in rapt attention. 'Thank you for coming out on such a cold evening,' she said, looking at each girl as if she had been waiting there just for them to arrive. 'I'm glad you are here tonight, each and every one of you. You are *exactly* where you are supposed to be because, as we know, the Universe does not deal in "accidents". This was meant to be. I want you to surrender to that knowing. Feel the peace which that surrender brings you. Allow it to fill your soul.' Samantha put a hand on her heart, asking the crowd to do the same. 'I breathe in love,' she said, and the girls repeated it as one. 'I breathe out fear,' she said, smiling when they chorused it back to her. 'That's right,' she said. '*That's right*. I can feel the release of energy in this room and it's amazing. Can you feel it, my loves? Can you feel your own power?'

The girls nodded their heads, murmuring *yes, yes, I can*. There was an easing of sorts, their shoulders falling, the knot that had been caught in their chests uncoiling. Such was the power of Samantha Miller. She would save them from their pain, their trauma, their difficult childhoods. The strained relationships with their parents – the fathers who ignored them because they'd wanted sons, not daughters, and the mothers who asked if they were 'sure' they wanted that second helping of mashed potatoes – 'carbs are *so* fattening, honey' – the men who fucked them and never texted again, the friends who talked shit out of the side of their mouths, and the other friends who gleefully repeated it back to them. This was a saturated market – so many broken girls with money to spend – and there were a lot of beautiful white women out there, selling wellness and crystal-encrusted yoga mats and fifty-dollar meditation candles, but none of them could do what Samantha Miller could. Authenticity was an overused word these days but the truth was, Sam had it. She'd been there; she had touched the bottom they all feared. She understood their despair but, more importantly, she understood the fury hiding beneath their smiles. She knew there was nothing more powerful than a woman finally given permission to scream.

'I know you,' Samantha said and the girls startled, as if afraid they had spoken out loud, revealing too much of themselves. 'I know you because I *was* you,' she continued, walking to the edge of the stage and sitting down, dangling her feet over the side. The hem of her jumpsuit rose, revealing silver python Miu Miu platforms, and there was a collective intake of breath. *She's so cool*, Sam could almost hear them thinking. Every magazine profile she'd ever been featured in had gushed that Samantha Miller was proof that you didn't need to wear sackcloth dresses to be spiritual, you could still care about your appearance and believe in a Higher Power. 'The Woman Making Spirituality Sexy!' the *Glamour* headline had screamed, and her manager insisted on using that as a tagline for all future books.

'Sexy sells,' Jane had said. 'And let's be real, Sam. Self-acceptance is more palatable when it comes from a woman who looks like you.'

'I arrived in this city with two hundred bucks in my pocket,' Samantha told the audience. 'I was nineteen and alone. I mean, I wasn't going to ask my parents for help, was I?' She paused, waiting for their murmurs of agreement. These girls had read *Willing Silence*; they knew why she'd been so desperate for independence from her family, financial and otherwise. They knew what her family had done to her. 'I slept on friends' sofas and worked in dive bars, using my tip money to party. And by party, I mean do cheap coke and have sex with any man who'd have me.' She chuckled ruefully and the girls did too, as if they also woke up in strange apartments with bruises speckling their inner thighs, scanning the floor for a used condom to see if they needed to pick up Plan B on the way home or not. 'But my life changed the night I met Lori Davis,' Sam continued. 'I was tend-ing bar at her bachelorette and she said she liked my style.' She shrugged. 'It was the late nineties. Everyone else in New York was cosplaying Gwyneth Paltrow but I was wearing acid-washed jeans and had shaved half my hair off.' Her mother would have hated that hairstyle, which was the reason Sam had done it, of course. Carolyn Anderson-Miller, who'd made her fortune from women's longing to be beautiful and who'd reminded Saman-tha every day since she turned thirteen that there was *nothing wrong with being pretty*. 'Lori gave me her business card and when I looked at it properly the next morning, I realized . . .' Sam paused and the girls found themselves leaning forward, urging her to continue, even though they knew how the story ended. They'd read it in her memoir, she had repeated it in dozens of interviews over the years, and yet still they wanted to hear Sam say it again, just for them. '. . . that Lori Davis was the editor-in-chief of *Blackout* magazine. I met her a week later for an informal chat and before I knew it, I was her second assistant.'

Second assistant and then first. 'You're doing well,' Lori told her, and Sam knew she should feel grateful. She was promoted to market editor, and packages began arriving to the office with her name on them, designer sunglasses and low-slung jeans and handmade panettone at Christmas, presents from PRs who wanted Sam to feature their employer's label's latest collection in the magazine. There were invites, too, gold foil letters on creamy vellum paper, and front-row seats at the shows, passwords for after-parties at a secret speakeasy in a Chinatown basement. It was fun, at first, but then she got bored. She went looking for trouble, her mother would have said. And she found it.

'I went to rehab when I was twenty-seven.' Samantha pushed herself to standing, brushing dust off the back of her jumpsuit. 'But it wasn't rehab that saved my life, it was *faith*. I'd been taught since childhood to have faith in external sources – my parents, my teachers, an almighty, all-seeing God – but once I took that faith and turned it inwards, when I made the decision to believe in myself above all else, that was when I came alive. Without that, I wouldn't be here today.' She signalled to the technician in the balcony, as they'd rehearsed earlier, and he turned the lights up in the audience so she could see her girls in all their glory. So young, their faces slightly shiny, patches of oil breaking out through foreheads and chins, mouths quivering with emotion. Her heart felt too big for her chest as she smiled at them, with their phones pointed at the stage, photos and videos taken and uploaded to TikTok and Snapchat and Instagram, tagged #TheQueen and #Samantha-Miller and, most importantly, #Chaste. 'I know you,' Samantha said again, but quieter this time. 'I know what you are searching for because I was searching for it too. It's a difficult time to be a young woman. The world can seem such a frightening place, can't it? We're living in an increasingly divided country.' *Be careful, Sam.* She didn't want to say anything that could be misconstrued as too political, not in this climate. 'But I urge you to see love where others would sow hatred, unity where they would sow fear. You are children of the Universe and you are powerful beyond measure. Once you believe that, nothing can stop you. Do you believe?'

She raised her hands, mouthing the words *thank you* as they clapped so loudly their palms stung. Oh, but she loved these girls, with their hopes and their dreams and their yearning so fierce she could almost taste its salt on her tongue. They always told Sam that she had saved them but they'd saved her too. They had given her a purpose, a reason to stay alive.

'OK. Let's do this thing,' she said, adjusting her headset as she opened the event up to audience questions. A few trembling arms went up, gulps as a microphone was passed to them. Their voices low as they asked the same questions Samantha was always asked at events like this – *How did you find the courage to leave your job at the magazine? I'm worried about money! What advice do you have for anyone who wants to write a memoir?* And then, there were the girls who stood and stared at her with hungry eyes, the girls who were too thin and too pale, their knuckles swollen red and cold sores puckering at the sides of their mouths, and they would ask Sam for help, *please, please help me.* They knew there was a better life waiting at the other side of this but they couldn't seem to find the key to unlock the door, and they were tired, couldn't she see how tired they were? She tilted her head, softening her tone as she reassured them that if she had managed to recover, so could they. There was help out there, but they had to reach out with both hands and grab it. She had been *sick*, Sam reminded them, so sick it was a miracle she was still here. But she'd clawed her way out of addiction because she believed that she was destined for greater things than an undignified death slumped over a toilet cistern. 'Do you believe in yourself?' she asked. 'Do you believe that you deserve to be happy and well?'

She wished she could take care of these poor girls, bring them home with her and nurse them back to health, every single one. In the beginning, she used to give out her cell number, told them to get in touch if they ever needed anything, but she couldn't do that any more. So often, the girls had no respect for her personal boundaries, expecting her to be all things to them – a surrogate mother, a therapist, a best friend. It was too overwhelming so now she just told them there was an online workshop that supported addicts on Shakti.com ('And it's running at a 20 per cent discount right now, you just need to give proof of purchase of *Chaste*') and wished them well on their journey. *Keep the show moving*, she imagined Jane saying, and she gave the stage manager an almost imperceptible nod, swallowing her guilt as he wrenched the microphone from the girl mid-sentence. She stood again, peering into the audience. 'You,' she said, pointing at a young Asian-American woman halfway down the auditorium. The event was being filmed tonight and Jane had said it would look better if there was at least *one* person of colour on screen.

The woman glanced at the row behind her then pointed at herself. 'Me?' she asked, and Samantha smiled.

'Yes,' she said. 'You.'

The girl appeared to be in her early twenties; she had dewy skin and shining black hair cut in a bob with sharp bangs. She'd smudged kohl around her eyes and she was wearing a cropped sweater with a checked mini-skirt, like Samantha had as a teenager when she'd developed an obsession with Liv Tyler in *Empire Records*. *Is that when you know you're old?* she wondered. *When you realize you wore the latest trends the first time around?*

'Hi, Ms Miller,' the girl said.

'Oh please, my love. Call me Sam.'

'Um, OK. Sam. I just wanted to say congratulations on your essay in *Blackout* today. I thought it was super . . . brave.'

'Aww, thank you. That's sweet of you.'

'I suppose . . .' The woman tightened her grip on the mic. 'I suppose I want to ask – why *this* book? Your work has been, like, totally transformative for millions of women, myself included.' Samantha looked down, a small smile tugging at her lips. No matter how many times she heard it, she still couldn't quite believe the impact her work had had, how big it had all become. It was beyond her wildest dreams, this life she had created for herself. 'You taught us it was OK to see ourselves as sexual beings,' the young woman continued. 'Just because we were female didn't mean we had to become wives and mothers, there was a different path we could take—'

'And I still believe that,' Sam interrupted. 'Nothing I've said or written – especially not in my new book, *Chaste* – has contradicted any of that.'

'Yeah . . . I guess,' the girl said, and there was the beginning of something, a minuscule shift in the atmosphere, so delicate Sam wasn't sure if anyone else would have picked up on it, but she'd been doing these events for a very long time and she was acutely sensitive to an audience's temperature. She could gauge by a passing cough or clearing of a throat if the girls were still with her or not. 'But this is your first book in over four years,' the young woman said. 'And I want to know why you would decide to write about *chastity*, of all things? Like, at this particular moment in American history when there are so many people in positions of power who would take advantage of that? And who, like, have done so in the past?' She faltered as the other women in the auditorium frowned at her, clearly annoyed that she would bring the mood down in this way – *What is this girl's problem?* she imagined them thinking – but then they turned to the stage again, looking to Samantha with curiosity, waiting to see how she would handle this.

She walked to the back of the stage, touching each neon pink letter and calling it out as she did so. 'C . . . H . . . A . . . S . . . T . . . E . . .' she said. '*Chaste*. Ever since I was a teenager, I've been saying that the idea of "virginity" is a patriarchal construct designed to control female sexuality, but I believe chastity is a very different thing. What's your name, sweetheart?' she asked, and the girl mumbled, 'Amy,' into the microphone. 'Thank you for your excellent question,'

Samantha said, and Amy couldn't help but smile in relief. 'The truth is, Amy, the modern dating scene has made sex disposable. It's made *people* disposable. I've come to believe that sex is sacred and we have to honour it as the force that it is. We shouldn't throw it away on those who are not worthy of us.' She could taste something sour in her mouth as she remembered the people she had tried so hard to make love her, how weak she'd become in the process. All the things she wanted to forget now. 'But it's not that I think we should become asexual or anything!' she said. 'Women have the right to pleasure. But is casual sex all that pleasurable? When female satisfaction is still seen as secondary to the male—'

'So, what are you saying?' Amy asked impatiently. 'That if we want to close the orgasm gap, we should just sleep with our best friends like you did?' There was a gasp from the audience, a smattering of nervous giggles.

'*Woah,*' a voice near the front said and the girls shifted in their seats, whispering to each other. Samantha was losing them; she needed to get this under control or the event would be ruined.

'I presume you're talking about my essay in *Blackout.*' Samantha pretended to laugh. 'Have the rest of you read it?' she asked the crowd, smiling when the girls shouted *yes, of course.* 'Well, then, you'll know the essay is about an experience I had with a friend when I was a teenager. I identify as straight – I'm attracted to men, I've only ever dated men – but I had the most intense orgasm of my life that night.' She stood in front of the neon letter A, hands on her hips, as she and Jane had practised; this was the pose which would look the most flattering in the photos, they'd decided. 'I chose today as the publication date for *Chaste* because it's my anniversary. I haven't had sex in two years,' she said. 'And I've spent a great deal of that time thinking about that night with my friend and wondering why I was able to let go in a way I never had before, and sadly, I never have since. This book is the result of that wondering. I believe that in reclaiming our right to be chaste, women will actually *destabilize* everything society has conditioned us to accept about our sexuality. Do you understand?' She looked at the young woman, and there was something on her face that Samantha recognized; she'd seen a flicker of it on other people in her workshops before. This girl needed her help, she realized, and she knew what to do. 'But I have a feeling that's not what you wanted to ask me, is it?' she said, and the girl shrank back, staring at Samantha with wide eyes.

'I . . .' Amy started. 'I don't know . . .'

'This is a safe space. You can be honest here. What is it you *really* wanted to talk about?' Sam asked gently and the young woman's composure cracked, a sob clawing out of her throat.

'I'm sorry.' Amy put a hand up to cover her face. 'When I read your essay earlier, I just . . . I can't imagine ever doing something like that.'

'You can't imagine doing something like what?'

'Something so . . .' Amy bit her lower lip to stop herself crying. 'You wrote about having sex with another *girl*. Aren't you scared of what people would say? My parents are— They're religious,' she said quietly. 'They wouldn't accept that. I wish—' Her voice broke. 'I wish I could be brave like you.'

'Oh, honey,' Samantha said, her heart hurting at seeing one of her girls in such pain. 'I wasn't brave when I left school. I wasn't brave when I came to New York, all alone. I was young and scared, just like you are. But I've learned a lot since then, and the most important thing I've learned is that you have to be true to yourself. This isn't about your mom and dad accepting your sexuality, it's about *you* accepting it. You have the power to change your world, right here, right now! I know you can do it! I believe in you!'

The girls began to applaud, shouting *yes, queen!* and Samantha wanted to throw her head back with the energy that was running through her, that electric shock stretching out her spine, ready to shatter her into a thousand pieces. This job could be difficult, it could be tiring, demanding. She had sacrificed so much to get where she was in her career – friendships, marriage, motherhood – and she had felt lonely at times, she could admit that. But none of that mattered when she was on stage and she saw these girls becoming whole before her, their broken hearts re-stitching because of her words. That was why she had been put on this earth, to help them. *Thank you*, she said silently, offering gratitude to the Universe for her gifts, and granting her an audience willing to receive them. *Thank you.* Then she looked the young woman straight in the eye. 'Tell me, Amy. Are you ready to change your life?'

As she came off stage, the jumpsuit clinging to her body with sweat, Samantha could see her manager waiting under a large, blinking EXIT sign. Jane was on her phone, scowling as she tapped furiously at the screen. 'Oh my god,' Sam said, half laughing. She lifted a hand, showing the other woman that it was trembling. '*Fuck me!* That was good. Did they get it all on camera? The energy was insane, we should use clips for Shakti's YouTube channel. Did you see that girl at the end? I was worried when she first started talking – there's always a tricky one, these days – but I got through to her, didn't I? I really think I made a difference.' Sam grabbed one of the hand towels stacked on a folding table, next to the bottles of smartwater and hand sanitizer. She dabbed at her forehead, then her chest. She waited for Jane to tell her that it had been awesome, that Sam was a star, that it was the best event she'd ever done. But the other woman just stared at her, an odd expression on her face.

'Sam,' she said. 'I think we have a problem.'

2.

'Jane,' she hissed as she tried to pull the key out of the lock, jiggling to get it free. 'Just tell me what's going on, you're freaking me out.'

Her manager had thrown a coat around her shoulders when they were still backstage at the Ballroom, insisting they leave immediately. Jane bundled her into an Uber, and Samantha could hear her tense conversation with the stage manager through the window.

'I have fifteen hundred women waiting in a line down there, I don't know what you expec—'

'Tell them she has a stomach flu or something.'

'A stomach flu? Are you fucking kidding me?'

'Say she had a family emergency, then. I don't care, man. You'll think of something.'

Jane climbed in after Samantha, slamming the door behind her. 'You have the address?' she asked the driver, a middle-aged white man with frosted tips who was blaring nineties hip hop from his iPhone. 'Turn that shit off,' her manager snapped at him.

'Is . . . is everyone OK?' Sam asked, her heart slowing to a painful thud. 'Has there been an—'

'It's nothing like that.'

'What is it, then?'

But Jane wouldn't say any more, holding a hand up to silence Sam when she tried to speak. 'Not here,' she said, tilting her head at the guy in the front seat. She stayed quiet as they walked through the building lobby, pressing her lips together as Sam smiled a hello at Alberto, her doorman, and made polite conversation in the elevator with Mrs Cohen, the elderly widow who owned the classic-six apartment on the floor above.

'OK,' Sam said once she managed to get the front door open. She hung her Max Mara cape on the coat stand, throwing her purse and keys on to the sideboard with a clatter. 'Are you going to tell me what all this drama is about? It had better be good, Jane. I can't believe you made me skip my signing. The girls will be devastated.' That was always Sam's favourite part of an event: meeting the fans, hugging them as they cried and told her how much her work had impacted their lives. 'And' – she tried to find some way of getting through to her manager – 'they might ask for their money back. The meet and greet was included in the ticket price.'

Jane closed the door behind them and leaned against its heavy wooden frame. She looked tired, her lean face almost haggard in the low lighting. 'Are you all right? Do you need some water?' Sam asked, concerned.

'Can we sit down?' her manager said, and Samantha led her into the living room. It was a large space with deep-set casement windows and intricate cornice mouldings running around the edges of the high ceilings, a faded Persian rug on the hardwood floor. She gestured at Jane to remove her heels before sinking into the smoky-grey velvet sofa. This apartment had been her first big splurge when the 'movie money', as Sam called it, came through. Everything in here – the French marble console and the embroidered linen cushions, the oversized paintings in vibrant oils and the hand-painted wallpaper in a whisper of duck-egg blue – it was all testament to her hard work, the sacrifices she'd made and the breathtaking success that had followed. Sam had never brought any of the men she'd slept with here, insisting they go to their apartments or a nearby hotel instead. It had felt too precious to sully in that way and she was glad of it, afterwards, glad she didn't have to live among the ghosts of their contempt and her neediness; the silence that had buried itself in the walls when the men left immediately after fucking her, like they always did.

'I need a drink,' Jane said, tucking the leather satchel stuffed with extra copies of *Chaste* into the side of the couch. She looked at her phone, then back towards the galley kitchen. 'Do you have any wine?'

'Of course I don't have wine here,' Samantha said, screwing her face up. 'I'm a recovering addict. What's *wrong* with you tonight?'

Jane held a finger up, finishing an email. A swooshing sound as the message sent, then she placed her iPhone on the coffee table, face down, and that was when Sam really began to worry. Jane never put her phone away, not even when they'd rented out the most expensive restaurant on Madison Avenue to celebrate *Willing Silence* selling seventeen million copies worldwide. It was something Samantha had chastised her for, saying that she should take Shakti's digital detox workshop, and Jane had rolled her eyes, replying, 'You can't afford for me to take a digital detox.'

'So,' her manager said. 'We have a situation.'

'OK,' Samantha replied slowly.

'It's about your *Blackout* essay.'

'Oh, come on! We were expecting a backlash. We're reclaiming chastity for a new generation; this isn't easy work. Whenever you introduce an idea to the culture, there's always criticism. Then, within a few years, poof! It's part of the mainstream and everyone has moved on. Don't panic, it'll—'

'It's not that.' Her manager smoothed her hair into a tight ponytail. Everything about Jane was neat, from the starched collar of her crisp, white shirt to the polished patent leather of her pumps, and even now, when she was as stressed as

Samantha had ever seen her, she looked as if she'd been freshly laundered. 'It's Lisa. She emailed me. She must have got my details from the site.'

'Lisa,' Sam repeated. The name didn't belong in her mouth, not here, not in this life. That was a name from before. Before the books and the movie and the money, before rehab, before the school in Utah, even. It was a name she had thought of every day while she was writing *Chaste*, but Sam hadn't said it aloud for a very long time. 'Do you mean . . . Lisa Johnson?'

'Lisa Taylor now.'

'Oh.' Samantha swallowed. 'She and Josh got married? Wow, I can't . . .' *Why didn't my mother tell me?*

Sam had looked Lisa up on Facebook years ago, but her privacy settings were so tight, all Sam could see was a profile photo of a sunset. She had sent a Friend request and a short message – *Hey girl! It's been forever! I'd love to catch up! S xo* – but she'd heard nothing back. She had looked him up too, of course, holding her breath – what would she do if he was single? Maybe he was living in the city now? They could go for lunch, or a quick drink after work, and who knew what might happen after that – but after trawling through dozens of Joshua Taylors, none of whom were him, Sam had given up.

'What did Lisa . . . Taylor have to say for herself?'

'She saw the piece. And she's not happy about it.' Jane cracked the knuckle of one thumb, then the other. 'You told me you'd make sure the friend couldn't be identified.'

'I did.'

'You used her fucking initial, Sam! That's not exactly high-level espionage. And Lisa Taylor definitely doesn't think you did a good job.'

'*What?* She's not the only person in the world whose name begins with L.'

'She says she's easily identifiable as the best friend.' Jane looked at her phone again. 'She spelled "identifiable" wrong, by the way. Fuck me, this email sounds three glasses of Chardonnay deep. But yeah, she says it's humiliating, she's still living in your hometown, she's worried what her husband will think, blah blah blah.'

'Right.' Samantha could feel the old resentment stir awake, scraping at her insides. 'Perish the thought that *Josh Taylor* might have to deal with any of his fucking . . .' She forced herself to take a breath. There was a place for anger, she would tell her girls at her workshops. It could be cleansing, especially for women who were so often told it was forbidden to them. But it could destroy you too, if you allowed it to burn through you like a wildfire. She had done enough therapy to recognize that it was easier to be angry with Lisa and Josh than to admit how much they had hurt her, how rejected she'd felt after they'd abandoned her when they no longer had any use for her. 'Has she actually read the piece?' she asked her manager. 'It's basically a love letter to our friendship. I don't get it.'

'I bet she doesn't want her friends thinking she's a dyke,' Jane snorted. 'I know women like that. When I came out, half my senior year stopped talking to me in case I'd get the "wrong idea". Like I would have had any interest in those basic bitches.'

'Yeah, but it's not the nineties any more. There must be *some* gay people in Bennford at this stage. And besides, I said in the essay we were both straight.' Sam walked out to the hall, rummaging in her purse until she found her phone. 'Listen to this,' she said as she scrolled through her Instagram messages. 'Hi Samantha! I never DM celebrities but I read your *Blackout* essay and I just *had* to contact you. I've never felt so seen . . .' She scrolled again. 'I love you, Sam! Your honesty inspires me to be braver . . . And this other woman sent a voice message and she was like, because of your essay I told my husband about a queer experience I had in college. She knows now she has nothing to be ashamed of and she never did.' Sam sat down on the sofa again, hugging one of the cushions to her chest. 'There are hundreds of messages like that. *Hundreds*. And that's just on Instagram. The new PA—'

'Darcy,' Jane reminded her. 'She graduated top of her class at Princeton last year.'

'Yeah, Darcy. Sorry.' Sam did try to remember her assistants' names but they were all so similar, with their shiny hair and liberal arts degrees and stories of ancestors who had arrived here on the *Mayflower*. 'Darcy had to take over my accounts because I can't answer all the messages myself. It's crazy. How many views has the essay had now?'

'One point four mill.'

'*Fuck*. We have something here. This is important.'

'I'm not saying it's not.' Jane rubbed her eyes but her mascara didn't budge; it wouldn't dare, Sam thought. 'But that's not the issue. I'm trying to explain, if you would just—'

'I don't want to get into ego here.' Sam threw the cushion aside and curled one foot under her, picking at the black polish on the other big toe. 'I'm just the vessel. I know I'm not important but the *message* is important. These labels we put on ourselves and our sexuality are so binary and we need—'

'What *you* need to do is to take a minute,' Jane interrupted her. 'What would you tell me if I was spiralling like this? Wouldn't you say that I should turn it over to my Higher Power or some shit?'

'Not now, Jane,' she snapped. 'I'm a human being having a human experience and I need to honour my truth. And my truth is that I feel really upset. I can't believe Lisa is throwing a hissy fit over a stupid essay. We're not in high school any more.' She bent down to the coffee table to grab the small, gold buddha she'd bought on a silent retreat in Chiang Mai and cradled it in her lap, rubbing its belly for luck. She breathed in, counting to four, and she breathed out, asking her spirit guides to show her the way through this. When she opened her eyes, Jane was watching her warily. 'I want to apologize,' Sam said. Such behaviour was beneath her, they both knew that. 'I shouldn't have snapped at you, that was unacceptable. Everything about Lisa . . . it makes me a little crazy, I guess.' She waited. 'Jane?' she asked when her manager didn't say anything.

'There's something else,' the other woman said. 'I'm not sure how to say this to you but . . .'

'What is it?' Sam clutched the buddha so tightly that her knuckles turned white. 'Did she say it didn't happen? Did she actually deny this?'

'Not exactly,' her manager replied. 'Lisa isn't denying it happened. But she says she remembers it differently.' Jane took a deep breath. 'She said what happened between the two of you . . . Sam, I think she's claiming it was sexual assault.'

3.

If you had asked Sam where she was in the moments after Jane told her about Lisa's allegation, she would say she knew she was in her apartment, the pre-war building on the Upper West Side with a view of the river from the rooftop. Jane was there, mouthing words that Sam couldn't seem to hear because she wasn't in her body any more, she realized; she couldn't feel her feet on the ground and her hands were clutching at the fabric of the sofa, as if to prevent herself from floating away. She felt so light, like she was dissolving to air. She was dimly aware of Jane wrapping a blanket around her, a Scottish tweed that smelled of her favourite perfume. Her manager sitting beside her, saying, 'We're gonna figure this out, Sam, I promise.' She wasn't sure of how long they sat there together in silence, how long it took for her to stop shaking, for the tectonic plates of her brain to slot back into place and for her to come back to herself, folding into her body again. Jane fumbled in her satchel, groaning. 'This was a bad week to give up smoking, wasn't it?'

'It's gross and it's eating your lungs,' Sam said automatically. She shrugged the blanket off. 'Forward Lisa's email to me. I want to read it myself.'

The message was rambling, littered with typos.

I just read your essay in blackout I cant believe you would write this about me. I'm mortified. You can't jsut say things like this. I'm a mother now. I have two girls. I cant have them reading something like this. How could you? It was private

21

sam what happened. you shouldn't have done this. That night . . . , I didn't want that to happen. I'm not like that. but when Sam wants something, it happens whether you want it or not. you just did it anyway didn't you? It didn't matter how i felt. You just took what you wanted without my consent.

Sam looked up from the iPhone, dizzy, and for a moment she thought she was going to pass out. 'Oh my god,' she said. 'She's implying that I . . .' She let the cell phone drop from her fingers as she lay down on the sofa, wrapping her arms around her head. She always told her girls it was important to cry, it was *cathartic*, but now, when she needed it most, she found it almost impossible to do so and she shook with the effort of trying to let go.

Jane waited until Sam was still, when the brittle sobs had stopped shuddering down her spine. 'Are you ready?' her manager said. 'Because we need to get our game plan together.'

They talked into the early hours of the morning, turning her apartment into a war-room. 'I don't understand,' Sam said, pulling strands of her hair out and letting them shimmer to the ground. 'I don't understand why she'd say something like this; it doesn't make any sense.' She looked at Jane. 'Why would she say this?'

'I don't know.'

'But *why* would she lie about something like this? Why would—'

'OK,' Jane cut her off. 'You've asked me that at least ten times. I get this is a shock but we need to focus. What are our options?'

'What do you mean, options?'

'We need to make this go away, before it becomes an actual problem. I suppose you could offer to write a retraction to the essay but it would hurt book sales.' The other woman winced at the thought. 'And it'll damage your credibility, long term.'

'Book sales? I've basically just been accused of *sexual assault* and you're worrying about book sales?'

'Yeah, well, this is where I earn my fifteen per cent.' Jane was calm, cracking her chopsticks in two and fishing some shrimp out of the takeout box she'd ordered at midnight, when it became clear she wouldn't be going home any time soon. 'I know this is upsetting, but it's my job to worry about things like that.'

Sam picked up her phone, scanning through the email again. 'You know, there's something not quite right about this. All these mistakes, that's not like Lisa. She was an honour roll student, she was . . . Do you think she's OK?'

'This is gonna sound heartless but I don't give a fuck. There's too much at stake here.' Jane stared into her Kung Pao intently, avoiding Sam's gaze. 'Have you thought about how this might jeopardize the Shakti sale?'

'It wouldn't.' She felt herself go cold. 'We're so close and Teddy has my back; he promised he'd take care of me.'

'He isn't the only investor. At the end of the day, there are millions of dollars at stake here. If the board decides you're a liability, Teddy's hands will be tied.'

'Shit,' she swore. Sam hadn't been convinced, in the beginning, that going public was the right choice for Shakti, but when Jane told her how much money she would get as a payout, Sam had gone quiet. With a deal that big, there was a real possibility she might get a *Forbes* magazine cover, one which described her as a mogul, a genius. Everyone in her hometown would read it. Lisa would too, and more importantly, so would Josh. She couldn't lose this deal, not now. 'I can't believe this is happening.' Sam covered her eyes with her hands. 'This is so unfair. I'm a good person. I don't deserve this.'

'Stop panicking,' Jane said. 'It's only an email right now, no one knows anything about it except us. We have time to fix it.' Her manager hesitated. 'I'm going to ask you this question just once and I need you to be totally honest with me,' she said in a low voice. 'Did you do it?'

Sam inhaled sharply. 'Are you for real? I'm a survivor myself, I would *never* do something like this.' All the nights she'd awoken from a sweating nightmare, convinced she could feel those hands on her body again, breaking her in two. The sound of their laughter as she fell back under, limbs flailing. It was the same time, every night – the body keeps the score, her therapist reminded her – and afterwards, as Sam tried to find sleep again, she would think – *I bet their bodies don't remember. I bet they sleep through the night easily.* 'I can't believe you'd even ask me that, Jane. Have you ever known me to lie?'

'No,' her manager admitted. It had often been a bone of contention between them, Sam's refusal to promote a product she didn't believe in, or give a quote for a book she didn't love, telling the other woman that her integrity could not be bought. 'But what's Lisa's motivation for doing this, then?' Jane made a face at the food, slopping the carton down on the coffee table. 'She could have just said it was an invasion of privacy and insisted *Blackout* take the essay down – why bring consent into it?'

'I don't . . .' Sam felt like her brain was short-circuiting, a childlike voice in her head whining *it's not fair, it's not fair* on repeat. 'Maybe it's because of Josh?' she tried. 'He hates me, and I doubt he was thrilled with the essay, he would— Oh shit.' She leaned back on the sofa, the blood draining from her face. '*Shit.* I know why she's doing this. In the interview—'

Her manager started to ask, 'Which interview?' because there had been so many in the week leading up to publication, but Sam cut her off.

'The one in *Blackout*,' she said impatiently. 'The one I gave to accompany the essay. I said in my next book I was going to touch on the ultimate taboo. Something I'd never talked about before, not even in *Willing Silence*.'

'You mean abortion?' Jane frowned. For years, they'd gone back and forth on the wisdom of Sam declaring herself to be pro-choice. Sam argued that one in four young American women terminated pregnancies, the sort of young women who were in her audience, but her manager had been reluctant, wary of alienating her Red State fans. 'Why on earth would you say that to a journalist without running it past me first?'

'I was exhausted,' Sam protested. 'I was just off the red-eye from London and it was my fifth interview that morning. The woman asked what my next book was about and I couldn't think of anything else to tell her. It just came out.'

'You're too long at this game for mistakes like that.' Jane shook her head. 'And why would Lisa care if you wrote about being pro-choice, anyway? What's it got to do with her?'

'Quite a lot, actually. I swore to Lisa I'd never tell that story.'

'Why not?'

Sam raised an eyebrow at her manager, watching as comprehension dawned on the other woman's face. 'Because it wasn't really my story to tell.'

4.

She watched as Jane gathered her things, wishing she could ask her manager to stay. *Please*, she begged silently. *Please, don't leave me here alone.* Jane stood, staring down at Sam. 'Go to Bennford in the morning,' she said. 'Whatever childhood drama you and Lisa have going on, it doesn't matter any more. You need to make sure that email doesn't get out. You're one of the most charming women I've ever met,' Jane said, but it didn't sound like a compliment. 'Now is the time to use those infamous powers of persuasion. Fix this before it becomes an actual problem.'

Her manager left and Sam was alone with her expensive, beautiful things, the smell of Chinese food hanging heavy in the air. The fear was dark water and she was shoulder-deep in it, tasting the rising tide. 'I didn't do anything wrong,' she said out loud, the words echoing in the empty apartment. 'I'm a good person.' She slumped to the floor, whispering, 'I'm a good person,' over and over. She needed someone here, somehow, to hold her and tell her everything would be OK, but she could not think of one person she trusted enough to tell this story to. *I am alone*, she thought. *I am so alone.*

Before writing *Chaste*, she would have gone out and found a man to go home with, to feel his skin against hers for long enough that she could pretend she was happy. But she couldn't do that any more, so she went to bed and the bad thoughts were like dandelion seeds scattering through the air, too many to count and impossible to retrieve. She thought of the email and she thought about what would happen were this to go public, the things people would say about her. She thought about that night and every other night she and Lisa had spent together – had she held her friend's hand too long? Had she accidentally touched Lisa in her sleep, and somehow not been aware of it? – picking through the rubble of their friendship to find the shrapnel, the wounds Lisa was claiming Sam had inflicted upon her. She was so afraid and her fear made monsters of the shadows, moving slowly towards her, and after an hour or so she got up, frantically searching through the wash-bags from her last European tour until she found the half-empty bottle of melatonin, swallowing two tablets without water.

She woke at 6 a.m., her mouth dry and her nightdress damp with sweat, fragments of strange, uncanny dreams breaking apart in her hands. After she showered, she knelt at her prayer altar and attempted to do a heart-opening meditation but she couldn't find stillness; not in the way in which she was accustomed to anyway, the calm blossoming in her lungs as she welcomed herself home. Today, all she could focus on was Lisa. Lisa's words, Lisa's email, the implication within. She couldn't stop playing out the worst-case scenarios – a Twitter pile-on, furious calls for cancellation. Her good name destroyed. Shakti closing down, her girls bereft, floundering without her guidance – and finally she kicked the blanket off her knees in frustration and phoned her therapist, using the private number Diane only gave to her 'special' clients. Sam waited in her office for the Zoom meeting to start, and as she pushed her chair back, she stared at the shelves lined above her desk. All the foreign editions of her first memoir, translated into thirty-seven languages around the world, a number one bestseller in most territories. A poster of the *Willing Silence* movie, its iconic shot of a young, blonde girl hiding under a single bed, a hand clasped over her mouth and a lone tear rolling down her cheek. There was a photograph of Sam with the production team on Oscar night, Anne Hathaway in a frothing tulle gown, cradling her statue for Best Actress as if it were a newborn baby. The *New York Times* bestseller list, cut out and framed, proof that she had, at one point, been the writer of the bestselling book in the whole country. *You are a success*, Sam told herself. *No one can take that away from you.*

'We've been doing this work together for years, Diane. You know me better than anyone else. Do you think I would have *sex* with someone without their consent?' Sam squinted at her therapist through the computer screen. Her eyes were tired from the lack of sleep, and the glare was irritating them. 'I—' She took a breath, steadying herself. 'I'm not capable of doing something like this, you know that, don't you?'

'What I know is this,' the older woman replied in her crisp, New England accent. 'We are all capable of being moral *and* monstrous, given the right circumstances. It does us no service to try and hide from our shadow selves.'

'Yeah.' Sam didn't have the patience for a lecture from Diane on the dangers of binary thinking today, not with everything else she was going through. 'I'm aware of that. I've been through the programme. I've done the twelve steps, I've made amends to all those I hurt. I know I've made mistakes, but don't you think it might have come up in our sessions before now if I had *assaulted* someone?'

'Samantha.' Diane tilted her head, visibly reluctant to appease her. Sam had seen many therapists over the years and she'd always prided herself on her ability to outsmart them, playing Chicken to see who would swerve first. They were either in awe of her success or impressed by it, saying how honoured they were to have her in their therapy rooms, *sit, sit, make yourself comfortable!* But Diane had no time for such games; she was one of the few people in her life who was disinterested in Samantha's charm, who seemed wary of it, in fact. She had pushed Sam to see how her need to 'mesmerize' every person she met played out in her friendships – how Sam kept people at a distance, afraid they would see beyond the dazzling charisma and be disappointed – and with the men she dated, too. It was Diane who'd first suggested Sam was not just a drug addict, but that her attitude to love and relationships might need exploration too. 'I'm curious,' the therapist had asked during one of their early sessions. 'Why do you feel the need to have sex with every man who will have you?'

'We both know memory is a delicate thing,' Diane said now. 'And while yes, it seems unlikely that the woman I know from our work together would commit such an act' – she held up a hand to stop her client from celebrating at this rare concession – 'don't you think it can also be true that Lisa might remember that night otherwise?'

'Please! There's a difference between blanking on what dress you wore to prom and forgetting you're a *sexual predator.*'

'Samantha . . .'

'I didn't do this.' She slapped her palm on the desk, her skin smarting in response. 'Do you have any idea how scary it is, that someone could just *say* something like this and you've no way of proving they're lying? After everything I've gone through . . .'

'I'm sorry.' Diane sighed, taking her glasses off and cleaning the lenses. 'This must be especially difficult for you, given your own history of sexual trauma.' She tsked in sympathy. 'You've been such a leading voice in this sector, too. Many of my clients reference your work; how helpful your disclosure of rape was during their own recovery. You should be proud of that, Samantha.'

'I am,' she said. 'But last night, when Jane left . . . I was sitting there, staring at my phone, and I realized I had no one to call. You're the only person I trust, Diane, and I have to pay you, for Chrissake.'

'What about Tatum? She's supposed to be your closest friend.'

Sam had met Tatum at a Yoga to the People class in the fall of 2009. She'd spotted someone in the front row with a red ponytail, pale arms covered in freckles, and she'd almost called out, *Lisa, is that you?* before she caught herself. Afterwards, she'd rushed to introduce herself, invited the other woman to join her for a green smoothie, and they'd been best friends ever since. But Sam wouldn't tell Tatum about this.

'Did you consider calling her?' Diane continued. 'We've talked about the importance of allowing people in.'

'I let Lisa in. And look how that turned out.' Sam dashed the back of her hand against her nose to stop it running. 'You know what's stupid? I *wanted* Lisa to read the essay. Even though they made it perfectly clear that I didn't fit into their lives any more, I thought maybe when she read the essay, she would remember how much we loved each other. Oh God.' Sam started to cry again. 'I thought I was over this.'

'Being abandoned by a friend is a primal wound, especially during adolescence. Those are formative years for the way we see ourselves in adult life. It's not that easy to "get over".' Diane waited. 'We haven't talked about what happened in a while. Would it be useful for us—'

'I can't. Not today.'

'OK.' Her therapist held her hands up. 'But perhaps you should phone Lisa? I know you're worried about her and it might help put your mind at ease, at least.'

'That's what Jane wants me to do. She wants me to drive to Bennford and persuade Lisa to drop this whole thing.'

'And what do *you* want to do, Samantha? What is your gut telling you?'

'I don't know. I guess the thing I keep coming back to is acts of service. I've made a career out of helping people, how can I not at least *try* to do the same with Lisa? Her email was . . . I don't think she's a well person.'

'It would be unethical of me to comment on someone who isn't a patient, so let's take a moment here to refocus, Samantha. Do you think there could be healing for you if you went home?' the older woman asked in a tone that suggested the right answer was *yes*. 'You never properly dealt wi—'

'I told you, I don't want to talk about that today.'

'I understand. But I'm going to ask you one more question. You might not like it but I hope you'll do your best to answer anyway.' Diane stared at her through the screen. 'What would it mean to accept that this is true, Samantha? That this is Lisa's truth and she believes what happened between the two of you was non-consensual. What would that mean for you?'

'But it's not true. I didn't do this.'

'OK,' Diane replied. 'But why don't we try it as a thought experiment. Can you imagine it for me, just for a minute?'

Sam closed her eyes, pretending she had woken up in a world in which this was true, one where she was just as bad as those men who had hurt her, and she felt as if the ground was giving away beneath her. A trap door opening and she was falling, falling, falling, and there would be no end to it, she thought, no release. She would just fall forever. She grabbed at the sides of the desk chair to steady herself. 'I didn't do this,' she whispered. 'You believe me, don't you?'

'It doesn't matter what I believe, but rather, what does Lisa believe? That's the real question here.' Diane picked at the silk scarf with her fingers, untying it. Sam realized she'd never seen her therapist's bare throat before, the creping skin gathering in folds, and it made her feel strange, as if the woman had stripped naked in front of her. 'And it seems to me, Samantha, like the only way you'll find the answer to that question is if you go home.'

5.

Sam could hear him calling her name and when she looked over her shoulder, there he was, fighting his way through a throng of sweating bodies as he held two cups of beer aloft. Josh had phoned her earlier, telling her about this party. Some kid from school – Sam didn't know the girl's name – whose parents had been forced out of town because of a family emergency and foolishly trusted their seventeen-year-old daughter when she swore she wouldn't throw a rager in their absence. 'We don't have any other plans for tonight. Should we go?' she'd asked him, already preparing to bribe Lisa's older brother with twenty bucks to buy her a six-pack of wine coolers.

'I don't care,' Josh had replied. 'Just as long as we're together at midnight.'

He handed her the beer, his eyes dropping to the ruched neckline of her spaghetti-strap dress. 'You look so hot, babe,' he said, leaning in to kiss her on the side of her neck. He traced his fingertips down her back and she shivered slightly, watching as a group of girls huddled in the opposite corner of the room stared at them, envy on their faces. Samantha Miller was the prettiest girl in Junior Year, Josh Taylor the cutest boy; it was inevitable that they would end up dating, that's what everyone said. They were perfect for each other.

'Babe, stop,' she said, pushing him away. 'Not here.' She grabbed his arm, turning it around so she could see his watch. 'What time is it?'

'Ten minutes till countdown,' he said, nuzzling her hair.

'Shit, where's Lisa? She went to the bathroom forever ago.'

Josh shrugged, wrapping one arm around her chest as he sipped at his beer. She wriggled out of his embrace and handed him the second red cup. 'Here,' she said. 'You take that. I'll find her.' She blew a kiss at him. 'I'll be back before you know it.'

'Have you seen Lisa?' she shouted over the pounding music to every kid she knew, but all she got in return was screwed-up faces and *what d'you say? I can't hear you!* She checked the bathroom and the kitchen, the garden, the garage where a game of Beer Pong had been set up, shaking her head *no* when the boys asked if she wanted to play. She went upstairs, muttering 'Shit, sorry,' when she opened a door to find a half-naked couple hooking up in the master bedroom, backing out as quickly as she could. Finally, she walked into a small room which looked like it belonged to a child – pale pink walls, a lamp made of seashells on the nightstand, a single bed with a patchwork comforter – and she could see Lisa through the window, the hood of her quilted jacket up over her head, sitting on the slate tiles of the flat roof. Sam grabbed the comforter, climbing through the open window to join her friend. Lisa didn't look surprised to see her; she just smiled, kissing the top of Sam's head as she huddled against her for warmth.

'What are you doing out here?' Sam asked, pulling the quilt up to her chin.

'It was getting too loud.' Lisa took a drag on her cigarette, blowing smoke out of the side of her mouth. 'I needed a time-out.'

'I thought you'd gone home.'

'Without saying goodbye? Never.' Lisa pointed at the sky, swirls of navy studded with specks of stars. 'Look at that,' she said. 'Isn't it beautiful?' Sam murmured her agreement, listening as the music turned off downstairs, someone shouting, 'It's nearly midnight, guys! Hello, 1999!'

'You'd better go find your boyfriend,' Lisa said, but neither of them moved. *Ten, nine, eight* . . . the chant began, and Sam slipped her arm around Lisa's waist, squeezing it tight. *Seven, six, five.*

She thought she could hear Josh's voice, calling her name again, *Sam, Sam, where are you?* but she wasn't sure; maybe she had imagined it, she told herself.

'No,' Sam said. *Four, three, two.* 'There's no one I would rather start the new year with than you.'

6.

🄾 2,922,452

The Bennford Inn was a Victorian-style mansion on the river, painted white, with arched wood decorating the eaves and high gables. Inside, its oak panelling and oversized oriental rugs offered a quaint charm, Sam supposed, as did the oil paintings of ships and stormy seas hanging on the walls. 'Hello,' she said, placing her overnight bag by her feet. She hadn't packed much; she didn't intend to be here for long. 'My assistant made the reservation but it should be under the name Miller.'

She smiled at the young man on the reception desk, a gangly boy with a shock of bright red hair whose suit jacket had a mustard stain on its lapel. His name tag identified him as 'Cody' and she watched him carefully as he checked her in, waiting for that half double-take which happened when someone recognized her, but it never came. He wasn't exactly her target demographic, to be fair.

'Welcome to the Bennford Inn,' he said, blushing; because he found her attractive or simply because she was female, Sam couldn't tell. 'I have your reservation here, Miss Miller. You're with us for three nights, is that correct?'

She nodded.

'Great,' he said. 'Would you follow me?' Cody grabbed her Louis Vuitton holdall before she could answer, leading her up a staircase lined with a threadbare plaid carpet and a rickety hand-rail, reeling off some local amenities she might enjoy during her stay. 'There are opportunities near by for hiking, biking, fishing, and boating, although it might be rather cold at this time of year!' he said. 'The town offers the quintessential New England experience, and is particularly pleasant if you enjoy antiquing. Do you need me to make a reservation at our restaurant for you?' he asked as he opened the door for her, and they were standing in a large room with a four-poster bed, the chintzy wallpaper matching the fabric of the chair by the open fireplace.

'I'm fine, thank you.' Sam paused. 'Cody, you're from here, right?'

He nodded his yes.

'Do you know the Taylors? Josh and Lisa Taylor?'

His face lit up. 'Yeah,' he said eagerly. 'Mr Taylor gave me my first job, in his company's office over in Stambury. I didn't even have my high school diploma but he still took a shot on me. I wouldn't be where I am today if it wasn't for him.'

'How nice. And what about his wife? Lisa?'

'Eh . . .' He cleared his throat, looking down. 'I don't know. I only saw her a couple of times when she would drop some-thing off to Mr Taylor. She seemed OK, I guess.' Sam was trying to interpret what this meant when he asked, 'Is there anything else I can do for you, Miss?'

'Sorry, what? I was distracted.'

He didn't reply. He stood there, an expectant expression on his face, and she felt suddenly afraid. *No*, she wanted to say. *I'm not like that any more.* In an alternative universe, the other Sam, the woman she had buried in a shallow grave, would have walked over to him and unzipped his fly, sinking to her knees and taking his dick in her mouth without another word being said. He might be shocked, as some of them had been, stuttering their thanks afterwards with such sincerity that it hurt her to hear it. Or he might be waiting for it, this boy who couldn't look at her without his cheeks burning red. He might know that was the sort of woman she was, grabbing her by the back of the head, telling her to *take it*. And the old Sam would have done it, like she had so many times before. She would have closed her eyes and pretended it was Josh Taylor she was kneeling before, Josh Taylor who gasped as he came in her mouth. She always pretended it was him.

'Are you OK, Miss Miller?'

'I'm sorry.' She fumbled in her purse for a fifty-dollar bill. A tip, that was what the boy was waiting for. She handed the money to the receptionist, waving off his protestations that it was too much. 'You've been very helpful, Cody,' she said, closing the door behind him.

She wasn't herself at the moment, that was the problem. She hadn't been able to sleep properly since she'd read that email and it was showing. She fell on to the bed, her body sinking into the mattress as she stared at a misshaped water stain on the ceiling, two black flies crawling across it. *Lisa thinks you assaulted her.* The bad thoughts came, fast and insistent. *She thinks it was non-consensual, what happened. Why is she doing this? This isn't fair.* She told herself she should unpack, hang her clothes in the antique wardrobe and smudge the room with sage to clear any lingering energy left behind from other guests. She needed to find Lisa after that, look into her friend's eyes and ask why she would lie about what happened between them – *But she won't want to talk to you. Lisa thinks you assaulted her. I loved that girl so much. I would never do this. I would never –* and Sam pulled the patchwork quilt over her head. No, the first thing she should do was phone her mother. Sam had intended to call her on the drive upstate but she felt herself shrink the closer she got to Bennford, like she was losing inches from her spine with each mile. What would she say to Carolyn? How would she even begin to explain this?

Her phone beeped and she reached her hand out, patting down the wooden locker to find it. She curled under the quilt again as she read the email from her manager.

> hope the inn is all right. darcy said the tripadvisor reviews were solid. listen ive been thinking & had an idea why don't you & Lisa write a book together?!!! it could be an exploration of the themes you raised in your essay but taking lisas side of the story into consideration too (as long as she's on message) I think it could be a great opportunity & would cancel any sug-gestions of assault. Win win. do you know what lisas financial situ is like rn? x

Assault. Even as she muttered 'What the fuck?' at Jane's impli-cation this was an 'opportunity' to sell more books, that was what Sam kept returning to. Her eyes snagging on the word, the utter impossibility of what it suggested. *Assault*. AssaultAssault-AssaultAssault. She said the word to herself so many times that it lost all meaning.

'Semantic satiation, that's what it's called,' Lisa had told her some day they were walking home from school together. Josh wasn't with them, or at least he wasn't there in Sam's memory, so it must have been tenth grade. Those perfect days when it had just been the two of them and there had been no com-petition for Lisa's time, her affection. Lisa whispering *we're so lucky* as they lay in bed on a sleepover, their fingers interlaced. *Imagine if your parents hadn't moved to Bennford? We might never have found each other.* 'It's a psychological phenomenon in which repetition causes a word to temporarily lose meaning and the listener perceives it as a meaningless sound,' her friend had continued. Lisa had always delighted in a new-found word, the more esoteric the better. It was Lisa who'd dreamed of becoming a writer, not Sam, but her friend didn't have that *thing* that marked her out as special: charisma, magnetism, whatever you wanted to call it. She could never have achieved what Sam had and maybe that was the problem. Maybe she'd watched as Sam became more successful than either of them could have ever imagined, and now Lisa wanted to see her fall.

Sam had turned forty the year before and her childhood was a land that seemed very far away. But there were certain moments that were so integral to the person she had become that they seemed to be picked out in technicolour, dazzlingly bright even now. Like the morning after Lisa's eighteenth birthday party. A stretch of arms, squinting against the harsh sunlight flooding her bedroom. The smell of stale breath and beer, a hangover dragging at her temples. Lisa had been in the bed beside her. Naked limbs and a tangle of red hair, her friend's skin freckled and flushed. Sam had smiled, thinking about how good it had been the night before. The little whimpering noises she had made, a hand over her mouth, whispering, *Shh, shh, someone will hear.* 'Morning.' Sam had bent down to kiss her again but Lisa had pushed her away.

'No,' she'd said.

Sam had stared at her. 'But yesterday, you . . . I don't understand. You were all over me last night, *you* were the one who started this. What's changed?'

Lisa didn't reply. She didn't need to; they both knew the answer. Josh Taylor and what he might say, that was all that mattered to Lisa now. She'd shuffled away on the mattress and retched, a hand to her mouth. It was that moment Sam was never able to forget afterwards, no matter how much she tried. She had remade herself into something new when she moved to the city after school, someone shiny and hard. She became the kind of girl other people wanted to be around; they couldn't get enough of her, she always had somewhere to go, someone to party with. But no matter how many lines of coke she snorted, no matter how many men she fucked, watching their eyes blacken with desire as she undressed, all she could think about was Lisa; that morning in her bedroom all those years before, and the disgust on her face. The shame was always there – it had caught in the back of Sam's throat that day and she had never been able to spit it out again.

She sat upright in bed, an idea forming. The phone number came to her easily; there were so few that she knew off by heart any more, but she had dialled this one a thousand times before. 'Hello,' she said when a familiar voice answered, older now but still with the authoritative tone of an elementary school teacher. 'Mrs Johnson? It's me. Samantha.' There was a slight pause and for a moment, she was afraid Lisa had told the old woman about the email. 'Samantha Miller?'

'Samantha!' Lisa's mother exclaimed. 'Isn't this a nice surprise? I don't think I've seen you since—' She stopped herself before she could finish her sentence with *your father's funeral*. 'Well, I see you on the TV all the time, of course. When you were on *Good Morning America*, I screamed so loud Rick thought I'd seen a mouse! Oh, you looked beautiful. I always knew you'd lose the weight. It was just puppy fat, I used to tell your mom, nothing to worry about.' Sam winced but she didn't say anything. There was no point with Mrs Johnson, she'd learned that years ago. 'I was so sad when you and Lisa drifted apart. I'd never seen two girls as close as you. She cried herself to sleep for *months* after you left for that school. I kept telling her you'd be home again for summer break but she was inconsolable. Although I suppose' – the older woman's voice became reproachful – 'with you being famous now, it must be hard to keep in touch with everyone.'

'I'm not that famous.' Sam curled her fingers into the palm of her hand. It had been *Lisa* who cut off contact, *Lisa* who decided she had to choose between her boyfriend and her best friend, and apparently Sam hadn't stood a chance in that contest. It was so unfair, she wanted to scream. 'But since I turned forty, it makes you re-evaluate things, doesn't it? I guess . . .' She hesitated. 'I'm hoping Lisa and I can reconnect.'

'Oh, for sure. A big birthday will put everything into perspective,' Mrs Johnson said and Samantha could almost see her, standing in that ramshackle house on Elliot Street. She would have her apron on, the one embroidered with pink roses, and the telephone cord would be tangled in a thick knot around her fingers. Sam could be sixteen again, pushing the front door open and calling out *hello!* to the woman grading papers at the kitchen table, before running upstairs to the cramped bedroom Lisa shared with her younger sister, Jill. The carpet matted with clumps of broken eyeshadow, a lava lamp spitting globs of orange, a stack of novels by the bed, Donna Tartt and *Wild Swans* mixed in with Jill's collection of *Sweet Valley High*. 'Speaking of birthdays,' Mrs Johnson continued. 'Do you think you'll still be around for Lisa's next month? Josh is planning a party. It'll be small, just family and a few close friends, but I'm sure they'd be happy to have you there.'

'It depends on work,' Sam replied slowly. 'My new book just came out; it's a busy time.'

When they were teenagers, turning forty seemed like an impossibility. 'The 27 Club, that's the way to go,' Sam had said, coughing as the weed burned the back of her throat. She'd passed the joint to Lisa, who pretended to take a puff before giving it back. 'Better to burn out than fade away, right?' she'd said.

'Who was that again? Kurt?'

'Neil Young, technically. But he had the right idea.' Sam had shuddered. 'I never want to get old.'

'Listen, Mrs Johnson,' she said now. 'I won't keep you much

longer but I need to ask a favour. Do you think you could give me Lisa's cell number?'

The old woman could do better than that, she said, calling Lisa's new address out too. 'Scout's honour,' Mrs Johnson promised, when Sam asked her to stay quiet about this, for she wanted her visit to be a surprise. 'They live in a lovely new development,' Mrs Johnson said, 'over on West Cross Street. Josh's real estate company did them. They're similar to your mother's house but much bigger, of course.'

'Of course,' Sam echoed, rolling her eyes as she hung up.

The GPS instructed her to pull the rented car down a narrow lane and take a sharp right; there she found a row of elegant houses, red brick and black railings and neat front yards. And then, at the end, number sixty-three. 'What the . . .' Sam muttered when she saw the Tudor-esque mansion with latticed windows, the perfectly manicured lawns surrounding a large water fountain. She parked on the opposite side of the street, staring at it open-mouthed. It was almost identical to the house she had grown up in, the same house she and Lisa had stood outside the day Sam was sent away to the school in Utah, their arms wrapped around each other so tightly it felt as if they were sinking into each other's bones.

'Promise you'll write,' Sam had said, her voice cracking.

'I promise,' Lisa replied. *I promise, I promise, I promise.* Sam remembered turning around in her seat as they drove away, staring back at Lisa. Her friend's red hair was whipped up by the wind and she'd clutched at the sides of her polka-dot button-up dress to hold it down. She became smaller and smaller, until Sam had to squint to see her, and then the car turned a corner, and Lisa was gone.

The porch light turned on outside the Taylors' house now and Sam shrank in her seat until she was out of sight, her heart pounding. She pulled her baseball cap down low, and waited a few seconds before sneaking a look. There were no lamps at this end of the street – she knew it was unlikely anyone would be able to see her in the car and even if they did, they would not expect it to be Samantha, not after all this time. She unrolled the window just a crack, as quietly as she could. There was someone on the deck, a woman, swamped in a huge over-coat, a muffler pulled up to her chin. Sam could see the flash of a lighter, a red pin-prick glow, then the woman leaned her head back, blowing smoke to the sky. The door opened and the woman put her hand behind her, hiding the cigarette, until she saw who was there. A man. *Him*. Samantha felt that old ache in her chest, made up of longing and sorrow, and she couldn't bear it. She sank in her seat again but she stayed there, listening to the sound of their voices. They were speaking too quietly to make out any words, save for the occasional burst of laughter. They sounded happy, the two of them, and some-how that made everything worse. Josh and Lisa were happy, smoking an illicit cigarette together on their front porch, while she was alone in the shadows, watching them. Lisa – despite what she had written in her email, despite what she claimed Samantha had done to her – was happy. Sam waited until she heard the porch door swing open and shut again, and the light turned off. She imagined them walking upstairs, hand in hand, whispering all the things they would do to the other once they went to bed. Sam pulled out of the estate's driveway, and as she drove back to the Inn she wondered why, if Lisa was sup-posed to be the victim in all of this, she was the one who got to be happy.

7.

⊙ 3,000,092

Sam couldn't sleep when she returned to the hotel that night; the mattress was too soft, the goose feathers in the quilted comforter making her eyes itch. She hadn't felt this afraid for a very long time. Her career had almost been an accident, she always said, something she had fallen into once she left rehab because she'd felt called to help others recover too. Handing out cheaply printed flyers on the subway and cramming half a dozen women into her studio apartment in Brooklyn for self-actualization workshops, the thrill of creating something new out of nothing, with only her heart to guide her. But success had come calling for Samantha whether she had intended it or not and now that she had tasted it, she didn't want to lose it.

She kicked the comforter off, sneezing as a few more feathers escaped. She unlocked her iPhone – there was an email from her editor, congratulating Sam on debuting at number two on the hardcover non-fiction list, and she let out a sigh she hadn't even known she'd been holding. Her last book had been a disappointment – it had failed to crack the top ten – and she'd embarked on an all-out publicity offensive to ensure the same didn't happen with *Chaste*. There were emails from her publicist, reminding Sam of a phone interview with *Bustle*, the short Q&A which needed to be completed for the *New York Times*, and confirming that she'd managed to reschedule

Sam's interview on *Today with Hoda & Jenna* for two weeks' time but the researcher for *Super Soul Sunday* wasn't being as accommodating, could Sam please call to discuss? A harried assistant was trying to set up a lunch date with Teddy, the co-director of the Shakti board (Sam forwarded that to her own PA with a note: *Delay as long as possible!!!*), multiple PRs 'reaching out', asking Sam to read this book on positive visualization and another book on the Law of Attraction and could she give it a cover quote please, this girl was going to be the next, well, the next Samantha Miller, all of which she could ignore. But there were three missed calls from Jane and a voice message too – 'Well?' Her manager's voice was tight. 'Have you talked to her yet?'

She checked Instagram and there were thousands of notifications, far too many to read. She had finally hit three million followers and people were sharing passages from the new book, as she'd hoped they would – she had written it that way deliberately; it wasn't so much a book that she'd pitched her editor as much as a series of Instagrammable quotes packaged together in a beautifully bound hardback – and uploading clips from the Ballroom event. She looked tiny in the white jumpsuit cut close to her body, the pink letters of CHASTE behind her. Delicate bones, wide eyes, and all that blonde hair; she was like a doll come to life. She stared at her sinewy limbs, the bones of her clavicle (*I always knew you'd lose the weight, it was just puppy fat!*), and she tried to feel grateful for the things her body could do rather than what it looked like. In her DMs, fans were sharing their stories; the terrible sex they'd had, the awful men they'd shared their beds with, the regrets that plagued them still. They wished they had read this book years ago, but they were determined now to stay chaste until they found someone worthy of breaking that vow with. *Thank you, Sam! Thank you for showing us the way! We love you!*

There were messages, too, from the super fans, the women who were the first to comment on every post, sitting in the front row at every event, their hands jerking up when it was time for audience questions. They were the ones who paid fifty bucks a month for her Shakti-Sister Membership, the private Facebook group where they had direct access to Sam. She shared her favourite meditations and green juice recipes there, organizing Zoom masterclasses and psychic circles to help members manifest their dream houses, jobs, relationships. She was thankful for their support – their fees amounted to just under two million dollars a year, after all – but it could be exhausting, trying to manage their expectations about how much of her time and energy they were entitled to. They were wondering where she was and hoping everything was OK, they'd heard she had to leave her launch party early because she had a stomach flu, or was it a family emergency? No one could be sure. Sam hadn't posted anything in a couple of days which was unusual – good engagement required frequent content, Shakti's social media team always reminded her – but it was particularly odd during a publication cycle. She scrolled through the comments (*I miss you, Sam!* shaktigirl00 wrote. *What's up, babe?*), liking as many as she could, until she saw that name again.

@Supernovadiabolique157 Does anyone else think it's bullshit Samantha is promoting chastity when her last book was *literally* about how hook-up culture can be 'empowering' for women? Seems like everything is empowering if Shakti can make a frigging dime off it.

Sam sighed. Whenever she'd posted recently, no matter how innocuous, that same username would appear, referencing interviews Sam had given years ago, pulling up ancient quotes that contradicted her current position on any given issue. She resisted the urge to delete the comment – she wanted her IG account to be a safe space for robust conversations, and that meant allowing criticism – but it felt unfair, this woman's inability to allow Sam to change her mind. People had to be allowed to make mistakes. We have to give others space to learn, to grow, she'd always said that. How would anything change otherwise?

She chose a flattering light setting on her LuMee case and went live on Instagram. 'Hey, my loves,' she said, smiling at the camera. She kept it tight on her face, not wanting to show too much of the patterned bed board – it was unlikely anyone would recognize it as the Bennford Inn but she wasn't taking any chances. 'I'm sorry I haven't been on here in a minute. It's been super busy with the release of the new book but I heard today that *Chaste* debuted at number two on the *New York Times* best-seller list! That's thanks to every one of you who bought the book.' She did a victory shimmy with her shoulders. 'I feel so lucky to have you as part of the Shakti family. This little community, *this* is why I do what I do. None of this would be possible without you.' She could see questions appearing on screen, one after the other, and she rushed on. 'Some awesome comments here but I don't have time for a proper #SamShares session today, 'k? I'm wiped from all the promo stuff and I need some self-care. Maybe it's worth thinking about that in your own lives. Do *you* need time out? Do you need to turn your phone off, get outside in nature and breathe? You deserve it, my loves.' She blew them a kiss and shut down the app. Her phone rang instantly, Jane's name flashing on the screen. She groaned and turned it on silent. Maybe her manager would—

Jane: i know youre there just saw your insta live. pick up

'Fuck,' she muttered as the phone rang again. Sam pressed it to her ear, saying as brightly as she could, 'Hello?'

'Have you talked to Lisa yet?'

'I just woke up. I'll go over there after I've had breakfast.'

'What's your game plan?'

'I don't have a "game plan", Jane,' she said irritably. 'I want to make sure she's OK.'

'This woman has implied you *assaulted* her. You do remember that, don't you?'

'Yes, and does that sound like the behaviour of a mentally sound person? I have a responsibility to make sure she's—'

'And *I* have a responsibility to make sure your career doesn't go up in fucking flames,' Jane cut across her. 'Go over there right now and sort this shit out.'

The steps up to the Taylors' house were the same as those at her childhood home: three broad steps to the front, wrought-iron railings shaped like curling ivy lining those at the side. The arched marble doorway set in red brick was similar, too, with its panelled door and stained glass cut into stars. The only differences were the two terracotta flower pots on either side of the entrance, stuffed with begonias and pansies, and the brass knocker in the shape of a lion's head. A Tesla SUV was parked in the drive – new, she noticed; Lisa and Josh weren't short of cash, clearly – and two pink bikes with glittering streamers abandoned on the lawn. She checked her Google Maps again; yes, she was at 63 West Cross Street. This was Lisa Johnson's – *Lisa Taylor's* – house.

She banged the knocker and waited, stamping her feet as plumes of smoke blew from her nose. January in Connecticut was always bitterly cold, and the air tasted like the promise of snow. She could hear muffled giggling and when the door opened, there stood two little girls, mirror images of one another. Twins, she realized, with their pigtails and corduroy dungaree dresses, one wearing a pink turtleneck, the other navy. They were miniature versions of Lisa, strawberry blonde hair and skin so pale you could trace the veins thatching across their hands, and as they smiled, Sam saw each girl was missing her front teeth.

'Hi,' she said, smiling back at them. 'What are your names?'

The girl on the left looked to her sister, waiting for her to answer. 'We're not allowed to talk to strangers,' the sister with the navy turtleneck said. 'My mom says it's not safe.'

'But I'm not a stranger. I was your mommy's best friend when we were your age.' She tried to look past them into the hallway. 'Can you get Mommy for me?'

Neither girl looked convinced, and they closed the door a fraction, their blue eyes peering up at her. 'We never seen you before,' the braver twin said, as if daring Samantha to contradict her. 'How can you be my mom's best friend if we never even seen you?'

'That's true,' Sam conceded. 'But that's because I live in New York City and I haven't been home in a while. I grew up here, though. In Bennford. I actually lived in a house near by.' A sharp wind cut through the bare maple trees surrounding the garden and she shivered. 'Can you get Lisa for me now? It's freezing out here.'

'Girls, who's at the . . .' He trailed off when he saw who was there, his face paling. When Sam was getting ready that morning, she had done so with careful deliberation, knowing there was a good chance she would see him. After she'd curled her hair and slicked her mouth with pink lipstick, she'd chosen her outfit – a slouchy sweater over leather leggings, ankle boots that were so high she felt as if she was on stilts – and she'd stared at herself in the mirror, marvelling at how glossy she looked, how *rich*. She'd been so preoccupied with wondering what he would think when he saw her that she didn't give enough consideration to how *she* would feel, faced with Josh

Taylor for the first time in twenty-two years. She'd secretly hoped that he would have gone to seed, his hairline receding and a soft belly straining against his shirt, but he looked remarkably similar to his teenage self. There was a little grey at his temples, a few more laughter lines around his eyes, and his nose looked different, as if it had broken and reset strangely, but he was still the sort of handsome that meant women would notice him when he walked down the street, nudging their friends in the line at Starbucks, mouthing *hot* as he gave his order to the barista. It was like the first day of ninth grade again, when she'd passed him in the cafeteria. He had turned tall and broad-shouldered seemingly overnight, his face tanned and his hair streaked with blond, laughing with his buddies as they grabbed a table near hers. There had been a quickening in her belly, a heat uncoiling inside her that she'd never felt before. Sam had spent the wasteland of her twenties looking for someone who would make her feel that way again – young and alive and like anything was possible. But afterwards, when those men were done with her, she would stumble into their bathrooms and stare at herself in the mirror, wondering at how far she had come from that fourteen-year-old girl who'd just wanted Josh Taylor to notice her.

'What—' Josh broke off, blinking rapidly. He put a hand on each of the girls' shoulders, pulling them back from the door.

'She's here to see Mom,' one twin said, looking up at her father.

'She . . . Lisa's not here,' he said. He was inching the door closed and Sam took a step forward, edging a foot in the way so he couldn't shut it in her face. He wasn't getting rid of her that easily, not this time.

'Where is she?' she asked and Josh said, 'She's gone—' He stopped himself. 'Please, Sam,' he said. 'Don't do this.'

'She went to the store,' the girl with the navy turtleneck

said, looking up at her father curiously. 'We ran out of milk and Mom said—'

'I don't think Sam's interested in that,' Josh cut in. 'She's a busy woman. I'm sure she needs to go back to the city now but we'll tell Mom she called, won't we?'

The twins chorused their agreement but Sam didn't move; she was worried that if she did, she would start to cry. She was furious with herself, to have allowed herself to be in a position where Josh could reject her again. When would she learn that these people were not to be trusted?

'Are you OK?' Navy Turtleneck asked her. She touched Sam's arm, stroking the soft fabric of her floral appliqué coat. 'Do you want to come in for a cup of coffee?' It was clear the girl was parroting something she'd heard her parents ask hundreds of times before; Sam doubted theirs was a household where guests were often left on the front porch in the cold.

'I don't think that's—' Josh tried, but she spoke over him quickly.

'I'd love to,' Sam said. 'Thanks so much, girls.'

The twins chattered excitedly as Sam unbuttoned her coat and pulled off her tweed fedora. Navy Turtleneck was called Martha, she said, and her sister in the pink turtleneck was Maya, and Sam recoiled. 'Sorry, what? I . . .' she said but she couldn't finish. Martha and Maya were *her* baby names; she'd told Lisa that a million times when they were teenagers. There was no way she could have forgotten; it had to be deliberate. Sam shook it off, trying to pay attention as the twins told her they were six and a half – 'But I'm two minutes older,' Martha said – and they were in first grade. Their teacher was Mrs Kelly. She was nice but she didn't go to their church, she went to a different one over on Fairfax Street – 'the *Catholic* one,' Martha said, pulling a face.

The foyer was large, with a pinewood floor and a domed

ceiling lined in gold-flecked paint, the split staircase covered with cream carpet. The walls were painted cream too, hung with a number of timid pastel paintings. *Bland*, the interior designer who'd helped Sam with her own apartment would have said, as he repressed a shudder at the baroque-style chandelier. 'Come on, slow-poke.' Martha took Sam's hand and led her into the kitchen. It was a traditional Shaker style, white cabinets with gleaming white floor tiles, a crown moulding on the ceiling and an ink-black splashback. Josh stood at the doorway, his lips pressed in a grim line.

'Daddy,' Martha admonished him. 'You're supposed to be making the coffee.'

'Sorry.' Josh filled the kettle with water from the tap. 'I didn't know if Samantha would want coffee; she's some sort of health guru these days.'

'What's a guru?' Maya asked and Josh said he wasn't quite sure. A shiver of excitement ran down Sam's spine even as she told herself not to read anything into it. It was only natural he would know about her career; the *Willing Silence* movie alone would have made it impossible for him *not* to know, but she couldn't help herself. Imagining Josh waiting until the twins were asleep and Lisa was out, at her book club or PTA meeting, and he would sneak into his study and turn on his laptop, searching for Sam's name. He would see what a success she had made of her life, despite what he and Lisa had done to her. Maybe he would wish he had chosen her then.

'And what are you up to these days?' she asked, as he reached up to grab two mugs from the top shelf of the cupboard. His sweater rose a little, a flash of taut stomach, and she swallowed, looking away.

'I'm in real estate,' he said.

'I wasn't expecting that,' she said, pretending to be surprised.

'What exactly were you expecting, Sam?' he asked, and she didn't say anything about the nights they had spent under her bed covers, whispering secrets to each other as the sky turned black outside. He wanted to be a teacher, he had said, working with kids from deprived backgrounds. He wanted to make a difference.

'Daddy's company is building a new mall over in Stambury,' Martha piped up, and Sam whistled.

'A mall,' she said. 'I'm impressed.'

'It pays the bills.'

'I bet,' she said, looking around at the glossy, lacquered kitchen. 'And what about Lisa? What does she do?'

'She takes care of us,' Martha said. 'It's a big job,' and Josh couldn't help but laugh.

'That it is,' he said, ruffling his daughter's hair. 'You keep Mom very busy, don't you?'

'I know a thing or two about that,' Sam said. She was prattling on, she knew, but she couldn't help it, she was so nervous. 'Being busy, I mean. Especially with . . .' She hesitated. 'My new book?' She watched him, waiting to hear what he would say about the book, the essay, Lisa's email, but he didn't react.

He just said, 'Good for you. I hope mint is OK. It's all I can find.' He slopped a mug of tea on to the marble-topped breakfast bar, and she wrapped her hands around it for warmth. They stared at each other, searching beneath these new faces with their fine lines and crow's feet for the people they had once been, and all they had meant to each other. The girls drifted away into an adjacent cubby from the kitchen, stuffed with their toys, board games and jigsaw puzzles. Martha made Ken kiss Barbie, screaming with laughter, while Maya settled down at a small table with a colouring book and a stash of pencils.

Josh waited until they were engrossed in their games before he said, 'What are you doing here?'

'That's not very welcoming.'

'Welcoming? I . . .' He looked lost for words. 'Sam, I don't know what you're up to, but I don't want any trouble.'

'Neither do I, believe me.'

'Then why are you here? We haven't seen you in—'

'Twenty-two years,' she said. She could have given him the months, the days, the hours since they had last seen one another, down to the exact minute. Losing him, losing Lisa – it had been one of the most devastating experiences of her life and yet it was obvious now that they had simply walked away from the bonfire, unscathed. Building this new life for themselves without a thought for Sam.

'And you just turn up on our doorstep?' He blew his breath out. 'What the fuck?'

'I don't want to be here any more than you do,' she said, annoyed with his attitude. 'But I have to talk to Lisa about that email. What else did you expect me to do, Josh?'

'What email?' he asked, but his phone rang before she could answer. He went to turn it off, grimacing when he saw the name on the screen. It cut off, then whoever it was tried again. The phone rang and rang, Josh's shoulders tensing with every new attempt.

'They seem pretty insistent,' she said. 'Must be important.'

A beat, Josh's agonized *shit*, then he grabbed his cell. 'Bill!' he said, forcing a note of joviality into his voice. 'I'm sorry about that, I . . .' He moved away, standing by the French doors that led into a formal dining room, his eyes still on her as he talked about some issues they were having with the new contractor.

'Tell me,' Sam said, walking into the alcove and crouching on her haunches next to the twins. 'What do we have here?'

It was five, maybe ten minutes later when she heard a key in the door and there was Lisa's voice. Deeper than the last time she'd heard it, and slightly huskier. Sam's stomach tightened at the sound of it, and she quickly fixed her hair. 'I know,' Lisa said. 'But it's just a phase . . . She'll grow out of it, you have to—' A pause. 'Oh, gosh. Of course, I would be the same if it was my girls. I didn't mean to sound dismissive. Why don't you come over tonight? I'll open a bottle of wine, and we can talk.' Lisa pushed the kitchen door open with her hip, her phone pressed between her ear and her shoulder, two brown paper bags in her arms. When she saw Samantha, sitting on the tiled floor of her kitchen, playing dolls with her daughters, she let one of the bags go slack. It slid to the ground with a bang.

'I have to go,' she said abruptly to the person on the phone, as the twins called, 'Hi, Mom,' without looking up from their game.

'I thought you said these dolls were regressive.' Sam waved one in the air, a perfect specimen of blonde beauty in a hot-pink mini-dress and stilettos. She knew she was being flippant but she couldn't help it; she was too anxious to come up with anything better. 'Anti-feminist propaganda, if I remember correctly.' She stood, tossing her hair to one side. Her sweater had fallen off her shoulder but she didn't adjust it; her collarbones were eye-wateringly sharp these days and she knew Lisa would notice. They had always monitored each other's bodies, silently weighing the other with more precision than the most sensitive of scales. But while these days, Sam was toned from daily Bikram yoga, Lisa was positively gaunt. She showed the signs of caring for small children far more acutely than Josh did – her skin was paper-thin, faint lines creasing around her mouth and her forehead. Her clothes were those of a suburban mom: dark-wash jeans tucked into knee-high tan boots, a matching purse and a lovely coat, belted, in a cream wool.

'Josh?' Lisa asked weakly, dumping the other bag of groceries on the breakfast bar.

'He had to take a phone call,' Sam said. 'Some guy named Bill.'

'Oh. Bill, of course . . . Yes. Yes, I . . .' She trailed off, her eyes darting to the twins.

'Are you OK?' Sam asked, pulling one of the stools closer to Lisa. 'Do you need to sit down?'

'I'm fine. What . . . what are you doing here?'

'Girl.' Sam narrowed her eyes. 'What do you think I'm doing here? My manager showed me the email you sent her. I've been freaking out, I can't—'

'Shh.' Lisa looked over her shoulder to see where Josh was.

Sam followed her gaze, realization dawning slowly. 'Wait,' she said. 'You didn't tell him?'

'I can't talk about this. Not now.'

'Well, when *can* you talk about it? You hardly expect me to just—' Sam hadn't noticed one of the twins coming up behind her until she was tugging on her sweater.

'I never showed you what Santa got me,' the girl said. 'It's a light-up karaoke machine. On Christmas Day, Mom and Dad got drunk—'

'We didn't, Martha.' Lisa frowned at her daughter. 'We had a couple of glasses of eggnog and we—'

'And they sang this old song about—' The little girl started giggling. 'About big butts!' She and her sister broke out in loud laughter, Lisa telling them to be quiet.

'Your father is on a work call, we have to be—' and then the door from the living room opened and Josh was rushing towards them.

'Sorry,' he said, flustered. 'It was Bill, I had to take it.' His hands on his wife's waist, pulling her back to him. 'Are you OK?' he asked, and he looked at her as if Lisa was a piece of fine china that he was checking for cracks.

'I'm fine, honestly,' Lisa insisted and her husband sucked his teeth, but he didn't argue. The three of them stood around the breakfast bar, mouths tense. Remembering what had happened the last time they'd seen each other.

'So.' Josh cleared his throat, looking from one woman to the other, his forehead creasing. 'How long are you in town for, Sam?'

'Will you bring the girls upstairs?' Lisa folded her arms across her chest.

'What? Are you sure you don't want me to . . . ?'

Lisa shook her head, and there was a glance between them, a wordless agreement. Josh clapped his hands and told the twins to follow him. 'Nope,' he said as their voices climbed into a piercing wail, demanding Oreos and milk – *we're hungry, Daddy*. 'I don't want to hear it,' he said. 'Let's go.'

'Martha and Maya?' Sam said when they were alone. She took a seat at the breakfast bar. 'That's . . . an interesting choice of names.' She raised an eyebrow at Lisa, waiting for the other woman to look sheepish, to apologize, but she did neither.

'What are you doing here, Sam? I think we made it pretty clear we didn't want to see you any more.'

'Lisa.' She felt like a child again, the last one to be picked when her classmates were choosing teams for softball. She wanted to run to her mother and cry, *The kids were mean to me in school today*. 'You can't still be mad about—'

'You don't get to tell me what I can and can't be mad about, not any more. Those days are long gone. I want you to leave now.'

'I can't just go,' Sam said. 'I came back to Bennford because I was worried about you—'

Lisa let out an ugly laugh. 'Worried about *me*? You came here because you were worried about yourself. At least tell the truth about that, if nothing else.'

'What did I ever do to you that was so bad?' The tears were close; Sam could feel them stinging the back of her eyes. 'What did I ever do that would make you hate me this much? That you would *lie* about me?'

'You can quit the act now. Have you forgotten about *Blackout*? Did you think I wouldn't see that essay?' She glared at Sam. 'What were you thinking?'

'I didn't ... Like, does anyone in Bennford even read *Blackout*?'

'How would you know what anyone here does or doesn't do? You haven't spent more than a couple of hours in this town since high school.'

'And whose fault was that? I only left because you wanted me to.'

'Don't start that shit again.' Lisa's chin jutted out. 'I never asked you to leave, the school in Utah was your idea. You *always* do this. You always twist everything. You just have to be the victim, don't you, Sam?'

'That's not fair! I'm not trying to twist anything. Your email scared me. You didn't sound like you, not when you're making accusations that I—'

'I can't do this,' Lisa said, crouching down to pick up the groceries she'd dropped when she first came in, repacking the bag of apples that had fallen out, a gallon of milk, a family-sized box of Cheerios. Sam watched as Lisa emptied the paper bags, then her friend said, 'I need you to leave. Now.'

'I'm not leaving. Not until you tell me what it is you want. Are you looking for a retraction to the essay?' Lisa didn't say anything so she continued. 'Are you—' Sam felt sick but she made herself ask. 'Are you planning on going public with this?'

'Would that be the worst thing in the world, Sam? For people to know the truth about you?'

'But it's not the truth! You know it's not the truth. We were both there that night and you know *exactly* what happened. What is wrong with you? How could you say something like this about—'

'What's going on?' It was Josh, closing the door to the hall-way behind him. 'We could hear you arguing upstairs; the girls are getting upset.' His eyes darted from one woman to the other. 'Sam,' he said faintly. 'Sam, what have you—'

'I haven't done *anything*,' Sam shouted. 'The two of you need to stop blaming me for shit I haven't even done. All I did was write an essay, which apparently is a crime now.'

'What essay?' Josh asked, confused. 'What are you talking about?' He looked at Lisa. 'What is she talking about, babe?' But Lisa slumped on to a chair as if she'd turned boneless. 'Babe,' he said. 'You're freaking me out. What's going on?'

'I wrote an essay,' Sam said slowly, for someone had to tell the truth and it looked like it would have to be her. 'It was promo for my new book. Talking about the night of Lisa's birthday.'

The blood drained from Josh's face. 'Sam,' he said. 'What did you do?'

'And then Lisa wrote an email to my manager,' she continued. 'Saying that what happened that night wasn't . . . Lisa said' – she had to take a second – 'Lisa said it wasn't consensual.'

'What?' Josh took a step backwards. 'No. No, that can't be . . . Lisa.' He went to his wife, lifting her chin so she was looking him in the eye. 'She can't be serious. You wouldn't . . . Why didn't you tell me about this?'

'Because we never talk about her, do we?' Lisa replied and the room seemed to shrink, the walls closing in and pushing Sam's face into those words, stuffing her mouth with their sharp edges. She thought about Josh and Lisa all the time and they never thought about her, just like it had been in high school. She was irrelevant again, the third wheel.

'I think you need to leave, Sam.' Josh stood by Lisa's side but he made no attempt to touch his wife again.

'Don't do this to me. I'm begging you. I don't deser—'

'Samantha, get out of here,' he shouted, and she jumped back in fright. 'I need to talk to my wife. Alone.'

8.

The last thing Sam expected when she walked into her hotel room was to find her mother there. Carolyn was sitting at the edge of the bed, her knees pressed together primly. The faded floral pattern of her wrap dress coordinated perfectly with the room's decor, as if she'd somehow planned it. Her hair was mostly grey now and gathered in a neat chignon at the base of her neck, showing off Grandma Anderson's pearl and diamond earrings. Her mother was still beautiful, even at seventy-six; her delicate bone structure had always done as much as her famously steady hand to persuade the wives of the Upper East Side that Dr Carolyn Anderson-Miller was someone they could trust with their expensive faces.

'Shit,' Sam said, clutching at her chest in fright. 'What are you doing here?'

'Language, please. Your father and I didn't raise you to speak like a fisherman's wife. And I think we both know the real question is, what are *you* doing here?'

Sam threw her coat on the back of the rocking chair, dusting snow off her hat. She sat down, staring at her mother. 'How did you even get in here?'

'The young man at the front desk was very obliging. He gave me a spare key once I explained the situation.'

'Explained what, exactly? That you wanted to break into my room? I'm pretty sure this is illegal, Mom.'

Carolyn smoothed down the material of her dress. She walked towards her and, for a moment, Sam thought she would hug her. She could smell her mother's perfume, the yellow and white bottle that looked like sun block, its citrus scent cut with sunflowers. Carolyn wore that fragrance because her own mother had given it to her when she was a girl, saying it was 'suitable', and that had been enough for Carolyn. She did what she was told. She didn't know why Samantha couldn't do the same; her daughter's life would be so much easier if she just followed the rules. 'Honestly,' she said, picking up Sam's coat and hanging it on the hook on the back of the door. 'I don't know why you buy such lovely clothes if you're going to throw them about willy-nilly. I couldn't believe it when I first came in here, the state of the room was shocking.'

'I was in a rush this morning and I—' Sam shut up. She didn't have to explain anything to her mother; she was a grown woman. She and her therapist had role-played this scenario many times, practising how Sam could stay calm and speak to Carolyn in a mature manner, and yet too often, when faced with her mother she reverted to behaving like a teenager, one second away from shrieking, *I didn't ask to be born, did I?* 'It was inappropriate of you to come in here without my permission,' she tried. 'You have to respect my boundaries.'

'Oh, I can't bear this therapy talk.' Carolyn nestled the handle of her handbag into the nook of her elbow, like the Queen of England. 'And I wouldn't need to break into your hotel room if you'd phoned to tell me you were in town, like a normal child would have done. Oh, but not mine. *My* daughter – who told me she couldn't *possibly* come home for the holidays, she was just *so* busy with work—'

'Mom, I took you to Tavern on the Green for dinner to make it up to you. We went to the freaking Rockefeller Center to see the tree! What more do you want from me?'

'And then' – Carolyn continued as if Sam hadn't spoken – 'she arrives back in town not even a fortnight later and I have to hear that she's staying in the Bennford Inn, of all places, from

Lydia Thomas, and good God, Samantha, you know what she's like. *Didn't you know?* she asked me, absolutely thrilled she was the one to tell me.'

'How did she hear I was in town? I literally just arrived yesterday; I've barely been outside the Inn.'

'Her niece is the assistant manager here,' Carolyn said with a dismissive wave. 'And that's hardly the point, is it?'

'Mom, I—'

'I don't want to hear any more excuses. Pack your bags. You're coming home with me.'

Sam's childhood was a lonely one, she would say in interviews. Her parents had been unsure if they even wanted kids; their careers were time-consuming, their lives in the city full of dinner parties and gallery openings, tickets for this play and invites to that exhibition. Sam had been the result of a missed pill, and that was how she'd always been made to feel – like a mistake. Not the son her father wanted, nor the pliant, malleable doll her mother would have shaped in her own image. With the help of guided visualizations to heal her inner child (which she'd insisted were readily available on Shakti so her girls could have access to the same healing she had), Sam had made peace with her past but still, she found herself reciting mantras as she drove to her mother's house – 'I am powerful. I am a Child of the Universe. I am worthy of love and respect' – and by the time she parked behind her mother's BMW, her damp palms were slipping on the steering wheel. She rolled down the window, staring up at her childhood home.

'Fuck,' Sam muttered under her breath. It was eerie, how similar the houses were. Had no one else in town noticed her former best friend playing Single White Female? Surely people had thought it odd when the Taylors had built a copy-cat mansion of their own?

'Samantha,' her mother said, turning at the front door. 'It's seventeen degrees out this evening and I'm not as young as I once was. I'd rather not get frostbite waiting for you, if you don't mind.'

She hurried to catch up to Carolyn. There were more photos hung on the chinoiserie tea paper from the hall to the living room: her parents' wedding and their honeymoon in Paris, smiling in front of the Eiffel Tower. Another, more formal picture from their thirtieth wedding anniversary, sitting on a sofa, their knees touching. They'd thrown a large party that night, erecting a marquee in the garden, caterers hired to serve Dom Pérignon in coupe glasses. Sam wasn't invited. 'Why must you always put it that way? You weren't *available*,' her mother would complain. Sam was in rehab at the time, going cold turkey in a facility in upstate New York, and the day of her parents' anniversary clashed with a family therapy session. It had been easy to reschedule – 'No harm done, darling!' her mother trilled on the phone – but that wasn't the point, Sam wanted to say. She needed them to show up for her. And once again, they had not.

The living room was decorated in shades of blue, the bespoke sofa and spoon-back chairs covered in a powder silk, and Sam sat, almost afraid to move – she hadn't been allowed in this room as a child and she was still nervous she would spill her tea on the rug, leave a ring mark on the walnut coffee table. She spotted a small photo in a silver frame, tucked behind a cut-crystal vase filled with calla lilies. It was one of her, this time, a small child blowing out candles, and next to her, staring at the red velvet cake in awe, was Lisa. This was her earliest childhood memory, her fourth birthday party – the lilac dress with white stars her mother had yanked roughly over her head, the staff at the local Chuck E. Cheese singing 'Happy Birthday' to her before clearing the table when she'd gone to use the restroom. There'd been another girl sitting in her place when she had returned, another cake. 'My first Bennford birthday,' she said, turning the frame around and showing it to Carolyn.

Her mother glanced at it, saying, 'No, that was in the city. We brought you to the Plaza, remember? Like Eloise.'

Sam looked at it again. 'Oh yeah, you're right,' she said, putting the frame back down. 'She lives close by; did you know that?' Sam checked her phone to see if her manager had emailed before tucking it into her bag. 'Lisa, I mean. Their house is the *exact* same as yours; it's so weird. Have you seen it?' Her mother had been about to pour tea into Sam's cup but she placed the pot down on the mirrored tray again.

'I have,' she said carefully. 'Joshua came to me when they were building and I—' She stopped herself. 'I didn't know you were back in touch with Lisa.'

'I'm not. We haven't spoken since high school, you know that. God. It was tough seeing her today. I don't know what I hoped would happen but . . .' Sam blinked away tears. 'Anyway. I'll figure it out.' She tried to smile. 'Oh, macarons! Are they vegan?' She reached down to take one and her mother grabbed her wrist. Carolyn's skin was ice-cold and her grip was surprisingly firm for a woman of her age.

'Don't start all that again,' she said. 'They've had enough trouble. Just let them alone, this time.'

Sam jerked her hand away, throwing the macaron back on the platter. 'You don't know anything about it, Mom. So why are you jumping to the conclusion that *I'm* the one in the wrong?'

It wounded her, how her parents always assumed the worst of her. Sam had made mistakes in the past, she was aware of that. She had hurt people when she was at the height of her addiction; she'd been unreliable, untrustworthy. She'd lied, she had stolen from friends and colleagues, she had done things that still made her uneasy to think about. Rooms she had woken up in, men she should never have touched. Limping home with unexplained bruises and vomit pooling at the back of her throat, trying to forget the night before. Her face pushed into a pillow that smelled of another woman's perfume, the way she had cried as a man called her *a dirty whore* and hadn't stopped to check if she was OK. Those men never stopped. Calling a car on the magazine's account before phoning in sick, hiding in her apartment for the rest of the day, popping diazepam to soothe the fear licking its tongue up her spine. She'd promise herself that tomorrow would be different, but after every tomorrow turned out to be the same, she couldn't even believe her own lies any more. She had done the work, she had recovered. Yet whenever she was back in Bennford, she could feel the old Sam pulsing beneath her skin. It was her mother's fault, she thought. It had always been Carolyn who knew where the stitches lay, how easily she could unpick the seams of this new identity Sam had made for herself. Carolyn was the one to blame.

'Joshua and Lisa could have been kinder to you when you were teenagers. I'm aware of that,' her mother said. 'But they're happy now. They've moved on. You need to do the same.'

'That's easy for you to say.' Sam got to her feet, her fingers itching to upend the Ottoman, knock over the teacups and saucers and those antique silver spoons her mother was so precious about. She probably preferred those fucking spoons to her own daughter; she certainly took better care of them. 'Why can't you ever take my side?'

'For goodness' sake, this isn't about "sides". You're not a child.'

'Just shut up and leave me alone,' Sam screamed, sounding exactly like the child her mother said she wasn't supposed to be any more. She stormed out of the room and slammed the door behind her.

She stood there, trying to catch her breath, when she heard

her mother say clearly, 'And of course they're not vegan. They're basically meringues.'

Sam had somehow imagined her bedroom would look the same as when she'd left it at eighteen. Padded bras on the floor, her Steve Madden slides kicked under the bed. It would smell of CK One and there would be nail polish scattered on her vanity table, a Fiona Apple CD and a stack of magazines on the nightstand. A time capsule, proof that she had existed and had a life here once. But her mother had other ideas, she could see. Carolyn had stripped the room bare, paving the floor with tiles and placing an old lamp she'd never liked on a vintage chest of drawers. There was a reupholstered Queen Anne chair, a pearl-and-bone inlay mirror, and a black-and-white photograph of a girl in a frilled dress smoking a cigarette hung by the lead-framed window. Of course her mother would not have kept it as a shrine to her, as if she'd died tragically and they couldn't bear to move a single tube of mascara. Carolyn wasn't exactly the sentimental type; even if Sam had died – and she could have, she thought fiercely, there were far too many times when she was close to death, stepping unsteadily into hot baths while she was wasted and the temptation to slip beneath the water was so great – her mother would have seized the opportunity to redecorate anyway.

She threw her bag at the foot of the bed and flopped on to the mattress, screaming her frustration into the pillow. She kicked her boots off and pulled the sweater over her head, lying there in her leggings and bra as she tried to catch her breath. She should phone Diane, set up an emergency Zoom session. Her therapist understood that these neural pathways were so deeply ingrained, it was all too easy to fall back into old patterns of behaviour. *The brain will always take the path of least resistance*, Diane would remind her. *Old habits die hard.* She could go on Instagram, too; she hadn't done a #SamShares in days and she knew, as upsetting as the confrontation with her mother had been, it might be helpful for her girls. They would identify with this struggle; they were young enough to appreciate how tempting it was to regress when you returned to your childhood home. *This is the work*, she would say, watching as the comments popped up on screen. *Hi from Brazil! We love you, Sam!* She always shared her pain in the hope it would ease theirs.

She touched the side of the bed, running her hand up and down, and she froze when her finger snagged on a tiny indentation in the wood. The bed board was different, a quilted jacquard in the same pattern as the armchair, but had her mother kept the old frame? She rolled off and tried to look underneath but it was too dark to see. She dug into her handbag until she found her phone, using the torch app as she scooted her body under. There was a reason why an image of a girl hiding under her bed was used for the *Willing Silence* book cover, and then again for the movie poster. Sam did this whenever her parents fought, arguing over the hours Carolyn worked, the magazine article her new practice had featured in – *The boys in the office had to show me. Do you know how that makes me look?* – her father had shouted that day, furious. She still hid under the bed when she was a teenager and she heard her mother's footsteps tapping down the hall. 'She's not here,' Carolyn would say when she found her daughter's room empty. 'I don't know what I'm going to do with that girl.' Snippets of her parents' conversation floating through the floorboards: *it's not natural* and *they were always too close*. Sam would put on her headphones, blaring Alanis on her Discman, and she'd scribble notes on the underside of the bed frame in black marker. *Parents fighting again, 10/16/1993* on one side, *I had a panic attack today, Dad told me to go to my room and have my* 'little freak-out' there, *07/27/1995* on the other. No one knew about this hiding place except Lisa. Sam had shown her one day after school, gesturing at the other girl to follow as she disappeared under the bed. Lisa holding up the torch to examine the messages written on the wood, reading aloud. 'I think my father hates me.' She had sighed, reaching out to hold Sam's hand. 'It doesn't matter if he does,' she'd said. 'Because I love you. I will love you forever.'

Now, as Sam hid under her bed again, she ran her fingers across the ragged wood, tracing the veins of her girlhood pain. Her phone buzzed – an email from Jane, the subject line screaming URGENT!!!!!! – and as she tried to climb out, her foot hit against something solid. She knelt on the rug and pulled it out, finding a large wooden box with geometric stencilling inlaid around the edges. It was beautiful, a mother-of-pearl clasp at the closure and a blue velvet interior, and she gasped in delight when she opened it. Carolyn had phoned her when Sam first moved to the city, saying a package had arrived from Utah and what did Sam expect her to do with this stuff? Burn it, Sam had said. What did she want with her memories now? She would make new ones, better ones. But her mother had kept everything. There were ticket stubs for the movie theatre, Polaroids of her and Lisa in the knee-high socks they'd worn after *Clueless* was released, their make-up turning bone-white under a camera flash. Tickets from a No Doubt concert in Hartford, dozens of fading Valentine's Day cards. There were her old diaries, too, held together with flimsy locks that she broke easily now, bubble writing on the front page demanding that the intruder KEEP OUT! She flipped through one, laughing at how intense she had been. *I can't believe Lisa told Becky about my crush on MK!!!!* she'd written in March 1997. Who was MK? she wondered. She couldn't remember having a crush on someone with those initials. *I will never forgive her for this, as long as I live. And then she pretended not to know what I was talking about when I said it to her! AS IF!! I swear, this is IT for us. If she comes over after school, I'm gonna tell her that. She and Becky can have each other!!!* The diary entry went on for pages, with precise details of how exactly Sam planned to punish Lisa for this transgression. It had clearly been important at the time and yet now she had no memory of this particular fight, reaching into the recesses of her brain and finding nothing. At the bottom of the box, there was a stack of letters. She stiffened when she saw them, the Comic Sans font, the computer ink smudged in parts.

I miss you so much, Mouse. Do you miss me too? It's so boring here. Have you made any new friends yet?

She scanned through the pages quickly. They were from Lisa, writing while Sam was at the school in Utah, and each one was signed off in the same way – *I will love you forever, Mouse.* That had been Lisa's family nickname when she was a kid because she was so shy, and when Sam had first heard it, she'd declared, *If you're a mouse, then I'm a mouse too.* While she was writing *Chaste*, she'd often thought about what it felt like to be best friends with Lisa. The almost obsessive affection they'd shared as girls, the constant urge to remind the other how loved they were, how much they needed one another. The night her father died, Sam had stared at her phone, wondering who to call. And there had been no one she wanted to talk to except for Lisa; no one else would understand how complicated her pain was, how she didn't know how to grieve the loss of someone she never really had in the first place. She'd cried then, not just for her dad, but for Lisa too.

Her phone rang. 'Hey,' Sam answered, one of the letters still clutched in her hand. She didn't want to let them go; it was as if she could still feel her friend's energy coming through the pages.

'Hey,' Jane shouted. The background was busy, voices yelling, the insistent beat of an old-school Prince track pulsating against the walls. 'Did you get my email? I just wanted to check in. See how things are going.'

'Where are you?'

'Out for dinner with Maddy and her people.' Maddy Morgan was one of Jane's other clients, a born-again Christian cornering the self-care market for Gen-Z women of faith. Her first book, *Blessed*, was an instant bestseller and while Sam wanted to be supportive – strong women uplift other women, she always told her girls – she'd lost a couple of opportunities to Maddy recently and it stung. 'They couldn't have a panel full of white women,' Jane had explained, 'it would have been a Twitter shit storm,' and Sam had smiled, pretending she wasn't paranoid that her manager was shifting more of her attention to the younger woman. Jane liked her, she knew, but Jane would always like her 15 per cent more, no matter where it was coming from.

'Have you spoken to L—'

'Yes,' Sam cut across her. 'I went over there today. Oh God, Jane, she looked so thin. I'm worried about her.'

'Has she said what she wants? Is she looking for money, a retraction, what?'

'I'm not sure. We didn't really get into that.' Sam could sense her manager's impatience so she rushed on, 'But you'll never believe what I found! It's this box full of letters Lisa wrote me when I was in Utah. There are dozens of them. Listen to this.' She smoothed the page out and began to read aloud. ' "Life is so boring right now, Mouse" – we called each other Mouse. Just a stupid nickname but . . . sorry, I know you're busy.' She cleared her throat and continued reading. ' "Nothing ever happens here, Mouse, it's the same thing every day. I hate that you're so far away. I cried myself to sleep last night. I miss you. I miss you so much." ' Sam stopped, her voice trembling.

'When was that written?'

Sam checked the date at the top of the page. 'About two months after I started school in Utah.'

'So . . . after she claims you assaulted her.'

'She didn't say assault, Jesus, she—'

'I don't have time to argue the semantics with you. The point is, she sent the letters afterwards. That's interesting, isn't it? How many are there?' her manager asked, sharply, and Sam could almost hear the ideas forming in that steel-trap brain of hers.

'Around two dozen.'

'And they're all like this?'

'Yeah,' Sam replied. She stretched her legs out, letting the letters rest in her lap. 'They're all signed off the same way, too. *I will love you forever.*'

'Aaaand there's the title for your new book. Yes! I am *obsessed* with this,' Jane said. 'We can pick the best, let's say, fifteen letters? And open each chapter with a different one. That's genius. Do you think Lisa kept the letters you sent back to her?'

'I don't know.' Sam couldn't even imagine broaching the subject with her, not if that afternoon's encounter was anything to go by. 'That's not the reason why I told you about these letters, I don't think it's—'

'I'm telling you,' Jane interrupted. 'This is a goldmine. The first week sales figures for *Chaste* are the highest you've had in years. Can you imagine the follow-up? What a hook – the friend you fucked as a teen becomes a global phenomenon while you're just a small-town mom. It's like *Three Women* on speed.'

'Jane . . . please. Don't put it like that. This is someone's *life* you're talking about. Why do I have to keep reminding you of that?'

'And why do I have to keep reminding you that your career is at stake here? If this gets out . . .' Jane paused, allowing Sam to picture it. The accusation going viral. Everyone having an opinion, using her pain as an opportunity to facilitate an Important Conversation. All the men who'd hated her since she had told the story of her own sexual assault, calling her a liar. *I bet Samantha Miller makes men fuck her when their dicks are soft*, someone had written on a subreddit devoted to tearing her apart, *otherwise she calls it 'rape'*. The old panic fluttered in her chest and she heard herself whimper.

'We need to be strategic,' Jane said, softer this time. 'Look at Glennon's last book. It was on the list for, like, a million weeks. That's what we want for you. You did it once; we both know you're capable of doing it again.' She paused. 'I wouldn't say this lightly but I think a book like this could be bigger than *Willing Silence*.'

'Woah.' Sam felt a kick of adrenaline in her stomach. 'Do you really think so?'

'I really do.' Her manager gave a harsh laugh. 'Jesus! I'm excited. I don't know how you do this shit but you are one of a kind, Samantha Miller. No one can touch you.'

Sam hung up and she gathered the letters, stacking them neatly into the carved box. She saw a photo then, one of her and Lisa. They were dressed like Drew Barrymore in *Mad Love*, white tank tops and unbuttoned plaid shirts over jeans, and their hands were clasped as they leaned in opposite directions, each holding the other up like they were playing a trust exercise at a corporate team-building retreat. She looked at the photo until the light grew dim, trying to ignore the fear beating inside her, like a second heart. They had loved each other once, Sam knew that to be true. She would just have to make Lisa remember it too.

9.

She was almost asleep when she heard Lisa say something. Sam groaned, pulling the duvet over her head. 'You do this every time,' she complained. 'I'm not watching scary movies with you any more if you're gonna freak out as soon as the lights are off. It's so annoying.'

'It's not that.' Lisa hesitated. 'I asked what it feels like.'

'What does what feel like?'

'You know.' Her voice dropped to a whisper. '*Sex.*' Neither of them said anything for a minute. When they were younger, they had talked endlessly about 'doing it', promising they would tell each other all the gory details immediately, yet Sam had lost her virginity two months ago and this was the first time Lisa had asked that question. Sam understood; it had been strange for her too, as if she was leaving Lisa behind, betraying her friend by experiencing something Lisa had not. Somehow, it had been easier to pretend it simply wasn't happening. 'Does it hurt?'

'A bit,' Sam acknowledged. 'In the beginning, anyway. That's why you have to be sure it's the right guy. Someone who'll take care of you. Like Josh, you know? But now . . . it's good,' she said, meaning how good it was for Josh, how desperate he seemed to be to push inside her, as if she was the only thing that could make him whole. After he left, promising he'd phone her later, Sam would stare at her naked body in her full-length mirror, not with revulsion, as she usually did, but with something akin to appreciation now that she knew the effect it

74

had on her boyfriend, how much it turned him on. Maybe she wasn't as disgusting as she had once feared, she thought.

'I think I'm falling for him,' she said quietly. It was the first time she'd admitted that but saying it in the dark made it feel safer, as if she could take it back if she needed to, insist Lisa must have been dreaming if she ever mentioned it again. 'I'm . . . I might be in love with him.'

'Shit, that's real. Has he said it to you yet?' Lisa asked, curling into Sam's side, her breath hot against Sam's face.

'No. But he will soon, I bet.' And she would say it back to him immediately. She wouldn't play any games, not with something as important as *I love you*. 'What if Josh is the one?' she asked. 'Can you imagine if I end up with my high school boyfriend?'

'Eh, excuse me?' Lisa joked. 'I thought *we* were supposed to be soulmates? When did you decide to throw me over for some dude?'

Sam reached for her friend's hand, feeling the scar burrowed there. She remembered the day Lisa had fallen off her front porch, her scream as she slashed the skin of her palms open on the concrete below. There had been so much blood, splattered on the ground and on Lisa's T-shirt, her neon-pink shorts, and yet Sam didn't panic. She'd walked into the kitchen, grabbed a sharp knife, and cut her own palm open, hissing as the blood bloomed in the soft flesh. She took Lisa's hand in hers, wound against wound, waiting until her friend had stopped crying. 'There,' she'd said, refusing to let go. 'We're sisters now.'

Her eyes were adjusting to the gloom, the edges of the room sharpening around her, and she watched as Lisa rolled on to her back, pulling at the neck of her old, flannel pyjamas as she waited for Sam to say something. Sam shuffled closer, leaning her head on the other girl's shoulder, listening to her steady breathing. 'You know that you'll always be the only one for me, Mouse,' she said, smiling as Lisa chuckled softly. 'Forever and ever.'

10.

⊙ 3,033,009

Sam had checked the elementary school's website that morning and it said that first grade was dismissed at 2 p.m. So, here she was at ten minutes to the hour, standing in front of a Starbucks across the street from the school gates, waiting. It was the same school they had attended as children, she and Lisa and Josh, a squat, one-storey building hunched around a small courtyard. She had worried there would be a drive-thru system, a crossing guard waving the SUVs on as soon as the kids climbed into the back seat, but instead, the mothers – and they were all mothers, she'd only seen one man in the group so far, and two young Hispanic girls whom she presumed were nannies – had left their cars in the parking lot and huddled together by the entrance. Their voices were loud, talking about Hunter's 'aversion' to math and who was supervising the school trip to the Discovery Museum in Bridgeport, and 'Did you book that clown? We had him when Caleb turned eight and the kids said it was the best party ever!'

She held back, watching Lisa. Sam had texted her multiple times since the confrontation at her and Josh's house but none of the messages had been read, the double ticks on WhatsApp remaining grey. Lisa was wearing a Canada Goose parka jacket, tight yoga pants with clog boots, and she stood a little outside the group, only half listening. Sam sent her another text (*Hey!*

76

It's me. Could we maybe meet today?) and she saw her friend look at the screen, and then stuff the phone in her pocket again without replying. Sam took a deep breath and began walking towards them, her heart beating a little faster. Had these women read the essay? Would they stare at her and Lisa, eyes glazing over as they imagined what had happened that night? Two girls experimenting, touching one another because it felt good, because they knew their bodies better than any teenage boy could be expected to. Or had Lisa confided in them about the email she'd sent? Would they believe her lies instead, picturing blurring shadows, a no made into a yes with a hand over a mouth? Sam felt like she was back in high school after a particularly messy Saturday night, wondering what the girls were saying about her behind her back, if this would be the day they decided to cut her out of their lives for good.

One of the group noticed her, clocking the Dries Van Noten coat first with a small nod of approval, her eyes widening when she realized who it was. 'Lisa,' the woman said, pointing behind her. 'Look.'

Lisa turned on her heel, her smile slipping into a panicked grimace when she saw Sam walking towards them. She was wearing heavy make-up but the layers of concealer couldn't disguise the shadows under her eyes, the pallor of her skin. She looked like she hadn't slept in weeks.

'What are you—' she started, but Sam spoke over her smoothly.

'We said we'd meet here before our coffee date,' she said. 'Don't tell me you've forgotten?' She smiled at the others. 'Hi, I'm Samantha Miller.'

The mother who had spotted her first said tersely, 'You don't need to introduce yourself to me.'

Sam stared at her. 'Becky?' she said uncertainly, for the girl she remembered had corkscrew curls and weighed at least a hundred pounds more. Despite the cold, this woman was in a cropped jumper, displaying washboard abs, and her hair was in loose waves, dyed a balayage blonde.

'It's Rebecca now,' she said. 'Rebecca Brown, that's my married name.' She cut a glance at Lisa. 'Why didn't you tell me Samantha was back in town?' she asked, but Lisa was rifling through her purse for lip balm, like she was trying to find something to do with her hands.

'Rebecca, come on,' one of the others said. 'Aren't you going to introduce us?' She smiled at Sam. 'I'm Melissa,' she said. 'I only moved to Bennford a few years ago. I'm sorry, I know this is super embarrassing but I have to tell you – I'm a huge fan of your work!'

'Oh, thank you.' Although not such a huge fan that she'd read the *Blackout* essay, it appeared. 'That's very kind.' Sam looked at the other two women, waiting for them to introduce themselves.

'You remember Nicole and Tiffany,' Becky said dryly. 'They were in our grade too.'

Sam exclaimed, 'Of course!' even though she could barely tell the women apart – they were just flushed cheeks and blonde bangs – but Nicole and Tiffany embraced her, gushing about how good it was to see her again, and Sam felt herself relax. They reminded her of a joke she'd made during Mr Petersen's English class and that night they had spent dancing at Heather King's house, and remember when Sam made out with Brandon Green in the boys' locker room in Senior Year? Principal Phillips gave them detention for a month!

'I haven't thought about that in years!' Sam laughed, marvelling at how recent it all seemed to them when so much of her childhood had faded to black, never to be seen again. It was like they were telling tales about another person, another life, memories that belonged to someone else.

'I'm jealous,' the new woman said wistfully. 'It sounds like you had a blast. I'm not friends with anyone I went to high school with any more.'

'It wasn't all that great. And you wouldn't have been allowed to be friends with Lisa if you'd gone to Bennford High,' Becky interjected. 'Samantha was *very* protective of her, weren't you?'

She looked like she might say more except Lisa put a hand on her arm, whispering, 'Leave it.'

Becky's jaw clenched but she nodded. 'But do tell us,' she said to Sam. 'Why are you back in town? I thought you wouldn't be caught dead here.'

'Oh, you know,' she replied with a wink. 'I hear the antiquing is great.' The women laughed and she could almost smell their excitement, a prickling heat rolling off them in waves. It was like this when she was on stage, too. Her girls, adoring her, drowning her in their hopes that she would heal them, that she would *save* them. She tried so hard to give them everything they needed and afterwards she would feel utterly hollowed out. Going home to her apartment alone, waiting for sleep to come. Wishing she had someone to hold her.

'I just want to say again,' the new woman said, 'how much I adored *Willing Silence*!' She didn't reference any of the books she'd written since, and Sam tried not to care.

'And the movie!' Nicole or Tiffany chimed in. 'How cool is it to have a *movie* made of your book? It was on TV a few months ago and I told the kids that I went to school with someone famous. They were actually impressed for once. Usually, they tell me I'm a loser.' She nudged Lisa in the ribs. 'Not like your two. I've never seen two girls who love their mama so much.' Lisa pretended to be embarrassed but the corners of her lips twitched with a smile.

'OMG, did you meet Anne Hathaway?' the woman she thought might be Nicole asked. 'What's she like in real life?'

'Annie is a sweetie,' Sam replied. 'And so dedicated to her art! She wanted to meet with me before and during filming, just to make sure I was happy with her interpretation of the character.'

'*Annie*, excuse me!' the woman laughed. 'One of us Bennford girls, BFFs with Anne Hathaway. I never thought I'd—'

'Never mind her,' the other woman broke in. 'I want to know about Oprah! I can't believe you went to her estate in Montecito! Did she gift you a panini press? I read in *People* she does that. You know,' she said, without drawing a breath, 'I've always thought Oprah and I would be great friends if we ever met.'

'I don't know about that, Tif . . .' A shadow passed over the woman's face and Sam corrected herself quickly. '*Nicole*. I think Gayle King might have the position sewn up.' There was more laughter but it was tinged with giddiness, as if they were kids again, cutting the last class of the day to hang out with the most popular girl in school. They were enthralled by her every word, trying to remember what she said so they could repeat it later – *Samantha Miller told me about the time she sat between Reese Witherspoon and Nicole Kidman at the Oscars. Oh yeah, Sam and I go way back!* – when she noticed Lisa, her mouth frozen in a rictus grin. She looked miserable and despite everything her friend had done, Sam hated to see her like this. That was the Golden Rule, she reminded herself, across all spiritual practices and religions – treat others as you would like to be treated.

She was about to ask Lisa a question when Becky placed her palm in the small of Lisa's back and nudged her into the centre of the group. 'Lisa,' Becky said. 'Tell the girls what Martha said when I was at *your place* the other night.' She looked at Sam as she emphasized the words 'your place', like they were teenagers again, competing for Lisa's affection. 'My goddaughters are *so* clever.'

The bell rang before Lisa could answer, a sharp, clear sound in the cold air, and the doors to the school were thrown open, the kids pouring out as if someone had picked up the building and spilled its contents on to the ground. They were wrapped up in scarves and mittens, and Sam was introduced to Hunter and Caleb and Mackenzie and Olivia and Emily and Liam, a series of names she promptly forgot.

'This is the person I was telling you about!' one of the women said. 'Mom's famous friend!' and the kids stared up at Sam, nonplussed. She could see Martha and Maya walking together, wearing quilted jackets with a fake fur trim, one in silver and the other in rose gold. The girl in the silver jacket slipped behind Lisa – Maya, she guessed – while Martha came to a halt when she saw Sam.

'Hey!' She pointed at her. 'You're the lady who came to our house the other day.'

'What? What's she talking about?' Becky asked as Sam crouched down until she was eye level with the kid, like she'd seen Lisa do.

'That's right, what a clever girl you are.' Martha didn't look impressed so Sam tried again. 'How was school? Was Mrs Kelly nice to you today?'

'You and my mom were yelling at each other,' the little girl said, her eyes darting between Sam and her mother.

'Martha,' Lisa hissed. 'That's not true.'

'It is true! I heard you! You were—'

'Be quiet,' Lisa said, and the girl stuck her bottom lip out, her eyes furious. 'It's not nice to tell lies.'

'Not still fighting over Josh Taylor, I hope,' Tiffany quipped, bending down to grab her son's schoolbag and telling him to keep his coat on, it was too cold.

Lisa blanched and Becky said, 'Don't be tacky, that was years ago.' Tiffany started to apologize but Lisa told her to forget it, it didn't matter.

'I'll phone you later, OK?' she said to Becky. 'Come on, girls, we have to go.' Lisa gripped the twins' hands, pulling them from their friends. 'Come on, I said.'

She hurried away without saying goodbye and Sam could see the confusion on the other women's faces, Becky saying, 'Was that really necessary?' and Tiffany spluttering an excuse. It was just a stupid joke, she said, they'd been talking about high school and all the old memories had come back. The women looked at Sam as if she might be to blame, and she knew she couldn't let Lisa leave like this. She couldn't allow any rumours about a rift between them to take root; the situation was precarious enough as it was.

'Lisa,' she called and one of the twins turned back, tugging on her mother's hand. 'You didn't forget about our coffee date, did you?' and, as she expected, Lisa paused, her shoulders hunching up to her ears.

She faced the group again and said tightly, 'Yes, sorry,' and she waited for Sam to catch her up after more hugs and kisses, reminders to check her Facebook later, she must have missed Tiffany's friend request, and Nicole warning her, 'You'd better bring us all to the next movie premiere, ya hear?'

Neither woman said anything as they crossed the street together, Lisa murmuring, 'That's nice,' as the twins told her about their day, how Mrs Kelly gave Jamie a demerit because he'd broken Mackenzie's pencil, and who they had played with at recess.

When they were outside the coffee shop, Sam said, 'Not

here,' because she couldn't bear the thought of trying to have a conversation this important in that tiny, cramped space, the twins demanding babyccinos, tugging on their mother's elbow, whining, *when can we go home, I'm bored.*

'I wasn't planning on getting Starbucks with you,' Lisa said tightly, herding the girls to the parking lot. When the SUV was in sight, Lisa handed Martha the car keys, telling them to sit in the back and put their seatbelts on, she would only be a few minutes. 'That's enough,' she said, when the twins squabbled about whether they would listen to *The Greatest Showman* or the *Frozen 2* soundtrack. 'Just get in the car and decide among yourselves, OK?'

Sam was quiet until she could be sure they were out of earshot. 'I'm so sorry, Lisa. I know you must feel I've, like, totally overstepped the mark by showing up here today. But I've been texting and texting and you wouldn't reply. I would *never* have done this but I couldn't get through to you any other way and I—'

'So, it's my fault you ambushed me at my children's school gates.' Lisa pulled at the right cuff of her coat, then the left. 'It's always my fault, isn't it?'

'Mouse,' she said, and the other woman half gasped at the old nickname. 'I'm not the one who wrote that email, am I?' Sam softened her voice. 'Why don't we go back to your house and talk this through properly?'

'We? *We* won't be going anywhere,' Lisa said, gritting her teeth. 'Because *you* are not coming to my house again. I don't want you anywhere near my children.'

'You can't be serious.' Sam looked at the ground, the dirty snow grinding to slush beneath their feet. The door to the Starbucks opened and she could hear the faint sound of music, an alt-country cover of 'Jolene' trembling on the frigid air. 'You can't honestly believe that I—'

'I don't want to talk about this! How can I make that any clearer to you?'

'Come on.' Sam willed herself not to cry. 'I haven't heard from you in twenty-two years and then all of a sudden, you email my manager and claim that—'

'What do you want me to say?' Lisa looked back to the car, a vein at the side of her throat pulsing. 'Do you want me to say it was a mistake? Fine. It was a mistake. I sent the email when I was drunk. I had too much wine and I shouldn't have sent it and I regret it. I take it back. OK? I take it back. Will you go now?'

'What?' Sam's head was spinning. 'I don't—'

'I said, I take it back! I take it back! Just leave me alone.' Lisa walked away, hunching her shoulders against the wind, and Sam hurried after her, grabbing her elbow.

'You can't just walk away from me *again*,' she said. 'None of this makes any sense.'

Lisa wrenched her arm away. 'I told you what you wanted to hear, didn't I? I wrote that email when I was drunk. It's all my fault, as per usual. You can go back to the city and get on with your life and you never have to think about me again.'

'Do you really believe that or are you just saying it to get rid of me?'

Lisa tilted her head. 'What do you care?'

'Of course I care,' Sam said, putting her hand on her heart. 'We were best friends. Of course it matters to me if you think I— if you thought I hurt you in any way. But I didn't, Lisa. Why would you say that I did?'

'I don't know.' Lisa looked at the girls in the back seat of the car, gesturing that she would be two minutes. 'I don't know,' she said again, softly. 'I was so out of it that night. When I woke up the next morning and you went to kiss me, I . . . I couldn't remember and—'

'I was out of it too.' Of the two of them, Sam had always been the most wasted at any party, the one who started drinking the earliest, the one who smoked the most weed, who did the most shots. 'I could barely stand by the end of the night, I lost one of my shoes and I stepped on a broken bottle and my foot was bleeding. But I still remember exactly what happened between us and it wasn't' – she dropped her voice – '*that*. You know it wasn't, Mouse. I don't understand why you're doing this to me. You're breaking my heart *again*.'

Lisa's mouth twisted into a grimace. 'How are you the victim in this already? *You're* the one who wrote that essay. That was private, Sam. That was just between us. I never even told Josh about it because I felt like . . .' She fumbled over her words. 'Like I had cheated on him with you, or something. I don't know. Or like I would be betraying you if I told him what had happened, which makes no sense either because he's my husband. I've been fucking tormented and you just went ahead and wrote a long-form piece about it! I can't . . .' Her breath was coming faster. 'Why did you write it? It was private, that night, it was—'

'I wish I hadn't written it, believe me, but I can't undo it now.' Sam stared at her friend. 'And I need to know if you're planning to go public with this allegation.'

Lisa hesitated, just for a second, then she shook her head. Sam took a half-step forward, almost dizzy with the relief. 'OK,' she said. 'OK. Then what are you looking for here, Lisa? Is it a retraction? Because I don't think that will play out the way you expect it to.' She took Lisa's hand in her own and her friend stared at their fingers intertwined, a strange yearning on her face. 'Either no one will see the retraction and this will have been a giant waste of time or it'll blow up, and the retraction *becomes* the story. Is that what you want? There'll be even more attention on you then. Josh too.' She looked inside the car window, where the twins were sitting side by side. 'And the girls . . . I can see what a good mother you are. They adore you. But when they're old enough to google their names, what will they find waiting for them?'

'Stop it.' Lisa was so pale even the freckles across her nose looked as if they were fading away.

A different group of women were walking from the direction of the school, fur-trimmed hoods pulled over their heads, and their faces lit up when they saw Lisa. The mothers climbed into their cars, shouting in their direction, 'Can you believe this weather, Lisa? And there's more snow forecast for tonight!'

Her friend raised a hand in greeting, calling back, 'It's wild, isn't it?'

Waiting until they were gone, a screech of tyres on tarmac, Sam said, 'Look at you, Miss Popular.'

'Turns out it's easier to make friends when you're not around. Funny, that,' Lisa said, and Sam made her mind go blank, pretending the dig hadn't hurt her. 'Tell me. Were you going to write an essay about what happened after the party, too?'

'How do you mean?'

'Give me a break.' Lisa looked around then mouthed the word *abortion*. 'You said you were going to write about the "ultimate taboo" in your next book. Were you actually going to do that to me?'

'It's an important subject, you always said that. You were the one who was out there fundraising for Planned Parenthood, weren't you?' Sam said. Lisa's face hardened so she quickly added, 'I was super jetlagged when I gave that interview. I wasn't thinking. But I would never have used any names.'

'Just initials, I suppose.'

'I don't have to write it. Not if you don't want me to.' Sam shivered as the wind cut through her. 'But I need to know you have my back in return. What you said in your email . . . it's not going to go any further than this, is it?'

Lisa crossed her arms across her body. 'As long as you promise you won't write about the abortion. It would have been the girls' brother or sister; they can't find out like that. You have to swear, Sam.'

'Hope to die,' she said, tracing an X over her heart. Lisa watched as she did it and, for a moment, Sam thought she might smile. But she just slumped. She looked exhausted, insubstantial, as if she might be blown away with the next strong wind.

'Fine,' Lisa said, opening the door to the SUV. 'I guess we're done here.' She climbed in the front seat, clicking her seatbelt in place, and fixed her rear-view mirror.

'Mouse,' Sam said and they stared at one another, silently. 'I think of you sometimes.' She paused. She needed to hear Lisa's answer but she was afraid of it too. 'Do you ever think of me?'

A shadow of something passed over Lisa's face but Sam couldn't tell what it was and she marvelled at that, that her best friend had expressions she did not know any more. Lisa pulled the car door shut and she said something but Sam couldn't hear her through the glass.

Don't go, Sam pleaded as the car drove away. *Don't leave me alone again.*

II.

She got another coffee, smiling at the barista and tipping him five bucks. Outside she hesitated, but decided to walk home despite the weather. The snow was coming down thickly, swirling a haze around the parked cars and street lamps, and she half tilted her head at the occasional person walking past, as if to acknowledge what a strange evening it was to be out for a stroll.

Her childhood home was only a few minutes' walk from the school, and she took a shortcut down Roosevelt Avenue until she came to Elliot Street. The Johnsons' house was in darkness except for one room, the glow from the television flushing it a dark blue, and there was her old house, right beside it. She had crouched behind those basement doors playing hide-and-seek with Lisa's older brothers; her mother had tied balloons to that rusting gate the day of her fifth – or was it her sixth? – birthday party. She couldn't remember now; all that was left was the smell of cotton candy, the glossy feel of wrapping paper beneath her fingertips as she tore the presents open. Her old bedroom had faced directly into Lisa's, and they would wave when they saw each other, rolling up the window and shouting, 'Hey, Mouse!' She would never have admitted this but sometimes she liked to sit in the dark and look into her friend's world, to see who she was when Sam wasn't around. She'd always been afraid that Lisa didn't love her as much, afraid of losing her, too. But she knew better than to show that level of need, for it was repulsive. There was always one person who loved the other a little more in any relationship and Sam didn't want it to be her. She contained her yearning, hid it deep beneath layers of personality – her quick wit, her charm – where no one would find it. Her mother had taught her that much.

She was about to turn left at the end of the street when she spotted the familiar corrugated roof, the giant yellow sign pointing at the front entrance, and she stopped in disbelief. Delilah's Diner was still open? They used to go there as teenagers, the guys ordering cheeseburgers, the girls sharing a single plate of fries, competing to see who could eat the least. Some of them were so shy, barely speaking as the boys joked about how some poor dude got a boner in Ms Martinez's class. But Sam gave as good as she got and the guys loved her for it. She was always invited to their parties, her name called across the cafeteria – 'Miller, sit with us!' And she would groan, saying she was tired of their bullshit when secretly she adored the attention. That's why Josh had liked her so much, her confidence . . . and the fact she gave the best head of any girl he'd ever dated, he said. He couldn't keep his hands off her. In the back seat of his car, in his basement when his mom was visiting her sister in Hartford, that one time in the Abercrombie & Fitch changing room at the mall, pressed against the cool glass of the mirror. Afterwards, he would tell her she was amazing, he was the luckiest guy in Bennford, and Sam was just happy that Josh was happy. They went to Delilah's together after school and she would invite Lisa to come too. 'I don't want to be that girl who dumps her friends as soon as she gets a boyfriend,' she'd explained, and Josh had shrugged. 'Whatever, Lisa's cool.' That was all Sam wanted, for her boyfriend and her best friend to like each other. She didn't see it coming, what they would do to her. She had never suspected they would betray her.

She pulled open the heavy door to Delilah's, giving it an extra tug when the stiff joints pushed against her. She remembered it as dimly lit, with grotty Formica-covered tables wobbling on the uneven floor, but it had been redecorated into a cliché of a 1950s diner in the years since. A black and white tiled floor, red leather booths, and an old jukebox in the corner, blasting Johnny Cash's greatest hits. She nodded at one of the waitresses as she slid into a corner booth by the window, dusting sugar off the large, laminated menu as she watched a group of high school kids sitting a few tables down. Delilah's must still be the cool place to hang out, she thought, as a Black girl with Bantu knots sat on her boyfriend's lap, a fair-haired jock type who wrapped his hands around the girl's waist as he kissed her. They were so young and in love, as fascinated with each other's beauty as they were with their own. They thought the world was theirs for the taking; they didn't know yet that they would make mistakes, do things they didn't think themselves capable of. The boy caught Sam looking and he bristled, giving her a *what's your problem?* scowl, and Sam fumbled with the menu, staring down at it intently.

'OK, honey, what can I get you?' The waitress, a middle-aged white woman with spiked short hair and a Southern accent, took a notepad out of her apron as she approached the table.

'Oh.' Sam couldn't think. 'A cheeseburger, maybe? Hold the pickles. Chilli cheese fries. And a chocolate milkshake.'

It was Josh's old order, she realized when the waitress returned ten minutes later, dumping the food on to the table. 'Are you really gonna eat all that junk?' she used to tease him when they were still together. 'What will Coach Sanders think?'

And Josh would stuff a few fries into his mouth and reply, 'Lisa will help, won't you?' Lisa was the only girl she knew who actually *did* eat whatever she wanted and never gained weight, while Sam's mother had brought Sam to this 'great doctor' in the city to help her manage her 'little problem'.

Dr Anat designed a special meal plan and it worked. The number on the scales dropped, the waistband of her jeans was looser, and she had felt more comfortable with Josh's hands moving low on her belly. She'd still try not to eat in front of him, sticking to iced water or Diet Coke, the occasional salad with dressing on the side, until the night he'd leaned over to stop her from getting out of the car. 'I've noticed . . .' He'd paused, his cheeks flushing. 'I just wanted to say . . . You don't need to lose any weight, Sam.' He pushed a strand of hair behind her ear. 'You're perfect just the way you are.'

The jukebox was playing the Beach Boys and the teenagers at the next table were gathering their coats and gym bags, talking about a geometry quiz they had in the morning as they paid their bill. Sam stared at the plate in front of her, the food greasy and hot. She hadn't eaten an animal product in ten years, and while she claimed she had gone vegan for health reasons, the truth was she just liked being thin. She saw the admiration in journalists' eyes when she outlined what she ate in a day – the zucchini ribbons and salt-cured olives for lunch, the seaweed salad and mushroom broth for dinner, the activated almonds she kept on hand to stave off any cravings – and she liked that too. She touched the burger with one finger, squishing the patty down until the ketchup and cheese were oozing out of the sides. She had a flash of that old hunger, the ferocious need to devour everything in her sight until she forgot herself and the world around her. She sank her teeth into it and she ate and she ate and she ate. There was a stickiness around her lips, something drip-dripping on to her beautiful coat, but she didn't stop. She couldn't stop until she was finished.

'Well, I never,' the waitress said, collecting the dirty dishes. 'I thought there was no way an itty-bitty thing like you was gonna eat all that food, but you must have been real hungry.

You want something else? The pie is good – we got pecan, blueberry or apple.'

Sam shook her head. 'No, thank you.'

She leaned against the windowpane, watching the snow fall outside. She felt dirty, sweat breaking out at the back of her knees, under her armpits, and she pulled her sweater away from her skin. She rested a hand on her swollen belly and made herself sit in that booth for another half-hour, staring at the vintage signs proclaiming *We're Always Open!* and *45c for a Hamburger!*, the beat-up guitar hanging from a string, and an old Coca-Cola poster with a cartoon brunette holding a glass bottle. She had got what she came here for – Lisa admitted she was drunk when she sent that email, that she had been angry because of the essay and she had lashed out, lying about that night they'd spent together. Why did Sam still feel so uneasy? She thought of Becky Stewart, her hand in the small of Lisa's back, the muttered asides. When had those two become so close? And what had Becky meant when she said no one else was 'allowed' to be friends with Lisa at high school? That wasn't true. Was this what it meant to be an adult, everyone reframing their childhood experiences to paint themselves as the victim? The words of Lisa's email came to her again – *when Sam wants something, it happens whether you want it or not . . . You just took what you wanted without my consent* – and fury worked its way up each bone of her spine and set solid in her jaw. False allegations like this meant it was harder for other women to be believed. It had made it harder for *Sam* to be believed when she'd told her story, all those years ago.

The jukebox turned off and the waiters mopped the floors and wiped down countertops, refilling the salt and pepper sachets, the sound of jingling as someone opened and closed the cash drawer. 'OK, ladies, I'm outta here,' a man with a New Jersey accent said as he walked out of the kitchen. He was very tanned and wore too much hair gel, a gold chain glinting just beneath his tight T-shirt, but he was around Sam's age and he winked at her, asking if she'd liked the food, and she smiled back.

'Yes, thank you.' She imagined walking over to him, murmuring in his ear, *Come with me.* She would bring him home and fuck him on her mother's Queen Anne chair, and he would grab her by the neck as he came inside her, groaning. The man walked out of the diner door backwards, grinning at her, and when he was gone, Sam closed her eyes. *Fuck*, she thought. *Not this again.*

'I'm sorry, honey,' the waitress said, gesturing at the plastic clock on the wall behind her. When Sam turned around, she saw the staff were waiting by the cash desk, their faces drawn heavy with weariness.

'Goodness, is that the time?' she said. She left a large tip, apologizing profusely. She'd learned over the years the importance of being polite to waiters and busboys, the check-in staff at the airport, the assistant at her dentist's office, because they were the ones who talked afterwards, their ten-second encounter repackaged as an amusing anecdote on social media. *I met Samantha Miller,* they would write, *and she was a total bitch!* Sam was never afforded an off-day. Women in the public eye could only have one personality type – *nice* – or everything they'd worked so hard for would be taken away from them.

She gasped when she walked outside, the cold wind biting at her skin. She reached for her phone, clicking on Google Maps. She had walked home from Delilah's enough times as a teenager to be able to do this blindfolded, but the snow was coming down so heavily that everything was blurred. She swiped condensation off the screen and saw she'd missed seven calls from Jane and a handful of texts from Tatum, her best friend in the city.

Tatum: I am SO sorry, my darling. I'm sending you so much love and light ✌️ ☮️ 🧘

Tatum: Remember, the Universe never sends us anything we're not ready for. The Chinese words for crisis and opportunity are the same, right? How can this be an opportunity for you? How can you use this experience as a tool for growth?

Sam frowned, about to text her friend back and ask what she was talking about, when her phone rang. 'Hey,' she answered. 'Can you hear me? I'm walking to my mom's house and it's, like, literally a blizzard here.'

'I can hear you,' Jane replied.

'Right. Here's the update. I think we're gonna be OK. Lisa admitted she sent the email when she was drunk. She was upset about the essay, and she was lashing out. I agreed that I wouldn't write about the abortion and now—'

'I'm on my way up there.'

'What?'

'I'm in a car. I should be in Bennford in less than an hour.'

'Jane, what are you doing? I'm going back to the city first thing tomorrow. I'll see you then.' She rubbed at her forehead. 'I need to get out of this fucking town as quickly as possible.'

'Have you been online this evening?'

Sam stopped walking. She was outside a closed-down hardware store, a faded *70% off all stock – everything must go!* sign still hanging in the window. She huddled under the wooden canopy, pressing the phone closer to her ear. 'No, I haven't even looked at my cell. I've . . .' She trailed off, not wanting to tell her manager the truth. That she had been sitting in a diner, bingeing on food she hadn't eaten in over a decade. Fantasizing about taking a strange man home with her, hoping he would break her in the ways she needed to be broken in order to forget. 'I haven't had a chance,' she said instead. 'Why? What's wrong?'

'I need you to turn your phone off until I get there. Do you hear me? Just wait until I'm there before you do anything.' Her manager hung up without saying goodbye and Sam was frozen, staring at the iPhone in her hand. *Don't look*, she told herself. *But why not?* a little voice inside her whispered back. That voice was familiar; she knew it all too well. It was similar to her own but warping, like rounds of tape pulled out of a busted cassette. A skeleton of burnt bones, urging her to jump. She had spent the last thirteen years learning to recognize those urges for what they were, developing coping mechanisms to help her ignore them, but her palms were sweating now, something turning in her stomach. *Just look. You can put it away once you know the truth. It's always better to know, isn't it?*

She unlocked her phone. And she looked.

12.

○ 2,589,788

Sam always made sure to highlight the fact that Shakti was a female-owned and -run company – all her employees, from the product design team to the copywriters and content creators, were women, and Sam insisted they offer decent maternity leave, childcare options, and flexi time for working mothers. It was the right thing to do, she said, but privately she admitted she didn't want a scandal about conflicting public-facing and internal values, like the other 'Girl Boss' companies torn to shreds by the feminist blogs – and yet here she was, standing in front of a group of old, white men in Shakti's head office on Howard Street, as her manager explained exactly how much trouble they were in.

'We initially thought this would die down in twenty-four hours,' Jane explained to the Shakti board. She had chosen one of her most austere suits for the meeting, a navy fitted jacket over a matching pencil skirt, a high-necked ruffled blouse underneath. Her dark hair was pulled off her face and she was wearing bright red lipstick, like war paint. 'Especially given this Reddit post is anonymous.'

'Disgraceful,' one of the men said. 'Whatever happened to due process? Innocent until proven guilty? It's just trial by social media these days and I—'

'That's all well and good, Scott,' Jane said, visibly irritated at being interrupted. 'But Shakti spearheaded a #WomenDontLie campaign off the back of Me Too in 2017. They have published literally *hundreds* of articles on the site debunking the myth of false rape allegations, insisting we believe victims.' She shot an apologetic glance at Sam. 'As you can imagine, a lot of Shakti readers are wondering if we're going to believe this particular victim or not.'

'She's not a victim,' Sam sobbed, grabbing a packet of Kleenex from her purse. 'I didn't do anything wrong!'

Teddy, sitting at the table beside her, put his hand on her knee and squeezed. 'What you're trying to tell us, Jane,' he said, 'is that we have one hell of a predicament on our hands.'

'I suppose we do.' Jane cleared her throat as she turned the laptop off. She'd prepared a PowerPoint presentation for the board to explain the situation and, like everything Jane did, it was thorough. She had included the full text of the Reddit post, reading it aloud at the beginning of the meeting. 'Samantha Miller is a sexual abuser' was the heading and the rest was equally devastating. ' "I've watched over the last decade as Samantha Miller has made a name for herself as an advocate for women," ' Jane read aloud. ' "As she declared her website was a 'safe space' for victims to share their stories, when all she's doing is using other women's pain to advance her career. Do you want to hear from a *real* victim? Here I am. I'm L, the friend she talks about in *Blackout*. I was drunk on the night Samantha Miller refers to in her essay and incapable of giving any kind of meaningful consent. And what do we call it when one person isn't capable of giving consent? That's right, ladies and gentlemen . . . It's sexual assault." '

It had been posted on Friday night and once it was shared on Twitter, it blew up almost immediately. The irony was, Jane kept saying, that if the post had been written at another time, it might have been a titbit of gossip among Sam's circles – the other thought-leaders at the forefront of the New Age revolution, the interns at her publishing house, the PR girls working on her campaigns. Embarrassing, yes, but Sam could have ignored it. But because her *Blackout* essay had gone viral, Sam was relevant in a way she hadn't been since *Willing Silence* was released. The tweets started from the men's rights activists, crying double standards, demanding that Samantha Miller be held to the same standards as a man would in her situation (*Cancel the fucking cunt*), right-wing trolls thrilling at the thought of a 'Queen of the Woke Brigade' being torn down by her own disciples (*I love watching the left eat their own, its fucking hilarious*). By Saturday evening, when she'd lost over four hundred thousand followers and #SamanthaMillerIsOver was trending, it was clear the story wasn't going to die on its own. A researcher at *Super Soul Sunday* and another at *The Today Show* emailed, cancelling Sam's upcoming interviews due to 'a scheduling conflict', and minutes later, Jane's phone had rung. She'd shown the screen to Sam, both of them tensing when they saw Teddy Jackson's name. 'Get back to the city,' he had said. 'The Shakti board has called an emergency meeting for tomorrow afternoon.'

'Just to be completely transparent, there's something else we're concerned about,' Jane said, taking the seat on the other side of Sam. 'It's not urgent – not yet, anyway – but I think we need to keep an eye on it.' She cleared her throat again. 'Sam's reputation isn't as, eh, *unassailable* as it might once have been. It's been a tough time for the wellness community. They're still trying to rebuild trust after the pandemic; a lot of these so-called gurus really showed their asses during that time. And there have been a few tweets about Sam's early career. The workshops, the "sweat lodges", and—'

'They weren't sweat lodges,' Sam interrupted her. 'There

was plenty of water and anyone who wanted to leave could go. I just turned the heating up in my apartment as we were practising breathing rituals.'

'In the middle of summer,' Frank, the vice president of corporate marketing for a software company, chimed in. 'In a-hundred-degree heat, that's asking for trouble.' He shrugged when Sam looked at him in surprise. 'I have a sixteen-year-old granddaughter,' he said. 'She sends me things to read, including the aforementioned Reddit post. In fact, I think it's fair to say Bella is the reason we're all here today.' He raised an eyebrow at her. 'Would we have heard about this from you otherwise?'

'No one was in danger,' Sam insisted, ignoring his question. 'It was a mind control exercise, to show the girls they were stronger than they realized. If they could find their inner peace, no matter how uncomfortable they were, they'd be able to apply that lesson in a real-life situation too.' She looked to Jane, hoping she would help her out. 'Most of the women found it transformative.'

'That's true,' Jane agreed, picking up the jug in the centre of the table and pouring herself a glass of water. 'And a lot of the fans have been pushing back online, telling stories about how Sam's work saved their lives. They're talking about eating disorders and addiction and sexual trauma; it's powerful stuff.' She paused and Teddy leaned forward so he could see her properly.

'But?' he prompted.

'But there's also been some conversation around the ethics of that,' Jane admitted. 'People saying Sam's not a doctor or a therapist and it's dangerous for her to behave like she is. There's been particular concern about her neural pathway work—'

'It's this Inner Child hypnotherapy programme on Shakti,'

Sam cut in when some of the men looked confused. 'You do a guided visualization to go back to a traumatic event in your past and you, like, reconfigure the memory. The results are incredible.'

'And by reconfiguring the memory, you mean . . .' Teddy gestured at her to continue.

'You change it. Not literally, obviously, it's not time travel. A psychologist developed it for the site,' Sam said. 'This is backed by cutting-edge science, you guys.'

'Yes,' Jane said. 'But as you can imagine, that has not gone down well online.'

It was *them* who'd brought that up, of course.

@Supernovadiabolique157 Is anyone going to talk about the fact Samantha Miller has been advocating *changing* past memories? How are we supposed to trust anything this woman says?

It had been quote-tweeted over 1,500 times.

'Added with some of the, eh, minor issues we've had in the past,' Jane continued, 'about the cookbooks "promoting ortho-rexia" and the unsubstantiated claims around some of Shakti's products—'

'We paid the fine to the District Attorney's office,' Sam argued. Her right leg was bouncing up and down and she tried to still it, pushing down on it as hard as she could with her hand. 'And we've completely overhauled the site since then, everything has proper disclaimers. This is ridiculous.'

'But what Jane is trying to tell us . . .' Teddy said as he adjusted his watch, the steel Breitling Navitimer that had once belonged to Sam's father. They'd been roommates at college and Carolyn had insisted Teddy take it at the funeral, saying, *Nate would have wanted you to have it*. Sam had been tempted to ask if her father had left anything special for her, but she knew he would never have thought of her in that way. Teddy was in his late seventies now and still handsome, his body lean, his skin tanned from regular vacations to Cabo. His eyebrows knitted together in concern as he flicked through the presentation Jane had printed out for each of them. 'Is that this doesn't look good. And it could hurt the company.' He looked around the table at each person in their turn. 'This needs to be contained. Urgently.'

'Here's the thing I don't understand,' said Leonard, a short man with tufts of thick, black hair under the cuffs of his pin-striped shirt. He was a partner in a prestigious law firm in the Financial District but Sam always thought he looked like an extra from *Goodfellas*. 'If you girls knew about this since the third of January, that's like what, a week ago? When you got the initial email from Laura—'

'Lisa.'

'—why didn't you come to us immediately?' Leonard continued, as if Jane hadn't spoken. 'Instead of running to Connecticut like a regular Jessica Fletcher.'

'He has a point,' agreed Scott, the equity analyst who seemed to have sweat stains on his shirt, no matter what the weather. 'You didn't stop to think that maybe we've seen similar shit in our time? We've been at this a lot longer than you, girls. We would have handled this quickly, *quietly*, and we would have made it go away.'

Jane bridled. 'Yes, well, I'm not sure Sam wanted it "handled" your way. That's not how things are done any more. Sam was worried about Lisa and—'

'Enough of the touchy-feely crap.' Scott looked at Sam. 'What's the deal with the friend? What does she want?'

Sam shook her head. 'That's what I can't figure out. There's no way she wrote that post. She even admitted to me that she'd sent the email when she was drunk and she didn't mean it. She just wanted this to go away.'

'*What*? You had an admission that she was lying?' he asked, his lip rolling in a sneer. 'What the fuck are we wasting our time for? Get her to make a statement saying this is baloney. Jesus fucking Christ, I flew in from Chicago on a Sunday for this horse-shit.' He looked at Teddy. 'Do you believe this?'

'It's not that easy,' Sam protested, the tips of her ears starting to burn. 'She won't take my calls, she won't answer my texts. And I don't know if she would be willing to make a statement anyway. She's a private person, she—'

'Give her enough money,' Scott said, rubbing his thumb and forefinger together. 'That's all these women want.'

'Excuse me?' Sam said, her voice dangerously low.

'Ultimately, I don't think we can wait around for Lisa Taylor to say something, one way or another,' Jane cut in before Sam exploded. 'This has gone far enough as it is. We need to put a contingency plan together immediately.'

The men agreed, talking about 'damage control' and 'crisis management' as easily as if they were recommending which cocktail bar downtown did the best Old Fashioned. They didn't seem to understand that what they were talking about were allegations that Sam had always taken very seriously. The day after the Harvey Weinstein story broke, she'd got a cab to the Shakti offices and called a staff meeting. 'This is going to be important,' she had said. 'I can feel it.' She'd been tracking similar stories since the company's inception in 2013, noticing the traction they got online. All these women desperate to tell their stories, desperate for their voices to be heard. Her chief content creator had been wary, unsure if this was just a 'celebrity thing' that would die out in a few weeks, but Sam was firm. She'd directed her staff writers to find as many women as they could, women who had been abused or harassed, women who had lost their job or left their industry or seen their career hindered because they refused to have sex with the man, or maybe they *did* have sex with the man and he wanted them gone afterwards, sabotaging them in increasingly cutthroat ways. And then, of course, there were the men who ignored the *no* and took what they felt entitled to anyway, walking away without a second glance. 'It shouldn't be hard to find them,' Sam had said as her staff scrambled to ensure Shakti would become the go-to site for this moment. 'Every woman I know has a story.' She'd taken a deep breath. 'Including me.'

It happened when I was twenty-six, she wrote in her editorial. *I'd gone out with some friends from the magazine and we met these guys in a bar downtown. They seemed nice, in the beginning. They invited us to a party at their place but the girls said they couldn't – we had work the next day, deadlines to meet – but I decided to go anyway. I thought they were good boys, you see.*

Their apartment was just off Gramercy Park – it belonged to his father, the cutest one said – and there was smoke and music and pills, and then there was nothing. I woke the next morning on their kitchen floor and my underwear was gone. I was bleeding. I couldn't understand that. I wasn't due my period for another two weeks. I didn't understand what had happened, yet. 'Hello?' I called out. 'Hello?' But no one replied. Flashes from the night before came to me, one face and then another. I couldn't keep my eyes open, I kept falling under but there was laughter, I knew that. That was what I would remember, when it was all done. The sound of those boys laughing at me.

Sam's essay went viral, causing the Shakti site to crash. 'Why didn't you speak up earlier?' she was asked. 'Why didn't you write about the rape in *Willing Silence*?' And Sam replied that she hadn't been ready, she wasn't even able to admit it to herself at that point. Her therapist diagnosed her with a form of traumatic dissociative amnesia – 'How convenient,' angry men on the internet yelled. 'Is this the new way of saying, *I'm a fucking liar*?' – but it was more than that. When faced with the bravery of the women who dared to speak out, even as they were called fantasists and gold-diggers, Sam felt she had no other choice. She'd told her story for the good of the culture and she had listened when other women told theirs. But those accusations were valid, those women were telling the truth. *She* had been telling the truth. This – whatever this was – was not the same.

Teddy coughed and the other men fell silent. He was the richest person on the board and therefore the most powerful, the hierarchy of male dominance asserted in some unspoken way. 'We can talk about this until the cows come home,' he said. 'But ultimately, there's only one thing that matters right now. And that's how the IPO is priced.' His face softened when he looked at Sam and she knew he was thinking of her father, of what Nate Miller would have expected his college roommate to do for his daughter. 'Sam, we both know that legally we can't ask you to step down. Not on the back of an anonymous post on the internet. And if it was just the' – he waited for Jane to supply the word *Reddit* for him – 'if it was just the Reddit thing,' he said, 'we could ignore it or at least we could try and wait it out. But if it ever became public knowledge that we knew there had been an official complaint from Lisa, we'd be in a lot of trouble for not taking appropriate action.'

'But she said herself that she sent that email when she was drunk!'

'If she's not prepared to admit that publicly,' he said, furrowing his brow, 'there's not much we can do with that.'

'Shit,' Sam muttered, her leg starting to shake again. 'What if I go back to Bennford and persuade Lisa she needs to sign this statement? Would that make a difference?'

'It would help, for sure,' Teddy said in a soothing voice. 'But in the meantime, we need to be seen to act decisively. This is a volatile environment and Shakti has positioned itself as a voice for this "movement". Which has been wonderful and, let's face it, profitable for everyone around this table, but these kids are demanding a new set of moral prerogatives which are almost impossible to satisfy.'

'Thanks for the lecture on woke culture,' Jane said dryly. 'Do you have a point with this, Teddy?'

He stood up, readjusting his beautifully tailored jacket, holding the print-out of the presentation aloft. Sam blinked and for a second, it was her father standing there. *Your mother told me what you did,* he'd said, his face twisting in anger. *You've ruined your whole life.*

'Here's what we are going to do,' Teddy said. 'We'll make a large donation to a sexual violence organization in Shakti's name. Then we're going to hire the crisis management firm that Scott recommended.' He nodded at the other man. 'After that, Samantha will announce her resignation from the Shakti board – temporary, of course, but no one needs to know that – posting some form of statement about how this isn't true but given the importance of believing victims, yaddi yaddi yah, she wants to step down to allow an internal investigation to take place.'

'A sabbatical, not a resignation,' Jane interjected quickly. 'We'll want final approval on the wording, too.'

'Let's just hear what the crisis management people have to say, OK?' Teddy replied. 'They're the experts.'

'But . . .' Sam felt like she was going to vomit, the fear was burning so fast up her throat. 'But Teddy, won't this make me look guilty? I didn't do this. You believe me, don't you?'

'Then why is she saying you did?' Frank asked, fiddling with his cufflinks when the other men turned to stare at him. 'I read a Shakti piece about how rare false allegations are a few months ago and it sort of blew my mind,' he said, sheepishly. 'I told you, my granddaughter is a big fan.'

'Lisa *said* that the email was bullshit.' Sam felt like she was going crazy, like she was banging on the walls of her nightmare and screaming for help but no one could hear. She'd always felt the same way about false rape accusations as she did about cancel culture – namely, that they didn't exist. It was only bad men with something to hide who were afraid of being 'cancelled'. But now they had come for her, and she hadn't done anything wrong. 'I'm innocent.'

'Innocence doesn't matter in this climate. Twitter just wants' – Teddy checked the notes again, reading the tweets from some of the men's rights activists aloud – '"a bitch to burn".' He shuddered. 'Honestly, it's disturbing the way they talk.'

'But what am I supposed to do?' Sam asked. This wasn't how she had expected the meeting to go. She thought Teddy would be on her side, that he would insist the board back her, no matter what. 'What am I supposed to do without Shakti? Without my girls? This is my whole life.'

'Listen to me.' Teddy put a hand on her shoulder. 'These people want blood and they won't be satisfied until they see your head on a stick. Just step away and give them enough time to cool off.' Everyone nodded, even Jane. Her manager picked up her phone, scrolling, moving on already to the next client, the next scandal that needed to be handled. Forgetting about Sam already.

'You can come back when this has died down,' Teddy reassured her. 'The mob will move on to their next target. They always do.'

'But Teddy, I can't just—'

'Trust me,' he said. 'Go home and wait it out. It'll be over soon.'

13.

After the meeting, she waited for her Uber outside the Shakti office, pushing her sunglasses on with trembling hands. She rushed through her apartment's foyer, her head down so she didn't make eye contact with the doorman. *Does he know? Does everyone know?* Her maid, the person who dropped off her dry-cleaning, the Uber driver who attempted to make conversation until he realized she wasn't listening; she was just staring out of the car window, dazed. Had they all seen the Reddit post? Did they know what people were saying about her online, the names they were calling her? Did they believe it?

Her apartment was quiet, save for the low hum of the heating system, the click-clack of Mrs Cohen's low-heeled shoes against the wooden floor upstairs. It was funny, Sam had always thought she was good at being alone. There had been relationships over the years: Gabriel, her French boyfriend, whom she'd dated for that last, terrible year before going to rehab. Oliver, the anaesthesiologist, who had left when Sam turned thirty-six and still refused to entertain a conversation about children. 'I told you from the beginning,' she'd reminded him. 'I told you I didn't want kids.' But Oliver had thought that was just something women in their thirties said so they didn't scare men off. He'd assumed she was playing it cool, pretending she didn't care about 'all that stuff' while secretly adding pictures of princess-cut diamond rings to her vision board. 'Why would you think that about me?' she'd asked him, baffled. 'It's like you don't have a clue who I am.'

Oliver had cried then, burying his head in his hands. 'Maybe it's because you won't let me in, Sam,' he'd said. 'Maybe it's because we've been dating for two years and I still don't know anything *real* about you.'

Later, she would post a short video on Instagram, telling her followers what had happened – they'd been so invested in her relationship with Oliver and she owed it to them to be honest. 'It'll be OK,' she'd said. '*I'll* be OK because I'm a strong person. A woman should never be reliant on a partner for her sense of self. If we're not happy alone, we'll never be happy with anyone else.'

But she was alone now, properly alone. She sat on her couch and stared at her phone, wondering who she should call. She couldn't think of anyone. Jane had instructed her to sit tight until the statement from the crisis management team came through and so she waited in her apartment for the next twenty-four hours, searching desperately for something to calm her. People had accused Sam of picking and choosing from different religious traditions like it was an à la carte menu, but now, when she needed it, none of her rituals brought her any peace. She tried transcendental meditation, homeopathic remedies, guided visualizations. She cast spells, she burned herbs, she lit candles. She took hot baths laced with Himalayan salts and surrounded herself with crystals – clear quartz, moonstone, Tiger's Eye. Healers came to the apartment: the past-life regressionist who said she and Lisa had been married in another life and reincarnated together to heal their relationship, and the angel therapist who promised to cut the psychic cords that bound them. Sam phoned her medium in Long Island, begging the woman for reassurance that she was safe, and then she crawled towards her prayer altar. Shuffling her tarot cards, asking the same question – *Will this go away?* She became frantic, shuffling the cards again and again, on her knees for hours at a time, searching for a sign that all would be well.

Her therapist left a message. 'I've heard about your situation,' Diane said and her voice was as serene as ever, as if the world wasn't falling apart. 'Call my receptionist and set up an appointment.' Her mother called too, asking how the business meeting went, and how was Teddy Jackson looking these days? Was Samantha returning to Bennford or staying in the city? Carolyn didn't mention anything about the Reddit post or the Twitter mob, all those strangers calling for Sam's head, but then, Carolyn was the only one out of her friends who didn't have a Facebook profile. 'This need to share everything is gauche,' her mother would say, wrinkling her nose. Sam had heard from so few of her own friends – the 'Spirit Mafia' WhatsApp group, her six closest girlfriends in the city (Ashley, Devon, Sawyer, Autumn and Harper – a reiki master, life coach, yoga teacher, shamanic healer and massage therapist respectively – and Tatum, of course), had also gone suspiciously quiet. Sawyer and Devon were the only two to get in touch, sending separate *hope you're OK* messages, so similar in their wording that Sam knew they must have written them together as they ordered their kale salads for lunch, another job ticked off their to-do lists.

The only person who stayed in regular contact was Tatum, who kept texting inspirational quotes.

> **Tatum:** everything happens for a reason!! Our souls are always reaching for growth and learning ✦ ✦

> **Tatum:** we create every experience in our lives, and thus the power to change lies within us!!!

And while she knew Tatum was trying to help, this sent Sam into a deeper spiral – *How did I create this?* she kept asking herself. *How?* She had been so careful, she'd chosen her thoughts wisely, she had put positive energy out into the world. She'd raised thousands of dollars for charity, tithing 10 per cent of her net earnings to her favourite causes. She hadn't done anything that would attract such darkness to her and yet here it was anyway; she was knee deep in it.

She kept trying to phone Lisa – 'Hey. It's me. Please, Mouse. I'm begging you. You have to help me' – but there was no response. She reached for her phone every few minutes to check when her friend had last been online, and the screen was blank, yet again, and then she would open Lisa's WhatsApp profile photo and stare at it. Sam presumed it was taken for a Christmas card; there was a candy-cane-patterned curtain as a backdrop, an artificial tree dripping in fairy lights. Lisa and Josh and the girls in matching snowflake sweaters, grinning at the camera. Why did Lisa get to have the perfect family and Sam did not? How was that fair?

She sent another message and another one, she phoned multiple times a day but Lisa never picked up, it just rang and rang and rang, until one morning, there was a distorted voice saying *your call cannot be connected at this time*. She opened WhatsApp again and the Christmas card photo had disappeared – had Lisa deleted her account? No, she realized with a sinking feeling, Lisa must have blocked her number. Her friend thought it was that easy to get rid of her, just as she had done when Sam went to Utah for final year. The letters had dwindled after a while, then petered out altogether. Mrs Johnson saying awkwardly, 'I'm afraid she's not here, dear,' when Sam had phoned, and then in Walgreens, the last time she'd been home for Spring Break, and she saw her friend and shouted *Mouse!* but Lisa had looked through her, as if Sam was invisible, walking out of the store without saying a word.

Tatum: Are you out of bed, boo?

Tatum: Send me a selfie once you're up and dressed, k?

If Tatum were here, she'd insist Sam go to her prayer altar and sit in stillness until a Higher Power showed her what she needed to do to get out of this mess. But Tatum wasn't here, was she? She should be – if she had any semblance of loyalty to Sam at all, she would be here – but despite the constant text messages, there were no suggestions made that Tatum come over to the apartment, no offers to bring a pot of her famous chickpea and spinach stew, like she had when Sam's father had died. But then again, Sam had always insisted she didn't need anyone – she was independent, a free spirit – and now that she did, now that she so desperately wanted someone to sit with her and hold her hand, there was no one there.

That afternoon, the crisis management person sent through a draft of the statement – 'While most of the things that are being said about me online are false, I have always maintained that it's important for women to be able to tell their stories without fear of retribution. I believe women but I also believe in due process and I don't think the two are mutually exclusive. I have decided to take some time away from Shakti in order to allow that process to take place and I look forward to returning once my name has been cleared' – and after she posted the Notes apology to her Instagram, Facebook and Twitter, she deleted the apps from her phone.

She hid in her apartment, the blinds drawn and the air growing thick with the stale smell of takeout food. She'd texted her maid, telling her not to come that week, and there was a stench from the unemptied trash and the clogging garbage disposal. She left the television on because she was too afraid to sit in silence with her own thoughts, and she watched blankly as young actresses with short dresses and shiny legs explained why this new role was the most challenging of their lives. She didn't check her social media, she didn't google herself. She didn't know exactly what people were saying about her and that made it worse, somehow, her imagination filling in the blanks. She felt as if she was standing at the edge of a very tall building, staring down at the ground below. Woozy with fear, but the temptation was there too, to just let go. She had been arrogant, declaring herself healed, saying there was no possibility of ever returning to that old place where the bad thoughts were the only things that grew. She'd publicly denounced Narcotics Anonymous years ago, saying the twelve-step programmes were too didactic, designed to keep people small, but she could see now she had been foolish to give up that support system. Even more foolish to give up her bag of tricks, the glass of wine and the diazepam bitten in half, an unknown man pushing her skirt up as he fucked her in a restroom stall, and the momentary relief it would bring her. She ordered food on Postmates, lining it up on her kitchen table – Hershey's Kisses and Sour Patch Kids, Twinkies and Tootsie Rolls – and she sat down and made a feast of it but it wasn't enough. She needed the total obliteration which could only be found in the other things. Then, she would be able to leave her self behind her. She would let her body be ravaged and afterwards she would feel nothing. That would be preferable to this, this gnawing desperation, the thoughts eating her brain like a mass of writhing maggots.

Sam: You can't do this to me.

Sam: I need you, Mouse.

She had tried to find other ways to get in touch since Lisa had blocked her number. She sent Facebook messages, a bouquet of flowers, muffins from a local bakery. Finally, she googled Josh's real estate firm and asked his secretary to put her through. 'You've some nerve, phoning me at work,' he said when he answered.

'Josh.' She was crying so hard she could barely get the words out. 'You know I didn't do this. You know me. Don't you?' She needed him to say yes. She needed someone from her childhood to remember her as good, to remember her the way she remembered herself.

'I—' He sighed heavily. 'Look. I know this must be really hard for you but I gotta be honest, I don't know what to believe here. And I'm not sure how you think I can help you. Lisa is my—'

'Get her to phone me. I think that's the *least* you can do for me, don't you agree?'

'Sam.' His voice was cut with the slightest edge of nerves and she was glad of it. Why did she have to be the only one who was afraid? She hadn't done anything wrong. 'Please don't do anything stupid, oka—'

'I need Lisa to talk to me. I'm all alone here. I have no one.'

'Fuck,' he cursed. 'I'll do what I can but I can't promise you anything.'

'But what about—'

'Listen,' he said sharply. 'It hasn't exactly been a piece of cake here either, Sam. But no matter what . . .' He was whispering now, almost inaudible. 'My first priority is to Lisa and the girls. Got it?' And he hung up.

Sam stared at the phone, saying, 'Hello? Hello?' and then she screamed so loudly her throat felt full of knives. They couldn't treat her like this. Lisa had started this mess; she would have to be the one who finished it, too. Lisa would have to write a statement denying these allegations whether she liked it or not. That was the only way Sam would ever know peace again.

She pushed the bed sheets away, sticky with crumbs of Lay's chips and chocolate chip cookies, and she flung the closet doors open; rows of red-soled heels and quilted leather bags, sequinned skirts and cashmere sweaters. She rifled through the hangers, yanking off what she would need. When she'd packed, she lugged the suitcase downstairs, waving away Alberto's offer of help. She was aware she must look very different to the Ms Miller he was used to, the glossy, smiling version who always asked about his mother's Alzheimer's and his father's heart surgery. When his daughter had died of leukaemia last year, she had insisted he get a month off with full pay, sending a tasteful flower arrangement to the funeral. 'How are you, Alberto?' she'd asked when he came back to work.

'Thank you, Miss,' he had said. 'You're the only person who has asked that.'

'It's late, Miss,' he said now, looking at his watch. 'You sure you don't wanna wait till tomorrow?'

'I'm fine,' she replied. She caught a glimpse of herself in the mirrored wall behind his desk, the T-shirt stained with chocolate, her eyes dark in her pale face. 'I'm fine,' she said again, but she wasn't sure if she was trying to persuade him or herself. The building's parking lot was eerie at this time of night, the dim lighting creating ghosts in the shadows, and Sam hurried until she found the Lexus her PA had rented the week before; thankfully, she had been too distracted to remember to return it. She piled the suitcase into the trunk, adjusted her seat and rear-view mirrors, and then she drove home in the dark.

It was past 3 a.m. when she pulled up outside Lisa and Josh's house. There had been fresh snow while she was away and the roof was smothered with it, a lopsided snowman winking at her from the front lawn. The twins had dressed it in an old waistcoat and she started when she saw it, a sense of déjà vu creeping over her. It had been Josh's in the nineties, she could remember his hands unbuttoning it as he smiled at her, or maybe it had been Brandon Green's? She had seen it before, whoever it belonged to. She stared up at the windows, trying to remember which one was the twins' room. She searched in the garden for a pebble, finding scraps of stone. Her aim was perfect, even after all these years, and by the time she tossed the third stone, she saw a light turn on, glowing red behind the heavy curtains. The window rolled up and a face appeared, peering down at her. They had done this so many times before, she and Lisa. Sam would wait until her parents were asleep and she'd creep downstairs, jumping from one step to the next to avoid the creaking floorboards, hushing the cat when it meowed from the kitchen. She would ride her bike to Lisa's house on Elliot Street, the wind whipping through her hair, her legs pedalling as fast as she could. The path that led to the Johnsons' front door was lined in gravel chippings and Sam would collect a small pile, tipping them at the room Lisa shared with her sister. The light would turn on, as it did tonight, her friend's face at the window.

'What are you doing here?' Lisa would ask when she came downstairs in her pyjamas.

'Oh,' Sam always said. 'I couldn't sleep without saying good-night to you, Mouse.'

She waited, remembering what her therapist had told her – *The brain will always take the path of least resistance, never underestimate that* – and the door opened, Lisa standing there in a white terrycloth robe and slippers, a silk eye mask pushed up into her hair. 'What are you doing here?' she asked.

'You blocked my number. What was I supposed to do? Did Josh hear m—'

'He's asleep.'

'And you weren't?'

'I'm not a good sleeper. I haven't been for years.' Lisa turned back into the house and Sam scrambled to follow, one palm on the wooden door to keep it open.

'No,' she said. 'I'm not going home until we talk about this.' She stared at the other woman. 'Did you write that Reddit post?'

'Keep your voice down,' Lisa hissed. 'You'll wake the girls.' She stepped back out into the red-brick archway.

'Did you write it?'

'I don't have to stand here and be interrogated like this, you know that? This is *my* house. And I'm going back to—'

'Josh, then,' Sam said. 'Did Josh do it?'

'Don't even try it.' Lisa stood up straight, tightening the belt on her robe. 'He would never do that to me. And besides, we don't have secrets from each other.'

'Oh, really? You didn't tell him about the email, did you? I think it's safe to say that you and Josh have plenty of secrets.' Sam leaned against the door frame. 'I still find it interesting, you know,' she said. 'That you didn't tell Josh about what happened the night of your party. What was it you said the other day? That you thought you were betraying him by hooking up with me?' Lisa hung her head, staring at the ground. 'Is that why you sent the email?' Sam asked. 'Because you thought it would be better for Josh to think you were "assaulted" rather than cheating on him?'

'I told you, I don't want to talk about that. Not the email, not the party, not any of it.' Lisa twisted the wedding band around her ring finger. 'You know what's funny? I was so panicked about the stupid *Blackout* essay and no one ever mentioned it to me. I don't know if it was because they hadn't read it or if they just felt embarrassed and thought it was easier to ignore it. But this Reddit thing—' Her mouth quivered. 'It's *everywhere*. Josh's brother in Philly, he sent the link to us first. And then a few moms from the PTA texted, pretending to "check in" on me when it was clear they just wanted the gossip. One even sent me the number of an "excellent trauma therapist" in the area if I wanted to talk to someone. Not that *she*'s ever needed to use a therapist, she was at pains to tell me. I feel like everyone is staring at me all the time. It's easy for you, living your fancy life in the city. I have to go to the grocery store and pick up the girls at school and wonder who's thinking I was . . . that I'm . . .' She swallowed. 'I didn't ask for any of this, Sam.'

'You wrote the email!' Sam hissed. 'This whole fucking mess is because you're a sloppy drunk who decided to take me down a peg or two. Well, congratulations, Lisa. You've succeeded.'

Lisa shook her head. 'You never take responsibility for anything, do you? Not with me, not with Josh, not with your parents. It's always someone else's fault.' She looked away, a tear rolling down her cheek. 'You told me this would all go away,' she said, her voice scared. 'You promised.'

'It will. But you have to trust me.'

'Trust you? Are you kidding?'

'Have I ever let you down before, Mouse?'

Sam reached out to take her friend's hand. This was how it had always been between the two of them. Sam would take charge, she would protect Lisa, and her friend would be happy to be taken care of. Their old, familiar dynamic, carved into their bones since they were children, was reigniting; she could see it taking form again before her eyes. Neither of them would be able to resist this. 'But you've got to make a statement about the Reddit post,' she said quickly, remembering what Teddy had said during the meeting. 'We both know I didn't assault you. You have to say that publicly, Lisa.'

'But you said that would only draw more attention to it. I can't deal with—'

'That was to do with a retraction for the essay! Things are a little different now, if you hadn't noticed. Have you *seen* the things they're saying about me online? I'm being destroyed. I'm—' Sam's voice cracked. 'I won't survive this. My career . . . I've worked so hard to get where I am, I can't lose it now.'

'It's just an anonymous Reddit post. Plenty of people are accused of being abusers and their careers survive, right?' Lisa half smiled at her. 'I read a piece about it on Shakti last month.'

'Don't try to be cute. And for your information, they were all men. Women don't get second chances, do they?' She wrapped her arms around Lisa's waist, pulling her close. The other woman froze, but she didn't pull away. 'It's terrible, having people talk about you like this, isn't it?' Sam whispered. 'Just imagine what they would say about your family if they found out about the abortion.'

Lisa drew back. 'Really?' she said and her tone was almost admiring, as if she had forgotten how devious Sam could be when she was desperate, the lengths she would go to in order to save herself. 'Blackmail? That's not very spiritual of you, is it?'

'It's not blackmail. It's the truth. I don't mind the truth being out there.' Sam paused. 'Do you?'

They both jumped when the hall landing light turned on. 'Lisa?' Josh's voice called, sleepily. 'Where are you, babe?'

'I needed some fresh air,' she hissed up the stairs. 'Don't wake the twins.'

'OK.' A padding of feet, a door closing, the lights turning off again.

'He's up early tomorrow,' Lisa explained, almost involuntarily. 'He has a big meeting. He'll be wondering why I—'

'Just tell him you came out here for a cigarette.'

'I don't smoke any more. I haven't in years.'

'But I—' Sam stopped herself. How could she admit that she had come to the house before, spying on Lisa and Josh? That she had seen them passing a cigarette between them that night.

She looked at her friend and she shivered. When had Lisa become such a good liar? 'Just listen to me,' she said, trying to ignore her uneasiness. 'This isn't going to go away by itself. It's too big for that now, you said it yourself – it's everywhere. I need you to say this is false and you didn't write that Reddit post. My team will take care of the statement; it'll be handled with the utmost care.'

'I'm not making a *statement*,' Lisa said, her face paling. 'I'm not a celebrity. I don't live in your world, Sam. I just want to ignore this and things will go back to normal eventually. There'll be a new scandal and who's gonna care about some housewife in the suburbs?'

'But—' Sam scrambled for a way to persuade her friend. 'Don't you want to figure out who did this? There are only three people who know what happened that night. Me, you, and Josh. If it wasn't one of us who wrote that post, who the fuck did? And what are they gonna do next?'

'You're scaring me.'

'Yeah well, I'm scared too,' Sam said. 'But we have to fix this and you might hate me right now, Mouse, but we have to fix it together. Don't you get it?' She tilted her head to the side. 'What if the next post on Reddit is about the abortion? Have you thought about that?'

'You said you wouldn't tell—'

'Who said it would be me? This person seems to know a hell of a lot about our lives. What if they know about that, too?'

'Fuck.' Lisa sat heavily on the porch, rubbing at her legs. 'Fuck, fuck, fuck.'

'Don't panic, *Jesus*. I'm gonna come to your house tomorrow and we'll figure out a plan. I've got you, Mouse, OK?'

'Josh won't like it. He's really upset about all this, he'll freak out if you turn up at the house again.'

'OK,' Sam said, thinking quickly. 'It's a few weeks to your

fortieth, right? Tell him you want me to help organize the party. He can't say no to that, it's your birthday.'

'Are you crazy? You think I care about a stupid party right now? I didn't even want to do anything in the first place but Josh insisted. I haven't celebrated my birthday since . . .' Lisa closed her eyes briefly. 'Why on earth would I allow *you* to take over the planning?'

'You want this to go away, don't you?' Sam said, clutching her friend's hand so tightly the other woman winced. 'Then you're going to have to trust me.'

14.

March 1999

When Josh told Sam he'd meet her after his calculus class, she didn't think much of it. She told Lisa she couldn't walk home with her – 'You suck,' her friend complained, 'I'll be stuck with *Becky*' – and Sam had laughed, promised to phone her later. Then she waited by the student parking entrance, like she and Josh had agreed, taking off her headphones when she saw him coming towards her. He was wearing the pale blue knitted sweater she'd bought him at Gap and she would think that was strange, later, that he wore her birthday present on the day he decided to break up with her.

'It's not you,' he said, jiggling spare change in the pocket of his baggy jeans. 'You're awesome, Sam. It's just . . .'

'Is this because of Saturday night?' she asked, a lump in her throat. They'd been curled up on her bed, his fingers tracing the bones of her spine, up and down, both of them somewhere between awake and asleep. *I love you*, she'd said under her breath and his body had tensed. He'd rolled away from her, silently, and the next morning he hadn't mentioned it, so neither had she. 'Because I was practically in a coma, Josh. I didn't know what I was saying.'

'It's not that.' He looked awkward, staring at the ground. 'Or maybe, I suppose . . . It just made me realize that something doesn't feel right. And I don't want to hurt you, Sam. I've never wanted to do that.'

Then why are you hurting me now? she wanted to ask him.

Why are you doing this? Is there someone else? But she could see Brandon and Chris over his shoulder. Josh's best friends were waiting by his ancient Ford sedan, throwing a football back and forth. They weren't looking at them, but it was obvious they were there as back-up in case Sam lost her shit. *That bitch is crazy,* wasn't that what they said when a girl cried after her boyfriend cheated or forgot her birthday or drove home drunk and crashed a car on their front lawn. Was that what they expected Sam to do? Fall to her knees and beg Josh to stay with her? Sam tucked her CD Walkman in her backpack, pulling the straps on to her shoulders. 'Whatever,' she said. 'This was getting boring anyways.' She smiled at Chris and Brandon as she walked past them. 'I'll see you all at Becky's party tonight, right?' she asked, putting a hand over her eyes to shield them from the sun. 'It's gonna be dope.'

She could barely remember driving home, inputting the key code with trembling fingers, waiting for the wrought-iron gates to swing open. Her mother's car was in the driveway and she called Sam's name when she opened the back door. 'Samantha? Is that you?'

Carolyn was in the living room, leafing through a copy of *Town & Country*, her shoes kicked off and her feet curled up underneath her. Her father was there too, saying, 'Hey kid,' without turning around from the window. He had developed an obsession with the neighbours' dog, convinced the Garcias had trained Coco to shit on the Millers' lawn rather than their own, and was keeping a log of every time it happened.

'You guys are home early.' Sam tried to sound casual but her voice shook.

Carolyn looked up from the magazine. 'What's wrong?' she asked, her eyes narrowing. 'Did you get in trouble at school?'

And with that, Sam spilled on to the couch, sobbing. She didn't know how to explain to her parents that it felt like her heart was breaking inside her chest and she thought she might go mad with the pain of it. She and Josh had been dating for six months and she was addicted to him, or to be more precise, addicted to the way he made her feel. It wasn't just that he found her attractive and wanted to have sex with her; she could have dated any teenage boy and they would have behaved the same way. Josh *listened* to her, he took her opinions seriously, he told her she was smart and funny. He made her believe that she was someone people could care for, if she let them.

'Josh,' she managed. 'He broke up with me.' Sam cried harder, curling into Carolyn's side, her tears soaking the delicate silk of her mother's blouse.

'Don't be like this, kid. Not over some stupid punk who doesn't deserve you,' Nate Miller said, frowning. He reached for his wallet, taking out two crisp fifty-dollar notes. 'Why don't you go to the mall with Lisa? Get yourself something nice. That'll cheer you up.'

Sam stared at the money, then her father. 'I don't want to go to the mall,' she shouted. 'I want Josh!' She caught her mother half rolling her eyes, and she said indignantly, 'I saw that,' and Carolyn shushed her as Nate backed out of the room, mouthing *you deal with this* at his wife.

'It's OK, sweetie.' She pulled her daughter back into her arms. 'I know it hurts now but it won't be like this forever. Joshua's a lovely boy but it was never going to last, was it? You're both in high school. You're just kids.'

'How can you say that to me?' Sam wailed. 'I'll never feel like this about anyone else, I know it. I have to get him back, Mom. I'll do *anything*, I'll—'

'Stop that. You're being ridiculous.' Carolyn got to her feet, gesturing at Sam to do the same. She stood the girl in front of the art deco mirror that hung above the fireplace, staring at her reflection in the glass. 'Look,' her mother said. Sam's mussed hair, her blotchy skin, her swollen eyes. 'Look at what that boy has done to you. Look at what you've *allowed* him to do.' She pulled Sam's shoulders back, forcing her to stand taller. 'You can't give a man the power to make you cry. That's what they want and if you're weak enough to give it to them, they won't respect you. There's always one person who loves the other a little more in a relationship.' Carolyn caught her daughter's eye in the mirror. 'Make sure it's never you.'

By the time Lisa had arrived at the house, throwing her bike on the front lawn and calling out her hello to Mrs Miller, taking two steps at a time in her rush to get upstairs, Sam had washed her face and reapplied her make-up. She was sitting at her vanity table, pulling tendrils out from her messy bun to frame her cheekbones, when Lisa burst into her bedroom. 'Oh my god,' her friend said, panting. 'Are you OK? I came as soon as I heard.'

Sam stiffened. 'Heard what?' she asked, but of course the story would be out there already. Becky Stewart had probably sent up an SOS flare the moment she caught wind of it. 'Girl, are you talking about Josh?' She pretended to laugh, dabbing on Black Honey lipstick. 'That's old news.'

'He's an asshole.' Lisa flopped on to the bed. 'I never thought he was good enough for you.'

'Shut up, you did not.' Sam threw her eyes to heaven. 'Anyway, I thought you were supposed to be the feminist here. You should be reminding me I don't need a boyfriend to validate my existence.' She turned around. 'You're not wearing that tonight, are you?'

Lisa was in jeans and a striped knitted cardigan, her red hair held back by two butterfly clips. 'How else was I supposed to get out of the house without Mom grounding me until graduation?' she said, sticking her tongue out at Sam.

'What did you tell her?' Sam asked and the other girl smirked, saying, 'An extra rehearsal at drama club.'

Sam shook her head. 'I don't know how you get away with that shit, my mother would never fall for it,' she said.

Lisa threw her arms up in the air, saying theatrically, 'That's because you're not an actooooor, darling!'

Sam threw a pillow at her, laughing. 'Neither are you, bitch.'

Lisa pushed her over so there was enough space for them both to half sit on the stool. 'We don't have to go tonight, you know,' Lisa said, laying her head on Sam's shoulder as they looked at themselves in the mirror. It was an eerie echoing of the scene with her mother earlier, although Lisa wasn't telling her to be strong, as Carolyn had. Her friend was looking at her with mournful eyes, remembering, no doubt, all the times Sam had said how much she liked Josh. *I think he could be the one, Mouse.* For a moment, Sam wanted to cry. *I loved him*, she wanted to say. *I loved him so much.* But she'd told Lisa the truth before and it had made her vulnerable. She wouldn't make the same mistake again.

'Of course we have to go.' She shrugged Lisa off. 'Becky's older cousin got two kegs.'

'But what about—'

'Why do you have to make such a big deal out of everything? I just wanna have fun tonight.' Sam stared at herself in the mirror again. She would sharpen her beauty, she thought, and use it as a weapon, and she would never allow anyone to get close enough to hurt her like that again. 'We're going to that party.'

15.

11 January 2022

'And I said, Lydia, I hardly think an art history degree from Barnard qualifies you to give medical advice.'

'Hmm.' Sam stifled a yawn. She was exhausted; it was almost 4 a.m. when she'd left Lisa's house the night before and she hadn't been able to sleep afterwards, her mind spinning as she tried to think of all the ways she could convince her old friend to make a statement declaring Sam's innocence. Lisa had to do it. *She had to.* 'Totally.' She was sitting with her mother in the small nook that curved off the kitchen in a C-shape. It was pretty, a bench in white wood curling around the oval table, latticed glass walls looking out on to the herb garden. Carolyn had been talking non-stop since Sam had joined her but she wasn't listening to her mother; she was reading the Medium post Tatum had sent that morning.

Tatum: I think you should see this. It's so unfair, what they're saying about you. I'm devastated for you 😔

The piece was short and not very well written, describing Sam as a 'quack' and a 'snake-oil salesman'. *No matter what you think about these allegations,* the author wrote, *if you think Samantha Miller is guilty or innocent, the conversation about her pseudo-scientific bullshit is long overdue. This is a woman who doesn't believe in 'disease', calling it 'dis-ease', and that illnesses (from cancer to*

HIV to the common cold) are all 'psychosomatic', just manifestations of a 'troubled mind'.

The writer said that Sam had been 'peddling conspiracy theories' during the pandemic, as if she'd been out there blaming 5G and chemtrails for the virus rather than urging her followers to do their own research. To call Sam anti-vax was entirely unfair; she was a former addict, she couldn't even take an Advil if she had a headache. She'd always maintained that she was pro-choice and pro informed consent and the site had never said people shouldn't take the vaccine, they'd just suggested a few things that could boost the immune system – there were Shakti's specially formulated vitamin D tablets called The Sunshine State, an oil to dab on your pulse points made of frankincense and tea-tree oil, and a gorgeous bloodstone pendant to ward off infection. This article was a deliberate misinterpretation of everything she'd said during that time. She scrolled down to the comments, her jaw clenching when she saw that username.

@Supernovadiabolique157 I used to be a fan of hers but the pandemic really put me off. She's dangerous imo.

@Supernovadiabolique157 And what about the Reddit post? When are we going to talk about that?

'Samantha?' Carolyn asked. 'Are you listening to a word I'm saying?'

She took the phone from her daughter's hand – 'Mom, you have to respect my personal boundaries,' Sam protested, but the older woman ignored her – and placed it face down on the table.

'It's rude to be on your cell while we're eating,' she said.

'We're not eating yet, are we?' she retorted. 'And Dad always read at the table, remember?'

When she was a child, she would come downstairs as soon as she'd washed her face and dressed in whatever outfit her mother had laid out the night before – plaid dresses and pink tights, ribbons for her hair and bows on her shoes – and peep into the breakfast nook. 'Your mom's gone to work already,' her father would say gruffly behind his *Wall Street Journal*, pushing over on the bench so she could sit beside him. When the breakfast arrived, Nate looked at the fruit and low-fat yoghurt the maid placed in front of Samantha, his mouth tightening, and she thought maybe he would say something, maybe he would tell the maid to take it back and make pancakes with chocolate chips for Sam instead, he knew those were her favourite. But he just sat there, watching as she ate the food slowly and when she was finished, still a little hungry, her father said, 'Mom only wants the best for you, kid. Remember that.'

'Did he?' Carolyn said, adjusting the cutlery. 'God, the nineties feel like a fever dream sometimes. You'll understand when you're older.'

'I *am* older, Mom. I'm forty.'

'Yes,' her mother said, surprised. 'You are, aren't you? I keep forgetting.' The maid walked up behind them, her hands mottled with burn marks and her thin-lipped mouth unsmiling. She'd prepared a tofu scramble for Sam, sprinkled liberally with turmeric and black pepper, and she couldn't help but look at her mother's eggs Florentine with a little envy, the spill of yellow yolk on the plate when Carolyn dug her fork into its heart.

'You were home late last night,' her mother said, taking a delicate bite of her eggs. She would eat a quarter of the portion then push the plate away, saying she was full. Carolyn had done this for so long, Sam didn't know if her mother really did have a tiny appetite or if she'd just trained herself to believe she did.

'Yeah. Thanks for leaving a key out for me.'

'I heard the door, it was almost four a.m. It's not safe driving in those conditions, surely you could have waited till this morning? Honestly, Samantha. I don't know what goes through your head sometimes.'

'I wanted to beat the traffic, OK? I think I'm old enough to decide what time I want to drive home at.'

'I worry. That's what mothers do, no matter how old their children are. You'd understand if you had kids of your own.'

'Hmm.' Sam heard the maid in the kitchen, the clatter of dishes rinsed in the sink and loaded into the dishwasher, a low chuckle at something Robin Roberts said on *Good Morning America*. 'What are your plans for the day?' she asked, changing the subject.

'I'm busy,' Carolyn said automatically. When her mother was still working and later, when she had to care for her husband after he was diagnosed with early onset dementia, Carolyn had never complained about her schedule, no matter how full it was. But the moment she'd retired, she was constantly 'busy', as if to be otherwise was to have succumbed to old age. 'I have Pilates at ten – oh, you should join me! Nothing makes you quite as lean as Pilates, that's why all the ballerinas do it – and then I'm having lunch with Lydia. After that, I'm—'

'But I thought you were fighting with Lydia,' Sam interrupted, her stomach sinking. She didn't want her mother gossiping over cappuccinos with Lydia Thomas; she seemed the kind of woman who would have an active Facebook account, spending her days liking politically charged posts, the jokes about 'wine o'clock' and 'Mommy Juice' even though her sons were well into their forties now, sharing GoFundMe pages for kids with cancer which she would call 'important' but never donate to. She imagined Lydia, one hand on

Carolyn's, as she told her what people on the internet were saying about her daughter.

'I'm not fighting with anyone,' Carolyn said in surprise. 'Lydia's a good friend of mine.'

Sam looked at her mother, weighing up her options. She knew something could be a big story online and never infiltrate the real world. She'd seen it before – an author who pretended her grandmother was bi-racial to sell her book about a Black family trying to buy a house in a 1950s Levittown development, the latest Karen to smile menacingly and say they were only 'asking questions'. Old, malicious tweets of a social media darling unearthed; the screenshots shared in the Spirit Mafia chat with multiple exclamation marks, Tatum declaring this was 'the end' of that person's career. But whenever Sam mentioned the same story to someone who didn't live online, like her therapist or her mother or her ex-boyfriend, they would look at her in baffled bemusement and say, *What are you talking about?* It was perfectly possible Carolyn might never hear about the Reddit post but still, Sam was nervous.

'I'm going to Lisa's later,' she said, reaching for the teapot and pouring some into the fine bone china cup. Her mother rested her hands on the linen tablecloth.

'Oh?' Carolyn asked. 'Why so?'

'It's her birthday party next month and I said I'd help out. Josh was planning some crappy little backyard get-together and I think she deserves a lot better than that. It's her fortieth, for God's sake, you'd think he'd make more of an effort.'

'I thought you were going on book tour; your schedule is usually crazy when a new one comes out.'

'Not this one. It seems to be selling all by itself.'

That's the good thing about a controversy, Jane had said during their last phone call. *It's free publicity. Book sales are holding strong. Better than ever, actually.* Sam imagined all those people, combing through *Chaste* until they found the passage about Lisa, looking for clues, the crumbs that would lead them to her guilt. Unfortunately, that was the only good news her manager had for Sam. Shakti had lost its biggest sponsor for its annual wellness summit, and a few of the speakers were starting to get cold feet; at least three had pulled out, saying they didn't think the 'optics' were right. The girls in head office were concerned, Jane told her, and Sam could tell by the edge in her manager's voice that they weren't the only ones. 'Don't worry,' Sam had said, hoping she sounded more confident than she felt. 'Lisa will make that statement, I promise you.' But what if she didn't? Sam's stomach tensed and she felt suddenly nauseous at the sight of the food, throwing her napkin on top of the plate to cover it up.

'Are you OK?' her mother asked.

'I'm fine,' Sam said. 'Just not very hungry this morning.' She ignored her mother's smile at this, and her own treacherous pleasure in response. 'Anyway, you've been nagging me for years to spend more time with you. And now that I'm home, you're not happy either?'

'I'm not saying that. I'm delighted to have you here, you know that. But it's just . . . shouldn't Joshua be in charge of the party planning?'

'I told you. *Joshua* was putting together a shit-show of a party. I offered to step in and take some of the pressure off and . . . well, Lisa and I thought it'd be a good opportunity for us to catch up.' She smoothed non-existent crumbs from the tablecloth, avoiding her mother's eye. She checked the time on her phone. 'I need to go or I'll be late.'

'Are you sure this is a good idea?' Carolyn asked, dabbing her mouth with her napkin. 'I don't want to see you get hurt again. The two of you together – you could be like a tinderbox at times.'

'What are you talking about?'

Her mother broke into peals of laughter. 'You don't remember the time I found that girl dragging you by the hair on the living room floor? She took a chunk out of your head; I was afraid you were going to have a bald patch.' She grew serious again. 'Please, Samantha. Be careful. I don't think things have always been . . . *easy* there.'

'How do you mean?'

Carolyn waved her away. 'I'm not entirely sure. I called to their house after the twins were born – I had a present for the babies, these darling monogrammed blankets – and when Lisa answered the door, she wouldn't let me in. I could hear the babies screaming in the next room and she looked exhausted. But then I was exhausted after you were born too and there was only one of you. I met Nancy Johnson for a coffee a few weeks later and she said Lisa was refusing to hire a nanny, that she wanted to do it all by herself.' Carolyn tsked. 'I didn't like to ask any more.'

'Do you see a lot of Lisa these days?'

'We stop and chat if we pass each other in the grocery store, but other than that, not really. She's devoted to those two girls, I'll give her that. Always taking them to soccer practice or buying materials for a science project. But she can seem sad at times, I think.' Carolyn looked at her daughter, her eyes sharp. 'And I'm not sure if the two of you "hanging out" is going to change that, Samantha.'

The Taylors' house looked deserted when she arrived. The bikes had been put away, there were no toys strewn across the porch, and the garage was shut. For a moment, Sam worried that Lisa had left at sunrise, packing her bags and telling Josh and the kids they needed to run. She banged the lion's head knocker as loudly as she could but there was no reply. She tested the handle, the door opening easily. 'Hello?' she called. It smelled sterile in there, like the floors had been freshly bleached, and she could hear voices coming from the kitchen. She crept closer, listening.

'It's just tough, you know?' a woman said.

'Of course I know,' Lisa replied. There was a clatter of something, as if she was stacking dishes. 'You want the best for her.'

'I . . .' The other woman hesitated. 'I'm happy she has Maya, but friendships can be so frigging intense at that age and I'd rather she have a big gang of girls than just one best friend. Does that make sense?'

'For sure,' Lisa said and she continued, inaudibly; Sam could only make out a word here and there. '. . . my own . . . I wish someone . . . different.' Lisa cleared her throat. 'Do you want me to talk to Martha? I'll be delicate about it.'

'Oh, would you?' The relief in the other woman's voice was palpable. 'I can't tell you how much I'd appreciate it.'

'What are friends for?' Lisa said. 'Goodness, look at the time, I'd better—'

Sam pushed the door open, smiling brightly at the two women. 'Sorry to barge in like this but I was knocking for *ages* and the door was open so . . .' It was only then that she realized who Lisa's guest was, the lithe woman in running gear and sneakers, her hair tied up in a top knot. 'Becky!' Sam said, ignoring the shock on her face. 'What a nice surprise.'

'I—' she stuttered, turning to Lisa. 'What's going on, Lis?'

'I thought you weren't coming until eleven,' Lisa said, checking her watch. 'It's only nine fifteen. I thought—'

'Oh, I've been up for hours.' Sam settled on to the stool next to Becky, unwinding the cashmere scarf from around her neck. 'I'm such an early bird these days. I like to get a run in before the world is awake.'

'Oh yeah?' Becky asked, sitting up straighter. 'I'm out the door by six most mornings. Just a quick 10k around Bluff Falls Park. Where do you go?'

'I can totally tell you're a runner. And you're hitting the gym too, right?' Sam squeezed Becky's bicep, inwardly smiling at the other woman's instinctive urge to flex her muscles. 'Welcome to the gun show, bitches! You look *amazing*.'

'Oh.' Becky was disconcerted, her cheeks flushing pink. 'Thanks. I worked really hard to get into shape.'

'It shows. Maybe we could go together some morning?' Sam smiled at her, and the woman smiled back, reluctantly. 'I need a few tips. I think I'm putting too much weight on my right ankle. It's feeling a bit weak.'

'Oh no!' Becky cried. 'That's the worst. OK, the first thing I would recommend is—'

'Didn't you say you had a spinning class, Rebecca?' Lisa interrupted them. She stood up, wiping her hands on a dish cloth. She was wearing a sheer blouse tucked into skinny jeans, a little risqué for a Tuesday morning, Sam thought; her friend had obviously dressed up for her benefit.

'It's not until ten,' Becky protested but she picked up her gym bag from the floor and got to her feet. 'So . . .' she said, looking from one to the other. 'What are you ladies up to?'

'We're planning Lisa's birthday party!' Sam said, clapping her hands together. 'The first of Feb. You can come, right?'

'What?' Becky licked her lower lip. 'I don't . . . you said you were cancelling, Lisa?'

'Yeah . . . um, the girls were heartbroken when I told them,' Lisa said, clearing her throat. 'You know how much they were looking forward to it. I felt bad.'

'Mackenzie never mentioned anything about it after school yesterday.' Becky's face fell. 'She is still invited, isn't she? She'll be so upset if—'

'Stop,' Lisa cut her off. 'The kids are all invited. Don't be silly.'

'Sorry. Sorry, I didn't mean . . .' She trailed off. 'Do you want me to help?' she asked hopefully. 'I'm good at this stuff. Marcus – that's my husband, Sam, he's the manager of the Savings Bank downtown – he likes to entertain a lot.' She dusted her shoulders off. 'I'm a regular Martha Stewart these days.'

'I think we've got it, don't we, Mouse?' Sam said, ignoring Becky's flinch when she used the old nickname. The other woman looked to Lisa, her mouth slack, as if asking for mercy.

'Come on,' Lisa said. 'I'll walk you out.' She could hear the two of them talking in the hall, an urgency to their voices.

'What are you doing? After everything—'

'Rebecca, I don't have a—'

Sam's eyes drifted on to the far wall and she saw a framed photo of their wedding day. Josh, handsome in his navy-blue tux, Lisa in a strapless dress and lace bolero, her hair in a stiff up-do and her mouth overlined with nude lipliner, and there was Becky, behind them, in a peach chiffon dress. *That should have been me.* Lisa and Sam were supposed to be the maid of honour at each other's weddings, godparents to each other's children, not Becky. They were supposed to spend their old age sitting side by side, waiting for death to come. Sam had never been asked to be a bridesmaid by any of her friends in the city and she'd always pretended she didn't care – 'Wearing the same dress as a bunch of other girls to a party?!' she would laugh. 'No thanks!' – but it had hurt, that no one loved her enough to want her in their wedding party. She heard a sudden burst of laughter from the hall, Becky saying she would phone later, the sound of an air kiss as they said goodbye. Then Lisa, pushing open the door, her face thunderous.

'We said eleven, Sam. I'm not sure what you're playing at—'

'Becky was your bridesmaid.' She pointed at the frame on the wall. 'I thought you couldn't stand her.'

'What are you talking about? I've always liked Rebecca.'

'What? You used to call her a loser.' Sam knew she shouldn't get heated – she needed to stay focused if she was ever going to get out of Bennford and back to her life in the city – but she couldn't allow Lisa to take their memories and reshape them to suit herself. 'You said—'

'Are we really going to sit here and argue about high school?'

'Fine,' Sam gave in. 'Where's Josh?'

'He's at work.' Lisa picked up the gallon of milk from the breakfast bar and put it in the fridge. 'Coffee?' she asked, and Sam said she'd rather have a herbal tea. As Lisa popped a pod into the Nespresso machine for herself, Sam took a quick photo of the piece of paper stuck to the fridge with an Elsa magnet, a schedule with the girls' after-school activities. It would be handy, she thought, if Lisa ever attempted to use the kids as an excuse not to see her. The kettle on the stove whistled and Lisa poured hot water over a peppermint tea bag. 'There,' she said, banging a Yankees mug on the bar in front of Sam. The two women sat in silence for a few minutes, the ticking of a clock on the wall, a slight slurp when one of them took a sip of their drink.

'So,' Sam tried after what felt like an eternity. 'Do you want to talk about your birthday?' Lisa ignored her, drinking her coffee. 'What about the cake?' Sam asked. 'Or we could go through the guest list? I'm not sure what—'

'Josh has everything covered.'

'Yeah, but his idea of a party and mine are very different.' Sam forced a laugh. 'I was thinking I could call a maid service and arrange for a deep clean the day before? They can come after too, to clean up, if you'd like. Anything to make things easier for the birthday girl!'

'Can you please stop pretending that we're friends?' Lisa pushed her stool away, the feet scraping against the tiled floor. 'We're not friends any more. And today is reminding me exactly why. I told you to come at eleven and you just arrived at whatever time suited you. I mean, I told you I didn't want to see you in the first place and you *blackmailed* me into doing it anyway. Why on earth would I want to be friends with someone who has no respect for me?'

'I do respect you! And I didn't blackmail you, I just . . . I didn't know what else to do,' Sam protested. 'I wanted to talk to you and you wouldn't—'

'You told me you had a plan,' Lisa interrupted. 'To fix this mess, to make everything go back to the way it was before the Reddit post. What is it? Tell me. *Tell me*, Sam. How are you gonna fix this?'

'I—' Sam didn't know what to say. Her 'plan' was to get close to Lisa again, to figure out why she would lie about what happened that night. After that, she needed to persuade Lisa to sign a statement swearing that Sam was innocent, the allegations were false, and then, only then, would everything go back to normal. It sounded so easy when she laid it out like that, and yet Sam had no idea how she was going to pull it off. She looked at Lisa, her throat tightening. 'I want us to be friends again, Mouse.'

'Stop calling me that,' Lisa spat at her. 'And you don't want to be my friend. You just want to save your own ass. Why can't you be honest about that, at least?' She propped her elbows up on the table, holding her head in her hands. 'This is my own fault,' she said quietly. 'Josh was right. I never could say no to you. What Sam wants, Sam gets. And I just let you get away with it because it seemed easier. But I can't do this any more. I need . . .' Lisa was struggling to hold back tears now. 'I need you to . . .'

'What do you need? Just tell me.'

'I need time,' Lisa said, looking at her with glassy eyes.

'Oh, Mouse,' Sam said, putting her hand on her friend's shoulder. 'I'm afraid I don't have any time to give you.'

16.

◎ **2,398,999**

Sam woke, disorientated, and she didn't know where she was. The room was dark, and a heavy dread settled in her bones as she sat up in the bed and remembered what had happened. The thoughts were racing – *Who wrote it? Was it Lisa? Was it Josh? And why? Why? Why?* – and she reached for her phone on the nightstand. She'd been awake until two in the morning, the glow of the screen burning against her eyes as she read the new comments on that Reddit post.

@Supernovadiabolique157 If she were a man, we wouldn't be 'waiting for all the facts', would we? #DoubleStandards

yeah, a man would of been cancelled already!

She unlocked her phone, squinting at the screen to find two new messages from Jane.

Jane: this isnt good

Jane: ill give you a chance to read & digest lets talk after

Her manager had sent a link to a piece on Jezebel. The header photo was of Sam, speaking at a workshop in Sydney maybe five years ago. It had been one of those events where the atmosphere was electrifying and she could sense the energetic shifts taking place in the girls, a flame sparked in their hearts, one by one. She so badly wanted them to have the lives they dreamed of, these beautiful, shining girls. 'Get down on your knees,' she'd been guided by a Higher Power to say. 'And raise your hands in a gesture of receiving. Allow the Universe to give you whatever you desire.' And all seven hundred of them had done just that. It had been so moving at the time but she could see now that it could be easily misconstrued as something odd, even sinister. Sam in her floor-length white dress, staring down at all those young women, kneeling before her, their arms outstretched as if to worship her. 'Fuck,' she hissed when she saw the name on the by-line. It was Tia Harris, a well-known Black feminist and writer. *Save me from these white women and their goddamn black squares*, Tia had tweeted less than five minutes after Sam had posted that very thing on Instagram, captioning it with her favourite Gandhi quote, *Be the change you want to see in the world* ♥

It's meaningless, Tia had tweeted that day. *It's literally the very least they could do and they waited until *now* to do it, when their silence might actually cost them something.*

She speed-read through the article, her mouth dry.

Much has been made this week of the anonymous allegations against Samantha Miller. I can't speak to that but I do believe we should have a conversation about Miller's stranglehold on the wellness industry. Where are the Black gurus? Where are the BIPOC leaders in this space? Why are the most successful teachers of yoga – a spiritual practice originating in ancient India – thin, white women? The sort of women who might, like Samantha Miller has done, name their company 'Shakti', even though what they preach is a Frankenstein-ed mish-mash of Hinduism, Buddhism and the Prosperity Bible, as far as I can tell. We've all heard the joke – Lord, give me the confidence of a mediocre white man. I say, Lord, give me the career of a mediocre white woman. Because that's what Samantha Miller is. Samantha Miller, in all her bland, basic glory, is the embodiment of white privilege and I, for one—

Sam couldn't read any more, closing out of the article. She checked Twitter and saw that a major journalist had retweeted the article. The replies under her tweet were piling up – *@Supernovadiabolique157 I'm glad people are *finally* ready to have this conversation! Samantha is dangerous imo* – and there was something else, a two-minute video, a compilation of different events Sam had done over the years spliced together. Row after row of white faces, Kid Rock's version of 'Sweet Home Alabama' playing over the top. Tia Harris quote-tweeted the video: *It's like Goop meets a Hitler Youth convention* 😳

Her phone rang, startling her. 'Fuck,' she muttered when she saw Jane's name. She rejected the call, then did the same when her manager attempted to get through a second time.

Jane: pick up

Sam: I'm in the middle of something

Jane: what are you in the middle of thats more important than this

Jane: we need to do damage control

Sam: I'm sorry, do you need me to do your job for you?

Sam: Plant a think piece about how dangerous anonymous allegations are. Stress that it could be *anyone* who wrote the Reddit post. A troll who resents what Shakti stands for. An MRA trying to discredit victims etc etc etc. It isn't rocket science.

Jane: this has gone beyond the reddit piece

Jane: we need to regroup urgently

No. Sam refused to believe that. That was the attitude of someone who believed she was helpless. It was the attitude of a
victim. Sam knew she was a powerful creator and she could
bend the world to her will. She could fix this. All she needed
was Lisa to say these allegations were false and everything
would be fine. Sam could go home, back to her old life. She
had always got what she wanted before; she wasn't going to
give up now.

Sam: I'm telling you. I have this under control.

Sam: btw I can't believe Tia Harris would write a piece like
that about me???

Sam: Like, I donated a LOT of money to ACLU during the
protests

Sam: Should we make those donations public? Would that
help?

Sam: Jane?

She waited an hour for her manager to text back. She went for
a run, checking her cell every couple of minutes to see if a
message had come through. Back home, she stripped her
clothes off, dumping them on the floor, and as she showered,
she kept glancing at the phone, face-up on the sink, hoping it
would light up. But as she wrapped a large towel around her
body, wiping steam from the screen, the only messages she'd
received were from an activewear brand promising 20 per cent
off their leggings and her horoscope app. She patted a vitamin
C serum into her skin, dotted cream under her eyes and
brushed her teeth. She checked her phone again. It was
7.30 a.m.; maybe Jane was in the subway and her signal was
gone. She could be meeting a client over breakfast, too; it
would be rude to text in the middle of a meeting. Sam pulled

on a pair of jeans and an oversized sweater, blasting her hair with a hairdryer. She sat on the edge of her bed, phone in hand, and she waited. And then, finally, it beeped.

Jane: i need to talk to you

Jane: something else has happened

17.

'Does the name Brooke Campbell ring a bell?' Jane hadn't even said hello when Sam had answered the phone, her tone brusque. 'She was an assistant of yours. We've just received a formal complaint from her, saying Shakti was a hostile work environment. And that you were a . . .' Jane paused. '*Demanding* boss. Actually, that's not quite how she put it. She said you made her life a living hell.'

'What? I would never—' A memory then, of a girl with a swishing ponytail and porcelain skin, her lower lip quivering. Sam was standing next to her desk, watching as she typed oh so slowly. 'Oh for God's sake, I'll do it myself.' Sam had snapped her fingers at the girl, telling her to get up from her seat. Sam took her place, sighing as she'd finished the email. She had been too slow, Brooke Campbell. Prone to silly mistakes, misspelling names of important clients, messing up Sam's diary. Once, she'd even booked flights for the wrong day and Sam had come very close to missing a speaking gig at Oxford University. Sam was a busy woman; she needed her PA to make her life *easier*, not more difficult. 'Yes,' she said, quieter now. 'I remember Brooke.'

'She's threatening to sue, Sam. The board are losing their shit,' Jane said. 'They've called another meeting tomorrow.'

'OK, I'll drive back to the city in the morning.'

'I don't think that's a good idea.'

'But this isn't fair! Brooke was incompetent; she wasn't cut out to be an assistant at this level. I did her a fucking *favour*. Any of those men on the board would have done the exact same thing but because I'm a woman, I'm a "bully". It's sexism, pure and simple. And why is she coming out of the woodwork now? I fired her, like, two years ago.'

Jane sighed. 'I'll handle it, OK?' And then, just before she hung up, she said, 'Wait, before I forget. There's been a guy emailing for you. He's pretty insistent.'

'Yeah? Who is it?'

'Some French guy? He said his name was Gabriel. Apparently, he needs to talk to you.'

Sam inhaled sharply. 'What did you say to him? Jane. What did you say?'

'I told him I couldn't give that information out, obviously. Why?' Her manager's voice was curious. 'Who is he?'

'He's my ex. It didn't . . .' She felt light-headed, reaching out for the bed post to steady her. 'It didn't end well. Jane. Listen to me. You have to swear you won't give him my details. This is really important.'

'Why, what—'

'Promise me, Jane.'

'Fine,' her manager gave in. 'I promise.'

The next morning, Sam woke too early, the back of her mouth sour, and she reached for the leather-bound diary on the nightstand to record her dreams, but all she could find were traces of salt and sweat, the blurring strangeness that was always there when she took melatonin. She checked her cell to see if Lisa had replied to any of her voice messages – 'Hey, Mouse. It's me. Again. I keep phoning and texting and you never . . . Look, I'm sorry for coming to the house again yesterday. I shouldn't have done that. I just thought maybe we could talk? I hoped . . . But you're right. You're right. You asked for time. I know you did . . . Just phone me, OK? When you're ready. Things are . . . things are bad here. I need your help' – but there was no reply. She pulled on her workout clothes and crept out of the house in the dark, the bitter air stealing her breath away. She ran until she was gasping, hoping to beat the fear out of her – *Gabriel is looking for you. He's back, Sam. He's come back for you, at last.* After her shower, she left another message.

'Hey, Lisa. It's me. I don't want to annoy you but I wanted to tell you about this dream I keep having. We're kids again, playing hide-and-seek. I'm in the basement and someone slams the door shut behind me. I can't find the light switch and I'm twisting at the handle, begging them to let me out. I'm screaming and screaming and then finally, the door opens and it's you, standing at the top of the stairs. You saved me, Mouse. Wasn't that what we always promised? That we would save each other if we were ever in trouble?'

The social team emailed, saying they were 'very concerned' about the latest stats; Sam was 'haemorrhaging followers', they said; did she realize she'd lost almost a million on Instagram alone? She'd been dropped by a few brands she had worked with for years: the organic food delivery service, the clean beauty face oil, the vegan collagen powder she mixed with her morning smoothie. A BuzzFeed listicle, 'Here Are All The Celebrities Who Have Unfollowed Samantha Miller', popped up on her timeline and she had to sit on her hands to stop herself from looking at the comments. An old video from an event she'd done years ago – it must have been 2009, she thought, she was still growing out the terrible pixie cut *he* had said would suit her – where a young woman disclosed her experience of rape. Sam, grasping the woman's hands. 'These predators can sense which girls to target,' she had said in the shaky recording. 'We believe we are worthy of abuse and then we attract that abuse to prove our core beliefs. But once you change the thoughts, you change your life. And then, my love, you will be safe forever.'

The reaction online was swift.

victim blaming much?

isn't this basically the same as telling her if she hadn't been drinking, it wouldn't have happened?

what more could you expect from Samantha Miller? She only spoke publicly about her own sexual assault after #MeToo & she could find a way to make money out of it

#BelieveWomen . . . unless they're the childhood best friend I guess 🖤

Sam squinted at the screen again and there it was, @Supernova-diabolique157. She clicked into the user's profile, scrolling through their activity over the last twenty-four hours.

Supernovadiabolique157 commented on *How The Pandemic exposed New Age Narcissism* r/whitefeminists

When are you going to talk about Samantha Miller? The stories I've heard about her.

Supernovadiabolique157 commented on *qAnon & wellness influencers* r/conspirituality

When are you going to talk about Samantha Miller? The stories I've heard about her.

Supernovadiabolique157 commented on *When the New Age and the Far Right Overlap* r/conspiracytheories

When are you going to talk about Samantha Miller? The stories I've heard about her.

She sent Jane a link to the profile. *I've seen this name pop up for some time now but it's getting super unnerving. Should we have someone look into this???* she wrote. It wasn't the first time Sam had attracted negative attention – there had always been over-zealous fans who formed unhealthy attachments to her, who seemed to think it was their God-given right to expect Sam's undivided attention because they'd read her book or bought a ticket to an event – but there was something about this that didn't feel right, a twist in her gut warning her of imminent danger.

Jane: its prob nothing

Jane: but leave it with me. ill get one of the IT guys to look for an IP address

Jane: btw another email from that gabriel guy. What do you want me to do

Sam put her head between her knees, trying to catch her breath. The panic was knitting the bones of her throat together; she was afraid she was suffocating. What did he want from her? What would he do when he found her? She reached for her cell again, dry-heaving with fear.

'It's me,' she sobbed. 'Please help me. I need you, Mouse. I don't care about what's happened between us. I don't care about that email, I don't care what you said about me. I'm alone and I'm scared and I need you. I can't go on like this. I can't . . . You always said you'd be there if I needed you.' Sam could hardly breathe, she was crying so hard. 'I need you now. I'm afraid I might do something—' And she hung up because she couldn't get the words out of her choking mouth.

18.

The windowpane rattled and Sam startled awake. There was a ping against the glass, and another, and she almost tripped over the armchair in her hurry to get to the window. A pale face below, staring at her. As soon as Sam saw her there, something eased through her, breathing calm into every cell of her body. For some reason, she knew everything would be OK now. Sam held a finger up – *one minute* – and she yanked a knitted sweater over her silk nightdress. She carried her ankle boots with her, only pulling them on once she had the front door open so she wouldn't wake her mother. It was freezing outside, her breath haunting the air before her, her fingers curling in an effort to keep the blood flowing through them. 'I saw the light in your room . . .' Lisa began.

'Come into the kitchen,' Sam said. 'It's too cold out here.'

'No.' Lisa was sitting on the porch, her hair in a scruffy bun, her grey pinstripe pyjamas tucked into rubber boots. She was wearing a puffer coat so comically oversized that it had to be Josh's. Sam waited, stamping from one foot to the other, and Lisa put a hand over her mouth, her face stricken. *'Oh my god,'* her friend kept whispering. 'I thought . . .' She moved her hand to her chest, catching her breath. 'Your voicemail earlier, Sam. You sounded so desperate and I thought . . . I was so worried. Josh said you'd be fine and that it wasn't our problem anyway, but I couldn't sleep. I thought you might have done something . . .' She faltered. *'Stupid.'*

'Oh shit,' Sam said, as she realized what the other woman was implying. 'I'm sorry, I wasn't thinking straight. There's—' *This man*, she wanted to say. *I am afraid of him. Afraid of what he'll do if he finds me.* 'I was scared I might relapse,' she said instead. 'Start using again, not . . . Oh, Lisa. I'm sorry. I'm fine, I promise.'

'I can see that now, can't I? But your message freaked me out. I don't know.' She rubbed the back of her neck. 'I don't even know why I'm here.'

'It's what we do, isn't it?' Sam said. 'The two of us. This is what we've always done.'

Lisa shook her head but she didn't disagree. 'Sit with me,' her friend said, patting the step beside her. 'Just for a little while.'

Sam did as she was told, rubbing at her bare legs, shivering. 'What were you thinking, coming out without a coat?' Lisa chided her, and she sounded so much like her mother that Sam laughed out loud. How was it possible that *Lisa* was a mom? How was it possible that the two of them were anything other than sixteen years old, best friends, blood sisters? Lisa shrugged her coat off and invited Sam to huddle under its warmth. She hesitated, but then it seemed easier to give in. This is what they did, she reminded herself. They gave in to one another. She would forgive Lisa and Lisa would forgive her because what other choice did they have? Sam nestled her head on her friend's shoulder and beneath the new perfume – the change of fragrance seemed an insult in a way Sam couldn't quite articulate – there it was, the way her best friend's skin smelled in the morning when they would wake in Sam's bed and immediately pick up whatever conversation they had fallen asleep in the middle of the night before. They sat there, nestled in Josh's coat, neither looking at the other. Staring out at the lawn, at the water in the fountain frozen solid, the grass dusted white with snow. It would melt tomorrow, it would be shovelled out of the way or made slush by people going about their days as if their small lives were of any great importance, but for now the world was untouched. It was theirs and it was perfect.

'The girls?' she asked.

'You don't think I left them alone, do you? Josh is at home.'
Lisa elbowed Sam. 'Don't any of your friends have kids?'

'Some of them,' Sam said. 'Mostly not.'

She'd found over the years that women had great intentions
in the beginning. *It won't change me*, they declared once two
lines appeared on the pregnancy test, but it always did. Eventually, Sam got phased out or she would phase herself out,
because their lives were so different; she had little interest in
the endless tales of piano recitals and pony lessons and infight-
ing in the PTA and she couldn't pretend she did. It hurt
sometimes but Sam had trained herself not to need other
people. It was safer that way.

'I started seeing a shrink last year,' Lisa said suddenly.

'Wow. OK. That's great.'

'Josh thought . . . we both thought it might be a good idea. I
struggled when the girls were born. It wasn't an easy journey
for us, you know. We'd been trying for a while.' She didn't look
at Sam, her voice flat. 'And nothing was happening.' She half
laughed. 'It's funny, isn't it? I was adamant in high school that
I never wanted kids – you know what it was like in my house.
There was always a new baby, someone trying to get Mom's
attention, and I didn't want that for myself.' Lisa bit her lip.
'But I guess there's a difference between not wanting something and not being able to have it.'

'Oh, Mouse. I'm sorry. I wish I'd known.'

'What could you have done? And after they were born,
things were . . . tricky, I guess you could say. I thought I had
everything under control for a while but during the pandemic
I was trying to home-school the twins and I was paranoid
Mom or Dad would get sick, so I insisted on doing all their
grocery shopping. And then I was afraid to go out anywhere
or meet anyone because I didn't want to bring the virus home

to them. It was just me and the girls and Josh, and I kept telling myself how lucky I was, I should be grateful. People lost their jobs, people *died*. But I just felt— It was like the walls were closing in on me and I couldn't breathe. And I had all of this *time*, you know? It was the first time I had stood still since . . . I couldn't sleep, I was drinking too much – I was always making an excuse to open another bottle of wine – and Josh said it might help. To talk to someone, I mean.'

'Did it? Help?'

'I suppose. She's nice. I wish I had seen her sooner, after the girls were born.' Lisa picked at the polish on her nails. 'They were so tiny,' she said quietly. 'I'd get this feeling in the pit of my stomach that I shouldn't be alone with them. Like they weren't safe with me.'

'Why wouldn't they be safe with you? You're their mother.'

'I don't know.' Lisa pulled her knees into her chest. 'I can't explain it. Just that something was wrong with me. And the therapist, she asked when I first had that feeling – that something was wrong with me, I mean. We went around in circles for months, trying to pinpoint it, until I realized it was after my birthday party. That night—' She wiped her palms on her pyjama bottoms. 'I was so drunk, Sam. I didn't understand why we would have done . . . *that*. I'd never felt that way about you before, so it just didn't make sense that we'd hook up out of nowhere. And I felt like I'd cheated on Josh and I never told him about it, not really. I hinted here and there, hoping he'd get the message. Then the essay came out and I panicked. I had a glass of wine and before I knew it, I'd drunk the whole bottle and I got really angry. You *promised* me you'd never tell anyone and then you write an essay and you use my fucking initial? How could you do that to me?'

'I'm sorry.' Sam rubbed her friend's back. 'I really am. I wasn't trying to cause trouble for anyone. But come on, Lisa.

You were flirting with me all night, you kept grinding up on me when we were dancing. Can you understand why I'm confused now that you've suddenly decided that I *assaulted* you?'

'I didn't . . .' Lisa whispered. 'I said I was sorry for sending the email, OK? I never meant for this to happen. And now it's just exploded, and all I can think about is that Reddit post. You were right: if it wasn't one of us, who wrote it? What if they know about the abortion? Josh will—'

'No one knows about that. It's fine.'

'It's not fine! Nothing is fucking fine!' Lisa shouted. 'I'm afraid to leave the house. I asked Rebecca to do the school run for me because I can't face the other moms. I'm afraid to go to the store in case I meet someone and all I'm thinking is, have they read it? Do they know? I feel like everyone is talking about me and I'm freaking out in case someone will say something to the girls in school, or one of Josh's colleagues will see it and think I'm a . . . a . . .'

'Thinks you're a what? I'm the one everyone thinks is a sexual predator, remember?' Sam had always said she didn't want to be a victim and yet now she could see that being a victim was a better option than to be falsely accused of something she hadn't done. 'I'm going to ask you this one time, Lisa. Do you actually believe I assaulted you?'

'I don't . . . I— *No.* I didn't mean to get you in trouble.' Lisa curled her hands into fists in her lap. 'I didn't mean for any of this to happen. I just wanted . . . I don't know what I wanted. But not this. I didn't want any of this.' She reached into the puffer coat for a scraggy-looking tissue, blowing her nose loudly. 'At first, I wanted to tell you how upset I was but the only thing we— *I* could find on your website was your manager's contact details. And the more I wrote, the more I thought about that night . . . I just got so worked up. I wanted—' She looked up with red-rimmed eyes. 'I wanted you to hurt as much as I did.'

Sam's jaw clenched. The temptation to scream at Lisa was too great; she was afraid if she opened her mouth, flames would spill out. 'I'm sorry you felt that way,' she said carefully. 'I know now that I should have been more sensitive in the way in which I wrote my essay. After all, it wasn't just my story to tell. It was yours too.'

'It doesn't feel like it's my story.' Lisa rubbed her nose with the back of her hand. 'Josh tells me one thing about that night and you tell me another, and neither fits with how I feel inside. I just wish I could remember.'

'Do you ever think,' Sam said, 'that if you've tried so hard to remember and you can't, maybe that means it didn't happen?' She looked her friend in the eye. 'Because it didn't, Lisa. I would never do that to *anyone* but especially not to you. I loved you. And I'm beginning to feel like I'm going crazy here. How can you see it one way and I see it totally differently? How does that work?'

'I don't know.'

It began to snow then, gently, like powdered sugar falling on their heads. Soon night would lift, the clouds turning navy then melting into that strange, fragile blue. The day would come and this, whatever it was, would be broken again. What were they doing? Sitting here, holding hands in the dark. It didn't make sense. She had betrayed Lisa by writing that essay, she'd broken her promise to take their story to the grave, and in retaliation her friend had set in motion something which was threatening to destroy Sam's reputation, her career, her life. These were unforgiveable actions, on both sides, and yet here they still were, together. It was as Sam had said: this was what she and Lisa had always done – they would fight, tempers flaring, sharp words sparking off one another like flint, and then it would pass and they would forget, falling into their easy rhythm of inside jokes and shared memories. The path of least resistance, as Diane would say. They were something more than friends, more than sisters even; they were two halves of the same person, only whole when they were together. And for all these years they had tried to forget that truth. Sam had spent a long time proclaiming it was unhealthy, their friendship, that what she had with Tatum was more boundaried, more sustainable. It was certainly less likely to burn to the ground and leave them both with smoke in their lungs and ashes in their hair, staring at the wreckage left behind. But it was never as good, she could admit that now. Sam wanted to be seen, for all her faults, and it was only Lisa who could do that. Lisa, who knew the worst things Sam had done, and loved her anyway. Sam needed her and, as she looked at her friend, she knew Lisa needed her too.

'Will you help me?' she asked.

'I can't.' Lisa went ashen at the thought. 'It's not fair to Josh or the girls. They don't deserve to be brought into this circus.'

'What about what's fair to me?' Sam felt tears pricking her eyes. 'What about what's fair to *real* victims? When women like you make false allegations, it just makes everything worse for the rest of us. You have to say the story is bullshit and that you have no idea who wrote the Reddit post.'

'I can't do that.'

Why not? Sam thought. If Lisa didn't write the post, surely she would be fine with saying so? She looked at her friend, paranoia trickling cold down her spine. What other secrets was this woman hiding from her?

'Not if it's going to bring more attention to my family,' Lisa continued. 'They don't deserve that.'

'OK. OK. I'm sorry.' She could sense a weakening in her

friend but she didn't want to push too hard, not yet anyway. 'We could always start off with something easy. What if you show up on my Instagram?'

'Why would I do that?'

'If people see you on my socials, they'll assume the Reddit post is false, right? Why would you be hanging out with me if it was true? And if people around town see us together too, they'll get the same idea. It'll make everything go away. That's what you want, isn't it? For it to go away?'

'I don't know . . .' she said, but Sam could tell she was relenting.

'You can be in the background, like the neighbour in *Home Improvement*.'

'Wilson?' Lisa laughed despite herself.

'Exactly! You'll be Wilson. A floating head behind a wooden fence.' She smirked at her friend. 'The top half of your face is your better side, anyway.'

'Excuse me.' Lisa swatted at her. 'I don't have a "better side". I'm not the one who insisted on having my photo taken from a certain angle, like you were Mariah fricking Carey.'

'I still do that. It's written into my contract.'

'No!' Lisa gasped. 'Oh, how the other half lives. I don't know why you bothered. You were always so beautiful.' Her hands went up to her hair as if to fix it, and then she let them fall again. 'Everyone thought so.'

'Not everyone.'

Lisa went quiet. A light turned on in the house opposite, a shadow walking past the window. The man who'd bought the Garcias' house, a surgeon at Mount Sinai, getting ready to drive into the city. A car alarm screamed a couple of streets away; a bird settled on a tree branch above them; a runner's feet pounding against the pavement, their breath heavy and fast. 'I should go,' Lisa said and Sam stood, leaving the coat behind. Her friend put one arm in, then the other, zipping it up. She walked carefully to the end of the footpath, checking for patches of ice, and when she was at the front gate, Sam called after her.

'Why did you build that house?'

Lisa turned back, staring at Sam, the mansion behind her. 'Do you really want to know?'

'Of course I do.'

She screwed her face up. 'It's stupid,' she said, 'but I didn't know your family was rich until you moved here. Up until then, I assumed we were the same. But the first day I saw this place, it made everything different. For me, anyway.'

'You never said.' Sam remembered inviting Lisa to the house for the first time, showing off her new room, the princess canopy bed and her own bathroom. Her friend crossed her arms against her chest, saying *it's OK, I guess*. The excitement leached out of Samantha's body, and she had felt stupid, as if she was acting like a baby with a new doll.

'I would have killed for a house like this. And when Josh and I were building our place, I wanted something that would make me feel . . . powerful, for once. I don't know. I can't explain it better than that. To be clear, it was just after the twins were born and I wasn't myself.' Lisa pulled a face. 'Josh hates it. Sometimes I wonder if we should move, but it's the girls' home now and it's close to the school and . . .' She looked away. 'It made it easier. Living in that house.'

'It made what easier?' Sam asked, confused.

Lisa tilted her head to the side, and she looked so young in the morning light, she could have been a teenager again. 'You not being here, I guess. Despite everything . . .' she said, and it sounded like the words cost her something but what, Sam could not tell, 'I still missed you.'

19.

'Looky looky what we have here.'

'Hey, Brandon,' Sam said, smiling tightly at him as she took her seat in homeroom. He leaned forward, his fingertips grazing her upper arm, and she resisted the urge to shudder. 'I had fun on Saturday night,' he said. 'Did you?'

She and Lisa had arrived at Becky Stewart's around 10 p.m. The colonial-style house with large shuttered windows was only two doors down from Sam's; their fathers were partners in the same law firm. 'Shit,' Lisa murmured when they walked into the Stewarts' kitchen. 'Don't look now but he's over there.' Josh was sitting on the dining table, his legs wide apart and his feet dangling off the ground. He was laughing at something Chris had said, his teeth white in his tanned face. 'Are you OK?' Lisa asked, and Sam snapped at her, 'Stop hovering, I'm fine.'

Brandon saw them, cupping his hands around his mouth and yelling, 'Oh shiiiiit. Call the cops cos we about to have an emergency up in here.'

Sam made a face at him. 'Get a life, Brandon.' She leaned in to kiss Josh on the cheek, inhaling his aftershave, spicy and warm, and the temptation to cry was so fierce, for a second she was afraid she wouldn't be able to stop herself. She moved on quickly to Chris and then Brandon, pretending she didn't have a care in the world. 'Josh and I dated for, like, six months. We're still friends, right?'

Josh looked relieved, saying, 'Yeah, of course we are.'

'Awesome,' she said, taking a vodka jelly shot and throwing it back, grimacing as it burned her throat. 'Now. Who wants to get fucked up?'

She didn't remember much after that. The night was a blank, snapshots of moments flashing here and there – another shot, 'No Diggity' on the speakers, Becky crying about a broken lamp, Lisa asking if Sam was all right, did she want to go home, she was super drunk. Brandon, his mouth on hers, his fingers digging into her soft flesh as if he wanted to leave evidence that he had been there. She opened her eyes. Josh, standing with a group of friends, staring at them. *Good*, she thought. *I hope you're hurting as much as I am.*

'We should do it again some time,' Brandon said as other students filed into the classroom, smirking at the sight of the two of them talking.

'Yeah, maybe,' she replied, tapping her lower lip with her pencil.

Lisa flopped into the seat next to her, flustered. 'I thought you were going to pick me up,' she said. 'I waited ages.'

'Shit, I forgot.' Sam turned away from Brandon, mouthing *help*. Lisa pulled her seat closer, taking a notebook covered in Bikini Kill's 'Rebel Girl' lyrics from her school bag, and opened it on her friend's desk.

'I didn't do my homework, can I copy yours?' she lied, and even though everyone knew Lisa was an honour roll student who hadn't forgotten to do her homework since first grade, Brandon turned away, talking loudly to the boy behind him, *yeah bro, the party was awesome, I was totally wasted.*

'Impressive,' Sam said. 'I nearly believed you myself.'

Lisa poked her in the arm with a pen. 'I told you, you have to be quick on your feet with my mom. I swear, if she watches any more *SVU* . . . Her new obsession is *semen-detecting* black lights, which, according to her, every parent of a teenage girl should have access to.'

'No!' Sam shrieked, and they dissolved into giggles, quietening down when Ms Martinez walked in, clicking her fingers at a boy in the front row to get his feet off the desk: 'Were you under the impression this was some sort of day-spa, Kyle? Because I can assure you, it is not.' Josh was just behind the teacher, sneaking in before she noticed him, sliding into his chair and reaching down to grab something from his bookbag. He looked at Sam then, and she thought, *It's happening.* Josh knew he'd made a mistake; seeing her with Brandon helped him realize how much he liked her, and he wanted to get back together. Then his gaze slid over her like water, landing on Lisa in the seat beside her, her head bent over her books and a chewed-up pencil caught between her teeth. His features softened, in some indescribable way that Sam had never seen before. *Oh*, she thought. *Oh, I see.* And she told herself she didn't mind, that she hadn't liked Josh Taylor all that much anyway.

That had been her first lie.

She didn't do anything about it, this new-found knowledge of hers. She didn't say anything to Lisa. She just waited. Months went past and nothing happened – Josh hooked up with Kristen, a sophomore with a C-cup and a lisp; Sam dated Brandon Green because he was persistent and he liked her and that seemed as good a reason as any – and she convinced herself she had imagined the look on Josh's face that day in homeroom. But then Becky Stewart approached her in the locker room before gym and while Sam was tying the laces on her sneakers, Becky said that Chris Williams had told her that Josh had told him he had a crush on Lisa but he was afraid Sam would freak if he asked her best friend out. 'Are you OK?' Becky said, her hand on Sam's arm. 'This must be, like, so hard for you.'

'Oh my god, Becky. Whatever.'

Becky wanted her to burst into tears so she could tell every-one that she broke the news to Sam and *she didn't take it well, the poor girl*. Becky would whisper into one ear and then another until she had the entire school convinced Sam was one prom date away from a nervous breakdown.

'What are you telling me for?' Sam said. 'Josh and I broke up months ago; I could care less who he dates.' She stifled a yawn. 'Come on, we're gonna be late for class.'

It didn't matter anyway, she told herself as she fumbled the basketball, the coach yelling, 'Look alive, Miller!' from the sidelines. Lisa would never say yes, not in a million years. Lisa would never do that to her.

20.

🅞 2,287,120

Sam scanned through her filtered DMs, wondering if there would be anything from Gabriel. She had blocked him years ago, but she knew if he wanted to speak with her, he wouldn't allow that to get in his way. But she couldn't see anything there. There was yet another message from Becky – *Hi Sam! Rebecca Brown here. Do you still want to go for that run around Bluff Falls? Let me know xxx* – and Sam ignored it, as she had done with Becky's other DMs. She took a breath, and pressed the Live button. 'Hi, my loves,' she said, smiling into the camera. She hadn't done this since the Reddit post had been published but she owed it to the fans to explain what was going on. Most of them had been loyal up to this point, getting into spats on Twitter in their efforts to defend her. *It was an anonymous post, we can't just cancel people!! The friend doesn't think Samantha abused her, they're planning a birthday party together! Haven't you seen Sam's latest Insta Stories? It doesn't add up!* They pointed to Sam's humanitarian work, her donations to women's charities, and all that Shakti had done to amplify victims' voices, calling it proof of her character. But Sam couldn't ignore the fact there was growing unrest, too. She was losing hundreds of thousands of followers every day, people asking, *Where are you, Sam? You've always told us to be brave but we need you to be brave now. Talk to us.* What would they say if they found out about Brooke Campbell, the law-suit calling Sam a bully? Would they still adore her then? She'd told her girls that it was OK to be angry, never think-ing they would become angry at her.

'Oh gosh, I look super washed out!' she said, walking towards the window for better light. 'I haven't been sleeping very well which I'm sure you'll all understand. And I want to be real with you, my loves, I haven't been eating great, either. I've been craving sugar and dairy and all the things I told *you* not to eat because it would lower your vibration. Wow.' She sniffed back tears. 'I didn't realize until I actually said it how afraid I was to admit that to you all. I thought I was letting you down, you know? I didn't want to scare you, either, especially my girls in early recovery. But at the same time, I had to be honest. That's what we do in this little community, we practise radical honesty. It's become a way of life for me, and I hope in time it'll be the same for you. But given everything I've been going through . . .' She took a shaky breath. 'It's been a lot. Because of my own history of trauma, this false accusation has cut me deep and I've been turning to food to numb out. That's why we all need to remember that it's important to use our words carefully. In a world where you can choose to be anything – be kind, my loves.' That was what Sam had spent her career telling people. Be kind. Compassionate. Forgive those who have hurt you, no matter how badly, like she was doing with Lisa. 'I'm a human being,' she continued. 'I'm flawed. I've never pretended to be anything else. But we put people on pedestals, don't we? We expect them to be perfect, to be fully enlightened beings. But we're all human, we all make mistakes. And that's OK.'

She put the Paris filter on the Stories and posted them, going into her inbox and scrolling through the newest messages to see the reaction. *You look amazing, Sam! Drop the deets on that skincare routine queen* 👑 . . . *im so sorry this hapened to you i hope your OK . . .*

@Supernovadiabolique157 You put yourself on that pedestal, Samantha. You only have yourself to blame.

She clicked into the profile again. It had no photos, no profile picture and it was following only one account, hers. She went back into her DMs and started typing. *Who are you?* The message was read instantly.

Typing, typing.

I'm just someone who wants you to be the person you're pretending to be, Samantha. Is that so wrong? After everything you've done.

A prickle of fear, and her heart beating faster. Sam wrote back only one word.

Gabriel?

21.

◎ 2,178,002

It was Josh who opened the front door today, his mouth setting when he saw Sam. 'Morning,' she said, stuffing her iPhone in her purse. She'd been using her burner account to look at Gabriel's Instagram on the way over, something she tried not to do very often. It still hurt, seeing him with his new girl-friend, how happy they both looked. Josh's hair was wet from the shower, a speck of toothpaste in the corner of his mouth, and she wanted to brush it away.

'It's not like you to be at home at this time,' she said.

'A meeting was cancelled.' He stood aside as if to let her through, then grabbed her arm, roughly. 'People in work told me they saw her on your Stories all week,' he said under his breath. 'I don't know what you're playing at but I'm warning you, leave Lisa out of this. Do you hear me?'

'Who's at the door, babe?' Lisa called from the kitchen, and the two of them froze at the sound of her voice. They looked at each other and something passed between them, a secret or an oath, she could not tell. But it was electric and Sam felt almost weak with the longing for him. How could she still want this man after all these years?

'Josh?' Lisa called again.

'It's just me,' Sam shouted. 'But I forgot something in the car, give me a sec.'

'Please, Sam,' he said weakly. 'Leave us alone.'

'I'm not doing anything wrong.' She wrenched her arm out of his grip. 'I just want my friend back. You've had her for long enough, don't you think?'

She hurried out to the rented Lexus, grabbing the cardboard box of pastries from the passenger seat. 'Oof,' she said aloud as she came back inside, shaking the cold off her. She was hanging her coat over the handrail when she heard Josh and Lisa arguing quietly.

'She's using you,' he said. 'She always used you and it kills me that you can't see it. You never could resist her.'

'I wasn't the only one, was I?'

'Not this shit again. I chose *you*, didn't I? *You* were the one I wanted.' Josh's voice was weary. 'Why are you doing this? Why are you letting this woman back into our lives?'

'I missed her.'

'*Missed* her? Are you kidding me? We have two beautiful children; I built you the house of your fucking dreams. When did you have the time to miss her?' Something muffled, one of them telling the other *shh, she'll hear*. 'You've accused this woman of—'

'It was a mistake. She wouldn't—'

'This isn't normal, Lisa. And I don't understand why neither of you are able to see th—'

'Got it!' Sam called from the hall, slamming the door behind her again but with deliberate force this time. She walked into the kitchen. 'I know you told me to quit it with the whoopie pies but if we don't treat ourselves, who will?'

It was untidy in there, a crunch of Cheerios beneath her feet, cereal bowls dumped in the sink, an apple core and a spill of orange juice on the marble top. Lisa was standing at one end of the breakfast bar, Josh at the other, and their faces were flushed.

'Are you staying, Josh?' she said, handing the pink cardboard box to Lisa. 'We could always use an extra pair of hands for the party planning.'

'Ah yes, the famous party,' he snorted. 'Sure. I mean, when *I* suggested a party for my wife, I was shot down. I was told the only thing she wanted was a few family members over for some cake. But when *Samantha* suggests it, suddenly we're talking about a live band and a porta potty, and all my golfing buddies are telling me they're "psyched" for this awesome party I'm apparently throwing.'

'Josh—' Lisa tried, but he threw a hand up to stop her.

'So no, I don't think I'm needed for party planning. It looks like you've got everything under control, Sam, as per usual.' He dashed into the utility room, grabbing a pair of sneakers. When he returned, he looked at Lisa first, like a lost little boy waiting for his mother to find him. Then, when Lisa turned away, he stared at Sam and his face distorted. *He hates me*, she thought with chilling clarity. *This man hates me.*

'I'm gonna head out for a run,' he said. 'Clear my head.'

They waited until he was gone and they giggled guiltily, the same way they used to as teenagers when their dads tried to make awkward conversation – *What classes are you taking this year, dear? What schools are you applying to?* – before giving up and leaving the room, like the girls had wanted them to do in the first place. 'Herbal tea?' Lisa asked, Sam nodding, and they fell easily into this new routine they'd created for themselves over the last week. Sam grabbed the plates from the cupboard next to the oven, unfolding the box printed with the name of the bakery in cursive script. As Lisa brewed a pot of chamomile tea for Sam, black coffee for herself, she instructed Alexa to find a 90s Jams playlist on Spotify, shimmying her hips when 'No Scrubs' started to play. Sam took a quick video, making sure Lisa was in the background. *Where my TLC stans at?* she typed across the top and posted it to her Stories.

'Oh,' she said when Lisa walked back to the table, looking down at her feet. 'You got the same shoes as me.'

Lisa had her favourite skinny jeans on but this time she was wearing remarkably similar ankle boots to the ones Sam had brought with her from the city. They had an identical rubber sole and eyelet lace-ups, but Lisa's pair had a sturdier heel. Sam had almost bought those ones herself before deciding the spiked stiletto was sexier, and looking at Lisa's now, she regretted that decision.

'They looked so good on you! I couldn't resist getting a pair. You don't mind, do you?'

'Hmm.' Sam gouged the creamy filling and licked it off her finger; it was sickly sweet but she ate it anyway. 'Aren't you hungry?' she asked, as Lisa tore a piece of the pie off and rolled it between her fingers before putting it down again.

'Not really,' she said, nudging the plate towards Sam. 'You can have it if you want.'

It had been a week since that night outside Sam's house, when they had sat on the snow-covered porch, waiting for the world to wake up, and every day since had followed the same pattern. Sam would wake up from dripping-sweat dreams of insistent hands and that pungent smell of tobacco, Gabriel's face appearing before her, asking what was wrong, didn't she love him any more? She couldn't go back to sleep after that, too afraid of what awaited her in the dark, so she picked up her phone, scrolling, scrolling, scrolling. Thinking about her follower stats and Brooke Campbell's lawsuit – at least that hadn't gone public, Jane said, they had to be thankful for small mercies – and the Reddit post and who could have written it. Her manager was slower to respond to emails now; *Chaste* had dropped out of the bestseller list and Shakti's traffic was down; the daily numbers being sent through were stark but Sam had to believe she could still fix this, she just needed Lisa to sign that statement. At around 10 a.m.,

Lisa would text – *the kids are in school, Josh is at work, the coast is clear* – and Sam would drive or walk over to the Taylors' house, posting polls for her followers' opinion on balloon arches for the upcoming birthday party, which bouncy house did they think the kids would prefer, should she get buttercream or frosted icing for the cake? Sometimes, she passed someone who looked at her oddly, and Sam told herself it could be because they recognized her. The famous author or maybe just the Millers' daughter, that girl who was two grades above them in school. But she hurried her step anyway, pulling her scarf up to cover her face. Afraid they might have seen the Reddit post and believed she was a predator who had assaulted her best friend.

When she arrived, Lisa would answer the door and they would sit at this table, and here were the things they didn't talk about: Sam's essay. The abortion. Lisa's email, her allegation. The Reddit post and who might have written it. They didn't talk about Josh, and they certainly didn't talk about Lisa's eighteenth birthday and what had happened after they went to bed that night. Instead, they pretended to talk about the upcoming party (What wine should they buy? Did they need to do a Costco run? Was a DJ necessary, couldn't they just use Spotify?), giving up quickly because Sam had outsourced most of the hard work to a party planner she used for Shakti's events and really all they wanted to talk about was their childhood. The games played, the scars incurred from climbing trees and falling off bikes, the parties they went to as teenagers, sneaking out of the house while their parents were asleep, the bottle of Patrón they drank before Junior Prom.

'I can't drink it to this day.' Lisa shuddered. 'If I even *smell* tequila, I feel nauseated.'

'Remember my dad found the empty bottle under my bed? And you said' – Sam broke into laughter – 'you'd gotten it as part of a ship-in-a-bottle kit? And he believed you!'

Lisa laughed too. 'I can't remember that. But it does sound like something I would do.'

She cleared the plates, scraping the rest of her cake into the trash. 'I have to say, I dread the day when my girls start doing that shit to me.'

'Ah, but your girls adore you, they'll trust you enough to tell you the truth. I was always so afraid of my father.' Sam shook her head. 'After you left, he gave me a lecture on "the dangers of hard liquor" and how I should be "careful" drinking around boys.'

'It sounds like he was worried about you.'

'What?' Sam stared at her. 'He wanted to *control* me, it was typical patriarchal bullshit.'

'See, I don't know if that's true. I've read some of the stuff you've said about your dad over the years and I'm not sure—'

'You're not sure of what, exactly?' Sam's voice was cool.

'He loved you.' Lisa worried at a strip of flesh coming away from her cuticle. 'Maybe it wasn't the way you needed to be loved but he did love you, Sam. I can't help but think that your view of your parents is stunted at nineteen because that's when you left home. You never really had a relationship with them as an adult, did you?' Lisa looked at her, as if daring her to disagree. 'But they just wanted to protect you; it's what parents do. I'm the same with Martha and Maya, even though I know they're gonna make their own stupid mistakes and there's nothing I can do about it. At least they'll have each other, like we did.' Lisa stacked the plates into the dishwasher then turned the tap on, running her hands underneath it. She shook the water off, reaching for a dish towel.

'Yeah,' Sam said, staring at the table. 'We took care of each other, didn't we?'

She held her breath, wondering what Lisa would say. It was a delicate dance they were performing, jumping from one subject to the next, testing to see if there were any landmines left behind. She knew she couldn't ask the one question she needed the answer to – *If we had each other, Lisa, then why did you choose him over me? Why wasn't I enough?* – so she kept quiet, for now. 'I still can't believe you're a mom.'

'I'm nearly forty. It's not that unusual.'

Sam threw the napkin at her friend. 'Ha ha, you're so funny. I can't believe we're forty, then.' She gave a mock shudder. 'It's terrifying.'

Lisa leaned her elbows on the breakfast bar. 'I don't know why you're worrying. You still look about twenty-eight, you bitch.' She winked at her. 'Give it to me. What have you done?'

'Nothing,' Sam insisted, relenting when Lisa scoffed. 'OK,' she said. 'I've had a tonne of chemical peels and lasers, like everyone else. And a *tiiiiny* bit of filler in my upper lip, just to even it out. But nothing else, I swear.'

'Don't give me that. Your forehead has barely moved since you've arrived back in town; it's hard to tell if you're angry or sad or happy or—'

'Fuck you,' Sam laughed. 'Ugh, fine. Just the teeniest dose of Botox.' She narrowed her fingers to demonstrate how small. 'Baby Botox, that's what they call it.'

'Samantha Miller! What about that clip? Every woman I know was obsessed with it.'

Sam didn't need to ask Lisa what she was talking about. During the press tour for *Willing Silence*, she'd said that she would never get cosmetic surgery. 'I grew up in a household where money was made from women's insecurities,' she had declared. 'And it makes me so angry. Why are we not allowed to age naturally, like men are?' It went viral, her fans applauding Sam for her refusal to give in to patriarchal standards of beauty, but it was easy to make such proclamations when she was still in her late twenties. As she crept closer to forty, she found herself wincing at her reflection under the bright bathroom lights, pulling her face taut at the sides to see what she would look like with a facelift. She didn't realize how important her beauty was until she felt in danger of losing it.

'I thought you were into all that natural stuff,' Lisa continued. 'I read some interview where you said you wouldn't even use Clorox in your kitchen, let alone put toxins into your body. How do you—'

'Everyone does it,' Sam said shortly. 'Literally everyone, including all of your faves who are shilling their face oil to you on Instagram.'

What right did Lisa have to judge *her* choices? Lisa, who married her high school sweetheart and moved less than two miles from her childhood home. Who cared if Lisa's upper lip was uneven or if her crow's feet were deepening? Sam wasn't a model but she was expected to look like one, hand on her hip and a wide smile for photo shoots to promote her new book. She always had to be camera-ready for daytime television slots with highly glossed presenters who would, no doubt, also deny their own visits to the dermatologist, crediting their suspiciously smooth foreheads to eight hours' sleep a night and good genes. Sam was still attractive, she knew, but only because that was what was demanded of her.

'It's not easy being a woman in the public eye, you know,' she told Lisa, not even trying to hide her irritation. 'I don't need you judging me on top of everything else. You don't know anything about my life.'

'If it's so hard, just quit. Enough with the pity party.'

'I can't just quit.' Sam pushed her chair away from the other woman. 'It's important, the work I do. It *helps* people. No one was there to help me, were they?'

'Sam.' Her friend looked at her sadly. 'You know that's not true. Your mom was there. Your dad too. They did their best.'

'Their *best*? Are you high? You saw how they treated me. Remember what was under my bed? All the stuff I had written there?'

'What are you talking about?'

'Come on. I showed you. I wrote that my dad didn't love me and you said . . .' Sam was blushing, almost too embarrassed to finish the sentence. 'You said it didn't matter because you would love me instead.'

'I don't know.' Lisa fiddled with the ends of her ponytail, frowning. 'I can't remember that.'

'You can't remember much, can you?'

'Well, some of us have been busy since high school. I'm sorry I don't recall every single thing we said to each other in minute detail. And what do my memories matter, anyway?' She narrowed her eyes at Sam. 'When I have you to tell me exactly what happened to me.'

'Give me a break,' Sam said, but her heart wasn't in it. She was thinking of her father, of the last time she'd seen him before he died. Things were getting out of hand; Carolyn had said she couldn't care for him at home any more. There had been too many accidents, too many near-misses. He needed to be somewhere where he would be safe. Sam had found Nate Miller in his study that day, his body shrunken in his old suit, and when he'd turned around to face his daughter, his eyes were cloudy. He'd flexed his two forefingers at her, telling her to come closer, he had something he needed to ask her. His voice was hoarse, worn out. 'Who am I?' he had said, and he'd looked so afraid. 'Who am I without my memories?'

'You know, you should be grateful,' Sam said now, pulling her seat into the table again.

'Grateful for what?' Lisa replied, her shoulders relaxing. They half smirked at each other, the way they always did after they fought. Ever since they were kids, they would scream and then they would laugh, forgetting about whatever they'd argued over because there was no point in holding a grudge.

Sam picked up her tote bag, checking her phone. The screen was blank. No texts, no calls, no emails. Nothing from Jane about the Brooke Campbell situation, but nothing from Gabriel either, she thought. The silence had come as swiftly as the storm before it had raged, and although she'd longed for that quiet, she found it unnerving now it was here.

'You should be grateful that I remember everything,' Sam said. 'I remember it all so clearly.'

22.

It was dark by the time she trudged home, wiping her boots on the mat before tugging them off and slotting them into the shoe rack by the front door. She should have got the other pair, the ones Lisa bought; they were far more practical. But that had always been her friend's way – she had held back, watching Sam carefully. Sam was the one who had to be brave and take risks, and then Lisa would follow after her, learning from the mistakes she'd made.

'Samantha?' her mother called. 'Is that you? We're in the living room. There's someone here to see you.'

She hesitated, her fingers around the door knob. For some reason, she was afraid it might be Gabriel there, that sly smile playing on his lips. He would have charmed Carolyn, admiring her home, complimenting her exquisite taste. Why did you never introduce me to this *delightful* young man, her mother would ask, and what could Sam reply to that? She opened the door, holding her breath, but it was only Becky Stewart sitting on the sofa, sipping a cup of coffee, an untouched plate of cookies resting on the table. Carolyn did a double-take when she saw her daughter. 'What happened? You're drenched.'

'I—' Her mouth was dry, the words sticking to her tongue. 'I walked home from Lisa's place.'

'In this weather?' Carolyn clearly wanted to say more but she restrained herself in front of their guest. 'Well, take a seat and warm yourself up. I can get some fresh coffee if you'd like? And the maid baked those cookies earlier. Rebecca was just telling me about her two little ones, um . . .'

'Caleb and Mackenzie,' Becky supplied helpfully.

'Yes!' Carolyn said. 'They sound darling. Children are such a blessing, your mother must adore them.'

'She does,' Becky said, placing her coffee down on the walnut table, and Sam could see her mother's eyes following it, checking to make sure she used a coaster. 'She's enjoying being a grandma far more than being a mom. Not as much pressure, apparently.'

'How lovely,' Carolyn said wistfully as Sam threw herself down on one of the spoon-back chairs.

'Sorry I didn't give you grandkids, Mom,' she said. 'Yet another way I've failed you.'

The older woman stood, fixing the collar of her dress. 'That's all right, I'm happy on my own. I've become used to it.' She turned to Becky. 'I'll give you two some privacy but it was lovely to see you, Rebecca. Take care.'

'Yikes, that was awkward,' Becky said when Carolyn was gone. She leaned back, waving at her face. She was wearing a long-sleeved top over high-waisted leggings, and a pair of high-end sneakers with fluorescent stripes. Did this woman have anything in her wardrobe except athleisure wear?

'What are you doing here?' Sam asked, too tired for niceties. She reached down for a cookie, feeling it crumble to sugar and dust in her mouth. She saw Becky's surprise as she did so, then a flash of triumph on the other woman's face.

'I wanted to reach out,' Becky said, fiddling with one of her tiny hoop earrings. 'But your maid said she wasn't allowed to give out your information when I phoned the house. I tried to request you as a friend on Facebook but—'

'I don't use Facebook any more; my social media team are in charge of it.'

'—and then I DMed you on IG a few times,' Becky

continued, as if Sam hadn't said anything. 'But still. No reply from Samantha.'

'Becky, I have, like, three million followers on Instagram.' *Not any more*, she remembered with a twist in her gut. 'I don't even see most of the messages.'

'I told you, my name is Rebecca,' she said tightly, pouring herself more coffee. 'Anyway. It looks like the party planning is coming along nicely. I got my e-vite today, very cute. I thought it might be a photo of Lisa and Josh, and the girls, maybe, but still . . .' She raised an eyebrow. 'Cute.'

Sam had found an old photo of her and Lisa, sitting on the front step of the Elliot Street house. They were in sun dresses, tanned feet in pink jelly sandals. She'd had the graphic designer at Shakti superimpose a *Happy 40th!* birthday sash on Lisa's tiny body, glittery balloons floating above their heads. It was perfect, she decided.

'I'd still like to help out, if I can?' Becky said. 'I'm not sure if I've mentioned it already but Marcus, my husband, he enter-tains a lot so I'm—'

'That's sweet but Lisa and I have it covered.'

'I just thought . . .'

Sam stood, one hand on the back of her chair. 'It was nice catching up but I have to shower. I'm going to get pneumonia if I don't change out of these clothes.'

Becky stood as well, pulling her oversized purse on to her shoulder. 'Sam,' she said, suddenly serious. 'I hope you know that things have changed around here. We're not in high school any more. Lisa means a lot to me and I don't want to see her getting hurt.'

'Who's going to hurt her, exactly?'

'Cut the crap,' Becky said, exasperated. 'I read the essay. You *humiliated* her. What were you thinking, saying that stuff about her? And then you just waltz back into town and act like you can pick up exactly where you left off?' She pursed her lips. 'God, you're the same as ever. You *always* did this. You always tried to control her and make sure you were her only friend. And now that you're back, Lisa doesn't want to meet up for coffee, she's too busy to chat at the school gate, she doesn't want to come to spinning class and sh—'

'With all due respect, Lisa is a grown woman. She can do what she wants.' Sam waited a beat, trying to find compassion for the other woman. 'Look,' she said. 'I understand you're hurting and I'm an easy target right now. But don't you think you're acting kind of childish? Not to mention the fact it's super inappropriate to come to my mother's house and yell at me because . . .' She half laughed. 'God, I don't know. Because you're upset Lisa doesn't want to spend as much time with you any more? What is this, eighth grade? Go talk to Lisa if you have an issue with her and leave me out of it.'

She walked towards the door, gesturing at the other woman to follow her. In the hallway, she grabbed the only coat and hat she didn't recognize from the stand, handing them to Becky. 'I think you should go.'

'Everyone's talking about it, you know,' Becky said as she slipped her arms into the puffer jacket. 'That Reddit post. It's a pretty serious allegation, Sam. If it was me, I'd be freaking out.' She tilted her head at Sam. 'And yet you seem so . . . relaxed about it all.'

'That's because it's not true.'

'Hmm.' Becky zipped up the front of her coat. 'A lot of the other moms have been talking, you know. Remembering how *close* you and Lisa were as teenagers. None of us could ever figure out why you guys fell out in Senior Year. It seemed strange, how you went away to that school and then we never saw you again.' She paused. 'I wonder why Lisa would write the post if it wasn't true?'

'She didn't write it.' Sam shivered as she opened the front door, an icy wind swirling around them, clinging to their skin.

'If she didn't write it,' Becky replied, stepping on to the porch, 'then who did?'

23.

'I have something I need to ask you,' Lisa said.

They were in Sam's bedroom. Sam was lying on the rug, skimming through the latest issue of *Cosmo*. She circled a few things on the fashion pages in black pen – a choker, a mini-skirt, a pair of Candie's clogs – so that when she left the magazine downstairs later, her father would insist on buying them for her. Nate Miller always wanted his daughter to have just as much as the other kids in her class, if not more. *What's the point of all this money if I can't spoil my little girl?* he said. Lisa had been restless since she'd arrived, refusing Sam's offer of a soda, disappearing to use the toilet once, twice, moving from the window to the vanity table to the bed and back to the window again.

'Oooh, very mysterious,' Sam said. 'What's up?'

And then Lisa told her. How Josh had been waiting for her outside her AP chem class. How he'd smiled at her, told her he liked how she was wearing her hair that day. He asked if she wanted to go to Delilah's some evening after school, just the two of them. 'What did you say?' Sam pretended to leaf through the magazine. She needed time to compose herself, to figure out what to do with her face before she could look up again.

'I said I'd have to ask you. You know girls come first with me, Mouse, I'm a feminist and I—'

'Oh my god.' Sam pushed herself to sitting. 'Why would

you say that? You've made me look like a total psycho; he'll think I'm obsessed with him. As if I give a damn who Josh dates.' Her hands were trembling slightly and she clasped them together, so Lisa wouldn't notice. 'What did he say then?'

'He said he understood and he'd wait for me to check with you.' Lisa rushed on, 'And I wouldn't even ask, but you and Josh broke up months ago and you hooked up with Brandon straight away. That boy is totally crazy about you, everyone knows that.'

'Yeah.' Sam thought of Brandon and his wet mouth, his insistent fingers. 'He is, I guess.'

'Oh my god, he *totally* is. That's what I said to Josh, and he said that was cool but he just . . . he wanted me to know how he felt anyway.' Lisa's skin was flushed a delicate pink and it was then Sam realized her friend wasn't nervous, she was excited. She was saying Josh's name in a way Sam had never heard from her before, like it was a secret, a blessing.

'Wait. Do you actually like him?' she asked, something sour curdling in the pit of her stomach. 'You said he wasn't good enough for me when we broke up.'

Lisa looked like she might disagree at first and Sam wouldn't have pushed it; she would have accepted her friend's denial and never mentioned it again. But Lisa didn't do that. She said, 'Yeah. I mean, come on. It's Josh Taylor. He's the hottest guy in our grade, not to mention the nicest.' She stood up, fixing the comforter. 'I never thought Josh would even look at someone like me, not after dating girls like you and Kristen. It's stupid.' She exhaled her breath through her teeth. 'It's probably just a bet. He's hoping to make the nerd prom queen, or something.'

'Firstly, you're not a nerd – I would never hang out with a nerd, thank you very much – and secondly, this isn't a remake of *She's All That.*' Sam got to her feet, putting her hands on her friend's shoulders. 'You're a babe.' Lisa snorted. 'You are,' Sam insisted, shaking the other girl gently. 'You're amazing. Any guy would be lucky to have you, including Josh Taylor.'

'Do you think?' Lisa looked up through her eyelashes.

'I know.'

'Whatever. It doesn't matter anyway.' Lisa grabbed her bookbag from the ground, pulling the fraying strap over her shoulder. 'I have to get home, I promised Jill I'd help with her math homework. I'll phone you after dinner, 'k?'

Then, almost like it was an out-of-body experience, Sam heard herself say, 'You know what? You should go on a date with Josh.' The dread-beat of her heart, faster and faster, everything in her body screaming *no*, even as her mouth kept saying the words. 'As you said,' she continued, picking up her magazine again. 'I'm with Brandon now.'

It wouldn't last long, she told herself. Josh would lose interest and move on to the next bimbo who flicked her hair at him. But then it was three months later and Josh had bought Lisa a heart-shaped locket for their 'anniversary', and he was wearing a shirt and tie to have Sunday lunch with Lisa's parents because he wanted to make a good impression. He walked Lisa to all her classes, leaning in to kiss her as he said goodbye, telling her he'd see her in the cafeteria for lunch. *Whipped*, that's what the boys were saying about him, but Josh didn't seem to care.

'Aren't they adorable?' Becky Stewart cooed, waiting to see Sam's reaction. And Sam pushed her feelings down as deep as she could, determined to be a good friend to Lisa, no matter how much it hurt her.

'Oh my god,' she replied, holding her hands in a heart shape. 'The cutest!'

She kept smiling, kept going on the awful double dates her friend insisted upon. Josh and Lisa on one side of the booth in Delilah's, Sam and Brandon opposite. Brandon's hand on her knee, and she itched to push it off, to tell him to stop *touching* her. She had come to despise him – the way he couldn't use chopsticks so always asked for a fork and knife when they ordered Chinese, how he was failing almost every class and thought it was funny, how he pushed her head down towards his crotch and it smelled of stale sweat – but she couldn't break up with him, not now. She sat there, laughing at Brandon's terrible jokes, when all she wanted to do was reach across the table and take Josh's face in her hands and tell him she still loved him. That she would always love him.

'I'm not in the mood,' she told Brandon when he dropped her home after Delilah's, his eyes darkening as he looked at her.

'You're never in the mood any more,' he said, reaching across and opening her door, gesturing at her to get out. 'Maybe I should find a girl who is.'

She stood on her front lawn as his car drove away. She shivered; she always wore her skirts shorter on these double dates, watching Josh's eyes skim over her legs. Feeling powerful again, if only for a moment. Inside, she walked towards the kitchen. She opened the fridge. Most of it was her mother's food – bags of salad, Ezekiel bread, chopped-up celery sticks – but stashed in the freezer were the things her father put on the grocery list, despite Carolyn's grousing about his cholesterol. A quart of Cherry Garcia ice cream, a box of Thin Mints. In a cupboard above the stove, Sam found chocolate chip cookies, Swedish Fish, a bag of peanut butter cups. She took small portions from each packet, piling her stash on the kitchen table, and stared at it. *You don't have to do this, Sam.* She crammed the candy into her mouth, piece by piece, until her stomach was so distended it was painful to touch. She crept into the downstairs bathroom, lifting the seat, and tried to be as quiet as she could. Afterwards, she flushed the toilet twice, then washed her hands, staring at the mirror. She looked high, her eyes huge, and she touched her face in the glass and smiled. That was what no one understood – the comfort of the purge, the perfect emptiness afterwards. For a moment, she had made herself holy.

She cleaned the kitchen, stacking the dishwasher and returning the packets of food to the cupboards. She heard footsteps on the stairs, the creaking of the wooden boards. It was her mother; she could tell by how sure-footed the person was, how light on her feet. Carolyn stopped on the bottom rung. It was as if she wanted Sam to know she was there, that she knew what her daughter was doing to herself in the dark. *Please, Mom*, she begged silently. *Help me.*

But Carolyn didn't come any further, she just waited.

'You were late last night,' she said the next morning.

'Yeah, we went to Delilah's after school,' Sam replied, shaking her head when the maid asked if she wanted cereal. 'I'll have a fruit salad and yoghurt, thanks,' she said, for she was going to be good today. She would lose five pounds and she would be beautiful and maybe Josh would want her back. The hope surged within her, getting caught in her teeth.

'What?' she said, when her parents glanced at one another. 'I'm being healthy. Isn't that what you're always telling me to do, Mom?'

Her father cleared his throat when Carolyn glared at him. 'Talking about being healthy, kid,' he said. 'My Ben & Jerry's was gone this morning.'

'I was hungry when I came in last night.' She kept her face as blank as she could. 'I wanted a snack. Is that a problem?'

'No,' he said. 'It's not a problem, per se. It just, eh, it feels like you've been snacking a lot recently.'

'Oh my god, are you saying I'm fat?' she said and he spluttered, 'No, of course not.'

'Like, I'll buy you more today, take a chill pill. And besides,' she added quickly, 'it wasn't just me. Lisa and Josh had some too.'

'Wonderful,' her father said, relieved. 'Did you hear that, Car? Lisa and Josh were here too. Just a midnight snack for the gang.'

He gathered his briefcase, kissing his wife, saying he had to run if he wanted to make his first meeting. He slipped Sam a fifty-dollar bill when Carolyn wasn't looking, winking at her, and when he was gone, Sam stared at the money in her hand. Was this to buy her silence? She had said only minutes before that they'd all gone to the diner for food; it didn't make sense that they would be hungry for ice cream when they came back to her house. Maybe it was easier for him to believe her lies. It was easier for all of them to pretend this wasn't happening.

24.

◎ 2,035,675

She was getting out of the shower when she saw her phone light up. Probably just another message from Tatum, she thought with a sigh, wrapping a bath towel around her. Her friend kept texting but only privately; no one had posted in the Spirit Mafia WhatsApp group since the day the Reddit post went public. Did the girls have a new chat? Somewhere they felt free to talk about Sam openly; this scandal, what it meant for Sam's reputation and career. Debating her innocence.

But it wasn't Tatum who had messaged. It was an email notification, a name she didn't recognize.

Hi Samantha! I hope this finds you well. My name is Alyssa Reed and I'm writing a feature for the *New York Post* about you and Shakti. I was hoping you might be able to help me out. The piece you wrote about your sexual assault was a seminal moment in the #MeToo movement but I've been speaking to a number of your former colleagues at *Blackout* magazine and none of them can remember the night in question you mentioned in that essay. In fact, all but one mentioned they found it odd that you said you went for 'after-work drinks' in a 'bar downtown', because you never socialized with anyone from the magazine during your last year there. I was wondering if you might be able to clarify?

I've also been in touch with an ex-boyfriend of yours, a Gabriel Marchand. He confirmed that in the 18 months you were dating, you never disclosed your alleged history of sexual assault to him.

Please let me know when is a good time to talk! My contact details are below.

Alyssa xo

Sam sat heavily on the toilet, staring at the screen. She'd dealt with criticism from the media before, journalists writing op-eds connecting the interest in the Law of Attraction to the sense of entitlement in American culture that had given rise to Trumpian politics, pointing to people like Sam as the architects of that shift. She'd always shrugged it off – moths would always be drawn to the light, she told her girls – but this was different. How had this woman found Gabriel? What else had he told her? She reread the email, then quickly checked Twitter, searching for the words 'Samantha Miller' and 'Blackout'. She scrolled through old articles she'd written for the magazine but she couldn't see anything that would have made the journalist start digging for dirt. Had the *Blackout* girls gone to Alyssa Reed? Told her – confidentially, of course; they didn't want to get anyone in trouble – that the story Samantha Miller was telling about her rape didn't *quite* line up with their memory of events? They weren't the first to have questions of Sam over the years; there were plenty of others who wanted more from her than she was able to give, asking for names, dates, locations. Police reports and hospital files. It was infuriating, she repeatedly said in interviews. Demanding Sam be 'specific' about her assault betrayed a lack of understanding of how trauma worked.

She should forward this email to Jane but she didn't have the stomach to do it. Her manager would only ask Sam what had 'really' happened that night, the night she had spent so many years trying to forget.

I can't tell you. But it's true, I swear. You believe me, don't you?

What would Sam do if there was silence at the other end of the phone? Where would she be if Jane admitted, no, she didn't believe Sam any more?

25.

'I'm ready to have sex with Josh.'

'What?'

They'd gone to the mall after school, heading straight to Contempo Casuals on the second floor. It was Lisa's grandparents' fiftieth wedding anniversary next weekend and Mrs Johnson was adamant she needed a new outfit for the occasion.

Lisa mouthed *shh*, tilting her head at Becky Stewart, only a few yards away, a pile of skirts hanging over one arm, rifling through the hangers – flick, flick, flick – with a ruthless efficiency that reminded Sam of her mother. The joyless way Carolyn did everything – the individual square of dark chocolate after dinner as 'a treat', the identical beige silk shirts hanging in her closet, the 5 a.m. aerobics regime before her work day – all designed to keep her life so tidy, so neat. Her mother made the denial of pleasure look like an art form.

Sam asked, 'Did you just say you're ready to fu—'

'Ugh. Don't be gross.'

Her friend had become prudish recently, refusing to tell Sam how far she and Josh had gone. It made Sam want to remind her of all the things they'd done as kids. Lying in bed together during sleepovers, pretending to play Mommy and Daddy. Bumping their bodies against each other in an approximation of what they'd seen in snatches of R-rated movies on TV before a parent swiftly changed the channel to something more suitable. It was Lisa who'd put a stop to their games once they started middle school, and Sam had agreed, wishing she'd been the one to call it first.

'I said, I think I'm ready for Josh and I to . . .' Lisa paused and it was clear she was going to say 'make love' but was afraid Sam would mock her. 'Have sex,' she mouthed instead.

'Okaaay. Why are you telling me here?'

It was a Thursday afternoon and the mall was busy, harassed mothers dragging snot-nosed kids into Filene's Basement, a group of pre-teen boys sneaking candy from the Sweet Factory, three girls cramming into a photobooth, screaming *'Cheese!'* An Aerosmith song was playing over the sound system and it was too hot in here; Sam could feel perspiration trickling under her breasts and she desperately wanted a shower. 'Like, we couldn't have had this conversation when—'

'I'm gonna try on a few things,' Becky interrupted. Beads of sweat were forming on her upper lip as she blew her bangs up her forehead. 'What do you think of this?' she asked, holding up a baby-doll dress.

'That'll be awesome on you!' Lisa cooed, pulling a *yikes* face when the other girl was out of sight.

'You are such a liar.'

'Come on,' Lisa said. 'What did you expect me to say?' She lowered her voice. 'I mean, is any of that even gonna fit her?'

'Don't be such a bitch,' Sam snapped. She picked up a halterneck in gold lace and checked the price tag, avoiding her friend's gaze.

'Jesus, I'm sorry,' Lisa said, rolling her eyes. 'Why are you getting so mad at me?'

'I'm not.'

'OK. Don't you have anything else to say?' She looked over her shoulder to make sure Becky was in the dressing room. 'About what I just told you.'

Sam replaced the halter on the rail. She was hungry; how

had she not realized how hungry she was? There was a McDonald's in the food court, a Taco Bell, a Sbarro. Could she leave now? Pretend to Lisa that she needed to use the restroom, and sneak upstairs. She could order quickly – a milkshake, some fries, maybe a slice of pizza – and sit in the corner, hoping no one saw her until she was finished. 'It's a surprise, that's all. I didn't know you were thinking of . . .' Sam trailed off. 'What's changed between you guys?'

'We've been dating for over six months now' – *Josh and I dated for six months too. Remember?* – 'and I'm going to be eighteen next month,' Lisa said. 'It feels right. You know I think the idea of "virginity" is a social construct designed to control female sexuality, but I kinda like the idea of doing it on my birthday. That way, I'll never forget. I'll be, like, forty and blowing out my candles and—'

'You'll turn to me and say, shit, it's been twenty-two years since I first did it?'

'Exactly!' Lisa laughed. 'And we'll be living in some cool apartment in Manhattan and—'

'I hope we're not still living together when we're *that* old.'

'—and we'll laugh, remembering the first time I had sex.' She shrugged. 'I don't know. I've waited this long, I want it to be special.'

'We don't have to do anything you don't want to,' Josh had told Sam that first time. 'I don't want you to feel pressured.' But she had wanted to be as close to him as she possibly could; she couldn't think of anyone better to lose her virginity to. She'd put a towel down on her bed, and he lay above her, propping his weight up on his elbows. 'I'll be gentle', he'd said, shushing her when she had cried out as he'd pushed inside her. 'It's OK,' he had said, kissing her. 'I'm here.'

Lisa held a high-waisted pencil skirt up to her body, a baby-blue top with cap sleeves. 'Do you like this?' she asked, turning to the mirror. 'It's the only thing I can afford right now.'

'You do know I have that top already, don't you?'

Lisa always did this. Sam would buy a floppy hat with a sunflower on the brim and Lisa would appear in the same hat two weeks later. Sam would beg her mother to pick up a Baby-G watch in Bloomingdale's and six months later Lisa would have saved her allowance to buy an identical one, shouting *twins* and clinking their watches together while Sam gritted her teeth in irritation and pretended not to be annoyed.

'I'm gonna get this,' Lisa said, ignoring Sam's question. 'Even though that's three months of babysitting money gone. Aunt Debra better not complain that the skirt is too tight or I will actually lose it.'

'Where will you . . . ?' she asked as Lisa paid for the clothes, smiling at the sales assistant who folded the skirt and top into a paper shopping bag. *There's a Cinnabon upstairs*, that voice whispered. *Baskin-Robbins. A Nathan's, and a Burger King. It wouldn't take long. And you'd feel so much better afterwards.* '. . . you know.' She widened her eyes.

'I'm not sure,' Lisa admitted. They walked to the entrance of the store, leaning against the window display until the mall cop told them to stop loitering. 'Josh's parents won't even let us go to his bedroom alone; we have to sit in the TV den while his mom hovers in the hall. It's so stupid. It's the new millennium, get with the programme!'

The music playing over the speakers changed, that low, insistent beat, *Oh baby, baby, how was I supposed to know, that something wasn't right here?*

'You know, I think my parents are out of town the weekend after your birthday,' Sam said. 'I'm pretty sure Mom has a medical conference in Portland or something and my dad is going with.' She waggled her eyebrows at her friend. 'A free house. You know what that means.'

'We're not having a party for my birthday,' Lisa groaned. 'It's too much pressure.'

'Bitch, you're the one who wants to be a famous writer. You'd better get used to the attention. Besides, did I say anything about a party? It'll be small. *Intimate.* You, me, Josh. Brandon.' Sam looked back inside the store. 'Becky will have to be asked too or she'll sulk until graduation.'

'Jessica Simmons?'

'Ugh, I can't *stand* her.'

'She is my lab partner,' Lisa pointed out.

'Fine. Wessica' – she said in a cartoon voice – 'can come too.'

'How magnanimous of you.' Lisa elbowed Sam in the ribs. 'That's an SAT word, look it up, dummy.' Sam stuck her tongue out and Lisa laughed again. 'Very mature.' She was quiet for a minute, then said, 'And maybe me and Josh could . . . you know. In the spare bedroom. It's just that my place is always so crowded and I don't know where we'll . . .' Her voice fell to a whisper. '*Do it*, otherwise.'

'Wow. I . . .' Sam thought of Lisa and Josh having sex in her house. She would be lying in her bed alone, hearing the creak of a mattress, the beat of a bed board against the wall, Josh's hushed assurances, *I love you, baby, I love you.* The words he had never said to her. 'Sure,' she said, pretending to check the time on her watch. 'Whatever.'

That evening, after she dropped Becky and Lisa home, she drove to the Taylors' house. There was a basketball hoop set up in the yard, a Ford Explorer that needed to be washed in the garage, a neatly trimmed lawn. It was so ordinary, it was hard to believe it could contain Josh, the boy she never stopped thinking about. Sam smiled at his mother when she opened the front door.

'Hi, Mrs Taylor,' she said. 'I'm a friend of Josh's from school. Is he in? I need to talk to him.'

26.

○ 1,999,123

They were in the parking lot opposite the elementary school, sitting inside Lisa's SUV. Lisa had run into Starbucks earlier to pick up their order and they sipped at their cups, Lisa humming to an old Boyz II Men song playing on the radio. The heat was blasting and they'd pushed off their coats, neither saying much except for Lisa's occasional murmur: 'It's really coming down out there,' and 'Gosh, how much more snow can we get this winter?'

'You OK?' Lisa asked, turning to Sam. 'You've barely said a word all afternoon.'

'What?' Sam asked. 'Sorry. I'm—' She paused, taking another sip of her tea. 'Just a little distracted, that's all.' She stared out of the window, watching the mothers at the school gate, their bodies oddly imprecise in their goose-down coats. She couldn't stop thinking about the email that had arrived yesterday. The journalist's perky tone, the *xo* after her name, as if they were friends. The audacity of it burned and Sam wished she could tell someone about it – her therapist, her manager, even the woman who was sitting beside her – and yet, it felt like her tongue had been cut out with the fear. It broke her heart that at the age of forty, she still didn't know who she could trust.

The kids ran out of the school doors, bundled into cars by

mothers who were not in the mood for dawdling in this weather. She could see Becky; she recognized those fluorescent-
pink sneakers. Becky hesitated, staring at the school before
climbing into her Jeep. Lisa's phone rang and she and Sam both
jumped, laughing at their nerviness. 'Hey, Becky,' she said as she
answered. 'Oh, did I? I didn't mean to. Rebecca, of course . . .
sorry. No, you're good, I sent Josh to pick up the kids. He should
be there any minute. I couldn't face the snow . . . Everything is
fine. Don't worry . . . Sure. OK, talk then. Bye.' She hung up.
'Rebecca,' she said to Sam, tucking the phone back into her
purse. 'Just wanting to see if the kids needed to be picked up.'

'Why did you lie to her?'

'What?'

'You said Josh would be there any minute to pick them up.'

'Oh, yeah.' Lisa pulled a face. 'It's just easier. I don't want to
get into a whole thing with her.'

'I can't believe the two of you are besties now.'

'Be nice, Samantha,' Lisa said in the same voice she used
with the twins. 'Rebecca is a good person. And a great mom,
too.'

'Come on,' Sam coaxed her. 'You know you wanna talk
shit. She can be intense, right? I've barely spent two minutes
with her since I got back in town and even I can tell that
already.'

'I guess . . . OK, sometimes it feels like all she wants to talk
about is high school. She's always trying to get the "old gang"
back together; she can't seem to let it go.'

'Yeah, that's weird. It's like, you have to move on at some
stage, don't you?' Sam picked at some dry skin in the corner of
her mouth. 'She came to my mom's house the other day.'

'*Rebecca?*'

'Yup. She said I was controlling you again, just like I did in
high school. Isn't that wild?'

There was silence then, except for the swish of the wipers and the radio presenter's voice, an ad for constipation relief, then one for an over-the-counter painkiller, as Lisa made her way into the slowly moving line of cars inching towards the school gates.

Sam asked, 'Does Becky know?'

'Know about what?'

'The abortion.'

'No, of course not.' Lisa's jaw was tight, her hands gripping the steering wheel.

'Why not? Isn't that something you'd tell your best friend?'

Lisa was about to answer when the twins clambered into the back seat, shouting *hi!* 'Hello, my darlings,' Lisa said, checking to make sure they had their seatbelts on. 'I missed my girls today!'

They beamed at her, chorusing, 'We missed you too, Mom!' and then Martha asked, 'Can we use the tie-dye kit Grandma Taylor got us for Christmas when we get home?'

'That sounds like fun! But first I'm gonna drop Sam to her house and—'

'No,' Sam interrupted. 'Can we go somewhere else first?' She put her hand over Lisa's. 'We need to talk about this.'

'OK,' Lisa said with a nervous smile. 'Let's talk.'

Mrs Johnson was standing at the front door when they pushed open the garden gate, the two girls running before them. 'Well, I never!' the older woman cried, limping on to the porch with the help of a crutch. 'I was in the kitchen when I saw the twins haring down the street and who do I see following? It makes me so happy to see you two together again. What a blast from the past!' Lisa's mom was thrilled to see her, Sam noticed; she obviously wasn't aware of what was being said about her online. Nancy Johnson had always loved being tan, lying out in the back yard for hours during the summer, slath-ered in baby oil, and Sam could see the signs of it now, the melasma on her cheeks, the ruddy discolouration creeping into her cleavage. She looked much older than Sam's own mother, even though they were roughly the same age.

'Are you OK, Mrs Johnson?' She rushed to help as the woman took the steps down to the garden path awkwardly, grimacing with pain.

'I'm fine, thank you, Samantha,' she said. 'I had an oper-ation on my back a couple of months ago and it's healing slower than I'd expected. I don't know what I would have done without Lisa! Bringing me dinner, sitting by my bed and chat-ting with me for hours. Honestly, I didn't hear a peep out of the boys and, of course, Jill is in San Francisco. She's a lesbian now, did you know?'

'Eh . . .' Sam was taken aback by the sudden change of sub-ject. 'I—'

'Auntie Jill and Auntie Poorna got married last year,' Martha said proudly. 'Maya and I were flower girls, which means you get to wear a dress and a flower crown and everyone tells you how pretty you are.'

'It was such a special day,' Mrs Johnson said, reaching out to stroke the back of Martha's head. 'And how are my best girls doing?' she asked. 'Do you want to come inside? This weather! It feels like it'll never stop snowing. I'll pour you a glass of milk – you don't want to be old like me and have issues with your bones, do you? – and maybe a grilled cheese sandwich. There might be cookies too, if you're lucky.'

The twins ran inside, Lisa calling after them, 'Only one each, girls, I don't want you ruining your appetite for dinner.'

Mrs Johnson told them they were crazy to insist on sitting outside. 'You'll freeze to death but on your own head be it,' she said, giving them an old blanket, its wool rough and scratchy. The two women sat on the porch swing, tucking the blanket over their legs. They listened to the muffled sound of the girls' laughter from inside the house, the creaking wood of the swing. Sam pushed away the clamouring thoughts about her Instagram followers and the Brooke Campbell lawsuit and that email from the *Post* – if the journalist had found Gabriel, what else would she uncover? What would this article say about Sam? – and she stared at her childhood house next door. The lawn was overgrown and the clapboard was peeling; it badly needed to be repainted.

'Do you remember,' she said, 'when we hung a string between our bedroom windows with tin cans on either side? And tried to use them as walkie-talkies? I don't know why we didn't just use the phone! Whose idea was it anyway?' she asked, although she knew it was probably hers. Sam had always been the ringleader, the one persuading her friend to skip class, to forge her mother's signature on a school report, to stay out past curfew. Lisa could never say no to her, not back then, anyway.

She stuck her tongue out to catch a flake of falling snow and she did a half-approximation of the Carlton dance when she finally succeeded.

'You always sucked at that,' Lisa said.

'The snowflakes or the Carlton?'

'Both. You're tragic.'

'Would a tragic person' – Sam gestured at her friend to lean in – 'give Brandon Green a hand job on this very porch swing?'

'You didn't!'

'Oh, but I did, my friend . . .'

'You swore to me that you didn't!' Lisa was trying her best to look horrified but she couldn't stop laughing. 'I was sitting on the step. I was, like, two feet away, you slut.'

'Excuse me. The Lisa I knew would *never* use such

IDOL

misogynistic language! What can I say? The heart wants what it wants. And apparently my heart wanted to jerk Brandon Green off.' They both cackled. 'Fuck, we were so bombed that night. Didn't we go pre-drinking in my hous—'

'No, it was my place. Remember? My dad drove us to Brandon's afterwards.'

'Oh shit, you're right! Becky puked in her purse in the back seat! And she just got out of the car, pulled down her skirt, and slurred, *Thank you, Mr Johnson*, as if nothing had happened.' Sam pulled the blanket up to her chin. 'The blessed teenage years. It's all ahead of you, Mommy. I don't envy you.'

'Can I ask you something?' Lisa said, waiting for Sam to nod her *yes*. 'Why did you decide not to have kids? You always said you wanted enough for a softball team. Such typical single-child fantasies, by the way. You'd have felt differently if you grew up in my house, believe me.' She rubbed the back of her neck. 'What changed your mind?'

'God. I don't know,' Sam said slowly. 'I guess I was worried the kid would be like me, and become an addict or have issues with food. I'd feel like it was my fault, you know? And then my career took off and everything got so *fast*. There was always another book to write, another tour to go on, and it didn't seem fair to bring a kid into that . . . It just never seemed to be the right time.'

And timing was everything, wasn't it? That's what Lisa had said when they were in the clinic's waiting room that day, their heads jerking up every time the nurse came back in, wondering if it was their turn. *It's not the right time.*

'Mouse,' Sam said, but she couldn't finish. She wanted to throw the truth out in front of Lisa like a dealer in an Indian bazaar, unrolling his rugs for inspection. She would tell her friend everything. About her relationship with Gabriel and how it had ended. The truth of what had happened to Sam, and the story she'd been forced to tell afterwards to protect herself. The words were caught in her throat and as much as she tried to cough them up, she couldn't get them out. She looked at her lap, blinking tears away.

'Sam. *Sam*. Why are you crying?' Lisa asked, and she pulled Sam into a tight embrace. They sat there, their bodies pressed against one another as Lisa murmured softly into her hair, as if she was one of the twins who had fallen and scraped a knee, telling Sam she would be OK.

'What are you doing? Get off her!' a man yelled, and they jerked apart to see who it was.

'Babe,' Lisa said in surprise. 'What are you doing here?'

Josh was standing at the garden gate in jogging pants and a fitted hoody, his face red. He was staring at them, Lisa and Sam sitting together on the porch swing, just like old times, and something like fear passed over his face. 'I thought . . .' He trailed off. 'Were you *kissing* her?'

'What?' Sam asked, wiping her eyes. 'No! I was upset and Lisa was comforting me. You thought we were making out?' She couldn't help but scoff. 'Josh, this isn't a porno movie. Girls don't have naked pillow fights at sleepovers either, sorry to ruin the fantasy.'

Lisa laughed at that and Sam did too, until they were both bent double. They couldn't seem to stop. They'd been like this as kids, uncontrollable fits of giggles infecting the other, back and forth, until Carolyn or Mrs Johnson would ask in a bewildered voice, *What's so funny, girls?* And no matter how hard they tried to explain the joke, their mothers never got it and somehow that made it even more hilarious.

'It's not funny,' Josh yelled, and Sam shrank back at the venom in his voice. 'None of this is fucking funny. Where are the girls?' he asked Lisa, grimly.

'They're inside. Josh, I—'

'No,' he said. 'I don't want to hear it. I can't understand why you're letting her come between us again. Haven't we been through enough?'

That wasn't right, Sam thought. It was *Josh* who had come between them, like a snake eating the core of an apple and splitting it in two. Lisa and Sam were too powerful when they were united, and Josh had been afraid of them, she could see that now. He'd wanted them apart, wanted them weakened so he could steal Lisa away from her without a fight.

'You're being ridiculous,' Sam said. 'I was upset, Lisa was trying to comfort me. I'm sorry if your internalized homophobia saw that as us "kissing", but get a grip.'

'Internalized . . . You know what? Fuck this. I would very much like for you to stop, stop, *gaslighting* me.'

Sam snorted. 'Gaslighting? OK, I never thought I'd hear myself say this but maybe feminism *has* gone too far?' She saw Lisa swallow a smile and Josh saw it too, his shoulders sagging in defeat.

'Why are you doing this?' he asked, broken. 'Seriously, Sam. What do you want from us? Because I can tell you one thing for nothing, if someone accused me of assault, I wouldn't be hanging around on their fucking porch swing.'

'Babe.' Lisa went to him, attempting to hold his hand, but he stepped away.

'No,' he said. 'I've tried to be patient. I've tried to understand this "bond" you two have but I can't. I know things have been difficult since the girls were born and I've done my best to support you, Lisa, and give you enough space and time to get better. But this is too much. You've accused this woman of sexually assaulting you' – Lisa tried to interrupt, 'No, that was a mistake' – but Josh continued anyway. 'And then you act like the last twenty-something years never happened and you've no other responsibilities except to be at Samantha Miller's beck and call. What about the twins? If she really is an abuser—'

'I am not an abuser,' Sam interjected, angrily.

'Shut up, Sam. For once in your goddamn life, can you shut the fuck up,' he shouted at her. He turned back to Lisa. 'If what happened was non-consensual, then why allow her anywhere near our daughters?' Lisa had started to cry quietly and Josh sighed, his face tired, but he didn't go to her. 'I'd like for you to go home now, Sam,' he said.

'Josh, come on,' Sam said. 'This is ridiculous.'

'I asked you to go home. Please respect our wishes, for the first time in your life.'

'I think I've respected your wishes plenty of times.' He looked as if she had struck him and she regretted her words immediately. 'I'm sorry,' she said quickly. 'I shouldn't have—'

'He's right,' Lisa said. There was an eerie blankness to her face, as though a veil had fallen over it, obscuring her features. 'You should go, Sam. This is a family matter now. It doesn't concern you.'

Sam stood, stumbling away, the world blurring before her. She kept her head down against the flurry of snow, warning herself not to cry – she had wasted enough tears on those people already – when she felt a hand on her shoulder, yanking her back. She screamed, clutching her purse to her chest, but when the person turned her around to face them, it was only Josh.

'What are you playing at?' he asked. There were flecks of snow trapped in his eyelashes and eyebrows, but even in his fury, he was beautiful to her. She wanted him so badly and she wanted to kiss his hard mouth until he said he wanted her, too. She had spent so long fighting her feelings for this man, trying to be a good friend, and for what? Lisa hadn't done the same for her, had she?

'You scared me,' she said.

'Scared *you*?' He poked a finger at her collarbone and Sam winced in pain. 'You don't think *I* was scared, seeing you and my wife back there acting like nothing had happened? I just want . . .' He was fighting tears and he dashed his hand against his eyes. 'I want my life to go back to normal.'

'And you think I don't?' she cried. 'My life is in ruins because of the two of you. I haven't been able to have a functional relationship as an adult because of the way you messed me up. I've never—'

'Stop with the bullshit.'

'It's not bullshit. I have to say this. I've been waiting to say this since I was seventeen. We were good together, weren't we? You and me? We had something special.' He didn't reply, he just stared at her. 'I loved you, Josh,' she said. 'You're the one who got away. If you and I had stayed together, I would—' She would be happy. She would be safe. She would never have met *him*. 'I've never experienced anything like what you and I had with anyone else, I—'

'If that's actually true – and I don't believe a word that comes out of your mouth any more – then it's pathetic, Sam. You're hung up on something that wasn't even there in the first place.'

'But don't you ever think about—'

'No.'

'Fine.' She put her hand on his chest. 'Then answer this. Do you believe that I assaulted Lisa?' He looked away. 'You don't, do you?'

'I don't . . . I don't know.'

'Come on! You don't think it's odd that she never mentioned it before now?'

'We never talk about you,' he said flatly.

'Josh. Listen to me. If you know these things aren't true, if you know she's lying' – Sam put a hand up to stop him as he protested, 'I never said she was lying' – 'then you have to help me. This could destroy me. If Lisa doesn't deny these allegations, I . . . I don't think I'll see my next birthday.'

'*Fuck*. I can't deal with this.' He blinked rapidly, trying to get the snow out of his eyes. 'I'm sorry, Sam, I really am. But I have to make sure Lisa is OK. You don't know what she was like after the twins were born. Things were . . .' He swallowed. 'She's not the girl you remember. She's fragile.'

'Fragile, right.' Sam shoved her hands in her pockets, trying to warm them up. 'You never seem to give any thought to how hard it was for *me* when I had to leave Bennford. Maybe I was "fragile" too, did you ever think about that?'

'I was eighteen, I was—'

'So was I! Why do you never seem to remember that?'

'I don't know,' Josh said. 'You always had your shit together. Not like me.' She could see on his face all the things he would never admit to, all the ways he had hurt her. He was sorry but he would never say it aloud because he was afraid she would use that apology against him. 'I was just a stupid kid.'

She stepped away from him. 'You're not a kid any more, though, are you? And you still haven't told her the truth.'

27.

○ 1,798,866

'Are you going to Lisa's house today?' her mother asked as they had lunch together. Carolyn took two bites of her Cobb salad, placed her hand on her stomach, and pushed the plate away.

'No,' Sam said shortly. When she was finished eating, she went upstairs and took the wooden box out from under her bed, flicking through the old photographs again. She paused on one – it was before Junior Prom, she and Lisa standing in front of the fireplace in their jewel-coloured satin gowns and cheap flower corsages. Sam had always known she was pretty. When she was a kid, strangers on the streets would squeeze her cheeks and ruffle her curls, telling her mother Sam could be a model. Carolyn had liked that; for someone who spent her days breaking women's bones to recast them as lovely, she placed a great deal of importance on the idea of 'natural beauty'. *Money can't buy good genes*, she always said. Sam looked at Lisa in the photo now, wondering if she had been pretty too – Sam had thought she was but it had always been difficult for her to be objective about her friend. Maybe she only thought Lisa was beautiful because Josh had chosen her.

Her laptop dinged and she hissed, 'Fuck.' Her phone lit up a split second later with an email notification.

Hi Samantha! Alyssa Reed from the *NY Post* again. I wanted to check in to make sure you received my previous email? It would be great to get a comment from you. Also, could you take a look at these emails (see attached) and confirm they're genuine? Thanks x

There were two screenshots: one of the original email Lisa sent the night of the *Chaste* launch (*I didn't want that to happen . . . but when Sam wants something, it happens whether you want it or not. you just did it anyway didn't you . . . You just took what you wanted without my consent*) and another, one from Sam. She checked the date and the time; it seemed she had sent it to her manager the morning after, but she couldn't remember writing it, it was like she'd done it in a fugue state. *I can't stop reading this bullshit email*, she had written. *And I still can't believe it. What the fuck is wrong with that CUNT?* Not quite the tone one might expect from a spiritual leader, Sam thought, and she started to laugh. She laughed so hard, she couldn't stop. What would come next? More think-pieces, brilliantly sharp columns about the difficulties in believing women when the abuser was a woman too. Arguing that Believe Women means Believe *All* Women. Wasn't that what Samantha Miller had always said, after all?

'This story will run in the *New York Post*,' she said aloud. 'Everyone you know will read it.' She laughed again, hysteria infecting the edges. This was what it was like, then, to see the monsters you worried over in the dark come to life, your greatest fears taking flesh and stirring awake. She forwarded the email to her manager, then phoned her. 'What are we going to do?' she cried when Jane picked up.

'About what?'

'About the email I just sent you!'

'Give me a sec.' The clacking of fingers on a keyboard, a hiss of breath. '*Fuck.*'

'What are we going to do? Should I deny it? And where did she get that email? Was your account hacked?' Sam could barely take a breath, she was talking so fast. 'How could you let this happen to me? It's your job to make sure things like this don't happen.'

'I change my password every two weeks.' Her manager's voice was tight. 'When was the last time you changed yours?'

'I . . . I don't know,' she lied. Sam kept forgetting the new passwords and, sick of getting locked out of her accounts multiple times a month, she simply used a slight variation on the same code for everything – ShaktiSam82 – for Netflix, Amazon Prime, her social media accounts, and . . . *oh fuck*, her email. The same accounts that countless interns and PAs had had access to over the years, she thought, the bile rising up her throat.

'Wait,' Jane said. 'What does she mean, you didn't reply to her previous email? What email? You know you're supposed to send any media requests to the crisis management people.'

'That's not important,' she brushed her manager off. 'The Reddit post was one thing; it was never confirmed as true. This is *proof* Lisa sent that email and she said what happened with us wasn't consensual.' Sam was shouting but she didn't care if her mother or the maid could hear her. They would find out soon enough anyway. Everyone would. 'What are we going to do?'

'Calm down. I'll phone the crisis management people and warn them this is coming. They'll get a plan in place. Fuck me,' Jane sighed. 'I feel like I'm fighting fires on all fronts right now. I spent the morning dealing with Brooke Campbell's legal team and now this? All we need is Ronan fucking Farrow to decide he wants to investigate the story for the *New Yorker* and we may as well kill ourselves now and get it over with.'

'Don't even joke about that. Can't we issue a statement? Three per cent of all assault cases are misreported, right? We could—'

'We could what? Accuse her of *lying*? Jesus, Sam. That's a PR nightmare waiting to happen.' Her manager blew out her cheeks. 'We need to draw a line under this, *now*. We'll see what the team says, but my instincts are saying that you should officially separate from Shakti. The company will go public in a few months, and you'll be rich enough to retire and never work again. Listen to me.' Her manager was serious. 'I've lived in this city long enough to know that the only thing these people can't forgive is poverty. If you have enough money, they'll forget everything. You'll be fine.'

'But what about my girls?'

'What about them?' Jane asked, exasperated. 'They'll find some other white woman to project all their hopes on to and make her a god instead. Come on. This is as good a time as any to take a break. You're out of contract anyway, remember?' Sam's advances had dwindled ever since the follow-up to *Willing Silence* hadn't done the business it was expected to and Jane hadn't wanted to sign a new book deal until *Chaste* was released, hoping the sales figures would give them enough leverage to renegotiate. 'I've been talking to the CEO of Glass House,' Jane continued, in a gentler tone. 'And he agreed you should get some rest. We can talk again later.'

'How much later?'

'I don't know. Maybe a year, eighteen months?' She could almost hear her manager shrugging over the phone. 'Louis C.K. waited two years before filming a new special. It depends. We have to see how this plays out.'

'You're comparing me to Louis C.K.? Are you for real?' Sam thought she was going to be sick. 'I can't,' she said. 'I can't do this.'

For who would she be, without her girls? Without an audience? It would just be her, alone in her apartment, haunted by the spectres of all the men who hadn't loved her enough, and the women who had tired of her, walking away without a second glance. Her career was all she had; she would be nothing without it. Why did no one understand that?

'You have to help me,' she pleaded. 'What about the letters she sent me? Surely they're proof this isn't true?'

'Do you have Lisa's permission to share them?'

Sam swallowed. 'No.'

'Sam, I don't think the optics of sharing them *without her consent* would look good right now, do you?'

'Fine, but I've been working on getting her to write a statement saying it's all false. I'm nearly there, I promise. And then I'll come back to the city and everything can go back to normal and—'

'Sam . . . It would have to be the most comprehensive statement in the history of the world to fix this shit, and I really can't see you getting something like that in time to stop this article, can you? *Jesus.* You went to Bennford to sort this shit out, like a grown-ass woman, and what have you done? Sat around posting throwback pics on social! This isn't high school. This is real life.'

'You think I don't know that? Let me assure you, I'm very much aware of what's at stake here. It's *my* reputation, *my* career. It's easy for you to tell me to retire; you'll still get your pay-out when Shakti goes public, won't you? I gave you those fucking shares as a thank-you for your "loyalty". Where's your loyalty now, huh?'

'I *am* being loyal. I'm trying to protect you as best as I can, but you're not making it easy for me.'

'I'm sorry I'm being so *difficult*,' Sam cried. 'Am I being too *emotional* for you, Jane? You wouldn't say that to your other clients, would you? Too afraid that Maddy fucking Morgan would run straight to TikTok and send her ten million followers after you. Well, maybe it's time I got a new manager, someone who will prioritize me and my "emotions" rather than whatever literal *child* they've decided is the flavour of the month.'

She stopped, waiting for her manager to respond. Sam wanted her to promise that everything would be OK, that she was safe. She wanted Jane to say she would take care of Sam, no matter what.

'Fine,' the other woman said. 'Maybe you should do that.' And she hung up the phone.

'Hello?' Sam tried, but there was no one there. 'Fuck,' she shouted, throwing her cell on the bed. She paced back and forth, muttering, continuing a one-sided argument with her manager. 'I made your career . . . You wouldn't be anywhere without me and you should remember that . . . You were *nothing* until you met me, you stupid—' She caught sight of herself in the mirror, her eyes wild, spittle around her mouth. She looked like a madwoman, like someone she might pass in the Village, talking to herself as she pushed a shopping cart full of trash along Avenue A. Sam crouched down, making small, keening noises like an animal. Everything was falling apart and she couldn't seem to stop it. *Samantha Miller is a snake-oil salesman, she's a fraud. She's a con artist. She's a conspiracy theorist. She's a liar. She's a predator, she's an abuser. When Sam wants something, it happens whether you want it or not. I didn't want that to happen. You just did it anyway.*

She grabbed her iPhone again, unlocked it and dialled Lisa's number. It rang out so she left a garbled voice message. 'I need you to phone me as soon as you get this, Mouse. It's an emergency, OK?'

She opened up the screenshot of her own email, hardly believing what she was reading. *What the fuck is wrong with that CUNT?* She had tried so hard to be an example to her girls, to be the light guiding them home, and what would they think of her now? They wouldn't understand that she had been flailing in that moment, lashing out because she was terrified. Sam was supposed to be better than this and if she wasn't, if she was no different to those girls staring up at her from the audience, then why should they follow her at all? How could they see her as their saviour if she was the same as the mothers who had hurt them, the fathers who'd rejected them? They would see behind the velvet curtain and there Sam was, small and insignificant, working furiously at the controls. They would never trust her now.

She picked up her phone.

'Hi, you've reached Lisa Taylor.' She sounded so happy, like she didn't have a care in the world. 'I'm sorry to have missed you but leave a message and I'll call you back!' A long beep.

'It's me.' Sam's voice was terse. 'Phone me back, Lisa. I'm serious. Phone me back right now.' She hung up and stared at the screen. 'Phone me back,' she said. 'Phone me back, phone me back, phone me back,' and she was screaming now, the empty room echoing her useless words back to her. 'PHONE ME BACK.' It was a howl, so spiked she thought it might shatter the windows. She flapped her arms, as if trying to shake it out of her – the choking panic, the bottomless fear. It was too much, these feelings swelling inside her. She needed to cut herself open, watch as the pain dripped on to the floor beneath her. *I need something to stop this.* The old voice, whispering to her, *Come back to me, come back.* She thought of diazepam, a pill in the centre of her hand. She would hold it to her mouth like communion and swallow it dry, waiting for its softness to seep through her, turning her spineless. She would curl up under the pillow in its daze and wait until the world became gentle again. It would make her forget everything. Her phone beeped and she grabbed it – maybe it was Lisa, maybe it was Jane, maybe – but it was from the crisis management firm.

Hi Samantha,

Jane forwarded the email from Alyssa Reed at the *Post*. I would like to schedule an urgent Zoom meeting to address this. We would also appreciate it if you could share this 'previous email' Ms Reed references in her message ASAP.

Please let me know your availability.

They had CC-d Teddy, she noticed, deleting the email without replying. Was this how it was all going to end for Sam? A false allegation? She had based her life on telling the truth and now she would be undone by lies.

She yanked the chest of drawers open, pulling on a knee-length skirt. She chose an off-the-shoulder top in the softest jersey and outlined her eyes in black kohl. Her highest ankle boots, clicking on the stairs and the tiles of the hall as she ran out of the doorway. Turning the wipers on. It was snowing again. Would it ever stop snowing? When she pulled up outside Starbucks, she checked her phone. The woman from the *Post* had tweeted:

I'm looking to talk to people about their experiences as part of the #SamanthaMiller fandom. My DMs are open #JournoRequest

@Supernovadiabolique157 Delighted to see this! The stories I've heard about Samantha Miller! Check your DMs.

It was a little after four o'clock and most of the children had gone home, but Sam knew from the schedule taped to Lisa's fridge that the twins took a movement class on Friday afternoons. She saw her friend park her SUV, pulling a beanie on over her red hair and clicking the doors shut over her shoulder. Lisa waved at another woman outside the school gates, leaning in for a kiss on the cheek, and they stood together, chatting easily. Sam threw her coffee cup in the trash can, looking left and right as she crossed the street, quickening her step in case the kids came out before she had a chance to talk to Lisa.

'Sam,' Becky said in surprise, still wearing those pink sneakers. 'What are you . . . Where's your coat? It's freezing today.'

Sam ignored her. 'You didn't answer my calls,' she said and Lisa took the slightest step back, staring at her in dismay. 'I've been trying to call you,' Sam said. 'You wouldn't answer your phone. Why didn't you answer?'

Lisa shook her head and she looked scared, eyes darting to Becky for help. Becky tried, 'Sam, do you want me to take you home? My car is just—'

'I'm sorry, was I talking to you? I don't think so.' Sam waved her hand, dismissing her. 'Buh-bye, bitch.'

Becky blanched. 'I . . .'

'This isn't high school, Sam,' Lisa hissed. 'You can't talk to people like that any more.'

'It's fine,' Becky said, swallowing hard. 'Don't make a big deal . . . oh look,' she said in relief. 'The kids.' She reached down to hug her daughter, a brown-skinned girl with her hair in braids. 'How was ballet?' she asked and the little girl grinned, her two front teeth missing.

'It was good, Mom,' she lisped. 'But we have to practise our dance.'

'What dance?'

Martha interrupted. 'There's a recital and Maya, Mackenzie and me were put in the same group.' She didn't seem pleased by this turn of events. 'It's because we have M names. I wanted to dance with Addison but Teacher said—'

'Don't be rude,' Lisa admonished her. Her daughter pouted

but leaned back into her mother's legs. Lisa pulled the girl's hair off her face, tying it into a high ponytail.

'We have to practise,' Maya piped up. 'Can we go to Mackenzie's house? She said it would be fine with her mom.'

'Did she?' Becky drawled, looking down at her daughter, who was staring up at her with pleading eyes. 'Oh, fine,' she sighed, handing over the keys and nodding her head in the direction of where she was parked.

'Are you sure?' Lisa asked over Maya and Mackenzie's squeals, as they ran towards Becky's Jeep, Martha dragging her feet behind them like a disgruntled teenager.

'Of course,' Becky said. 'Unless you want me to stay and—' She looked at Sam, then back to Lisa. A glance between the two of them, a slight shake of Lisa's head. 'Sure thing,' Becky said, hurrying after the kids. 'I'll drop them home this evening, 'k?'

Lisa and Sam stood there as Becky's car pulled out, the girls blowing kisses from the back seat. Then, without saying another word, they walked away from the school, stepping aside as a group of kids raced past, their oversized backpacks banging against their spines.

'Was that really necessary?' Lisa said under her breath.

'It's Becky. Who cares?'

They turned a corner down a quiet side street, lined with identical picket fences and clapboard houses. No one was out in their gardens, it was too cold for that, and Lisa came to an abrupt stop. '*Rebecca* is a good friend of mine, actually, and I don't appreciate you embarrassing her like that. It's totally un—'

'Did you get an email from a journalist?' Sam cut in. 'Someone from the *New York Post*? Her name is Alyssa Reed.' Lisa's eyes darted to the ground, then up again, settling on a point somewhere past Sam's shoulder. 'You have, haven't you?' Sam said with a sinking feeling in her stomach. 'Why didn't you warn me?'

'I didn't reply to it.'

Sam clicked her fingers in front of her friend's face, demanding she look at her. 'What are you talking about? You *have* to reply. If you reply, there's no fucking story. You need to email her and say you lied because you were drunk and jealous of me – you've always been jealous of me, haven't you? – and you made all this up.'

'I can't do that.'

'Email her back. Email her back right now and say this was a mistake. Tell her I was a good friend and I would never have done anything to hurt you. Do it, Lisa.' Sam's voice was rising and Lisa looked around in alarm to make sure no one could overhear. 'Email her now, for fuck's sake.'

'I can't get involved with this. It's too much; this is way beyond anything I can cope with. Josh and I were talking and we agreed . . . it's better if you and I don't see each other any more. I don't want to get in the middle of some big newspaper story, Sam – can't you see that's an impossible situation to put me in? I don't want that level of scrutiny on my family. I have to put the girls first and get on with my life.'

'What about *my* life? I swear to God, I keep going over and over what happened that night, trying to find even the slightest hint that you were uncomfortable. And there's nothing! You were the one who instigated it in the first place. The only thing I could think of that might have made you mad is that maybe the two of us hooking up the same night you lost your virginity made it less "special" or something, but that's ridiculous, what self-respecting forty-year-old woman still cares about losing their—'

'That wasn't the night I lost my virginity,' Lisa mumbled and Sam stumbled back, unsteady.

'What did you just say?'

'Josh and I . . .' Lisa pulled the sleeves of her top down over her knuckles. 'We had sex before that.'

'But you told me—'

'Sam. You literally just said that no self-respecting woman would care about when they lost their virginity.'

'But you *lied* to me. Why would you lie about something like that?'

Lisa threw her head back as if she was screaming at the sky. 'I had to!' she shouted. 'You were being so weird about it. Like, you *insisted* on throwing that stupid party that I didn't even want in the first place just so you could say it was the "perfect opportunity" for us to do it in your house. You wanted to be in control of everything, Sam. And then when we did hook up, I was afraid to tell you because I thought you'd freak out. Like, how is that normal? What did it have to do with you? Rebecca said—'

'You told *Becky* about it?'

'She's one of my best friends,' Lisa said, ignoring Sam's flinch. 'She was the one who showed me your essay in *Blackout* in the first place. And when I told her that wasn't how I remembered that night, that I thought maybe—' Lisa stopped herself. 'She said I should email you. She was the one who found your manager's contact details.'

'Wait. Becky was there when you sent the email?' There was something bothering Sam, something she needed to recall but could not. The memory was wriggling out of her hands, like a fish flapping out of water. 'OK, then. Let me ask you this – what exactly did you tell Becky? Did you tell her that you were the one who knew what to do? I'd never even touched myself before that night; you were the one who said it would feel good. *You* showed *me* what to do. Did you tell Becky that' – Sam was gasping with fury now – 'when you came, you were whimpering and you—'

'Stop it! Someone will hear you.'

'I don't give a fuck if anyone hears me.' It was true, she realized. She'd been cautious for so long, choosing her words with care to make sure they didn't reveal more than she'd wanted them to. It had been a dance, her entire life, and she was tired. 'What else do you and Becky talk about? Do you ever talk about how you were the one who stole my boyfriend in the first place? How does that fit in with your moral code, huh?'

Lisa pressed her fingertips against her temples, as if she had a migraine. 'Are you serious? You and Josh dated for six months when we were kids. It was barely a relationship.' Her face hardened. 'I'm done with this now. But I just want to get one thing straight. I went to you as soon as Josh asked me out and—'

'What was I supposed to say? If I said no, he would have told everyone I was a psycho bitch who wouldn't let any other girl near him. You shouldn't have asked me! You should have *known* how I felt.'

'I went to you,' Lisa said, 'because I'd already turned him down. I didn't even *want* to go on a date with him. I wasn't interested in Josh; you were the one who was obsessed with him. The only reason I told you was because I didn't want you to be blindsided if you heard from someone else. But you *insisted* I say yes, Sam. You made me use your house phone to call him and say I'd love to go out with him, if he was still down. You chose my outfit, you even did my make-up, saying you knew exactly how Josh liked it.' She braced herself as another gust of cold wind curled under the trees. 'You kept saying we'd be perfect together.'

'That's not true, that's . . .' Sam trailed off. It was like she was flipping through a photo album and watching the colours leach out, the images fading to nothing. Her memories were so intertwined with Lisa's that sometimes she could not decipher which were hers and which were not. Perhaps, she thought, because they had shared everything as girls, their stories belonged to one another, too. 'That's not how I remember it.'

'What's that thing you always say? "This is my truth." Well, it seems like there's your truth and there's my truth and there's nothing in between.' Lisa dashed her hands against her eyes, refusing to allow herself to cry. 'How can anything be true, then? How do you know what's real?'

She walked away, ignoring Sam calling after her. 'Mouse. Mouse, please come back!' Her friend hurried her step, turning around a corner, and Sam cursed under her breath. Her phone rang, and she dug into her purse to get it. 'Yes,' she answered irritably.

'Is this Samantha Miller?' the voice on the other end asked.

'It depends on who's asking.'

'Eh, it's Mike. From the IT department at Shakti. I'm calling cos we got that IP address for you.'

'What are you talking about?' she asked, her head hurting.

'You know,' he said, and she could hear the sound of some papers rustling in the background. 'The Instagram account? Supernovadiabolique157?'

28.

'Sam. What are you doing here?' The woman opened her door, doing a double-take when she saw who was waiting on the porch. She had changed since Sam had seen her last, now wearing grey sweatpants and an oversized men's shirt, both caked in old paint stains, and she had a silk scarf holding her long hair off her face. Sam could hear music blasting from another room, a song she recognized from a television advert but couldn't quite place, and in the background there were kids chattering and laughing. The house was lovely, Sam had to admit: a raised ranch style surrounded by mature trees, a wooden swing set and playhouse in the front, and a covered pond to the side. It was a little outside of Bennford, in an area Sam hadn't been to before; it had taken her twenty minutes to drive there from the school.

157 Sterling Way.

'Did Lisa send you?' Becky asked, fiddling with her head scarf. 'I told her I'd drop the twins home after dinner. Is everything OK?'

'This has nothing to do with Lisa,' Sam said, leaning against the door frame. 'You know, we have really great guys working in Shakti's IT department.'

'OK,' Becky said, confused at the change of subject. 'That's nice.'

'Yeah. It's amazing what they can do these days. Just between you and me,' she said conspiratorially, 'I've been dealing with this awful troll on social media. These keyboard warriors, they think they can say *anything* and get away with it. But my guy tracked the IP address.'

When the IT guy had called out the name and address, Sam had found she wasn't surprised. There was relief, at first, that it wasn't Gabriel, but then there was a strange sense of inevitability, as if some part of her had known the truth. Supernovadiabolique157. Here she was, in the flesh, after all this time. 'One five seven.' Sam knocked on the slate plaque hung on the side of the porch, engraved with the house number. 'What a coincidence.'

Becky walked on to the porch, closing the door behind her. 'I don't know what you're talking about, Sam, but I think you should probably leave.'

'You see, here's the thing. I've been thinking about that Reddit post and I realized only four people could have written it.' Sam counted on her fingers. 'Me, Lisa, Josh, and my manager. Now, it wasn't going to be me, was it? And it certainly wasn't going to be my manager; she likes her commission far too much for that. I wondered about Josh, I really did, but in the end I decided he wouldn't want this going public; he has just as much to lose as I do. And Lisa? She doesn't have the balls to do something this sneaky. So. Who else knew? It's interesting, when you came to my mother's house last week, you acted like you didn't know anything about it, but today I find out that Lisa *had* told you about that night. Not only that, but you were the one who found my manager's contact details on the website.' Sam did a slow clap. 'How clever of you, Becky.'

'I don't know what you're talking about. You can't just come to my house and accuse me of—'

'Shut up,' Sam snarled at her. She grabbed Becky's elbow and pushed her on to the steps of the porch. 'It was you, wasn't it? You wrote that post. What is *wrong* with you?' she paused. 'What would Marcus think, if he knew what an evil bitch his wife is? I can't imagine his clients at the bank would be too impressed. They mightn't be as keen to come for dinner in the future. What a shame that would be. After all, you're a regular Martha Stewart these days, aren't you?' Sam stretched her arms out in front of her. She still wasn't wearing a coat and she saw the skin turn to gooseflesh but she couldn't seem to feel the cold. 'And . . . I'd have to check with my lawyers but I'm almost certain impersonating Lisa online is illegal.' She tilted her head to the side. 'Maybe that's the worst part of this all. You were supposed to be her new best friend. Why would you do this to her?'

'I had to,' Becky said, wrapping her arms around her legs. 'I had to protect Lisa from you. I knew she would never stand up to you by herself.'

'Is that your story now? Is that what you're telling yourself?' Sam paused. 'Indulge me for a minute. Let's say – just for argument's sake – that you wrote the Reddit post to destroy me. And you put your own needs in front of your best friend's in order to do so. What would it mean to accept that as true?' Becky paled, stuttering, and Sam cut her off before she could speak again. 'You can't, can you? Because that would destabilize your view of yourself as a good person, and that just feels too dangerous, doesn't it, Becky?'

'My. Name. Is. Rebecca.' She pushed herself to standing, inching her mouth closer to Sam's, and for a moment Sam thought the other woman would kiss her. Her breath smelled of mint, a layer of peach fuzz on her cheeks. 'And you're right. I didn't write that post for Lisa. I did it because you deserved to have your life ruined.' Becky bared her teeth in a facsimile of a smile. 'I've been watching you for years, do you know that? Thinking, at least in movies, the prom queen peaks in high school. But not Samantha Miller! You went from strength to strength. Hanging out with movie stars and travelling all over the world, and your fancy apartment and all these fans who *adored* you. And I tried to believe that you had changed – it made it easier to believe that maybe you were different from the girl who bullied me and—'

'I never bullied you,' Sam protested, a twist of fear in her gut. Wasn't that what her former PA was accusing her of too? Saying Sam had been such a terrifying boss that Brooke Campbell was still battling anxiety attacks, two years after leaving Shakti. 'I *never* would have done that.'

'Cut the crap. You made it so obvious you couldn't stand me. You never asked me to walk home with the two of you and I lived two doors down, Sam, we were going in the same direction! You'd invite the boys over when your parents were out of town, and I'd be sitting in my bedroom alone and I could *hear* you. I could hear the music and the voices and the, the . . .' Becky's face turned red as she stumbled over her words. 'You didn't think that maybe it might have been nice for me to be included?'

'Included? You were always there, Becky. We couldn't get rid of you. And I was always lovely to you; it was *Lisa* who talked shit behind your back, if you must know the truth.'

'Wow. You've really rewritten history for yourself, haven't you? You don't remember asking if I was' – Becky put on a Valley Girl accent – 'like, *actually* hungry if I so much as looked at a sandwich? Talking about how you'd rather die than be as fat as Kate Winslet when we went to see *Titanic* and, the very next day, saying she reminded you of me? Insisting I try on your velvet tube dress in Freshman Year when we both knew it wouldn't fit in a million years and you just wanted to humiliate me? You made my life miserable and I've had to watch for the last ten years as you made a career out of being *kind*, preaching about the importance of "connectivity" and "collectivity" and all this shit about treating others as you'd want to be treated. I thought I was losing my fucking mind.'

'I'm sorry, I didn't know you felt like this,' Sam said, trying to touch the other woman's arm, but she jerked her off.

'Oh, fuck that,' Becky said. 'You *did* know, you just didn't care. The only person you cared about was Lisa, and you wanted to keep her all to yourself. She was the only thing that mattered to you. Well.' A slow smile spread across her face. 'Her and Josh, I suppose.'

'I said I was sorry.' Sam sat on the step of the porch, patting the empty space beside her. Becky flopped down too, as if she didn't have enough energy to hold herself upright any longer. 'I was going through a lot back then. I had bulimia, did you realize that? I was struggling too. You can't hold me responsible for what I did as a teenager; we were all assholes.'

Becky gave a harsh laugh. 'I don't think an eating disorder is a good excuse for bullying someone, Sam. And if you do, then you haven't done quite as much "work" on yourself as you might like to believe.'

There was a shout from inside the house, one of the twins complaining that Mackenzie had spilled her jar of water all over the table. 'My painting is ruined!' the girl wailed.

'I'm coming,' Becky called over her shoulder. She stood up straight, pulling her shirt down to cover her thighs. She looked at Sam. 'You know, I wasn't sure if I believed Lisa, at first, when she told me what happened that night,' she said. 'She can be . . . inconsistent, and it's not like I haven't caught her in lies before. Telling me Josh is picking up the kids when I can see her car in the parking lot. Or when she told me she was going on a "trip" for a couple of weeks and Josh confided in me – privately, of course – that she'd had a breakdown. That was bad, that time.' She let out a low whistle. 'I had to pick up the pieces but she never mentioned it again afterwards. It was like we were supposed to pretend it never happened. I love Lisa but I've learned to take a lot of what she says with a pinch of salt.

But then I thought about it.' She paused, looking Sam up and down. 'And it did seem like something you would do.'

· 'I didn't—' Sam broke off. 'I don't have to stand here and defend myself to you. I didn't do this. There's no proof, there's no case, there's nothing. Because it isn't true.'

'Hmm. Funny, I remember an editorial you wrote for Shakti,' Becky said. 'It was a couple of years ago now, maybe 2018? You wrote that the first, most vital step in this movement would be to give survivors our unconditional trust. "Even with proof",' Becky recited the words off by heart, ' "whether that's medical evidence or an admission of guilt from the perpetrator, survivors are still rarely believed in a patriarchal society." ' She smiled at Sam. 'It was an excellent piece. It really made me think.'

'I'm a good person,' Sam said weakly.

'Oh, Samantha,' Becky said as she closed the door in her face. 'Isn't that what every rapist thinks?'

29.

She got in her car, reversing out of Becky's driveway. Her legs were shaking, and her chest was so tight it hurt to breathe. She needed somewhere to sit, to calm down and gather her thoughts, but she couldn't go home, not now. She didn't want her mother to see her like this. She drove through the town centre, her heels catching in the mat beneath the pedals as she came to a screeching stop outside Delilah's Diner.

'What'll you have?' the waitress asked, an attractive Hispanic woman about the same age as Sam.

'Just an iced tea,' Sam said, and the waitress glanced out of the window.

'On a day like this?' she said. 'You must be warm in your blood.'

When the tea arrived, Sam sipped it and she started shivering. Whether it was from the shock or the cold, she did not know. *Rapist.* She kept replaying that moment, the sneer on Becky's face as she said it. She wasn't . . . she would never do that. Sam would never hurt another woman in the way that she herself had been hurt. It was impossible. She was a good person. Her phone lit up and she grabbed it, hoping it would be Lisa.

Unknown Number: Hello Sami! I hope you are well! I have been trying to get your manager to give your email to me but c'est impossible. A woman from a New York paper contacted me asking about us and I did not know what to say to her

She checked the profile photo on WhatsApp, and when she saw who it was, the nausea was so swift, so severe, she almost vomited all over the table. Her heart was pounding as she forced herself to read his next message. He must have got a new number; she had blocked his old one. She couldn't take it any longer, the texts at 3 a.m., saying he was remembering what had happened. Touching himself, thinking about that night. Did she ever think about it too? he asked.

> **Unknown Number:** I hope everything is good. I have been watching your success from afar. It is very exciting! You must be proud

> **Unknown Number:** If you are in Paris again soon, text me. We will go for drinks? Love, G xx

> **Sam:** I don't want to talk to you, Gabriel. Please don't contact me again

She blocked him, then threw her phone in her bag. She would have to get a new number again, she thought. Would she spend the rest of her life running from this man? Would she be looking over her shoulder until she drew her last breath?

When she had awoken that morning in Paris, she'd limped to the bathroom. Gasping with the pain as she'd peed, the urine stained with specks of blood. Her period wasn't due for weeks; she remembered being confused by that. She didn't understand what had happened, yet. Her mind was blank, like a tape which had been erased. She'd crept back into his warm bed. His hand moving lower on her stomach as he'd whispered in her ear, *Last night was fun, non?* And she loved him so much that she'd said, *Yes, it was?* A yes with a question mark, an uncertain yes. She had allowed him to fill up her empty spaces with his memories because it was easier that way. It was only on the flight home to New York that she had begun to cry. That was when the terrible thought came to her and it wouldn't leave, no matter how hard she tried to push it away – that it wasn't right, what had happened. That he wouldn't have done that to her if he loved her.

In the months that followed, there would be the smell of a certain brand of cigarettes, the way someone tossed their hair out of their eyes, a stranger's crooked smile on the subway, and Sam would start to sweat, tasting vomit. She told herself it was nothing, she was just being dramatic. Even when she'd started to have the nightmares, waking up with a scream trapped in her chest, still, she had stayed with him. They'd dated for six months after that, and she kept smiling at him and at those men, too; she didn't want to make things awkward. She didn't want to embarrass them by asking too many questions; how gauche of her that would be, how *American*. Creeping doubts began to rise in her, filling her lungs, but she told herself that she was partly to blame, she'd been so high that night. She'd taken too much ketamine and she had embarrassed Gabriel by falling around the club, barely able to stand. Even afterwards, when they'd broken up and she'd finally gone to rehab, Sam didn't want to ruin his life. He was a good guy, he wasn't . . . he wasn't *that*. So, she said nothing. She watched him move on and meet someone else, a younger woman than her, prettier as well. Sam wondered if he did the same thing to that girl, and if she said nothing too.

The journalist with the *Post* was right – it hadn't been post-work drinks with the girls at *Blackout* that had led to Sam's assault. What she had written in her #MeToo essay for Shakti wasn't the full story. She didn't want to be sued but she was afraid, too, that if she said it had been her boyfriend, someone she'd loved, trusted, no one would believe her. People claimed they wanted the truth but when faced with it, it was too messy for them to accept. The truth often felt like a story, one with plot holes, an unreliable narrator. Sam had told the world a half-truth because she knew that would be easier for them to believe. 'Someone' raped me was more palatable than *that* husband did it, *that* father, *that* son. That newsreader smiling at you through the television, that musician whose song you chose for the first dance at your wedding. It was easier to make monsters out of faceless strangers than the nice, ordinary men who worked in your office, who let you skip the line in the grocery store, who held the door open for you at the bank.

Sam was still friends with a few of those men on Facebook, Gabriel's gang; for some reason, she couldn't let them go. She'd watched over the years as they met women and got married, confetti thrown outside a quaint church in the French country-side. Some of them had daughters, baby girls in pink bows and ribbons. After #MeToo, those men wrote long posts about how 'as a father of daughters', they felt it was important they added their voices to the movement – enough was enough, the time was now, when would women be free? They wanted their girls to be safe. That wasn't too much to ask for, was it?

The waitress brought the check, leaving the piece of paper on a small saucer. 'We're clocking up,' she said and Sam lingered at the cash desk, waiting, until the kitchen doors swung open. It was the same chef from the last time, pulling his wool jacket on. 'I'm out for the night, ladies,' he said, and then he saw Sam. Taking in the tousled blonde hair, the top falling off one shoulder and exposing creamy skin, her nipples clearly outlined beneath the thin material. She held his gaze, smiling slowly at him. The bell jingled as he left and she slung her handbag over her shoulder, hurrying after him.

'Hey,' she called and he turned on his heel, surprised.

'What's up? Do you need—' he asked, muttering *woah* as Sam pushed him against the brick wall outside the diner, a flurry of snow dislodging from the corrugated roof and falling on their heads. Her tongue against his, her hands snaking behind to clutch at his ass, grinding her hips into his until she could feel him get hard.

'My car,' she said. 'It's over—'

'Right,' he said dumbly and she took his hand. She'd parked the car down a side alleyway and she told him to get in first. When he was sitting, she unzipped his jeans and he pushed them down, his dick springing free from his boxers. She moved on to his lap, one knee on either side. Her skirt bunched around her waist; she wasn't wearing underwear. 'Do you have a—' he started but she cut across him, saying, 'I'm on the pill,' sliding him inside her before he could protest. His face screwed up and he groaned, his fingers tightening on her arms. She hadn't had sex in so long and it hurt. She winced but still moved against him, smelling the grease off his skin, his hair gel sticky against her chin.

'Fuck,' he said. 'Fuck,' and he bucked his hips as he came and she was glad of that, glad it was over. His breath slowing, his grasp on her loosening. She looked out of the window. It was snowing again.

'Holy shit,' he said, brushing her hair out of her face so he could see her properly. 'You're really pretty.' His eyes were a little too close together, and one of his teeth was grey, dead at the root, and she could not bear to look at him any longer.

'What did you say your name was again?' he asked.

'I didn't,' she replied, rolling off him. His softening dick, flopping on to his pimpled thigh. She reached across him, opening the car door. 'I think you'd better go,' she said.

She drove home alone, the radio turned off. She didn't want to hear any music; she didn't want a song to remind her of this moment for the rest of her life. 'You are disgusting,' she kept repeating aloud. There was something rotten inside her. She had spent so many years trying to keep the darkness at bay but she couldn't resist it any more; her blood was surging, urging her towards its shadows. 'Look at yourself. Look.' She stared in the rear-view mirror when she parked outside her mother's house. A stranger's semen dribbling out of her, her make-up smeared across her face. She could pretend all she wanted but this was what she truly was.

A lamp turned on as soon as her key was in the door and there was her mother, sitting on an armchair in her silk pyjamas and nightgown, her face shiny with night cream. 'Where were you, Samantha?' she asked.

'I was out.'

'I can see that,' Carolyn replied as Sam threw her car keys on the console. She stood there daring her mother to comment on her bare legs, the fact she was not wearing a bra. She smiled, a baring of teeth, and Carolyn flinched.

'I'm sorry,' Sam said. 'Do I not look pretty enough, Mother?' She strode past, Carolyn getting to her feet and holding her back by the elbow.

'I'm worried about you.'

Sam laughed. Once again, she found she couldn't stop, giggles hopping off her tongue like hiccups. 'Why are you worried about me *now*? Why weren't you worried about me when I was a teenager? When the maids were telling you that food was disappearing from the fridge? Didn't you think that was strange, Mom? Didn't you think you might have reason to worry about me then?'

'I didn't know.' Carolyn's shoulders tensed up around her ears. 'In the beginning, I just . . . I didn't know.'

'You *did* know. You just ignored it. Because that's what we do in this family, isn't it? We pretend everything is fine even when it's not.' And it hadn't just been her parents. On sleepovers, she and Lisa watching scary movies, bags of candy between them, and she would sneak off to the bathroom, running the tap to muffle the sound of the vomiting. Lisa would look at her oddly when she returned but she never said anything and, in her silence, Sam tasted her friend's collusion. No one had cared enough about Sam to try to help her. 'It was obvious I was falling apart, Mom, and you did *nothing.*'

'I didn't know what to do. You were so headstrong; you wouldn't listen to a word we had to say.'

'Don't you dare blame me,' Sam hissed. 'I was the child; you were the parent. It was your *job* to protect me. And what did you do? You brought me to some diet doctor to "fix" me. Because that was all you wanted, wasn't it? The perfect little doll to show off to your friends.'

'What?' her mother said, confused. 'A diet doctor? What are you talking about?'

'Don't play dumb. Dr Anat?'

'Samantha.' Carolyn stared at her. 'Dr Anat was one of the best eating disorder specialists in the city. She was recommended by one of my partners in the practice. Jackie's daughter also had issues with food, remember?'

'What? No. No, she was . . .' Sam remembered the waiting room. The tan leather couch. The same girl leaving the doctor's office five minutes before Sam's appointment began every week, her red-rimmed eyes, her braces. They avoided eye contact but the smell of the girl's perfume – sweet, floral, some celebrity fragrance Sam had sniffed at a drugstore before but couldn't recall the name of – filled the room, even after she'd gone. Then Dr Anat would open the door.

'I'm ready for you now, Samantha,' the woman would say, standing back to let her through. They'd sit opposite one another in the small, windowless room and Dr Anat scribbled in her notebook as she asked Sam questions about how her week had been. She always tried to tell the doctor what she wanted to hear.

'I don't . . .' Sam trailed off.

She had been talking about her childhood for so long, viewing it as something akin to a performance piece to be acted out for interviews and panel discussions, that she wondered if she could not tell what was real any more, and what was just a story, and the thought was terrifying. 'But I went to the city,' Sam tried. 'During summer break. I overheard you talking to a woman in your office. She was telling you about her daughter, about the . . . the vomiting. And you said, *That's just what they do at that age.* It's no big deal, you said.'

'I don't remember saying that.' Her mother edged closer, slowly, as if Sam was a wild animal who might start easily. 'But if I did, I'm sorry. I know I let you down in a million ways. But I tried, Samantha. I really did.' She put her hand on Sam's arm and Sam stared down at it, at Carolyn's wrinkled fingers, the emerald engagement ring flanked with two square-cut diamonds. Her mother was getting older. She would die one day and that ring would be Sam's. This house would be hers, too. She would have all the things she'd ever wanted and she would be alone forever.

She looked at Carolyn, and she imagined what her mother must see. Could she smell the sex off her? Could she smell the badness in her, too? Sam thought of that man's hands on her skin, the bruises he must have left in his efforts to make her body his own, and she could taste bile at the back of her throat, bitter.

'It wasn't enough,' she whispered. 'I needed more from you.'

'I know.' Carolyn pushed her daughter's hair off her face, like the chef had done earlier, but not with awe, as he had, at her beauty. She looked at Sam as if she saw her for all that she was, and she loved her anyway. Sam bowed her head again. Carolyn would never understand the aching emptiness at the centre of her, a gaping black hole so ravening that nothing would escape its hunger. *Run*, she wanted to warn her. *Run.*

'Are you OK?' her mother asked gently.

'I don't know,' Sam answered. 'I don't know what I am any more.'

30.

January 2000

Sam heard the creak of a door opening but it wasn't her mother. There was no scent of sunflowers and citrus, no frustrated sigh as she took in the state of her daughter's bedroom – the clothes thrown on the floor, make-up stains on the rug, wet towels dumped on the comforter. *Why must you insist on being such a slob, Samantha?* It couldn't be her father, either. He hadn't come into her bedroom since the day Sam got her period, as though some invisible line had been drawn. She had been fourteen, a late bloomer, her mom said. Lisa got hers nearly a year before and Sam had said *eww, gross*, pretending she wasn't jealous. Later, tired of Lisa and Becky complaining about menstrual cramps, asking to be excused from gym because it was 'that time of the month', Sam had lied and said she got hers as well. Then, when it had finally happened, the shock of blood in her underwear, she had no one left to tell.

The person walked past the bed frame and Sam could see a pair of battered Keds, the laces undone, the scuffed soles.

'You haven't done this in a while.' Lisa squatted down, crawling underneath the bed to join her. They lay there for a few minutes, listening to the sounds the house made around them.

'How was the anniv—' Sam couldn't say any more. She was in a tank top and boxer shorts but she was still sweating, the cheap tequila oozing out of her pores.

'It was cool,' Lisa said, tracing her fingers across the words etched into the wood. Sam had a flash of relief that she hadn't written anything there about Josh choosing Lisa over her; it felt as if it would make it real, if she did that. 'Granddad gave a speech, saying he'd known from the first minute he laid eyes on Grandma that she was the love of his life. Everyone cried, even Aunt Debra.' She paused, waiting for Sam to say something. 'Did you have fun at Chris's party? I'm pissed I couldn't go.'

'It was fine.'

'Josh said it sucked. He . . .' She hesitated. 'He said you had another fight with Brandon. Do you want to talk about it?'

Sam put a hand up to stop her friend – *I can't do this right now.*

'OK,' Lisa said. She stretched her arms above her head, muttering 'ow' as she hit something. 'What's that?' she asked, flipping over on to her stomach to investigate. 'Ooh, did you get new kicks?' She grabbed hold of the shoebox, pulling it towards her.

'No,' Sam blurted out. 'That's private.' Her diary was in there, but there were other things, too, mementoes from her time with Josh. Ticket stubs from movies they'd seen together, a docket from Delilah's after their first date. A Valentine's Day card he'd given her. There were photos, too, grainy Polaroids snapped when they were in bed together, their faces flushed, skin raw from kissing. One of her alone, in a spaghetti-strap top and panties. She hadn't wanted him to take it, saying 'stop it' as she pushed him away, thinking, *I'm too fat.* Meaning, *I'm too much.*

'You're beautiful, Sam,' he'd said, raising the camera at her again. And she had felt beautiful in that moment, just because he'd said so.

'I said leave it,' she snapped and Lisa apologized, pushing the box away from her. She propped herself on her elbows, looking down at Sam.

'You all right?'

'Just hungover,' Sam managed. She closed her eyes but that made it worse, the floor tipping to the side beneath her. *Don't puke, don't puke.*

'I know how to distract you,' Lisa said.

Her friend told her a story, then, the same story she'd told Sam many times before. How they should never have been raised in a town like Bennford. It was too small, too provincial for girls like them. Everyone knew everyone else's secrets, whispering about the illicit affairs and embezzled money and failed business ventures. How much this neighbour's car had cost, and had they seen the Wilsons' new pool? The way the moms always cleared up after the cookouts while the dads stood around talking about football and didn't even offer to help. What scared Lisa the most was that no one else in town seemed to care. They'd all assimilated so well, sinking into their lives with such precision that they didn't even know they were drowning.

'But that won't be us,' Lisa said. 'We're gonna move to the city after graduation and get an apartment together. We'll work shitty jobs and I'll write at night; I'll have my first play finished by the time I'm twenty. And you . . .' She laughed. 'Oh, Sam, I don't know what you're going to do. But I know it'll be spectacular.'

'What about Josh?' Sam risked turning to the side so she could look at her friend, and the queasiness sloshed in her head. Lisa paused and it was clear she had forgotten about her boyfriend, just for a second, and she wasn't sure how he fitted into these plans for world domination. *I would never forget about him, if he was mine.* If Josh had loved Sam, she would've been happy to stay here, to buy a house a few streets away from her parents, and raise their children together. Two girls, Maya and Martha, and a little boy called Josh Junior. The perfect family.

But Josh didn't love her, that was the problem. He would never love her.

Sam grabbed her friend's hand and said, 'You'll always choose me, won't you? No matter what happens?'

Lisa curled up on her side, facing her. 'Don't be silly,' she said, stroking Sam's hair. 'It's you and me, Mouse. Forever.'

31.

⊙ 1,675,232

Sam: Lisa, please. Please text me back

Sam: I need you to talk to the reporter from the Post. You have to tell her this isn't true

Sam: I don't know what Becky has been telling you but you can't trust her.

Sam: You have to believe me. I'm asking you, just phone me back OK?

Sam: Lisa?

'Hi, Josh. It's me. Sam. I've been trying to call Lisa all day and I can't get through to her. I think she's blocked my number again. Can you get her to ring me? Please?'

'Josh, it's me again. I'm not fucking joking. The two of you can't just . . . you can't just *do* this to me. You can't just decide I'm a piece of dirt on your fucking shoe that you can discard whenever you want. Listen to me, Josh, and listen good. You don't want to push me on this, OK?'

'Hey. It's me. I'm sorry for that last message. I'm tired and I'm . . . I need to talk to her, Josh. I need her to fix this. I need . . . Please. Just get her to call me.'

@alyssareedNYP I'm still looking to talk to people for that story I'm doing on #SamanthaMiller. Nothing too big or too small. My DMs are open #JournoRequest

32.

◉ 1,650,674

'Samantha?' Carolyn said. 'Are you awake?' She sighed when there was no reply, a clatter of cutlery on ceramic. 'I'll leave this here for you.'

Two days had passed since her confrontation with Becky, since she'd fucked that chef in her car, and she had not been able to leave this room since. She knew her mother must be itching to throw back the curtains, open the windows. Strip the sweat-stained sheets and duck her daughter's head under a cold shower, snapping her out of this funk, but Sam refused to speak to her. All she could do was lie in bed, thinking about Gabriel, how easy it had been for him to text her, and how casually he had done so. Did he not remember what he and his friends had done to her? Or had he retold the story, convincing himself that Sam had been a willing participant, that she'd wanted to be used like that?

She waited until she heard the click of the door closing again and scurried over to the chest of drawers where her mother had left a stoneware platter, a bottle of Evian water, fresh fruit, a glass jar of coconut yoghurt. She took the tray and hunkered down on the ground, eating as quickly as she could. Her pyjamas were dirty, stained with dribbles of yoghurt, and she could smell the sour ripeness of her body. She stuffed the food into her mouth, then she crept back to bed, crawling under the covers, and slept for the rest of the day. Later, she was never sure what time, her mother would return. 'I'm here if you want to talk,' Carolyn said every time, picking up the tray and leaving again.

Sam pulled her phone out from under the pillow, checking Twitter.

@alyssareedNYP Some jaw-dropping stories about #Samantha Miller in my DMs. Keep 'em coming #Wellness #Guru #Idols

Alyssa had emailed Sam, asking for a comment. *If you could get back to me by the 2nd of February*, she wrote. *My deadline is the 3rd. Thanks!*

Sam forwarded it to the crisis management person, who promised they would write a statement and put an aggressive strategy in place as quickly as possible. All she could do was wait, remembering everything she had ever done or said that could be used against her – the off-colour jokes she'd made on Twitter when she was in her twenties and snarkiness seemed the best way to get likes online, the wellness experts she'd insisted be removed from panels when they were getting too popular for Sam's liking, the dubious porn she watched late at night when she couldn't sleep. The world was changing, and Sam had sensed it was coming for a long time. It began with kickback about the use of the name 'Shakti', accusations of cultural appropriation, and Sam had listened. She didn't believe, as many of her contemporaries did, that 'you can't say anything any more!'; she never wanted to be defensive or react-ive in the face of criticism. As she'd told her team, white people had to do the *work* now, didn't they? They had to show up. She'd chosen *White Fragility* for the Shakti book club and the conversations had been *fascinating*; it had really opened her eyes. She'd noticed the girls at her events were becoming more politically engaged, wondering what Sam's stance on immigration was, did she think the rich should be taxed more, what was she doing to help dismantle capitalism, and to welcome trans women into the movement, what were her opinions on this bill, this senator, this statement? It wasn't enough any more that Sam said she was a feminist, posting a photo of her Spirit Mafia crew on International Women's Day with multiple hashtags (#WomenEmpoweringWomen #StrongWomen #WhoRunTheWorld). These new girls wanted to know the specifics of her feminism, the boundaries it encompassed. They wanted more from her and she had finally been ready to give it to them, now that she felt sure it would not cost her too much, or at least it would gain her enough new followers to make up for those she would inevitably lose. Was it too late now? Would there be anyone left to listen once this article was published in the *Post*? It was so unfair, all of it. She'd worked hard and done her best to help others – did she really deserve to have her life ruined because of something that had happened when she was a teenager? She'd always presumed – no, she thought fiercely, she'd *known* – that Lisa had wanted it just as much as she had. The signals were all there: her friend had moaned into Sam's mouth, her back arching as she'd climaxed. It wasn't like what happened in Paris, that dark room with four men, taller than her, stronger too. The smell of cigarettes, the whispers, the laughter. Sam hadn't been given a choice.

She pushed herself to sitting, the blood rushing to her head. It was nearly Lisa's birthday. Sam had told people to arrive at 2 p.m. and although her friend insisted she didn't want gifts, Sam had texted everyone saying she'd made a generous donation in Lisa's name to St Jude Children's Research Hospital and that they should feel free to bring presents if they wanted. *Our girl deserves it!!* The guests would park outside the house on West Cross Street, and gasp at how beautiful the place looked, the flower arch over the footpath studded with hundreds of white roses, the garlands of lilies wound around the wrought-iron gates. There would be a string quartet in the hallway, wait staff with trays of champagne and a specially designed cocktail ('Lisa's Libation', she'd called it, made of gin, lime juice, green tea extract, and agave syrup). There would be a full buffet, too, a roasted salmon with cold salads, a selection of breads, dips and crudités, with salted caramel cheesecake, macarons and chocolate fondants for dessert. The four-tier birthday cake Sam had commissioned from the best bakery in the city was due to arrive in the morning, a delicate confection of butter-cream icing and a lemon drizzle centre. It would be perfect.

She'd insisted on paying for everything; it would cover all the birthdays she had missed in the last twenty-two years, she told Lisa. She signed the checks for the DJ who had been instructed to play nineties hits all evening, the magician and the bounce house to keep the children entertained in the back yard, and the two nannies to make sure they didn't injure themselves. She'd done everything she could to ensure that Lisa had the party of a lifetime – to show her that Sam still *knew* her, better than anyone else ever would – and had Lisa shown any gratitude? Had Lisa thanked Sam for her generosity? *No.* Her friend wouldn't even expect her to turn up; she thought Sam would slink back to the city, the same way she'd fled to Utah in Senior High, doing whatever she could to give Lisa the 'space' she claimed she needed. Lisa had fucked her over when they were teenagers, abandoning her supposed best friend when Sam had needed her most, and now she wanted to destroy Sam's life. She was like Shiva, the god of destruction, the Tower card incarnate. She wouldn't be happy until Sam was buried alive and she had dug the grave herself.

She thought of the letters stacked neatly beneath the bed and imagined the words drifting off the page, pushing the box open to float to the sky. She could see them on the ceiling, arranging and rearranging themselves, dancing in the dark for her alone.

It doesn't matter what happened, Mouse. We're still us. We will always be us. Can you ever forgive me for what I've done?

Where had that Lisa gone? she wondered. Had she even existed in the first place?

33.

There were bodies everywhere. People on the stairs, more sitting on the floor, swigging from red Solo cups as they threw their heads back and laughed at jokes that seemed hilarious after three vodkas in Samantha Miller's house, waiting for Josh and Lisa to arrive.

'Shh,' Sam said, turning off the lights. 'He texted to say he'll be here in a few minutes.'

A few of the girls screamed in the darkness, one complaining, 'Whoever is touching my butt right now had better quit it, it's not cool.'

'Shut up,' Sam hissed as headlights turned into the driveway, a car coming to a slow stop outside. A murmur of voices, the doorbell ringing once, twice.

'That's weird,' she heard Lisa say. 'It's open. And why is—'

'SURPRISE!' they shouted as Sam flicked the lights on. Lisa recoiled, her eyes moving from face to face, as if she was counting how many people were crammed into the hall. Costumes were mandatory for the night, Sam had insisted, so there were a couple of Neos from *The Matrix*, a Ghostface, and the usual slutty versions of a nurse, a cowgirl, a cat. She'd invited most of Senior Year and everyone said yes; no one was going to pass up the opportunity for a party at the Millers'.

'Are you surprised, Mouse?' Sam said, wrapping her arms around Lisa's waist.

'I thought we said that—'

'It's your eighteenth,' Sam dismissed her. 'Josh and I have been planning this for ages! You hardly thought we were gonna spend the night playing Scrabble or some shit, did you?'

Josh laughed and Lisa's face fell for a split second, so quickly that no one else would have noticed but Sam.

'Hey,' Sam said. 'It'll be awesome, I promise. We love you.' She smoothed down some frizz at Lisa's hairline.

'Yeah,' Lisa said faintly. 'Thanks, Mouse. This was really cool of you.'

'Hate to break up the love fest,' Josh said. 'But I gotta run out to the car and grab my costume.' He winked at Lisa. 'I think you'll like it.'

'Wait, I don't have a costume.' Lisa smoothed down her dress. 'Although I do love this—'

'Don't worry,' Sam said. 'I have you covered.' She took her friend by the hand and led her through the crowd, bleary-eyed people turning to wish Lisa a happy birthday, hugging her, *Did you guess? Did you have any clue?* Up the stairs they went, passing couples kissing, grinding against each other, and Brandon and Chris were sitting on the top step, both dressed as Austin Powers. Chris was rolling a joint, licking at the paper, and Brandon reached out, sneaking his fingers up Sam's leg as high as they could go.

'Stop,' she said, swatting him away.

'What are you supposed to be, anyway? Some sort of princess?' he asked with a sneer, dropping his hand back in his lap.

Sam looked down at her outfit, the cream slip dress cut on the bias, the pearl-beaded rosary. She'd scrunched her hair with mousse, slipped a plastic tiara on, coated her mouth in bright red lipstick.

'Isn't it obvious?' Lisa said, pulling Sam away. 'She's Courtney Love at the Oscars, dumbass.'

In Sam's room, she sat on the edge of the bed. 'So,' she said in an overly casual voice. 'What's going on with you and Brandon?'

'Boooo! I don't want to talk about that douche bag.' Sam made a gagging noise. 'This is *your* night. My baby has turned eighteen.' She clasped her hands over her heart. 'You're all grown up now.'

'Your birthday was, like, last August.'

'Yeah, and those extra six months gave me a real sense of maturity. You'll understand in time,' Sam replied, laughing when Lisa picked up a cushion and threw it at her.

'But seriously,' she said as Sam dragged her to standing, bringing her to the closet. Piles of wrinkled clothes fell out when she opened the doors and Lisa bent to pick them up, *ooh*ing wistfully at the strapless Calvin Klein dress Sam had got for Christmas, worn once, and promptly forgotten about. 'Do you think you'll get back together?'

'Ugh, I doubt it,' Sam said. 'And who cares? It's not like it would've lasted past graduation, right? I thought we agreed no boyfriends for our first year at college. Gotta sow those wild oats, baby.'

'Hmm,' Lisa murmured. 'Speaking of boyfriends . . . Josh has been a bit—' She hesitated. '*Weird* since Chris's party.'

'Weird, how?' Sam asked, rifling through the hangers to find the paper shopping bag she'd stashed at the back of the closet.

'I don't know. A bit distant, maybe? I can't put my finger on it.' Lisa paused. 'You didn't see anything, did you?'

'How d'you mean?'

'The night of the party. Josh, he didn't . . .' Lisa trailed off but her meaning was clear.

'Girl!' Sam was incredulous. 'You think I saw your boyfriend *cheating* on you and didn't say anything? You tripping.' She let out a low *yesss* as she spotted what she was looking for. 'He was probably scared that he'd let it slip about the party. I told him I'd literally murder him if he ruined the surprise.'

Lisa laughed. 'OK,' she said. 'OK. You're right.'

'I'm always right,' Sam said, handing her friend the shopping bag. 'Now, get this on you. Chris rolled me a spliff earlier, you want some?' She lit it and handed it to Lisa, who coughed as the weed burned the back of her throat.

She passed it back to Sam, saying, 'Oof, that's strong,' then pulled the yellow polka-dot shift dress over her head so she was standing there in her underwear. Her body was perfect, Sam thought; it was like a model's. Her legs were long and her stomach lean, her tiny tits barely filling out the strapless bra.

Lisa held the costume up to herself in the mirror in confusion. 'But . . . but it's the same as yours?'

'No, remember? It's Amanda de Cadenet.' Sam had had both dresses especially made, but the second one was particularly beautiful with its lace bodice and sheer tulle at the hem; she knew Lisa would look stunning in it.

'I'm not sure,' Lisa said, frowning. 'It's a bit . . . Can't I just wear my own outfit?' But Sam had unclipped her friend's bra already – the black wouldn't look right and the applique flowers on the lace would cover Lisa's nipples anyway – and removed the butterfly clips, fitting a cheap blonde wig over Lisa's hair, before grabbing the spare tiara that matched her own. She took the tube of red lipstick from her vanity table and smeared it across Lisa's mouth.

'There,' she said, turning her friend to face the mirror, the two of them standing side by side. 'We look hot.'

Lisa's smile was frozen, and she swiped the half-empty bottle of vodka on the table and took a swig from it, gagging at the sharp taste.

'Woah.' Sam widened her eyes. 'Someone is ready to get this party started. You good?'

'I'm fine,' Lisa said, about to wipe her mouth with the back of her hand but then, remembering the lipstick, she stopped herself. 'I'm just . . .'

'Nervous?' Sam asked. 'It's not that big of a deal, don't worry about it.'

'What's not a big—' She cleared her throat. 'Oh, *that*. Yeah. Of course.'

'You've waited so long to have sex, it's only natural you freaked out. But it'll be fine! Josh loves you.' Sam linked arms with her friend, staring at their reflection. The tiaras and silk dresses, the lipstick, the tousled blonde hair. They were like twins; they could easily be mistaken for each other in the dark. 'But not as much as I love you, Mouse.' Sam leaned her head on her friend's shoulder – she didn't know if it was the weed or the vodka, or just this strange, sudden understanding that they were adults now, and things were destined to change between them after they left for college, no matter how much she wanted them to stay the same, that life would have its way with them and there was nothing she could do to stop it – and she wished she could unzip Lisa's body and step inside, inhabit her friend fully. She wanted them to become one entity, their veins woven in and around each other so they could never be unravelled again. 'Remember that.'

34.

⊙ 1,635,631

An Irish intern at *Blackout* had told Sam once that the first of February meant the start of spring in her country. They celebrated St Brigid's Day, she'd said, the goddess of midwives and abortions, and Sam had always found it ironic that Lisa shared a birthday with a saint who emptied the wombs of unwilling mothers. Every year on this day, she would think about Lisa's birthday and she would think about the termination, and how the two had become inextricable in her mind. The start of one life, the ending of another. Sometimes she imagined parallel universes to this one, a world in which she had been the one to marry Josh, not Lisa, and he held her hand in a delivery room as two tiny girls slithered out of her, bald cries taking their place among the elements. Or another dimension, where she and Lisa raised that lost baby together, sister moms, like something from a Bravo reality show. A little boy, this time, and he would have Lisa's red hair and Sam's heart-shaped chin. Created of Lisa's blood and Sam's flesh, their child entirely.

She slipped on the outfit she'd chosen, a blush-coloured crepe dress with cape-like sleeves and a fringed hem. She curled her hair and applied her make-up with care for she had to look more than beautiful today, she had to be irresistible. This was her last chance to fix this mess, after all.

'Hello, my loves,' she said, holding the camera higher for a better angle. 'I'm just getting ready to leave the house. It's finally Lisa's birthday! I'm sorry I haven't been on here much lately but the party planning has taken up soooo much of my time. It's not every day your BFF turns forty, right?!'

She took a mirror selfie, staring at the image on her phone. She remembered Gabriel's text – *I have been watching your great success from afar* – and she went cold, as if she could feel his eyes on her. But still, she posted the picture to her main grid and tagged every single thing she was wearing even though she knew there would be comments underneath asking, *Where's your dress from, Sam? What mascara are you wearing?* She waited, watching the words appear.

omg 🔥🔥🔥

where is this dress from Sam? is it true to size?

kill yourself, you fucking cunt

wow i cant beleve what some of you r saying have you never heard of #bekind

you should be in jail bitch if u wer a man u wud b

Oh please, because men are so *consistently* convicted of rape and sexual assault? Your strawman arguments aren't going to work here, troll

Shut up libtard 👇

LEAVE SAM ALONE!!!!!!!!!!!!!

'Jesus,' she hissed in fright as her mother pushed the bedroom door open, a tray of food in her hands. 'Knock, much?'

A smile spread across Carolyn's face when she saw her daughter, out of bed and dressed for the first time in days. 'Oh, Samantha, you look—' Then she stopped. 'Where are you going?' she asked, placing the tray on the antique luggage rack by the door. 'Not where I think you are, surely? That's not a good idea.'

'I don't remember asking your opinion,' Sam replied, peeling off a small bunch of grapes and popping one into her mouth.

'Why do you even *want* to go?' her mother asked, sitting heavily on the bed. 'After what that girl said about you . . .'

Sam stiffened. 'What are you talking about?'

'Samantha, come on. I'm seventy-six, I'm not Methuselah. I do know how to use the internet, you know.'

Sam looked at the ground; the shame rushing through her was so hot, she could hardly bear to maintain eye contact. 'Why didn't you say anything, Mom?'

'I thought you would tell me in your own time. But then you've always been so . . .' Carolyn sighed. 'Oh, Samantha. Why didn't you ask me for help? What is this *need* you have to try and control everything?'

'So, you know . . . you know what Lisa said . . .' Her breathing was drawing fast, snagging against her ribs. 'Are you—' The words were breaking in half and she couldn't catch her breath; it was coming faster and faster but she couldn't fill her lungs again. Her head was so light and she dropped to her knees, clutching at the ground beneath her, trying to find something to hold on to. She was going to pass out, she was going to— *I might die*, she thought, panicked. If she couldn't find a way to breathe, then she would die here.

'Samantha.' Her mother crouched beside her. One hand on Sam's back, the other on her heart centre. 'You're fine. It's just an anxiety attack, OK? Breathe in.' She inhaled slowly, urging Sam to copy her. 'And out.' She exhaled. 'In,' Carolyn said again. 'And out.' She waited until her daughter did as she was told, then she took Sam's left hand in hers and she held her close, whispering, 'You're safe. You're safe, sweetheart. I'm here now.'

Sam could feel the tension in her chest unspooling, her limbs loosening, and she collapsed into her mother's embrace, spent. She apologized – she was ruining her mother's silk shirt – but Carolyn shushed her. 'Cry as much as you need to,' she said. 'It's good for you. Cathartic.' She waited until her daughter's sobs slowed, and she kept her mouth pressed against the back of Sam's head, kissing her hair.

'Are you ashamed of me, Mom?' she asked.

'What? Of course not,' her mother replied. 'This isn't your fault. I can't even imagine what you must be going through, dealing with something like this. I could wring Lisa's neck, I really could. What is she thinking, lying like this? I *know* you.' Carolyn looked at Sam with such tenderness it made her want to cry again. 'I know my daughter. You're incapable of such a thing.'

'Did you . . .' Sam sniffed loudly. 'Did you read my essay? The one I wrote about Lisa?'

'No. I made the decision a long time ago that I wouldn't read any of your work. It felt like I was reading your diary.' She tucked Sam's hair behind her ears. 'I wanted to give you space. Maybe that was the wrong thing to do.' She sighed. 'I feel like I've spent most of my time as a mother doing the wrong thing.'

'Giving me "space"? Is that what we're calling ignoring my career?' In the beginning, Sam would tell her mother about an award she'd won, or what position her book was on the bestseller list, which actresses were vying for the main role in the *Willing Silence* movie, and she was always met with silence, Carolyn grimacing as if Sam was being uncouth discussing such things over dinner. After a while, Sam made the decision to stop telling Carolyn anything, answering with a curt *fine* when her mother asked her how business was. 'You can stop with the Perfect Mom act now.'

Carolyn said, hurt, 'I may not have been perfect but I tried my best. We both did.'

'Your best? Does "your best" include packing me off to Utah? You and Dad couldn't wait to get rid of me, could you?'

'Oh my god. Are you ever going to quit it, Sam? It's just the two of us here, you can drop the act now.' Carolyn stood up again, putting her hands on her hips. 'I've held my tongue for long enough. I haven't been *allowed* to ask questions, have I? Any time I've even *tried* to bring this up, you've cut me off for weeks and I . . . I don't have anyone else left, Samantha. Your father is dead. You're my only child. I can't lose you too.' She touched her fingers to her eyes to stop the tears. 'I didn't want to send you away. You came to us and showed us those brochures, saying what a "great opportunity" this school would be. We'd never even heard of the place. But you were so determined, like you always were, and we—' Carolyn rubbed her hand against her forehead. 'We didn't know what to do. You had been refusing to go to school, you weren't talking to Lisa, and when we found out what the two of you had done—'

'You were disgusted, I suppose.'

'Please. You think I don't have friends who've had abortions? I wouldn't judge *any* woman for making that choice, let alone a schoolgirl. All we cared about was the fact you refused to get out of bed for weeks. You wouldn't see Dr Anat, your eating was out of control, you weren't even trying to hide it any more. There was vomit *everywhere*, I just . . . I didn't know what to do.'

'Stop it.' Sam had thought she was being clever, that she'd hidden her little habit well and no one had noticed how bad things had become. She didn't want to believe she'd been a problem, someone who had been pitied rather than envied.

'Your teachers told us you'd missed too many classes to graduate and you'd have to repeat final year. Your father and I, we just wanted you to sit your SATs and get into a good school,' Carolyn said. 'We didn't want you to fall behind. And the place in Utah, it was beautiful, wasn't it? You were close to the mountains and you went skiing and hiking and there was fucking *horse therapy*' – Sam flinched; her mother never swore. She said it was unladylike and spoke to a limited vocabulary – 'and then Lydia Thomas is showing me an interview you gave to the *LA Times* about a "correctional school" and "solitary confinement", and I could see people in town looking at me like I was evil, sending my only child somewhere like that.'

'I . . .' Sam trailed off. She tried to think of an excuse but, for the first time in her adult life, she could not find one. 'I'm sorry,' she said, wretchedly. 'Mom, you have to believe me. I never thought it would get so big. I just . . . I needed a story in the beginning. The publicity team at Glass House kept asking how I was any different to all the other privileged, white women writing their memoirs, how was I going to differentiate myself? I didn't know it would turn out like this.'

It had become clear early on that Sam would need to embellish parts of her life – she knew if she wanted all the broken girls out there to identify with her, she would have to say she was broken too. So she highlighted her trauma, omitted to mention that her parents had paid her rent when she'd first moved to the city as it didn't quite fit the scrappy, self-made mythology she had created for herself – but she was a storyteller after all, that's what artists do. They create their own legends, their own lore. She had never expected the story to become so deeply rooted in the culture that she couldn't dig it up again. 'And I did hate it in Utah,' she tried. 'I was miserable there, I—'

'Being miserable is different from being abused, Samantha.'

'I know!' she shouted. 'You think I don't feel awful about that? But Mom, of all people, you should understand how hard it is to be an ambitious woman. It makes people uncomfortable. They want to hear that you've struggled too, that you're not just some spoiled brat who's had everything handed to them on a plate. I did what I had to do to get ahead! If a man did the same thing, he'd be lauded as "visionary" and "determined". I needed—'

'Yes, I get it.' Her mother held her gaze. 'You needed a story. But why did that story have to involve your father? The things you said about him . . . you broke his heart.' Carolyn's face crumpled. 'And then . . . Before we knew he was sick, Nate was getting so confused. He kept coming to me, asking if it was true. Asking if we had sent you to one of those schools and he just' – her mother was sobbing now – 'he was afraid he couldn't remember.'

Sam bit down on her lower lip as hard as she could to stop herself from crying too. She had never wanted to hurt her father; she'd only wanted him to pay attention to her. To tell her he loved her, just once. 'Look, I'll admit I fudged a few details on the school in Utah.' Her mother snorted at this but Sam ignored it. 'But everything else I said was true. Dad *was* emotionally distant. He never showed affection, he just threw money at me as if that would solve everything. My therapist says that emotional avoidance is a contributing factor to addiction! Dad owed it to me to at least *try* and bear witness to my trauma.'

'He was a man of his time,' Carolyn said, patting the pocket of her cardigan and pulling out a linen handkerchief. She dabbed at her eyes. 'You think he was running around the place, telling *me* he loved me? Of course not. But I knew by his actions that he did.'

'Why are you defending him?' Sam scrambled to her feet, glaring at her mother. 'He was jealous of your success. He hated your career, he—'

'He was a good man. He wanted . . . oh, Sam. He wanted so badly for things to be different for you. He tried his best, you know he did. And you're right, my job was hard for him. He'd been brought up to believe that the man takes care of his wife and he felt as if he had failed in some way because I didn't want to be taken care of, not like that. I *wanted* to work.'

'And he should have been supportive of that!' Sam said. 'Why are you defending him?'

'He was a good man,' Carolyn repeated. 'And a good father.' Sam laughed harshly and her mother shouted, 'Stop that! He *adored* you, Samantha. We only moved to this godforsaken town because he wanted you to have the childhood he could have only dreamed of when he was a kid. He phoned that school every evening to check in on you and you never took his calls. You wouldn't come home for Thanksgiving or Christmas, you never sent him so much as a birthday card. He insisted we pay your rent for *years*, that dump in Brooklyn and then that one-bed in Chelsea—'

'Only because he didn't believe in me!' Sam hadn't wanted to take his money, but she couldn't afford to work at the magazine otherwise, not with the pittance they were paying her. She'd felt a hot flush of shame on the first of every month when the check was deposited in her account, the constant reminder that her father thought she was incapable of succeeding without his help. 'It was humiliating!'

'Oh, stop acting like a spoiled brat. Your father grew up poor,' her mother said tightly. 'He had *nothing*. Even after he got the scholarship to Harvard, he felt like an outsider, and that certainly wasn't helped by the way my parents treated him. Did he have a chip on his shoulder? Maybe. But he was determined that you would never feel the same way, Sam. He wanted you to have everything you ever wanted. He worried about you all the time. And when . . .' Carolyn squeezed her eyes shut, as if she couldn't bear to remember. 'We hadn't heard from you in weeks. He couldn't sleep, he was up all night pacing. *Something's wrong*, he kept saying. He insisted on driving into the city and he went to your apartment. Your neighbour said you hadn't come out in days. Nate thought you were dead, he thought . . .'

This was the story Sam had heard later, during their family therapy sessions. Her father had banged on the apartment door, so hard that his knuckles bled. Then he panicked, driving into the wood with his shoulder, screaming out with the pain. The door half came off its hinges, and he rushed inside. *Samantha*, he shouted. *Where are you?* He found her on the bathroom floor, in a dirty T-shirt and panties, unconscious. He called 911 and waited for an ambulance to come, holding her limp hand as he prayed to a god he didn't believe in to save his daughter. After Samantha's stomach was pumped, the doctor explained to her parents that she had suffered an accidental overdose – given the level of cocaine, sleeping pills and OxyContin in her system, she should be dead – and Nate Miller decided there and then that Sam would have to go to rehab.

'I didn't want you to go,' Carolyn said now, wiping her eyes. 'I didn't want people knowing our daughter was a *drug addict*. But Nate said the most important thing was that you were alive. All he wanted was for you to be happy.'

'You can't actually believe any of that.' Sam crossed her arms. 'Dad wanted me out of the way, and making me go to that shithole rehab was the most convenient way to do it. I've spent my entire life chasing after emotionally unavailable men because the father figure I had in my formative years was—'

'Jesus Christ. You're forty years of age, Samantha. When are you going to stop blaming us and take responsibility for yourself? Or maybe that doesn't suit this "narrative" you've created to make yourself sound . . . I don't know. More interesting?

More tortured? You said it yourself, you needed a good backstory.'

'That was just about the school,' she protested. This was so typical of her mother, to use something Sam had said when she was feeling vulnerable and turn it against her. 'But this is my truth, Mom. You have to respect that.'

'If it's not *the* truth, what's the point?' her mother asked, but Sam didn't answer. She sat at the vanity table and pumped cleanser into her palms, massaging it on to her face until it was clean again. She began to reapply her make-up – the glowing skin, the plump lips, the arched eyebrows – painting her beauty back on, like it was armour.

'Please don't go to this party,' Carolyn said, but her voice was weak, as if she knew she had already lost the argument. 'Haven't they hurt you enough?'

Sam caught her mother's eye in the mirror. 'I am, as you so kindly reminded me, an adult now. I know what's best for me. And what's best right now is that I persuade Lisa to sign a statement saying the Reddit post is false. Then I can go back to my life in the city and forget about all of this.' *But what about the lawsuit? What about Gabriel? What if he won't leave you alone?* that little voice whispered, but Sam pushed it away. Lisa was the key to fixing everything; she had to be. Sam had no other options left. 'Isn't that what you want too?'

'I want you to be happy,' her mother said. 'And I don't think this is the way to do it.'

'And I think you're wrong about that,' Sam said, fluffing out her hair. She looked beautiful and terrifying all at once, a Valkyrie riding to battle. 'I'm going to that party.'

35.

February 2000

Sam was gripping the sides of the sink and she let go. A mistake, she thought, as she stumbled on her heels. She grabbed hold of it again and tried to make eye contact with her reflection. The plastic tiara was caught in a tangle of hair and the pearl rosary necklace had broken off; she wasn't sure where it had gone and her costume didn't look right without it.

Someone banged on the door – 'Come on!' a high-pitched voice whined outside. 'Some of us are, like, dying to pee here!' and then another girl, saying, 'What about the toilets upstairs?'

'They're locked,' the first girl said. 'This is the only one we can use.'

A fist on the door again: 'Hurry up!'

Sam had just made herself get sick, forcing two fingers down her throat. She'd skipped dinner – *eating is cheating*, she'd texted Becky earlier – because her dress was so tight, the material clinging to her body, and she wanted people to think she looked thin in it. Or, to be precise, she wanted *Josh* to think she looked thin. Wasn't this what he wanted? A girl made up of edges? Josh, who was dressed as Brad Pitt in *Fight Club*, with a cigarette hanging from his lips, his bare chest daubed in fake blood. The heat in her lower belly when she saw him, how fierce her need tasted. She had pulled Lisa into the hallway, where some friend of a friend had set up his decks and was blaring Fatboy Slim, and they'd danced together, twin visions in their silk dresses and diamanté crowns. She'd watched him as he watched them, eyes moving from one girl to the other. He had looked perplexed, as if he wasn't sure which one of them he wanted.

'It's ridiculous,' she heard the girl outside say. *Becky*, she realized, that's who it was. 'Like, shouldn't it be her and Josh in a couples costume? It's so weird.'

'I know. They act more like a couple than Josh and Lisa do.' The first girl's voice dropped. 'What does Brandon think of it?'

'Does Brandon *think*?' Becky replied. 'He's just happy to get some. They don't call her Samantha Sucks for nothing.'

Sam flushed the toilet, washing her hands and rubbing mascara smudges from under her eyes. 'Hi girls,' she said. It was Becky and Jessica Simmons standing outside, both dressed as Britney Spears in knee-high socks and fluffy pink pigtails.

Becky stuttered when she saw who it was – 'I, I, I didn't—' and Sam put a hand up to stop her.

'I can't believe you would say that about me,' she said, her voice cracking. 'I thought you were my friend, Becky.'

Jessica winced. 'Oh my god, Sam, we didn't know you were in there. We were just kidding, we . . .' She went to hug her, wrapping her arm around Sam's shoulders.

'You didn't say anything,' she whispered. 'It was *her*.'

She waited until Jessica had stood back before she allowed herself to look at the other girl. 'Why are you always so mean to me, Becky?' she said, touching her baby fingers to the inside corners of her eyes to stop the tears from smudging her makeup. 'You're such a bully.'

'What?' Becky gasped, looking to Jessica for support, but she just sipped her drink, eyes wide. 'That's not true!'

Becky grabbed at Sam as she pushed past but Sam wrenched her arm away. As she walked off, she could hear Jessica admonishing the other girl – 'Not cool, B,' and Becky's breathless defence, 'That's not fair, I didn't' – and Sam tilted her head up, sniffing back tears. *'What a bitch.'* She would have to talk to Lisa about this; Becky couldn't be trusted, not if she was going to be saying shit like that behind Sam's back.

'Hey guys,' she said, flipping her hair over her shoulder when she saw Chris and Brandon still sitting on the stairs, passing another joint between them.

'Miller! You want some?' Brandon asked, but she shook her head.

'I'm good,' she said and he shrugged, putting it back between his lips.

'You sure? That shit is tight.' He half coughed, handing it to Chris again.

'Have you guys seen Lisa?' she asked. 'I told her to wait here for me.'

Chris flicked ash into his beer can. 'She and Josh went upstairs,' he said, holding his hand out to Brandon for a high-five. 'Dude's gonna get lucky tonight.' They both cracked up, clearly high.

'Cool,' Sam said. 'Enjoy yourselves, guys.'

She forced herself to walk up the stairs slowly, as if she was calm and had all the time in the world, but the dread was swelling thick in her chest. She had thought it would be better if they did it here for the first time so she would feel involved, so she would feel important, but that was a mistake. She couldn't allow them to have sex, she realized, it was the only tie Sam still had to Josh that her friend did not. Once that was gone, what would she have left? What would make her special in Josh's eyes then?

She checked her bedroom, finding it empty. Her parents' room was locked, but down the hall she could see a light on in the smaller guest bedroom. She tiptoed towards the door, ear pressed against the wood – why was she always the one standing in the shadows, listening to other people live their lives? she wondered – and she tested the handle; they hadn't locked it and it opened easily. 'Fuck,' Lisa hissed. She was sitting on the bed, her dress up around her hips, while Josh was kneeling on the ground before her, his head beneath her legs. She bucked away, pulling the hem of the dress down, and Josh looked up, his lips glistening.

'Oops,' Sam said but she didn't leave, turning to close the door behind her and giving them a second to tidy up. When she faced them again, Josh was glowering at her, and Lisa was fixing her hair, her cheeks and chest flushed red. They stood at one side of the bed and Sam at the other, and she didn't like that. It should have been her and Josh together, or her and Lisa; *she* was the one they should have chosen, not each other.

'Can we help you?' Josh said, his voice clipped.

'It's just' – she reached into her bra, pulling out the plastic baggie she'd tucked inside there earlier – 'I got a lil somethin' for the three of us.'

'What is that?' Lisa asked, peering at it.

'It's your birthday present, Mouse,' Sam said, sticking out her tongue and waiting for Lisa to copy her. She placed the pill in her friend's mouth, the faint outline of a dove on one side, a single line fracturing the other. She put one on her own tongue too, gagging at the acrid taste. 'What about you?' She raised an eyebrow at Josh. 'You don't want to be the odd one out, do you?' And he grabbed the bag from her, swallowing the remaining pill without a word.

'What happens now?' Lisa asked nervously.

'We wait,' Sam replied.

36.

She rang the doorbell to the Taylors' house, ignoring the nerves slithering in the pit of her stomach. She smoothed her hair down, watching through the glass panel as a body came towards her.

'Hey,' she said brightly when one of the blonde women from the school gates answered. Sam held her breath for a second, afraid of the reaction she might receive, but the woman didn't seem shocked to see her; there was no expression of disgust, no attempt to close the door in Sam's face.

Instead, she gasped with delight. 'Hello!' she said. 'Come in, come in.'

'How are *you*?' Sam cooed, hoping the woman wouldn't realize she'd forgotten her name. 'And how are the little ones?'

'Oh, they're having an awesome time! It's like a wonderland in the back yard,' she replied, making a face that Sam was familiar with from her mom friends in the city, the *my kids are so adorable* face, even if said children were breaking Sam's furniture or performing hara-kiri on their screaming siblings. 'I just adore that dress,' she said as Sam threw her snake-print leather trench on the back of a chair. 'Where's it from?'

Sam waved her off airily. 'It's this little Italian brand I discovered when I was on book tour in Europe,' she said. 'You wouldn't know it—' She paused. 'Nicole?' she guessed and the other woman smiled.

The French doors between the kitchen and the dining room

were thrown open, people gathered in small groups to chat, grabbing champagne and arancini balls from the passing waiters. She couldn't see the musicians but she could hear them, her skin prickling with goosebumps when she realized it was 'Rebel Girl' picked out in delicate strings. *That girl, she holds her head up so high. I think I wanna be her best friend, yeah.* What were the chances that this song would be playing when she walked in? It had to be a sign from the Universe that she was doing the right thing, she was sure of it.

'Samantha,' Nicole said, touching her arm. 'Did you hear me?'

Sam shook her head. 'I'm sorry,' she said. 'I was distracted by the music.'

She had led Sam to the nook off the kitchen which the twins used as a playroom; it had been cleaned up today, all of the toys and books and jigsaws packed away. There were a couple of women there – was that Jessica Simmons? She looked so old, her skin crinkling around her eyes, her forehead a mass of deep wrinkles. And there *she* was too, her mouth tight with fear as she saw Sam walk towards them.

'Look who it is!' Sam paused and Becky visibly braced herself, waiting for Sam to tell the other women about her dirty little secret. Sam leaned in, as if to whisper in Becky's ear, inwardly smiling when she gulped loudly. 'There,' she said, picking a piece of lint off Becky's shoulder. 'Perfect.'

The women all wore similar dresses, fitted sheaths with lace sleeves, blood-red pedicures in open-toed court shoes. 'We hear you're responsible for all this,' Nicole said. 'My fortieth is next month if you're interested.' She and Jessica Simmons giggled as if this was the funniest joke they'd ever heard.

'More champagne, ladies?' A waiter held out a tray. He was young, maybe mid-twenties, his body lean and his dirty-blond hair slicked back from his face.

'Yes, please,' Sam said, holding his gaze as she took a glass.

There was a moment between them, a rush of something moving through her, and she didn't know why she had denied herself this for so long. This power, this understanding that she could weaponize her face and her body to make people respond to her in whatever way she wanted. It was delicious.

'Phew,' Nicole said when the waiter moved away, pretending to fan herself. 'You could cut the sexual tension between you two with a knife. You are so *bad.*' She leaned in and Sam could smell the brined salmon from her breath. Was this what she would have become if she had stayed in Bennford? A middle-aged housewife wearing two pairs of Spanx and a dress she'd found on sale in T.J. Maxx? The waiter would never have looked at her like that then, a glint of promise in his eye. Wasn't that what she had wanted? To be different? To be *special*.

Nicole nodded at Sam's glass. 'I thought you didn't drink?'

'Technically, I was a drug addict,' Sam said. 'Not an alcoholic. Unless there are plates of cocaine being passed around, I'm good.'

'That's not funny,' Becky said, looking behind her. They could see the kids in the garden through the window, their faces painted like tigers and pirates and unicorns. The magician was pulling a rabbit out of his top hat, and the two nannies occasionally glanced up from their iPhones to check everyone's limbs were still attached. 'This is a *family party*,' she continued. 'There are no drugs here. I don't know what kind of people you hang out with in the city, but in Bennford we don't—'

'Chill out. It was a joke.' Sam rolled her eyes at the other two women and Nicole drawled, 'Yeah, lighten up, Becky,' a half-glance at Sam to see if she had her approval.

'It's Rebecca,' Becky tried weakly, but no one was paying attention. Jessica and Nicole moved closer to Sam, touching the cape sleeves of her dress, asking where did she get her shoes, her bag was Alexander McQueen, wasn't it? She gathered her hair in a knot at the back of her neck, tossing it over one shoulder, and that was when she saw them. Josh and Lisa, standing by the breakfast bar. Josh hadn't shaved; there was a shadow of stubble on his face, and his jaw was working furiously as he stared at her. Lisa was wearing a midnight-blue velvet jumpsuit, her hair styled in a milkmaid braid, and her expression was miserable, her cheekbones prominent in her thin face. Watching Josh watch Samantha, for once. It had been the other way around for long enough, Sam thought as she raised a glass at them in greeting, smiling her hello.

'Is Lisa OK?' she asked out of the side of her mouth. 'She looks . . .'

'Poor Lisa. She can be a bit up and down, you know,' Jessica said. 'Some days she's great, and then there are weeks where . . .' She made a face. 'It's the twins I feel sorry for. And Josh too, of course.'

'That's not fair,' Becky said sharply. 'Lisa's been through a lot.'

'Yeah, sure,' Jessica replied, only half listening. Her gaze drifted over Sam's face, down her body. 'You really do look good, don't you?' she said. 'I was hoping it was just Photoshop or filters or something. It's depressing.' She waved her empty glass at the waiter, beckoning him to come over. 'Bottoms up, girls,' she said, taking a swig from the new glass.

They talked about their kids then, the math tutor who had worked *wonders* for Nicole's son, the tennis classes in Stambury which were *impossible* to get into, a book on child psychology every mother simply *had* to read, it was *transformative*. 'I can't believe Abigail is starting high school in the fall,' Jessica said. 'How is that possible?'

'When Mommy and Daddy love each other very much,' Sam began, and they laughed eagerly.

'Ha, ha,' Jessica said. 'But you guys know what I mean.' She turned to the others. 'Girls can be such bitches at that age. Do you remember when someone spread a rumour in Senior Year that I' – she dropped her voice – 'had sex with Brandon and Chris? Like, *together.*'

'What?' Sam ignored Becky's death-stare. 'I never heard that.'

'It obviously wasn't true,' Jessica said. 'But everyone went along with it anyway. And it wasn't the boys who ostracized me, you know? It was the girls.' Her eyes were glistening with unshed tears. 'I'm fine,' she said when Nicole rubbed her back, making soothing noises under her breath. 'It was years ago. It's just with Abi . . . it's bringing it all back, I guess.'

Sam sighed. 'After the month I've had, I can safely say I know a little something about unsubstantiated rumours,' she said. The other women were visibly shocked she'd brought it up, then quickly murmured, *Yeah, I heard about that* and *It's so terrible* and *People think they can say whatever they want on the internet these days.*

'Absolutely,' Sam said. 'Although I do try to have compassion for the trolls.' A smile at Becky, watching the ugly flush creeping up her face. 'They must have no lives of their own. It's pathetic, really.' Becky looked at the ground, gripping the stem of the coupe glass so tightly she might shatter it. 'Girls aren't born inherently bitchy,' Sam continued. 'It's a learned behaviour. So much of the work that I do – with Shakti, especially – is offering a new model of what it means to be a woman. I want young girls to see their female peers as collaborators rather than competitors. That's crucial if we want to enact real change, don't you think?'

'Oh my god, you're amazing!' Jessica said, and Nicole fell over herself to agree. They gushed about how great Sam was, how grateful they were she was doing this work; their daughters were lucky to be growing up in a world where companies like Shakti existed and that was all thanks to Sam.

'You're too kind.' Sam tucked her white envelope clutch into her ribcage. 'But if you'll excuse me, ladies, I must use the restroom.'

She moved through the crowd, her elbow grabbed by one woman and then another, saying how much her books had meant to them, the impact her work had had on their lives. They told their stories in quick, urgent whispers – the man who followed them home from the subway, the man who pressed his body against theirs in the copy-room and pretended it was an accident, the man who said he loved them while breaking their fingers, one by one. The memories were carved into their bones, echoing in their ears as they tried to fall asleep at night. 'I'm haunted by him,' one woman said. 'And I bet he doesn't even remember my name.' Sam held their hands and reminded them of how strong they were; they were more than women, they were warriors.

'You are braver than you know,' she said, reciting her lines off by heart, for this happened every time she left the house. These women and the worst things that had ever happened to them. Their darkest secrets, spilling so easily, showing Sam their fractured bones in the hope that she would mend them. 'Believe in yourself,' she said, 'and nobody can hurt you ever again.' Maybe that was what she was selling; the impossible promise of safety. Maybe that was all these women wanted, in the end.

When she finally reached the bathroom, she sat on the toilet checking her phone, but there was still no reply from her manager. She flushed, pulling her underwear up. In the mirror, she watched herself as she drank the glass of champagne in one gulp. What would her therapist say if she could see Sam now? Or her old NA sponsor? Would they be disappointed in her?

'Oh,' she said when she walked out and found Josh standing there, waiting for her. 'Hey. Are you enjoying the party?'

'What,' Josh asked her through gritted teeth, 'and I cannot stress this enough, *the fuck* are you doing here?'

'It's my best friend's birthday, how could I miss it?' she said, twirling a piece of hair around her finger like she did in high school. 'After all, I did pay for everything. But you're used to me paying for things that should be your responsibility, aren't you?'

His face twisted as if he was trying out different responses in his mouth, seeing which one tasted the best. Finally, he spat out, 'Fuck you, Samantha,' but it was feeble; he sounded more afraid than anything else. He pushed her back in the bathroom. 'I saw your post on Instagram about the party but I thought to myself, there's no way she has the balls to turn up today. Not after we expressly told her we didn't want her to come. And yet here you are!' His eyes flashed with anger. 'Why can't you let us alone? I don't want to make a scene, not today. This is Lisa's birthday and she's been through enough. But it's time for you to—'

'You always hated me and Lisa being friends, didn't you?' she cut in. 'You'd do anything to keep us apart, even now. You're afraid of me, Josh. Admit it.'

'Afraid of you? It was *twenty-two years ago*.' He dropped his voice to a furious whisper. 'When are you going to get over it? The rest of us have moved on, Sam. When will you do the same?'

'Maybe I'll "get over" it when you take responsibility for once in your life,' she hissed back. 'You piece of—'

'Oh, sorry,' a woman said, pushing the door open. 'I didn't know there was anyone—*Josh?*'

It was Becky, her gaze darting between the two of them, and Sam felt such a flash of fury, the only thing that would sate it would be to lash out and strike the other woman across the face. But she couldn't do that in front of Josh. It would only give him a legitimate reason to kick her out. She had to behave herself, for now.

'What's going on here?' Becky asked.

'Nothing,' Josh said brusquely. He pushed past her, and there was a trace of cologne in his wake, something cut with musk, a present from Lisa, perhaps, or the girls. The perfect gift for the perfect father. When he was gone, Sam turned to the mirror, checking her make-up.

'I don't think Lisa would be happy to see you in here alone with her husband.'

Sam leaned against the sink. 'Oh really?' she asked. 'And what would you know about what Lisa wants?' She raised an eyebrow, waiting for Becky to beg for forgiveness, like she did when they were teenagers.

'Lisa's my friend.'

'I'm not sure if that's going to be true for much longer. Not after I have a little chat with her about everything.'

'Are you going to tell her?' Becky asked, swallowing.

'I haven't decided yet,' Sam said, a corner of her mouth quirking up. 'Anyway. I'd better get back to the party.'

Becky held her hand out to block the door. 'Fuck that. You're not leaving,' she said. 'Not until you apologize to me for everything you did in high school. You hurt me, Sam.'

'What about how *you* hurt me? Talking shit about me at Lisa's eighteenth? "Samantha Sucks", wasn't that it?'

'What are you talking about?'

'Oh, please,' Sam said impatiently. 'I was in the toilet, you and Jessica were on the other side of the door in your Britney costumes – slutty schoolgirls, *ground-breaking* – and you said all the boys at school called me Samantha Sucks because I gave such good head.'

Becky stared at her, open-mouthed. 'You're crazy,' she said, and she backed away, as if she was afraid. 'You're actually crazy. That's not what happened. I wasn't even dressed as Britney at the party. I went as Wednesday Addams. And besides, I doubt you went to the restroom by yourself all night; you wouldn't let Lisa out of your sight for two seconds. What were you afraid was going to happen? That she and Josh might actually get a second alone? It was tragic.'

'Oh, sweetheart,' Sam said slowly, for she knew this woman so well, she knew where the scar tissue was tender. 'I'm not the tragic one here. Look at me. I'm rich. I'm beautiful. And most importantly, no matter what happened between us, Lisa actually loved me. Can you say the same?' She tapped her fingers against her lower lip. 'Do you know what she told me last week? She said you were stuck in high school, always trying to get the "old gang" back together. Lisa doesn't like you, Becky, she *tolerates* you. The same way we tolerated you in high school.'

'That's not true,' Becky said, her voice wavering. 'That's not . . .'

'But you know it *is* true, don't you? Deep down, you know no one likes you. No one even wanted you here today, Becky. Maybe you should just go home.' Sam checked her reflection again, tousling her hair, then turned to leave.

'I saw you that night, you know,' Becky called after her. Sam went very still, wondering what she was about to say. 'I saw what you guys did.'

'Me and Lisa?' she asked, and she was almost glad of it; there would be a witness, then, an alibi, someone who could prove that Sam was telling the truth. Maybe Becky had seen how Lisa had been the one who touched Sam first. How Sam had said, 'I don't know how to do that, I've never—' and how Lisa had hushed her.

'It's OK, Mouse,' her friend had said then, pressing her mouth against Sam's. 'I'll show you.'

'Not exactly,' Becky said. 'I followed you upstairs at the party. And I saw you. You, Josh and Lisa.'

'I don't know what you're—'

'I saw the three of you together,' Becky said. 'I know what you did.'

37.

Sam didn't know who had started it that night, whose idea it had been in the first place. It was such a long time ago. All she could remember now was the drugs faltering in their veins and the three of them stripping their clothes off because they were too hot, their nakedness almost incidental. Someone had touched her first, or had she touched them? She couldn't remember. But it was all she had wanted, she'd realized, as Josh moved inside her while Lisa kissed her gently. Sam had needed them to love her most of all. She'd needed to be the home they both returned to.

'So that's how you get your kicks.' Sam affected a bored tone, turning back to Becky. 'Creeping around, spying on other people. God. You're even more pathetic than I thought.'

'I didn't—' Becky's face was burning. 'I didn't stay there and *watch* or anything. I left straight away; I was in shock.'

'Sure you did.' Sam adjusted the fringed hemline of her dress, trying to buy herself time. Besides her therapist, Gabriel was the only person to whom she had ever told that story. The hot, sticky evening in his tiny apartment in the 17th arrondissement, when he had whispered, *Tell me your fantasies, Sami.* His surprised laugh then, an arched eyebrow as if he could not quite believe it. 'You are full of surprises,' he said.

Later, when she'd gathered up enough courage to tell him she wasn't certain about what had happened that night with him and his friends, Gabriel had smiled, pulling her close. 'But you said you liked to share, non?' he'd whispered into her ear. 'I thought that's what you wanted.'

'Here's the thing.' Sam paused, taking a step closer to the other woman. '*Rebecca*. You should be very, very careful about what you say next. It was such a long time ago, wasn't it? And we were all drinking that night. I don't know about you, but I was wasted. How can you be sure that you're remembering it right? That's a pretty big claim to make if you're not one hundred per cent certain.'

'I know what I saw.' Becky's mouth was set.

'What exactly did you see? Three people lying on a bed? We were probably just asleep. It was a high school rager, not a sex party.' She rolled her eyes. 'You can say whatever you want about me, but do you honestly believe that *Josh and Lisa* were having threesomes in Senior Year? It was Bennford, not the Upper East Side.'

Becky hesitated. 'But I thought . . . No, I'm almost certain that—'

'Why don't you go and ask them?' Sam stepped aside, gesturing at Becky to walk past. 'Go right on up to them and say, hey guys, quick question – *did the two of you fuck Samantha Miller at the same time twenty-two years ago?*' Her voice was mocking, making it sound utterly ridiculous. 'I can't *wait* to hear their response.'

'I'm not going to just . . .' Becky stuttered. 'I wasn't going to do it like—'

'I wonder what everyone else will think,' Sam interrupted. 'Knowing you've made up this . . . *fantasy* for yourself.' She paused, and Becky blushed so violently she looked as if she might be having a stroke. It was just too easy. Sam put her finger to her lips and murmured, 'Ssh.' 'Maybe it's for the best if we keep this little story between us, hmm?'

When she returned to the party, the string quartet was playing 'Jump Around', everyone a little loose around the edges. A hint of a slurred word, champagne slopped on to suit lapels and dripping into décolletages. Sam gestured at the hot waiter, taking another two glasses from him with a wink. She knew she was drinking too quickly, her voice becoming louder, her laugh more insistent, but she didn't care. Josh and Lisa were huddled in the corner of the kitchen, their faces tight, but everyone else found her charming, the way they always had since she'd become famous. Her every joke was hilarious, her every thought profound. It was one of the best things about being a celebrity, she'd always thought, having a captive audience. Becky had disappeared, gone home to lick her wounds, Sam presumed, but she discovered Brandon Green and Chris Williams by the chocolate fountain, still best friends, it turned out, although Chris's hairline had abandoned him, receding further and further away from his forehead, and Brandon's football muscles had thawed to fat. After a few jokes about her memoir ('I can't believe I only got a one-line mention!' Brandon complained. 'Did I mean nothing to you, Miller?'), they coaxed her into telling stories about the most famous people she'd ever met.

'And that's when I told Jay,' Sam said, 'if you're gonna buy a basketball team, at least make it one people have heard of. The goddamn Knicks would be better than that bullshit.'

'Wow,' Brandon said, his eyes bright. 'I can't believe you're friends with Jay-Z and Beyoncé.'

'Oh,' Sam psshed him. 'I don't think anyone is actually "friends" with Jay and B. I had to sign, like, a *serious* NDA before that party.'

'Still,' he said. 'It's awesome. You've really made it, Sam.'

She smiled at him, then glanced over at their wives, Jessica and some woman she'd never met before, lean and hungry in their tight dresses, pretending not to care that Samantha Miller was flirting with their husbands.

'So, tell me. Which of those Rugrats are yours?' She pointed out of the window to the crowd of kids racing around the back yard, high on sugar and corn syrup. The two men followed her gaze, trying to find their children among the mass of bodies.

'I need my glasses,' Chris muttered, while Brandon complained about the face paint confusing him, saying, 'Four of my five are out there somewhere.'

'Five kids! You don't mess around, do you?'

'Don't get me started,' he groaned. 'Abi, my oldest, is the only one not here. She's at home making TikToks or whatever it is fourteen-year-old girls do in their spare time.' He took a sip of his beer. 'She's a mystery to me.'

'Teenage girls were always a mystery to you, Green.'

She laughed and she thought she saw something stirring in his eyes when Chris said, suddenly, 'There he is! The dude with the Spider-Man face paint. That's Jackson.'

'He's cute.' Jackson tugged at the end of the nanny's sweater. 'The poor girl,' Sam said as the young woman picked the little boy up, settling him on her hip. 'Pamela Anderson's body but that face, *yikes.*' Chris and Brandon cracked up and Sam took another swig of her champagne, trying to drown the guilt needling her. *This is why you shouldn't drink. You say bad things. You do bad things. What would your girls think if they could see you now?*

'So.' She nudged Brandon in the ribs. 'You and Jessica Simmons. Well, well, well.'

'I haven't heard anyone call her Jessica Simmons in a while,' he said, self-conscious. 'But yeah' – he held up his hand, showing the ring on his fourth finger – 'sixteen years next May.'

She licked the corner of her mouth and saw him notice it, his eyes on her lips, then darting away again. 'There was me thinking you had carried a torch for me all this time.' She laughed, expecting Brandon and Chris to do the same, but they just stared at her, taken aback. She laughed again – *I'm just kidding!* – but even she could hear how strained it was. Brandon cut his eyes at Chris, as if saying, *Man, did that just happen?* and Sam knew she'd badly misjudged the situation. She never did that when she was sober; she was always so careful, trying to figure out what it was people wanted from her and giving them exactly that, watching as they fell in love with her, or more precisely, fell in love with the way she made them feel.

'Ehh, speaking of wives,' Chris said, looking over his shoulder. 'I'd better go find mine. It was great seeing you, Sam.' He looked her up and down. 'You really do look good, you know.'

'It was just a joke,' she said to Brandon when Chris was gone. 'Can't anyone in this town take a joke any more?'

'Sure we can.'

She licked her lips again, taking another sip of her champagne. 'Sam,' he started, then wavered. 'Are you all right?'

'Of course I'm all right. I'm great,' she said, looking around for the waiter. 'If I could just get another drink, I'd be fan-fucking-tastic.'

'No, I mean it.' He was staring at her, an expression of pity on his face. 'You don't seem like yourself.'

'Oh, really? And how would you know? We dated, like, a million years ago. A lot of things have changed since then, haven't they, Brandon?' She dropped her gaze to the folds of his soft belly and he flushed, pulling at his striped shirt and standing up straighter. 'Like I said, it was just a stupid joke. I was never that into you anyway, it was . . .' She trailed off.

'Don't worry, it was pretty clear who you were into,' Brandon said wryly, glancing over at Josh. 'But I still cared about you. I always knew you'd be a big deal, Sam, even when we were kids. You were unstoppable.' He stuffed his hands in his pockets, frowning. 'You know, I was excited to see you today.

Just to congratulate you on everything, tell ya how proud we all are of you. But you're different to how I thought you'd be, you're . . .'

'I'm what, Brandon?' she said, clutching her empty glass. 'Please do enlighten me.'

'You seem lost.' He touched her shoulder briefly then cleared his throat in embarrassment. 'I hope you find whatever it is you're looking for, Miller.' He left her alone and went over to Jessica Simmons, muttering something. Self-loathing tore through her, gutting her insides. She was next to the table covered in a white linen cloth, and she stared at the multiple three-tier cake stands laden down with cupcakes, 'Lisa's 40th' scribbled in pink icing. She imagined taking a tray and bringing it to the bathroom, sitting on the cold floor while she devoured each one, trying to fill the wasteland burning empty inside her.

Her phone beeped and she opened her clutch to grab it, performing her role as a Very Busy Woman for anyone who was watching and wondering why Samantha Miller was standing by herself. She hoped it was Jane but it was just an email from Equinox, informing her that a place in their 7 a.m. Reformer Pilates class had become available. She tapped out a message to her manager (*I'm at Lisa's party. Should have her statement soon. Let's talk strategy afterwards*) and then scrolled through her inbox, waiting for a reply that never came.

She looked up and saw Josh, taking the birthday cake that *she* had paid for from the fridge. He grabbed a pack of candles from a drawer and began sticking them in haphazardly. When they were all lit, he moved towards Lisa, his mouth open to start singing, and Sam panicked. She had to prove to Lisa that she loved her before it was too late. She rushed into the centre of the room, clapping her hands to get everyone's attention.

'Hi, you guys,' she cried, using her best stage voice. All the guests turned to her and Josh stopped, the cake still in his hands. He returned it to the countertop, blowing out the candles. 'I just wanted to say a few words,' Sam said, waving at the quartet to cut the music. 'Thank you all for coming today, I know my girl really appreciates it. Right, Mouse?' She raised her glass at Lisa as the guests cheered, *Happy Birthday!* Josh was behind his wife now, his hands on her waist, and she leaned into him, her face tense. 'As many of you know, Lisa and I have been best friends since we were— Oh my god, how long is it? Mrs Johnson, you'll know?' She looked into the crowd for Lisa's mother, smiling as the older woman held up four fingers. 'Since we were four? I feel old now,' she said, pretending to wipe sweat off her brow. 'We grew up together, our houses were side by side over on Elliot Street. Our bedroom windows were actually directly opposite one another so we'd lean out and yell, *Hey Mouse, whatcha doing?* The neighbours loved that, as you can imagine.'

She paused to allow some polite titters. 'I was an only child but I never felt lonely because Lisa was my soul sister.' The guests *aww*-ed at this and she could see some pointing their phones at her to record this moment, and she straightened up, tilting her chin so she would look thin in the videos. 'We did everything together – our moms used to joke that we must have been separated at birth. And I know we drifted apart after high school, which is something that happens to a lot of us,' she said, gesturing at the guests as if to say, *right?* before remembering that most of the people here had never left Bennford. They saw their old classmates every day, at the gym and the school gates, at the grocery store or at church. She recalibrated, saying, 'But really, what this has taught me is that the friends we have from childhood are more important than *any* we could meet afterwards,' and she saw them nod at this. They liked that, they liked being told they were correct to stay here, that there was nothing for them beyond the boundaries of this town.

'I'm so happy to have Lisa back in my life. As some of you will know, I haven't been home in a while.' Chris pretended to boo at that, his wife telling him to be quiet. 'But when I came back this time,' Sam said, 'I found something under my bed.' She caught Lisa's eye. *Remember? Remember how you would come into my room and I would be hiding there? You would duck down and join me, holding my hand?* She reached into her handbag, pulling out a clutch of pages, waving them in the air. 'Look at these! They're letters Lisa wrote me when I went to Utah to repeat Senior Year. Now, you'll be glad to hear I only brought the PG-13 ones!' She winked at a stony-faced Josh.

'Here goes,' she said, unfolding one of the pages. ' "I miss you so much, Mouse",' she read aloud. ' "Things are not the same without you. I feel so lonely . . . When will I see you again? Everything is better when you're here." ' She pursed her mouth at the crowd. 'I know,' she said as they all murmured *aww* again. 'So cute, right? And there are, like, dozens of them. Lisa' – she turned to the other woman – 'you were the best friend a girl could ask for. I feel blessed to have you in my life and I can't wait to see what the future holds for us both. I hope your forties are your best decade yet and they bring you love, light and healing. OK, everybody.' She held her glass aloft, gesturing at the guests to do the same. 'It's time for a toast! Happy Birthday, Lisa!' And they all chorused, *Happy Birthday!*

The string quartet picked up their instruments, falling into the Birthday Song as fast as they could. 'The cake,' Sam mouthed at Josh but he just stared at her, dumbfounded. She walked towards them, her eyes on Lisa, waiting for her friend to rush and embrace her. But Lisa didn't move; she didn't react to any of the guests hugging her, wishing her a happy birthday.

'Well,' Sam grinned, kissing her friend on the cheek. 'Are you enjoying your party, Mouse?' She looked around. 'I think we can call this an unqualified success.'

Josh's hand was there, pushing her away from Lisa, and she stumbled, hissing at him to be careful.

'What are you doing?' he said, but Lisa told him to leave it, she would handle it.

'Just keep my mom distracted, OK?' she told him under her breath.

'You'll handle what, exactly?' Sam asked through a fake smile, mouthing *thank you* at a guest a few metres away who shouted, 'That was a beautiful speech!' in their direction.

'Why don't we get the cake?' Lisa said, pretending to smile too, and the two of them huddled in the corner, their backs to the room. 'Show me those letters,' Lisa said as Sam struck a match, relighting the candles. She handed her friend the clutch bag, watching as Lisa snatched the crumpled papers, rifling through them, her eyes scanning from top to bottom.

'Oh, Mouse,' Sam said. 'These letters reminded me of how much we loved each other. We did love each other, didn't we? You have to remember that.'

Lisa's hands shook, dropping the letters. Sam crouched down to pick them up from the floor. 'Be careful,' she said, stuffing them back into her bag. 'Those are precious to me.'

'Sam,' Lisa said in a low voice. 'I didn't write those.'

'What?'

'I didn't write any of them. You did,' Lisa said, and Sam grabbed one of the letters, reading it again. They were typed out, addressed to Mouse and from Mouse, the same Comic Sans font on every single one. 'All of those letters are from you,' Lisa said, and she was afraid, Sam could hear it in her voice. Lisa was afraid of *her*. 'Did you hear me, Sam? They're all from you.'

38.

Her father's hand on the top of her head as she slumped in the armchair, staring out of her bedroom window for the last time. How pale the sky was today, she thought, just the faintest whisper of blue. Nate Miller smelled as he always did, of expensive aftershave and the cigarettes he swore to his wife that he had quit years before.

'I'll miss you,' he said. A deep sigh, coming from the centre of him, as if it was being dragged from his gut. 'Oh, kid. Your mother told me . . .' He stopped and there was silence until he muttered, 'I don't know what to say.' Her father took his hand away, but she could still feel the warmth it left behind.

'I've ruined my whole life.'

'Of course you haven't ruined your life. You're so young, Sam. You don't see that now but . . . it will get better, kid. I promise.'

She went outside to where her mother was waiting next to their Cadillac, three suitcases lined up by the open trunk. Carolyn's blonde hair was in a low chignon and she wore her grandmother's pearls and a tailored shirtdress in white linen. She glanced at her Cartier watch, saying, 'We'll be late for the flight if we don't hurry.'

'Just a few more minutes, Mom. Please,' Sam said, a hand over her eyes, staring in the direction of Elliot Street. She couldn't go, not yet. She had to wait until Lisa arrived.

Things had been strained for the last few months, the

gossamer-fine thread that connected them stretched so thin it threatened to break. Lisa wouldn't talk to her; she wouldn't answer Sam's phone calls. She looked through Sam as if she was invisible, and after a while Sam began to feel like maybe she was. She would go to the school bathroom and trace the outline of her reflection in the mirror with her fingers, just to be sure that she was still there, that she still existed. Or maybe it was Lisa who had become the ghost, a shiver of perfume left behind by her locker, a flash of red hair as she disappeared into a classroom. Sam had never thought their school was particularly big until she'd lost Lisa within its walls. So, she waited until darkness fell and she crept out of bed, stealing downstairs. Cycling to the house on Elliot Street, the wind in her hair, her feet pedalling as fast as they could. A pebble thrown, a window pushed up. Lisa's pale face.

'What do you want, Sam?' she asked when she came downstairs. She looked unwell; she was gaunt, dark circles like ash around her eyes. *I want you, Mouse. I need you.*

'There's a school in Utah,' Sam said instead. 'I think I might go. Give you and Josh some space to . . .' She had hoped her friend would be horrified at the idea of losing her, insisting Sam stay. Lisa would choose her, not Josh, because that's what they did.

'Maybe that's for the best,' Lisa had said and she turned around, walking back into the house.

That had been two months ago and they hadn't spoken since. But Sam knew her friend would not allow her to leave Bennford without saying goodbye. Lisa would be here soon and they would cling to one another, their arms wrapping around each other so tightly it would feel as if they were sinking into each other's bones. *Promise me you'll write*, Sam would say and Lisa would cry, *I will. I promise, I promise, I promise.*

'We have to go now, Samantha,' her mother said gently and

Sam nodded, climbing into the front seat. The key in the ignition, a Bikini Kill song playing. *In her kiss, I taste the revolution.* Sam slammed her hand against the radio; she could not bear to hear that song now, reminding her of all she had lost. She turned as the car drove away, pretending that she could see Lisa behind her. Her friend's red hair whipped up by the wind, clutching at the sides of her dress to hold it down. Waving goodbye as she mouthed, *I love you, Mouse. I will love you forever.*

39.

Sam pushed her way through the party guests – she felt like she was stoned, moving in slow motion, everyone talking in long, drawn-out sentences that made no sense. She needed to get outside, she couldn't breathe in here, but people were grabbing at her to say *that was a super cute speech*, and *I'm glad you and Lisa have patched things up, you guys were always so close.* A young woman wearing high-waisted jeans and pool slides stopped her. She was Olivia's nanny, she said, like Sam should know who Olivia was. She was such a huge fan of Sam's work; *Willing Silence*, like, literally changed her life. 'Can I have a selfie?' she asked, her arm already outstretched, smiling for the camera. 'Thank you so much!' the woman said and Sam replied, 'No worries!' as if everything was fine.

When she got to the front porch, she sat down heavily on the snow-covered step and started to shiver, the cold settling into her. She buried her head between her knees, trying to stop the panic from knitting her ribs together. *I didn't write those . . . I didn't write any of them.* And there, behind Lisa's words, she could sense a trace of something new, or something old, rather, surfacing again. The house mistress in Utah saying, 'Another letter for you, Samantha,' handing over the envelope, *return to sender* stamped on the front. How had she forgotten?

She felt horror singe her insides, like a naked flame held too close to the flesh. Was she going crazy? Could it be early onset dementia – these things were genetic, weren't they? She would be like her father, her fingers prised off her past until she was untethered, unmoored, falling through the abyss for the rest of her life. *No. No.* People forgot things. Her mother did, Lisa did too, and they weren't crazy. Sam had been through so much, of course her brain would try to shed painful memories in an effort to protect her. She couldn't discount the effect the drugs would have had, too – the molly, the ketamine and all those pills, those dodgy prescriptions from backstreet doctors in the Village. They must have eaten away at her brain, leaving gaping holes behind. She gripped her knees even tighter, terror gritting her teeth.

'Here.' She felt something warm on her shoulders.

She looked up and it was Lisa, draping Sam's snake-print trench over her body. The other woman shut the door behind her, but Sam could still hear the party rattling at the window-panes, the music and chatter and laughter. It sounded like they were having the time of their lives.

'What are *you* doing here?' she said as Lisa sat on the win-dowsill, pulling her own coat tightly around her.

'I was worried about you.' She patted down the pockets, pulling out a Marlboro packet.

'I thought you said you didn't smoke,' Sam said as Lisa put a cigarette between her lips, lighting it. She inhaled deeply, tilt-ing her head back to the sky.

'I guess I lied,' she said.

'You're good at that, aren't you?' There was no reply, Lisa taking another drag on her cigarette. 'What is *wrong* with you?' Sam asked.

'What's wrong with me? I'd love to have an answer for you, I would love to be able to tell you exactly what's wrong with me, but I don't know.' Lisa took a shaky breath, resting her hand on her knee, flicking ash to the ground. 'I'm sad,' she said, so quietly Sam had to lean in to hear her. 'I've been sad for a long time.'

'You got Josh,' Sam said. 'You got everything I ever wanted, and you have the audacity to sit there and talk to *me* about being sad? You think I haven't been sad? You think what happened didn't affect me?'

'I'm sorry,' her friend replied, staring at the cigarette in her hand. She stubbed it out, throwing it into the bushes. 'I . . .' She stopped, as if she had forgotten mid-sentence what she was trying to say. 'I just want this to be over.'

'There's only one way for that to happen.' She stood up, moving closer to Lisa. She held her friend's gaze as she fished Lisa's iPhone out of the jumpsuit's pocket, ignoring her friend's intake of breath. 'Email my manager,' she said, handing Lisa her phone. 'Email and tell her what was written in that Reddit post is a lie and I'm innocent.'

'I can't do that.' Something broke on Lisa's face as she spoke, like an elastic band pulled too taut before it snapped. 'I can't lie for you. Not any more.'

'Lie for me?' Sam stepped back, nausea blistering her tongue, and she was afraid she might vomit all over her shoes. 'No,' she whispered. 'You can't be serious. You said you wrote that email when you were drunk. You said you didn't mean it. You kept saying it was a mistake. Do you . . . do you actually believe I assaulted you?'

And with that, the other woman came undone, her shoulders hunching in towards each other. 'I didn't . . . I don't think you meant it,' she said, her mouth quivering. 'You're not a bad person, Sam, you're not . . . you're not *that*. But it wasn't right, what happened. *I* don't feel right. And I don't want to ruin your life.' She looked up at Sam, her eyes desperate. 'I never wanted that.'

'You're lying. You're *lying*.'

'I'm not.' Lisa sniffed her tears back. 'Why would I lie? Why would anyone lie about something like this? I wish I had never written that email. You were right, this mess is all my fault. But I couldn't stop thinking about that night. It didn't happen the way you said it did, Sam, and you can't just rewrite history.'

'I'm not the one who has been rewriting history.' She tilted her friend's chin up so she would meet Sam's gaze. 'I presume you still haven't told anyone? About the abortion, I mean?' Lisa shushed her, saying *please*, but Sam ignored her. 'Hmm . . .' She pretended to stroke her own chin. 'Maybe I should go back into the party and make another speech. I wonder how they'll react? I'm sure your mother will have plenty to say about it, anyway.'

'You know what?' Lisa set her jaw. 'Do whatever you want. I'm tired of you holding this over me. And why should I care, anyway?' She stared Sam right in the eyes. 'I wasn't the one who was pregnant.'

40.

March 2000

They sat together in the waiting room, Sam and Lisa. Avoiding looking at anyone else – the harried woman in her forties with a ring on her wedding finger, the couple in their twenties having a hushed argument, the girl who looked even younger than they were – as Sam stared at the posters about sexually transmitted diseases on the wall. Waiting for the nurse to call the fake name she'd written on the forms, beckoning her to follow. 'It's not the right time,' she had said when Lisa had asked if she was sure. Sam was too young to become a mother; she was only a baby herself. Besides, how was she supposed to explain to people what had happened? That she, Lisa and Josh had a threesome when they were high on ecstasy, and she was pregnant as a result? It was like an episode of *Jerry Springer*. Things like this didn't happen to girls like them, that's what Sam's mother had always told her – girls with options, money, shining futures lying ahead of them. This was the right choice. It was the only choice. After it was over, Lisa drove her home, helping Sam limp upstairs. She lay in bed, pressing a hot water bottle to her stomach to ease the cramps. No one had told her it would hurt this much, she thought. Lisa pulled the armchair over to the window and she was staring outside, the setting sun bathing her in pale, yellow light. It was only then that Sam saw her friend was crying.

'I'm sorry,' Sam said. 'I just . . .' Neither of them spoke again for a long time.

'It was probably Brandon's baby,' Lisa said eventually.

'Maybe,' Sam said, but they both knew that wasn't true. Her eyes were closing, she was drifting away on the painkillers, somewhere between awake and asleep, when Lisa spoke again.

'It should have been me,' she whispered.

'You don't want this.' Sam had the strange sense that she would remember this moment for the rest of her life, that she would look back and see this as the end of something she could not even name now. She was only eighteen and yet she felt so old, as if she had lived a thousand years.

'He's my boyfriend, not yours,' Lisa said fiercely. 'This should have been *our* decision, just the two of us. You shouldn't be involved. Josh thinks the same, he said—'

'Josh was perfectly happy at the time, wasn't he? Thrilled, if I remember correctly.' She propped herself up on her elbows, wincing in pain. 'Have you told him about afterwards? What we did . . . what happened between us when he passed out?'

'I'm never telling him that. I'm never telling *anyone* about that. I just want to pretend all of it' – she gestured at Sam, the hot water bottle, the painkillers on the locker beside her – 'never happened. I can't do this. I'm sorry, I can't.'

'Mouse,' Sam tried, stretching her hands out, but her friend stepped back, just out of reach.

'I can't,' Lisa said again.

She left without another word and Sam listened to her friend's footsteps on the stairs, hurrying across the hall, the bang of the front door behind her. She kept screaming, begging Lisa to come back to her.

41.

1 February 2022

'I'm sick of protecting you and Josh,' Lisa said. 'If you want to tell everyone that my husband knocked you up, go right ahead. I don't care any more. I've spent years thinking about the party and the abortion and everything that happened that night, over and over again, and I'm tired of it. Josh is fine and you're fine, both of you seem so fucking happy. Like, it's so easy for the two of you to forget while I'm *broken* by it. It's not fair. I'm done, do you hear me?' She put her hands on the back of her head. 'I'm done with this.'

'Stop making yourself the victim.' Sam spat the words out. 'You left me alone after we got home from the clinic. I could have bled out in that room for all you cared. I would *never* have done that to you.'

'Yeah, well.' Lisa's mouth twisted like she had tasted something sour. 'I would never have kept touching you after you said no.'

'Stop saying that, stop it, stop it,' Sam screamed and Lisa was on her feet, turning as if she could see through the house and into the back garden where the children were, afraid the twins might hear. 'You're a liar,' Sam hissed. 'That's what women like you do – you lie. You stole my boyfriend, the only man I ever loved, but that wasn't enough for you, was it? You stole my life, too. This should have been my house, my family. You even stole my fucking baby names. Martha and Maya were *my* names, they were mine. You couldn't let me have anything, could you? You even copied my fucking boots! You had to steal everything from me because you couldn't get it by yourself; you wouldn't have a clue how to do it alone. And now – after I've spent so long working and working, building a career that a pathetic little housewife like you could only *dream* of – you want to steal that from me, too?' Sam could feel spittle running down her chin but she couldn't stop, not now. 'You and all your ambitions of being a writer? Ha! What did you do? You did *nothing*. Because you're not like me, Lisa. You've never been like me. You don't know what it's like to be this fucking hungry. I'm hungry for *everything*.' She jabbed her finger in the air for emphasis. 'For love, for money, for acceptance. To be valued. To be special! And I made myself into this. I made myself a fucking idol for millions of women around the world. They'll do anything I tell them to do, *anything*. I fucking *own* them. And I'm telling you now, you're not taking that away from me. Do you hear me?'

The fury was crackling inside Sam, like wood eaten by flames. She despised Lisa in that moment, despised them both for what they had done to her, and how easily they'd walked away afterwards. She could feel the anger licking at her insides, swirling hot at the back of her throat, and she took a breath before continuing. 'Poor little Mouse,' she said, and her voice was preternaturally calm now, as if it belonged to someone else. 'I have something else I want to tell you. Something I've wanted to tell you for a very long time.' She sat beside Lisa on the windowsill, cuddling her body into the other woman's, ignoring how Lisa tensed at her touch. 'Do you remember that party at Chris Williams's?' Sam asked. 'The one you couldn't go to because of your grandparents' anniversary?'

'No,' Lisa said, for high school had been such a long time ago. It was difficult to remember every little detail.

'Oh, come on,' Sam said, stretching her legs out in front of her. 'You couldn't go cos you were in Boston with your family, but I went. And Josh went too.' She felt her friend stiffen beside her but she continued anyway. 'We got so drunk, all of us. Brandon and I had this huge fight – God, we were always fighting, weren't we? I don't know why I even pretended to like him. I think I just stayed with him because it made things less *complicated* for you, Mouse. I was always trying to make things easier for you.' She tucked a piece of stray hair behind her friend's ear. 'Anyway. Josh walked me home and he hugged me, saying he was glad we could be friends again, that I was "so cool" not to let any of that stuff get to me, like other girls would have.' It had seemed important then, not to be like the other girls. She reached down to hold Lisa's hand. 'But we never meant to hurt you. It's important you know that.'

'Please don't do this.' Lisa was very still. 'Please.'

'I asked if he wanted to come inside,' Sam continued, ignoring her. 'There was always wine in the fridge and my parents never noticed if any was missing, you remember what they were like. And Josh did hesitate, it's important you know that. He did think of you, even if only for a second.' She traced her fingers up Lisa's arm and then down again, circling her wrist, measuring how small the bones were. The other woman still didn't pull away, her eyes glassy as she stared at the ground.

Afterwards, Josh had rolled off her and he'd started to cry. He didn't want to, he had said, he didn't mean to . . . He loved Lisa, he loved her so much. He'd begged Sam not to tell and Sam had promised she never would, *cross my heart and hope to die*. She had liked that, the idea that she and Josh had a secret, something only they knew. A bond between them, one that could never be broken.

'It was a mistake,' Sam said. 'We'd been drinking so much, you know? You can't hold someone responsible for what they do when they're drunk. But we didn't want to hurt you. You believe me, don't you? We never wanted to hurt you. And that would have been it.' Sam was crying, the tears running down her face. It was such a relief, she thought, being able to confess to the worst thing she had ever done. 'Except I missed my period the next month.'

'No,' Lisa whimpered. 'This isn't true. You're lying.'

'Why would I make this up? As soon as I went to the doctor, I knew the dates didn't add up.' She grabbed Lisa's face, forcing her friend to make eye contact again. 'Think about it, Mouse. Remember how scared I was when I found out I was pregnant. I didn't have much time, did I? But I decided to just let you think it had happened the night of your birthday party. I wanted to protect you. Everything I've ever done has been to protect you.' Lisa gasped but Sam refused to let her look away. 'That's why Josh has been trying to get rid of me since I arrived back in Bennford. He was afraid I would tell you the truth.' Sam made a face. 'All these secrets you two have been keeping from each other . . . What kind of marriage is this?'

'I don't believe you. I don't. Josh would never do that to me.' Lisa folded over her lap like a rag doll, heaving as if she might be sick, and Sam rubbed her friend's back, feeling the bones of her spine protruding through the skin. 'No,' Lisa whimpered. 'Don't. Don't do that, please,' and Sam started at the words.

No.

Don't do that.

Please. No.

An electric jolt running through her, pumping her heart faster. It was as if she had found a door in the middle of an empty field, leading nowhere, and when she stepped through it, she'd fallen into another world. Walking slowly through a dream she'd had many times before but forgotten upon awakening, shaking it off her like water. She was standing at the edge of her childhood bedroom; it was night-time, a makeshift bong and an empty vodka bottle on the nightstand, the air so thick with stale beer she could almost taste its heaviness on her tongue. Josh was lying on the floor, snoring, and there she was, too. Sam could see herself. Eighteen and desperate to be loved, desperate to belong. She was so young, just a girl, really. She had thought the world was hers for the taking; she didn't know yet that she would make mistakes, do things she didn't think herself capable of. She watched as this younger Sam folded her body around Lisa's, telling the girl she loved her, she loved her so much. But this wasn't right – in her memory, Sam recalled Lisa mewling in pleasure, arching her back, calling Sam's name. But here, *here*, her friend was crying quietly in the dark – *don't do that, please, please* – and Sam was whispering, *shh, shh, someone will hear. Don't cry. Don't cry, Mouse.* One hand over Lisa's mouth, the other moving lower, while Lisa stayed so very, very still, her eyes fixed on the wall opposite. Frozen.

Sam gagged at the image, something unbearably wild twisting in her gut, and her hands began to tremble. No, this wasn't right, she wouldn't – *what would it mean to accept that this is true, Samantha?* – she didn't mean to, she didn't – *what would it mean to accept that this is true, Samantha?* – but she wasn't like *that*, she wasn't like them, this was different, this was different, this was – *what would it mean to accept that this is true, Samantha?* She crouched down on her haunches, touching the tips of her fingers to the wooden decking below, waiting for her breathing to settle again. This was different, she told herself again and again, carving the letters into her heart. Sam was a good person. She hadn't done this to hurt Lisa, she'd simply wanted to bring her friend back to her, to remind Lisa that Sam was the one who loved her the most. Lisa and Josh had treated her so poorly, they had left her to drown. Was it any surprise that she had reached out for something to keep her afloat? Sam had made mistakes; she'd never claimed to be perfect. But she wasn't like Gabriel, or those men in Paris with their dark hair, their thin fingers, that smell of tobacco. Those men had been adults; they had known what they were doing, what they were taking from her. Sam and Lisa, they'd just been stupid kids. They'd all been drinking that night; they had taken pills; they'd been smoking weed. She was out of her head, she didn't know what she was doing. This wasn't her fault, any of it. She was a good person.

'Lisa,' she tried, but the other woman backed away, one hand out to keep Sam at a distance.

'You have to leave,' Lisa said. 'I'm begging you.'

'Mouse. I didn't mean to hurt you. I would never—' Sam felt like something was breaking inside her, and with sudden, terrifying clarity, she understood that if it did, there would be no putting it back together again. There would be no return from this. She had to save herself. She focused on her breathing, as she had done so many times before, and she visualized a bright light flaring through her body, cleansing these bad memories to nothingness again. This wasn't true, what Lisa was saying. She was a good person. Her friend was creeping through Sam's memories, readjusting the colours to suit herself, and she had almost convinced Sam of it too.

'We were kids,' she said sharply. 'I don't deserve to have my life ruined because of something that happened a million years ago. What about you, Lisa? Were you really so perfect back then? When that rumour was going around about Jessica Simmons fucking Chris and Brandon, did you speak up and say it was bullshit? You bought a fake ID to buy beer when we were sixteen – should I have called the cops on you? We broke into the Garcias' house when they were on vacation so we could go skinny-dipping in their pool. You drove my dad's car after we drank half a bottle of Jack Daniel's and you didn't even have your fucking licence! Do you think *you* deserve to have your life ruined because of all of the dumb shit you did as a teen-ager? Or is it just me, Lisa?'

'Please. Just leave me alone. What will it take for you to leave me alone?' Lisa tore her hands through her hair. She had looked so beautiful, in the beginning, and now she was ruined. 'What will it take for you to leave and never come back?'

'Don't say that. We can work through this. It's only two weeks since you came to my mother's house, for fuck's sake. You said you'd missed me all those years. Was that a lie?'

Her friend looked up at her, her eye make-up smeared. 'You can still love someone who hurt you. Was that a lie?'

'But I didn't *mean* to hurt you, Mouse. It was a mistake. You made mistakes too! We can forgive each other, right? Isn't that what we do?'

Lisa's face contorted in agony and she put her hands over her head again, rocking back and forth. Sam could feel something shift inside her as she watched her friend, something hardening. Lisa was crying so hard it sounded like her ribs might crack in two and really, what did *she* have to cry about? She had this beautiful home, two daughters who adored her. She had Josh. Sam was the one they had abandoned. She was the one whose life they'd tried to destroy with their lies. She was the real victim in all of this, but the difference between her and Lisa was that Sam would never have claimed that identity for herself. She was too strong for that. Gabriel had once described her as a cockroach, saying she could survive anything. *It's a compliment, Sami*, he'd said when she'd huffed, and maybe he had been right. And so, too, she would survive this. She knew exactly what she had to do.

'Fine,' she said in a clipped voice. 'I'll leave. But not before you do something for me. Get your cell out. I want you to send an email to my manager.' She waited for Lisa to take her iPhone out of her pocket. She could barely hold the device, her hands were shaking so badly. 'Dear Jane,' Sam dictated, gesturing at Lisa to type out exactly what she was saying. 'I am writing to you today to retract the false allegation that I made against Samantha Miller.'

Lisa couldn't do it; her entire body was convulsing, her teeth chattering. Sam took the phone off her with a sigh and tapped at the screen. 'I only started this because I was jealous of the amazing life my old friend had made for herself,' Sam said aloud as she typed the email, watching Lisa to see her reaction. 'I have been envious of Samantha for a long time but I know now it's unfair to destroy her life and her incredible career because of my own issues. Her work is too important for that. Sam and I have reconnected over the last few weeks and I've come to realize how much her friendship means to me.' Lisa broke out in a sob but Sam ignored her. 'Samantha is innocent of everything I have accused her of,' she continued, 'and I apologize not only for hurting her, but also hurting the cause of every real victim of sexual violence who comes forward. Yours sincerely, Lisa Taylor, née Johnson. Et voilà,' she said with a flourish. She sent the email to Jane, CC-ing the journalist from the *New York Post*, then handed the phone to Lisa. Her friend slid to the ground, her back against the door frame, and she buried her face in her hands as she wept.

'Stop crying,' Sam said. 'I promise, this is going to fix everything. I told you to trust me, didn't I?'

Sam's cell lit up, Jane's name on the screen. 'What the fuck?' Her manager's voice, high and excited. 'Is this for real?'

'You should know enough at this stage not to doubt me. I said I would get the statement and I did.' Sam pressed the phone between her ear and her shoulder as she belted her trench coat. 'I want you to contact that woman from the *Post* and make sure the story is dead in the water. OK? And ring

Darcy for me. Tell her to get my apartment ready; I'm on my way home.'

She hung up – she and Jane needed to have a long conversation when she returned to the city. It was time her manager prioritized her; Sam needed to feel *valued* and she didn't think that was too much to ask for – and clicked into the Uber app, booking someone to pick her up in five minutes. Her mother would return the rental, she thought as she stood there, the tiny car moving on the screen, closer and closer to West Cross Street. A Toyota pulled up outside the house, and an older man in a red baseball cap rolled down the window, asking, 'Samantha?'

'Yes,' she called back. 'That's me. Just give me a sec.'

She crouched down, pulling Lisa's hands away from her face. 'Your beautiful make-up,' she said. 'Oh, Mouse.' She hugged her, her arms wrapping around Lisa so tightly it felt as if she was sinking into her bones. 'Do you remember our song? They were playing it earlier when I arrived and it made me think of you. *In her kiss, I taste the revolution,*' Sam sang softly and Lisa shuddered in response. 'I want you to know I don't hold any grudges against you, no matter what's happened. I want us to stay in touch. Promise you'll phone some time, 'k? Maybe we can get lunch when you're in the city, my treat.' She squeezed Lisa's hands as tightly as she could. 'Come on. It was good, that night, wasn't it? With us? Don't say you don't remember, Mouse. You know it was good.'

Her friend's eyes were haunted. 'It doesn't matter what I say, does it?' Lisa said, desperation carving through each word, hollowing it out. 'You'll tell this story the way you want to, anyway. That's what you do, Sam.'

'Lady,' the Uber driver called. He tapped at his watch. 'I don't got all day.'

Sam nodded. She walked towards him, that strange feeling

of lightness flooding her limbs again, like she might float off the ground and take her place among the stars. The car smelled of stale smoke and a vanilla air freshener, the leather seats worn and scuffed. She touched a hole in the fabric, feeling the spongy material beneath her fingertips.

'Manhattan?' he asked, looking at his phone. 'That's going to cost a—'

'It's fine.' She unlocked her phone, about to text into the Spirit Mafia group to let her girlfriends know she was on her way back to the city, when the screen flashed with a message from Jane to her and Teddy, explaining that Lisa had retracted the allegations of abuse. *We still have a long road ahead of us if we want to rehabilitate Sam's image,* her manager wrote, *but this email will do a lot to stop the situation from getting worse, at the very least.*

This was what would happen next, Jane said. Lisa's statement would be made public, posted on Sam's social media channels. Brooke Campbell would be paid off handsomely, as well as reminded of the stringent non-disclosure agreement she'd signed when she was first hired at Shakti. Teddy would have a phone call with his friend at the *Post* – just a little chat, nothing formal. Man to man, you know – and this friend would encourage Alyssa Reed to look the other way; after all, there were plenty of other stories that were far more newsworthy than a wellness guru's spat with her childhood friend. The email from Sam calling Lisa a lying cunt would disappear into thin air. Then she would arise, like a phoenix from the ashes. Triumphant.

People love a comeback, Jane said, *especially when it's a beautiful white woman.* They wanted to believe in second chances, and Sam wanted so desperately to be given one. She could almost taste it, the sweet rush of her glittering career, reformed and reshaped, using this unpleasant experience as a teachable moment. It might even bring her more success, in the end. She turned in her seat as they drove away, staring back at Lisa, standing on the front porch, alone. Her red hair whipped up by the wind, clutching at the sides of her jumpsuit. She watched as Lisa became smaller and smaller in the rear-view window, until Sam had to squint to see her. Then the car turned a corner, and her friend was gone.

'Do you mind if I turn up the music?' the driver asked.

'Sorry?'

'The music?' the driver asked again. 'Can I turn it up?'

'No, don't do that,' Sam said, fastening her seatbelt. 'Please.'

She didn't look back again for that was her past now, and as she always told her girls, it didn't do anyone any good to dwell on the past. She would return to the city, to her busy, busy life. She would send private DMs to the people who had supported her – she'd kept a Notes app list of those who had spoken out against her so that when this was all over, she would remember exactly who had remained loyal. She made a note to speak with Jane, too, asking her manager to sort out the situation with Gabriel; that was nothing a little money wouldn't take care of, and she'd never have to think about that man again.

Lisa would be fine, of course. Sam had done this to protect her; she knew her friend wouldn't have survived the public humiliation of that story running in the *Post*. She would appreciate what Sam had done, in time. In a couple of months, it would be like this had never happened. Lisa would be happy then. They would all be happy. Her phone beeped, and she frowned at the screen. It was a WhatsApp message from a number she didn't know and when she checked it, the profile photo was of Becky and her surprisingly hot husband, lying in fringed hammocks on a sandy beach.

Becky: I can't believe you left without saying goodbye.

Sam rolled her eyes. Becky was pathetic, she thought, as she adjusted her dress, leaning forward to ask the driver to turn the heat up. She half smirked, reading the message again. After everything that had happened, she *still* thought she could be Sam's friend?

Becky: I had a present I wanted to give you.

A video appeared in the chat, uploading slowly. When it was done, Sam clicked on it. It showed red brick to begin with, someone moving slowly through bushes and trees, the only sound that of the heavy breathing of the person recording it. *What the fuck is this?* Creeping and creeping, a hand reaching to push some branches out of the way, and there was Lisa's front porch, the wooden decking and snow-covered steps, the flower arch and the lilies wound around wrought-iron railings. Sam inhaled sharply when she saw herself come into view, ugly with rage as she stood above a cowering Lisa, shouting at her.

I'm hungry for everything, she screamed. *For love, for money, for acceptance. To be valued. To be special. And I made myself into this. I made myself a fucking idol for millions of women around the world. They'll do anything I tell them to do, anything. I fucking own them.*

Sam's vision was contracting, darkness nudging around the corners, and her breath was coming in desperate, dry gasps. The woman in the video said so clearly, *I don't deserve to have my life ruined because of something that happened a million years ago*, and Sam could hear someone moaning, *no, no*. It was only when the Uber driver turned around in alarm, asking, 'You good, lady?' that she realized it was her. She went on to Twitter, her hands shaking, praying to God to protect her, to stop this from happening, but she immediately saw that she was tagged in a new YouTube video. *Samantha Miller Meltdown*, it was called. She watched the first few seconds, a desperate wail crawling out of her throat when she realized it was the same video Becky had sent to her. She rang Jane, begging her to 'take it down, get it taken down, Jane, please', but there was silence on the other end of the phone, there was nothing, *there was nothing*, and all Sam could do was watch as the video was shared and reshared, thousands of times in a matter of minutes. Twitter and Facebook and Instagram and Snapchat and TikTok and YouTube and countless WhatsApp groups. It was like a virus spreading, mutating, gathering speed. There would be no stopping this now. She opened her mouth and she screamed and screamed and screamed.

Becky: Oh, Samantha.

Becky: You didn't think I was going to let you get away with this, did you?

Song credits

Lyrics on p.192 from '. . . Baby One More Time' by Britney Spears, written by Max Martin and produced by Max Martin and Rami.

Lyrics on p.264, p.284 and p.299 from 'Rebel Girl' by Bikini Kill, written by Kathleen Hanna, Billy Karren, Tobi Vail, and Kathi Wilcox.

Acknowledgements

I feel very lucky to have Juliet Mushens, agent extraordinaire, in my corner. Thank you for your brilliance, humour and determination – you are a force of nature.

I'm so grateful to Frankie Gray. Your vision for what this book could be surpassed my own, and I'm indebted to your incredible skill and insight. Working with you has been such a pleasure.

With thanks to everyone at Transworld and Penguin Ireland who worked on *Idol* – Imogen Nelson, Tenelle Ottley-Matthew, Viv Thompson, Tabitha Pelly, Fíodhna Ní Ghríofa, Izzie Ghaffari Parker, Vicky Palmer, Ruth Richardson, Laura Garrod, Emily Harvey, Tom Chicken, Gary Harley, Louise Blakemore, Sophie Dwyer, Laura Ricchetti, Natasha Photiou, Oli Grant, and Claire Gatzen. Thanks to Irene Martinez and Phil Evans for the beautiful cover.

Thank you to Catherine O'Brien in Ennis, who sent me so much material on 'conspirituality' and gurus gone wild, and to Aoife Murray for sending me articles on anything #GirlBoss. Thanks to Angela Koh for giving me an update on the New York fashion world, and to my early readers, Sophie White and Katie Webber. With thanks, too, to all the amazing authors who read *Idol* and gave early quotes.

Thank you to the Arts Council of Ireland for their support, and Maynooth University for welcoming me as their Writer in Residence 2022. Thanks to Sarah Bannan and Sarah Moore Fitzgerald for their advice and kindness.

As always, I owe so much to my two beta readers – Catherine

Acknowledgements

Doyle and Marian Keyes. Cat, thank you for being so honest with me (and for persuading me to change the ending!). Marian, you are the North Star for many Irish writers, and I am no different. Thank you for your infinite generosity and wisdom, both as my friend and as an author.

And lastly, I want to thank my wonderful family, my dog Cooper, and all my friends for their love and support.

About the Author

Louise O'Neill grew up in Clonakilty, a small town in West Cork, Ireland. Her first novel, *Only Ever Yours*, was released in 2014 and won the *Sunday Independent* Newcomer of the Year at the Irish Book Awards, the Eilís Dillon Award for a First Book and the *Bookseller*'s inaugural YA Book Prize. Her second novel, *Asking For It*, was published in 2015 to widespread critical acclaim. It spent fifty-two consecutive weeks in the Irish top 10 bestseller list. Both novels have been optioned for screen.

Louise's first novel for adults, *Almost Love*, was published in 2018, followed shortly by *The Surface Breaks*, her feminist reimagining of *The Little Mermaid*. Her second novel for adults, *After the Silence*, was published in 2020 and was an instant bestseller in Ireland. It won Crime Novel of the Year at the Irish Book Awards and has also been optioned for screen. *Idol* is her third adult novel.

Louise has a weekly column in the Irish *Sunday Times*.

Reading Group Guide

- Discuss Sam's viral essay in *Blackout* magazine. Was Sam right to write about her and Lisa's sexual encounter without Lisa's knowledge or approval?

- Think about the #MeToo movement and the current discourse around the importance of believing women. How easy was it for you to believe Lisa's allegations? Did you find yourself doubting or questioning her story at any point?

- Throughout the book, Sam appears to have trouble recalling certain events in her life. Have you ever had an experience where you remember an event from the past differently from a sibling, parent, or friend?

- Social media and modern celebrity/influencer culture are a prevalent theme in the novel. Did Sam come across as authentic to you? Discuss the ways in which her online persona differs from, and aligns with, who she is in her real life.

- Did the media and public's response to the sexual assault allegations surprise you at all? What did you think about the ways in which Sam handles the online response throughout the book? Did you sympathize with her?

- Sam often expresses feelings of resentment and betrayal towards Josh and Lisa for building a life together without her. Why do you think this is? Are these feelings justified?

– Think about the events that take place during Lisa's 40th birthday party. What did you think about Sam's behaviour and her speech? Were you surprised by the way in which she acts?

– Consider the reveal about the person behind the troll account targeting Sam. Did this come as a surprise to you? Did you have any other ideas about the identity of @Supernovadiabolique157 while you were reading?